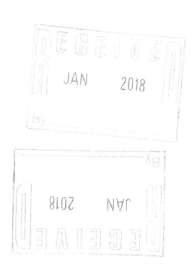

GHOSTS
IN THE
MACHINE

ALSO BY RICHARD FARR

The Babel Trilogy
The Fire Seekers
Ghosts in the Machine
Infinity's Illusion (forthcoming)

The Truth About Constance Weaver: A Novel
Emperors of the Ice: A True Story of Disaster and Survival
in the Antarctic, 1910–13
You Are Here: A User's Guide to the Universe

GHOSTS
IN THE
MACHINE

The Babel Trilogy
BOOK TWO

RICHARD FARR

SKYSCAPE

SKYSCAPE

Published by Skyscape, New York

The publisher wishes to dedicate this book to Nick Harris. We hope he enjoys it, wherever he's reading from.

www.apub.com

Amazon, the Amazon logo, and Skyscape are trademarks of Amazon.com, Inc., or its affiliates.

ISBN-13: 9781477817896 (hardcover)
ISBN-10: 1477817891 (hardcover)
ISBN-13: 9781477827918 (paperback)
ISBN-10: 1477827919 (paperback)

Cover design by Will Staehle
Book design by Jason Blackburn

Printed in the United States of America

"A butcher's sharp blade liberates the flesh from the bone. But the words of the Architects are sharper still: they liberate the mind from the body."

—*From the Akkadian Version, translated by Morag Chen (compare Hebrews 4:12)*

"History is repeating itself. I know a lot of history, and I'd rather it didn't."

—*Professor Derek Partridge*

"Science begins with doubt."

—*Fang Lizhi*

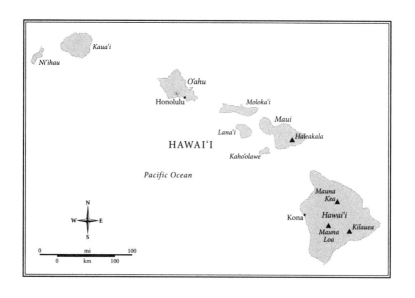

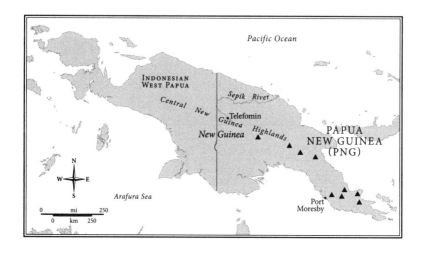

A MESSAGE TO THE PLANET

According to the Seraphim the message that follows was written by their founder and leader, Julius Quinn, shortly before his death—or "ascent," as they claim—on Mount Ararat. It is being reprinted as a new introduction to *Anabasis*, his account of his interaction with the so-called Architects.

Anabasis has been described as "the founding scripture of the world's newest religion" and "a conversation with the gods." Quinn himself vigorously opposed the use of such language. He denied that his movement was a religion or faith and described the Architects only as "free intelligences."

Anabasis (the word means "ascent") is now available in 147 languages, and has been read by an estimated 300–500 million people worldwide. Ironically, one of Quinn's key messages has been that the proliferation of human languages and cultures began only because—in the period of "doubt and rebellion" that led up to the catastrophic eruption at Thera in 1628 BCE—humanity drifted away from the "true voice" of the Architects.

Our immediate task, Quinn has said, is to "reject these inauthentic cultural influences and return our minds to their origin."

Do you experience tastes and sounds, pleasures and pains—but also an inner self that is conscious of itself? Are you, in short, a human being? Then we, the Seraphim, salute you, for soon you will join us on the stairway. After five thousand years, humanity's ignorance of its own true nature is drawing to a close. We are poised now to rise together and join the dimension of the infinite.

Deep in our past, we were animals. By slow degrees, over hundreds of thousands of years, we evolved into the cleverest of all animals. But our full humanity was given to us only when the Architects first enabled in us the capacity for language. Since then we have had understanding, and have found, in our myriad ways, how to cope with the great gift that comes through language—the full inner light of consciousness.

And yet how painful our humanity has been, this temporary way station between the animal body and the infinite mind! Animals experience, but they do not plan and build, hope and fear, because they have no sense of a self that continues into the future: it is their great good fortune not to live, as we do, under the savage lash of time. Time is the medium through which we experience the frustration of our hopes, the sense of our limitation, and the well-founded terror that the self, which we carry within us like a guttering candle in a jar, will be extinguished in death. No wonder we have invented so many new languages, ideologies, and religions in our desperate attempt to understand the paradox that we are minds trapped in the decaying prison of the body. No wonder that so many of our ideas contain, like flashes of lightning, hints of the astonishing truth!

Hear the news, then. Hear the truth.

The period during which we humans have been conscious of ourselves as unique individuals is a mere eyeblink in the larger story of our development.

A mere stage, like childhood. And now, at last, our waiting—our very history—is coming to an end. Just as we left our animal nature behind on the way to becoming human, now we are ready to leave our humanity behind and become what people throughout history have mistakenly called "gods."

No longer will we be mere animal bodies.

No longer will we be self-conscious minds imprisoned within bodies.

In the next inevitable stage of our development, we will become free intelligences. Eternal thoughts. Untethered from the physical world. Immortal.

Prepare your mind for this transformation; prepare your inner self. Listen to the original language that we corrupted, the language of the Architects—for they want us to come back; they want us to be with them; they have announced that we are ready at last!

Em-DA-chol

Ul-KO-vok

Ret-YEM-an

Ar-QA-het

When you are ready, when your mind is ripe, they will come for you. Do not be afraid. For it will be time then to leave your body behind.

To leave time itself behind.

To rise up at last and become what you are.

$$\triangle$$

New calculations indicate that, although much smaller than the eruption at Thera, the "Ararat event" unleashed energy equivalent to over eight hundred kilotons, concentrated at first in a narrow column that seems to have triggered the main eruption. Due to the scale of the ensuing devastation, neither Quinn's body nor those of approximately a thousand followers have been recovered. Eyewitness accounts are almost exclusively from Seraphim converts who survived unscathed on the lower slopes to the north of the mountain, and even their accounts vary widely. A much larger number of survivors became Mysteries—or Partials, as the Seraphim prefer—their bodies still functioning, at least for a time, but their minds and personalities gone.

What really happened there continues to be disputed across the globe by scientists, religious leaders, and others. Not in dispute is the fact that global rates of conversion to the Seraphim, far from faltering, increased exponentially in the wake of the "event." This is, they say, both an effect and a cause of "the growing power of the Architects to aid us in our coming transformation."

PROLOGUE

A THOUSAND GODS

You were standing motionless on the snow, like all the others, with your face tilted up toward the sky and your hands raised in greeting.

"There!" I shouted.

Mack didn't hear me, which wasn't surprising—I was competing with 130 decibels. I leaned across the instrument panel, pointed, and shouted again. "There! Daniel and Rosko. Do you see?"

Wrestling with the controls, struggling to make the big machine do his bidding, he glanced to his left and nodded. Even in that moment of life-threatening crisis there was an aura of relaxed control about him.

"Go," he mouthed, even before the helicopter's wheels had made contact with the pad. "Help them. You'll have to be quick."

Snow and ice, stained pink by the evening light, were cascading onto the pad. Smoke and steam were so totally everywhere that you couldn't tell which was which. As if by magic, Rosko had emerged from the crevasse, covered in blood, and was struggling up the slope toward you from fifty paces away. The Seraphim were standing silently, or chanting, or on the steeper sections they were beginning to stumble and fall as the ground shook. It was still a couple of hours to sunset, but the full moon had risen into view over the shoulder of the mountain, indecently big and close, like an airbrushed fantasy planet from the cover of an old comic book. Not far to our right, Mount Ararat's first lava flow in centuries was hissing and sliding—a lazy, venomous, red-eyed snake, mooching for new victims.

And—

And—

It was hard not to stand there in the doorway and just stare. The sky, which should have been blue, was turning before our eyes into an upside-down oil-black lake. And a thousand gods—spirits, disembodied souls, angels, demons, Architects, what the hell did I know?—were swirling and foaming and materializing out of it, taking on human and yet not-human shapes as they dripped down toward the shiny, bright faces of the entranced, eager-for-immortality Believers. That counts as a Don't-Miss, Five Stars, Bucket-List roadside attraction, don't you think? But it grabs your attention even more, when it contradicts everything you've ever believed, because your whole life you've been a science-minded, unapologetically rationalist, don't-give-me-that-crap atheist.

This is not happening. That's what I said to myself. *Morag, this is so so so not bloody happening. It's just an illusion. A hallucination. An extra-deluxe, high-octane, ultra-high-pixel-density nightmare.*

I hate it, D; I totally hate it when I don't believe a single word I'm telling myself.

Your dad's voice came floating back to me. He may have been an arrogant pain in the neck, but he was also my mentor, my hero. William Hayden Calder, famous linguist: hunched over our Akkadian translations at the big table in his Seattle office, unearthing buried civilizations for a living. "Don't misunderstand me, Morag," he'd said to me once. "My position isn't simply that ghosts don't exist and souls don't exist and gods don't exist. I'm not saying that we have bad-to-zero evidence for those *particular* things—though, sure, bad-to-zero evidence is what we have. What I'm saying is the whole category of what people call 'the supernatural' is a crock, a confusion."

"Why?"

"Simple. If you can't make sense of something—if it seems to lie beyond your understanding—then you've nothing but bad reasons for claiming that you 'know' it's supernatural. On the other hand, if eventually you do make sense of it, bingo: the temptation to call it supernatural evaporates. History of science in a nutshell."

Thunder and lightning explained as Zeus having a snit: that was his favorite example. I'd always agreed with him, and I'd always thought that Julius Quinn, his former student turned Alternative Messiah, was merely a super-charismatic BS artist, like all the other people in history who've claimed they're just back from a personal interview in the Big Office Upstairs. Even when Iona became obsessed with the disappearances in Bolivia, even when the "disappeared" turned out to be Mysteries—and even when she died, and we saw a hint of this same craziness in those blurred frames of video, I wasn't ready to believe so much as a syllable from our Mr. Quinn. But Ararat forced me to give him and his Seraphim this much: I might not have, and they might not have, the slightest effing clue what the Architects were, but they were *real*.

They came down like fast-acting stalactites from the roof of a cave. At first each one was just a viscous column, and they hesitated, as if picking out one of the individuals below: only then did they begin to take on the outline of a human form. The supplicants (Applicants? Angels? Victims? You tell me!) stood rigid, with their arms held out in greeting, poised on the cliff edge of infinity with joy on their luminous upturned faces.

Amazing—and when you've been raised by a couple of archaeologists, so you know the world's mythologies like the back of your hand—well, all things considered, it would have been nice to get a spare five minutes, sit down with a notepad, and concentrate on the details.

"You'll have to be quick."

Oh. Right. Sorry, Mack, yes, have to be quick. Because—

Because *shit shit shit* one of them is above you.

You, Daniel Calder.

Right now.

Don't look at it, D! Please! Don't look at it!

But it was there especially for you, so you looked at it.

Daniel, run!

But you didn't run. You were already beyond running. You just stood there looking up, like all the others, mesmerized. In that pose, you might have been one of those Greek statues of an athlete that they found standing, javelin arm forever raised, on the seabed at Antikythera. A track-and-field snapshot in solid bronze. The hero of the games, anticipating forever the laurel wreath of victory.

I hauled the door open and jumped down onto a pile of snow and ice. My foot hit a jagged block at an angle and I spun sideways, turning my ankle and cutting both hands. Rosko had started running up the slope toward you; when I picked myself up and looked again, he was already halfway there. Yelling was pointless—neither of you could have heard a thing from that distance, not over the deafening triple protest of the blades, the engine, and the mountain itself—but I yelled into the thin air until my throat hurt.

"Daniel! Daniel, it's me. Morag. We're over here; can you see us? This way! Rosko, you have to move faster. Now, Rosko. Now!"

Cheerleading the impossible. You must both weigh eighty kilos—sorry: 180 pounds—so how he even picked you up, I'll never know. Somehow he got you over his shoulder and started half-carrying, half-dragging you toward me. I ran, or stumbled, to meet him halfway. It was only then that I saw how bad his injuries looked. No words between us. We made it to the open door, where I pulled more muscles than I can name getting you both on board. Before I'd even had time to get your bums into seats, the helicopter lurched sideways, smashed in the tail by a block of ice. Our bearded, grinning, rifle-toting Armenian friend shouted, "Hang on to something!" before managing to give us a foot or two of lift and steer us crabwise off the steel deck.

I buckled you both into the second row and half-jumped, half-fell into the copilot's seat on Mack's right as he veered away and down. We passed right over a tongue of the lava flow. The heat radiating off it was so intense, I wondered if we'd light up. A shred of lint, sucked in too close to a bonfire.

Once it was behind us we dropped like a stone. It took only a few sickening, theme-park minutes to leave that horrible scene and most of Mount Ararat's five thousand meters behind. The pale-brown moonscape beneath us—rock, dust, gullies—looked like a beach raked by a bear's claw. The whole machine was canted over to one side, the nose was tilted too far down, and we were seconds away from violent death.

"So far, so good!" Mack said, as if everything was going way better than expected. As if he was Dad, we were the kids, and this was a Sunday drive to the beach. When he looked at me with a mad gleam in his eye, as if to check that I was having fun too, I didn't know whether to feel better or worse.

Funny how many regrets a mind can dwell on, in the almost infinitely expandable space of a single moment. We were about to say our last good-byes to the world from inside a fireball of shredding metal, and I had all the emotions you'd expect, including the purest and most cowardly physical terror, anger that this was a situation over which I had no control, and "a kind of philosophical panic" (I here quote the great German thinker sitting beside you, Rosko G. Eisler) at the thought of my own extinction. But that was just the start. I managed also to regret that I'd never see my parents again. Regret that I'd never become the world-famous anthropologist, linguist, and discoverer of lost civilizations I'd planned to be. Regret that I'd never know how to adjust my personal belief-space to fit the fact of oily, strangely attractive beings materializing into semihuman form out of a clear sky, precisely as Julius Quinn had predicted they would.

It even entered my mind, like the scent of honeysuckle captured in passing, that I'd never see a Certain Other Person again. Or find out what feelings that person might have about me. Or—let's face it, Morag, shall we?—almost certainly not have about me.

⚠

The mountain was behind and above us. I couldn't see most of it, but the eruption seemed to have stopped. A small fist of smoke was rising from the summit. It blurred into the rolling bank of unnatural darkness that kept parting, re-forming, and concentrating in the sky above. Several darker points within that darkness dripped down, a viscous goo extending down like molasses toward the crowds of people still grouped in rings around the summit.

The Architects, still at work.

And the Seraphim faithful—but it wasn't a *faith*, Julius Quinn had insisted, hadn't he? It wasn't a *faith* because it wasn't a *religion*, even if everyone, including me, kept calling it that. No: it was *the truth*—and those who called themselves the Seraphim because they had accepted the truth were still there, still waiting to accept their infinite reward.

We were following the line of a deep gully. Its edges reminded me of saw blades, and there were more gullies on either side. I was supposed to be saying something helpful, like *What about landing over there? I see a place over there!* Only, there wasn't enough *there* to set down a phone.

There was a sickening drop, a half second of zero-g during which my brain decided to brighten up its last moment with a picture of Einstein, clothes rumpled and hair wild, in delighted free fall: the light-bulb moment when he gets it that acceleration and gravity are the same thing.

Mack slapped at the dashboard and said something in Armenian that was probably unprintable; it must have worked, because our descent rate corrected itself so abruptly that my stomach tried to escape through my sinuses. We leveled out after that, which was good. Not so good was the fact that we were flying almost sideways.

"The tail must be damaged," he said. "I can't keep us in the air much longer."

A band of green appeared. A smear on the windshield? A trick of the light. But Mack pointed at it. "Crops. That's the Aras River valley. Ten kilometers."

Small farms came into view. Fields. Even a few trees. Behind us, Ararat still loomed; the curve of the slope made it look like we were trying to outrun a tsunami. We flew almost straight for a minute, but as the helicopter slowed down, it slewed hard to the left again, like a supermarket trolley with a jammed wheel. We sunk to ten or fifteen feet off the ground but kept moving. There was a sound I mistook for the squeal of a pig—our tail section dragging through the branches of a tree—and, after hanging motionless for a second, we went to the ground like a dropped brick.

By pure chance, the wheels were level. By pure chance, we landed in plowed soil, or the impact would have snapped our necks.

"Help Daniel," I shouted. From behind one of the seats I grabbed a bag with a big red medical "+" on the front. I unbuckled Rosko, took his good arm, and threw us both out the side door.

There was barely time to get him away from the slowing rotors and collapse on a low mound of earth before the true eruption came.

The pulse of light was the pure, pure white of a bleached sheet. Nothing like lightning: though it seemed to come from the summit, the whole sky lit up; the whole atmosphere lit up.

What happened next was a monster version of what Rosko had shown us on that video of when your mom was killed in Patagonia. The spherical bubble of pressure started at the summit and moved out silently toward us like a magic fishbowl, kicking up a line of snow and dust to mark its progress across the scree. Mack was still in the helicopter, helping you to the door. I had time only to scream a useless warning.

"Watch out!"

It was like being punched, hard, not in one place but all over at the same time. It blew me off my feet, hurling me past where Rosko was seated and into the dirt. I felt as if someone had jammed their thumbs into my ears and a knee into my gut, and every inch of my exposed skin crackled and stung. I looked up to see you and Mack thrown from the door of the helicopter as the pressure wave picked it up on the other side. The whole machine balanced over you, motionless, then continued to topple sideways. You and Mack were lying right beneath it.

"Move move move!" I screamed. At the last possible moment, he grabbed you to him and rolled. One of the rotors slowed the fall for a moment, but the blade snapped off and bounced sideways into the grass like a vaulter's dropped pole. The lower edge of the airframe came down and met the ground, missing you by inches.

For a few seconds, we thought it was over, then we felt a powerful *thump* in the ground beneath us, like a giant was trying to break out of the earth with a hammer. Another thump. Then three more in quick succession.

The summit was a pristine white cone—

A pristine white cone—

But a moment later it had gone, and what remained was a broad white Puritan's collar of snow surrounding a vertical column of fire.

We crouched or stood, immobilized by the sight. It unfolded before us in absolute silence. But of course it did. We were miles away, and it took more than a minute for that awful sound to reach us.

Roaring? No. Booming? No. Imagine a giant dragging truck-sized rocks in a chain-mail bag across the steel deck of a ship. It was an unholy choir of fifty notes, all combined into a single deafening howl. It snapped us out of our amazement, and we fled, but the ground was trembling so hard that even Mack and I kept losing our footing. Rosko understood the danger, but his jaw was rigid from pain, and I was afraid that at any moment he would faint and pitch face-first into the earth. And you'd been reduced to a chameleon's slowness, like someone trying to recall what movement is. Mack and I had to take turns pulling you along.

A dark wall of vapor and pulverized rock was pouring down off Ararat's higher flanks. Judging its size or speed was impossible. After we'd gone half a mile, pellets of smoking rock began to fall around us. Fires started in some of the drier grass, forcing us to run faster while breathing the smoke. We passed a farm building as several large chunks hit the roof. The sound they made was odd, hollow, unexpected—like arrows thudding into the wet bole of a tree.

"This way," Mack yelled, peeling off to the left. My eyes were streaming. My throat burned. I had your arm in mine and turned you toward him, but a mini-meteor of burning material arced into the ground a few steps ahead and brightened at the moment of impact. It was like seeing a video clip of a firework played backward. When I'd guided you around the foot-deep smoking pit, Mack was nowhere to be seen.

A moment of panic—then I heard Rosko's voice: "Over here."

I followed the smudged outline of his back, climbing and stumbling on the rutted, stony ground. A hundred yards later the chunks of rock stopped coming down. A few more pebbles, then grit, then nothing. A cloud of ash was still coming our way, but we'd reached the river.

The central column above the mountain was thinner than I expected, a slender black mushroom stalk reaching thousands of feet into the sky. But the summit had cleared already, the earlier smoke dragged higher by the convection currents, and the strange blackening in the sky itself, which had come with the Architects, was nowhere.

It wasn't a neat, symmetrical eruption. The north side of the summit, where we'd been, was almost intact, but the south side had radically changed shape. A vertical plume at first, followed by a massive sideways collapse away to our left—like Mount Saint Helens. The whole once-beautiful mountain had been turned into a horseshoe. It hadn't lost much height, just a big chunk of its core, and it was now a deep, crab-shaped caldera, its claws grasping out to the southeast.

I thought of Babel again—both Babels. The ruined ziggurat at Babylon, under the outline of which I'd dug and studied with Jimmy and Lorna and your dad, which for so many centuries had been misidentified as the original site of humanity's divine spanking. And the vaporized mountain at Thera—Strongyle, as they'd called it: the round island—which had turned out to be the true site, so much earlier, of an enigmatic transaction between promises and demands, belief and unbelief, human beings and something both more and less than human.

So. Another great mountain breathes fire, and once again the gods announce their arrival with charred corpses, shattered rock, and stunned survivors promoting strange, strangely enticing beliefs. ANCIENT MESO-POTAMIAN GODS RETURN TO WREAK NEW HAVOC UPON THE HUMANS THEY FOOLED ONCE BEFORE! Now there's a theory—if you're a sucker for headline-making supernatural woo-woo. Me? Not so much. For me, well trained by Bill Calder, being forced to take it seriously was like being thrown into the sea with my hands tied.

I set out the medical gear and did what I could to fix up Rosko's wounds. He was bruised all over, cut and scraped all over, but neither his mangled hand nor the gash on his head were life-threatening. I found an aluminum tourniquet in the bag, and stabilized the hand by putting his whole forearm in a sling. Lorna's voice came back to me as I did it: *Nooo, gurrl, not like that. Like thuss. Aye, aye, well, not so terrible. Now untie the knot and gie't another go, eh? Tighter thuss time.* I looked south, toward Baghdad, and allowed some superstitious corner of my brain an attempt to sense whether they were OK, to sense whether they were alive. Nothing, of course—which proved nothing, of course.

Rosko's head wound was still oozing blood. I dabbed off the worst, squirted on half a bottle of Betadine, and packed it with gauze. When I tightened a bandage over it, he gasped.

"Scheisse!"

That must have been the moment when I started the habit of talking to you all the time. It was a way of mastering the panic. Up to that moment, I'd been too focused on staying alive, and keeping you and Rosko alive, to think much about what had happened up there, but I was aware of you next to me, frantically aware of the need to assess your mental state and engage with you, to in some way hang on to you, as if at that moment you might be drifting out of reach. I could feel panic rising in my throat like a wave of nausea—so I started chatting.

"Can't take this boy anywhere, can we, Daniel?" I said, stealing a glance in your direction as I administered water and pills to Rosko. "Do you remember Patagonia? You saved Rosko's skin there, and he just returned the favor. But he's a mess all over again. What do you make of his injuries? I see two broken fingers and the head wound. On the bright side, none of the major arteries came to the party, did they? Back and legs seem to be OK too, so all those expensive titanium spare parts they installed after your little adventure on the Torre Sur must be working. Anything to add to that, Dr. Calder? No?"

I was willing you to speak, to say something normal, to snap out of it. But you didn't respond. You were looking at me; I felt that in some sense at least you were following what I was saying, but your face was a mask of puzzlement. I felt a hot flare of emotion, fear that I was losing you mixed with anger at myself, and even resentment at you—as if you were rejecting me. I made a conscious effort to suppress the thought and blundered on.

"Well then, what else does Trauma Specialist Morag see? Collarbones look OK. Ribs, can't tell about the ribs, but that doesn't matter because there's squat we can do about ribs except advise the patient to abstain from wrestling and sex. What our German friend needs is a fancy, complicated piece of kit called a hospital. But they forgot to squeeze one of those into the medical bag, so we're going to have to look after him as best we can. Aren't we? Yes? Good."

Rosko seemed to understand what I was doing, but he didn't join in. It was me he addressed, catching his breath between each short sentence.

"I was in the crevasse. Right behind him."

"I know."

"A slab of ice came down off the opposite wall. Size of a car. Size of a truck. It was going to kill me for sure. Instead it fell to one side and trapped my hand. It was like it was looking at me, waiting, thinking about whether to make my death slow or quick. But it shifted the other way instead, released my hand, jammed itself across the crevasse at an angle. Funny, almost. It was going to kill me, and then it seemed to change its mind, and it was the only reason I was able to climb out."

He paused and took several huge, gulping breaths, like sobs. "I felt it, Morag. It was awful. I was there, and I saw. I saw it, felt it, taking him."

"Don't, Rosko."

But he wouldn't stop. "It was like I was inside him and inside the Architect at the same time. I could feel him being stretched out, emptied out, each little element of his experience, his feelings, his memories, and his sense of himself. Being extracted from his body in infinitely small grains. Like sugar being sucked up through a straw."

"Rest," I said. "Try not to talk."

"Remember what I told you about the accident in Patagonia? How I was falling, and I knew I was going to die?"

I dabbed at his face with an antiseptic wipe. "Aye. You said you felt calm about it. Accepting."

He nodded. "Like it was meant to be. And when I didn't die, when I woke up in the hospital, I felt terrible, as if I'd been rejected. This was the same. For a minute, when I managed to climb out of the crevasse and get to Daniel, I felt that I was no longer inside my body. I was up there, with them, and I wanted to be with them."

"With the Architects? And you wanted them to take Daniel?"

"I had to fight it. It was like, the whole time I was running to him, grabbing him, and getting him back to you, I was having a sort of argument with myself about what was best. It's—I'm sorry, it's hard to put into words."

A minute earlier I'd not wanted him to talk about it; I'd not wanted to know, not yet; now I was frustrated that he couldn't be more articulate.

"Try," I said. "Try, Rosko. I'm a mite confused right now. Atheist Encounters Ancient Gods? It's hard to process. I've been trying not to believe my own eyes. So far, you're not helping."

He shook his head. "I can't help with that. I don't know what they are, Morag. But believe your eyes is all I can say. They're real, and it's like they want to take a person's experiences to another place."

"Which is what Shul-hura's religion was preaching three thousand years ago in Babylon, according to the tablets Bill and I translated. It's also what Julius Quinn says in *Anabasis*. Taking our experiences out of the body to some place where they don't depend on the body. All of which makes no sense, because the mind depends totally on the brain. All that afterlife stuff is rubbish."

"I'd have agreed with you completely, until today."

"So you're telling me you're a convert to the Seraphim now?"

"I don't know what I'm telling you. It's too strange. I want to know why part of me did believe that their taking Daniel was in his own interest—and another part of me didn't believe it. And I want to know why I felt sorry for them: Why did I feel that these gods, or whatever the hell they are, were needy and desperate? And why did I sense that they wanted Daniel, but not you or me?"

You weren't listening to any of this, or you didn't seem to be. You were crouched close to me, alert but calm, rubbing a pinch of dirt between your fingers like a tracker scanning the ground for evidence. I allowed myself a sip of optimism. Your body language wasn't right for a Mystery. More nearly normal than that, more relaxed.

"Daniel," I said, crouching next to you. "It's Morag. *Look at me.*"

You were still wearing your dad's down mountain jacket, the one he'd slipped off and passed to you on the summit, before the fight with Mayo and the fall into the crevasse. A madman's bar chart of drying blood stretched from its collar all the way down one sleeve; right at the end, near the Velcro cuff, there was a rust-colored handprint. It looked as if you'd been bleeding from the neck, but the red cells were all Rosko's, deposited there when he'd carried you. I grabbed your wrists. "Daniel Calder. Please. Look at me."

You did. And with a flood of relief I saw, or thought I saw, that it was you. Not that awful blank look of the Mysteries. But your eyes held mine for only a second, before darting away, settling on my forehead, my nose, my eyes again, my chin. As if you didn't recognize me—or as if you didn't even grasp that I was a person. Your gaze came back to me again, and slid off me again. Drawn back to the river.

"Daniel, what happened up there?"

You said nothing. It was as if you were waiting for me to notice something, and I had to blink away tears and control my breathing before I did. In the earth at your feet, right in front of me, you'd scratched a crude outline of the mountain, complete with the double peak: Ararat and Little Ararat. But the top of the main triangle was open, and a single curled line rose from it. The symbol of the Seraphim.

"What does it mean, D? That they're right? That you're one of them now? I don't understand. All I want to do is bring you back."

You drew a circle on the ground, around the outline of the mountain.

"What's that?" Rosko said. "The earth?"

You didn't say. Your only response was to reach down with your splayed fingers and rub the image away.

Mack was standing forty or fifty feet away, on a rock at the edge of the riverbank. He turned in a slow arc, with one hand up to shade his eyes. In the other hand he had a small military-green compass.

"Where are we?" Rosko asked.

"I was right. This is the river Aras. We're still in Turkey, but that"—
he pointed to the other bank, a hundred meters away—"is Armenia."

"This is the border?"

"Yes." He pointed to the northeast, where a tower was visible on a
ridge. "See that? Khor Virap. It's a monastery. Come on."

I hate water—have I ever mentioned that? Just in case, I'll mention
it again: I hate water. I hate it so much that I never learned to swim.
Even when we'd found a place where the Aras was only fifty yards wide,
I had to endure the humiliation of it being impossible to hide the fact
that I was scared out of my wits. The river was shallow enough to wade,
mostly, and there was a gravel bar in the middle, but Mack had to help
us over one by one: Rosko because of his injuries, you because it seemed
you might at any moment sit down in the current and let it carry you
away, and me because I was rigid with terror. The lines of current in the
water looked like alligators to me; they always do.

When we emerged on the other side, with my heart rate back below
120, a thin veil of ash reached us. We found ourselves in vineyards that
had already turned gray: arriving in Armenia was like walking into a
crumbling black-and-white photograph. We reached a dirt road and
followed it north, up a shallow slope that rose above the vineyards.
Soon we saw the river again, below us, and a shadowy outline of the
mountain.

You stopped, as if to catch your breath. "Come on," I said, taking
your arm. "We need to keep going." But you resisted, turned, and that
was when you looked me in the eye for the first time. It was like you
were trying to remember something, or put a difficult idea into words.

"Tell me what happened up there," I said. "Describe it. Talk to me,
Daniel Calder."

You said nothing—but it wasn't that you looked like a sleepwalker;
you didn't have that creepily empty, classic Mystery stare. You looked
intensely preoccupied, like someone trying to solve a difficult puzzle
under time pressure—or like someone who just received news too bad

to take in. You turned back to the mountain again and raised one arm, as if you were about to point to it. But the gesture was odder than that. You held your palm up flat, as if pressed against an invisible pane, and spread your fingers wide, grasping at something you couldn't reach.

When you spoke, that first time after the eruption, the accent was your own, but not the pattern of intonation. Not the pitch either, which was higher than usual, more feminine. And every word seemed to cost you struggle, effort:

"Kor-QET-si—"

"Kor-QET-si, dol-ETH-mor, uk—"

"Kor-QET-si, dol-ETH-mor, uk-WAI-jen, voh-DJE-mun."

There were tears in your eyes. Tears in mine too, because you'd taken me in one minute from thinking you were a Mystery to thinking that perhaps, if possible, it was worse than that.

Who were you? What mind, what consciousness, was in there, behind those familiar eyes?

At least you switched back to English briefly after that. "They'll come back," you said quietly, in almost your own voice. But the next thing you said, at least it wasn't in the language of the Architects, but it came out with a great anguished struggle, each word a burden. It was like you were possessed by someone, speaking in tongues. The "other" voice, coming through yours, was clearer now, not American, and oh, I knew it so well. It could almost have been mine.

Your mother. "It's everything, Daniel. Everything and nothing. If only they'd known."

You bent over, choking and gasping, and her voice came again.

"Everything and nothing. If only they had known. They'll come back. Stop them, Daniel. Before it's too late."

PART I:

AFTERMATH

Chapter I

The Universe Vanishes

Don't worry, I'm going to tell you the whole story. Everything you missed, everything you were robbed of, everything that happened at the edge of your understanding when you were present but absent. Yes, the whole story of what I tried to make sense of, and what I tried to do to help you, and what happened instead. But I can't do that, can't give you a true picture of what happened out there in the world, without you knowing what I was dealing with privately, inside me, *in here*. (The public and the private. Facts versus feelings. *Is* and *seems*. "A theme to which we'll return," as your dad liked to say in his lectures. Oh aye.) And I want especially to make one wee detail of my inner emotional geography totally clear.

OK by you if we do that?

Cards on the table, before we move on?

So. The short version is that when we got back from Ararat, your famously brilliant, logical, levelheaded sister was a sniveling, useless mess. A mental and emotional farm-fry. Exhausted, rattled, a bag of nerves without a clue. I wanted answers, and I wanted them yesterday, and I had to face the fact that I didn't even know what questions to ask. Oh, and I was desperately, desperately *thirsty* for you to recognize me and say my name; failing that, to answer a question, or ask one; failing that, to at least say something I could understand. But you weren't there. Your will, your motivation, your *self* wasn't there—or else it was there, but it was buried under layers of rubble, like an earthquake victim, trying and failing to claw its way back to the surface.

"It's everything, and it's nothing," you'd say. "It's everywhere and nowhere. Now."

"What is, D? Are you talking about the Architects? Are you talking about something you saw, something you experienced when they were there?"

"It's light, everywhere. It's a—, it's a—"

"A what?"

"A kind of perfection."

"What is?"

"A hunger."

"Daniel, please—"

"No bodies. No emotions. No time."

"Daniel—"

Then there'd be five minutes of silence, or a day of silence, and you'd suddenly say: "They will return for us."

That was the kind of thing that came out, when you spoke, and even the half-lucid moments were erratic and fleeting. You had a foot in two worlds, and you were fully present in neither of them. Limbo: isn't that what Catholics call it—like, a traffic jam in the afterlife, when you've departed but you can't arrive? Ninety-nine percent of the time you were silent, enigmatic, and unreachable. And on top of that you scared the crap out of me by shifting without warning between a manner that was relaxed, as if you were just an amused observer of the human comedy, and a burning anguish that only your eyes could articulate. Above all else, I wanted to find a way to bring you back, to rescue you from whatever had happened up there, but both your anxiousness and your long silences reminded me of the worst rumor from the outside world. One by one the Mysteries were "coming to a stop," as someone had said, "like battery-powered toys when the juice runs out." For all their superficial physical health, the people the Architects had left behind as blanks, as empty husks, were dying.

What was I to believe? What was I to do? Why could I no longer even concentrate on what to believe or do? One thing I did, even though I'd kind of guessed it'd be useless, was persuade Gabi Eisler to be the designated grown-up and take you to a doctor, then a neurologist, then a shrink. Three pale balding men in their fifties: they could have been brothers.

Or parrots on a perch: "We can do nothing for these people."

I was really just going through the motions—no stone unturned and all. But "these people"—how dare they? Violent impulses aren't usually my thing, but I imagined them saying what they were so clearly thinking—*The Mysteries are a lost cause; let it go; we shouldn't waste resources on them*—and then I imagined punching their oversized noses.

It wasn't their fault. I just wanted them to have answers because I didn't. So much for the cool, intellectually hyperconfident, somewhere-on-the-spectrum savant. So much for the miniature know-it-all, blinking cutely in the glare of the Shanghai TV lights. That's who I was supposed to be, D. That's how I'd been *constructed*. An adult genius in a child's body. A thinking machine. A once-in-a-lifetime phenom. *Daughter of archaeologists can speak twelve languages, has "unmeasurable" IQ,* et cetera, et cetera, et bloody cetera. I'd spent seventeen years surrounded by those bright, tinny trumpet notes of amazement and ignorant praise. And now, when I needed it most, my confidence in my own understanding, even my own mental stability, was no longer just lower than people had come to expect. It was zero.

Nobody suggested we move back into your parents' house, or use it, or even visit, and at the beginning I was way too fried to argue with Gabi Eisler's brittle hausfrau efficiency. She welcomed us, fussed over us, and laughed too loud in short bursts, like a person with depression in a smiley-face T-shirt. She also shoveled enormous quantities of heavy, wintery food at us—chili with corn bread, sausages with shredded red cabbage and mashies, great steaming bricks of beef-and-mushroom lasagna. You ate it all, mechanically and without interest, like an engine that needs fuel—and you still lost weight. Me, I pushed it around on my plate, tried to make the right noises of gratitude, and gave most of it to you or Rosko when she wasn't looking. When she thought I wasn't looking, she'd reach out and touch his damaged face, her eyes bright with tears. She was trying to pretend—to me and to herself—that she'd forgiven me for nearly getting him killed. She was trying to pretend, also, that you weren't giving her the creeps.

She made up a temporary bedroom, two camp cots divided by a curtain in their half-finished basement. It smelled of old paint and dryer lint. And maybe it was the physical claustrophobia, or the guilt and helplessness I felt every time I looked at you, or my fears for the future, but down there I felt myself turning into a person I just didn't much like.

I was pissed off with Gabi and Stefan for their frosty hospitality— as if they owed me any other kind! I was pissed off with all the people whose brains I'd have picked, if only they hadn't all been so inconsiderately dead. (Julius Quinn. Mayo. Both your parents. Derek Partridge.) I even got pissed off with Rosko, because he'd totally clammed up about Ararat; oh aye, and because one afternoon he actually said, "Morag, what are you so pissed off about?" Boy, did that do the trick!

Giving me a constant stream of advice was one of his techniques for not talking about himself.

"You have to sleep more, Morag. And eat more. And drink less coffee. Maybe get away from Seattle to somewhere you feel safer and can relax. Some friends of my parents have a poky little cabin out on the Olympic Peninsula that we could use. At least put some drops in your eyes—they look terrible."

I wanted to say to him, *Thanks, yes, excellent advice, Rosko, and I appreciate the concern, and now please, please would you bugger off, because yes, OK, the drops, I'll do the drops if you insist, but right now I need to concentrate on, uh, whatever it was I was thinking about a minute ago, and could you at least not stand in the light like that, because this cuneiform of Shul-hura's that I'm rereading, which by the way seems to suggest that the Architects said they'd come back when we were ready, is a swine to read in the best of circs, the individual wedges small as a rat's teeth, and—*

My eyes were red because I was getting even less sleep than normal. Also because every third time I looked at you, I had to take a deep breath, steal five minutes of privacy in the loo, and cry. And the sadness, the sense that I'd failed you, was combining with a rising tide of anxiety that threatened to breach my seawall and drown me in pure salt panic. Deer in the headlights? Ha. It was more like deer just galloped off a cliff. When I did get two straight hours of blissful unconsciousness—or, more likely, two straight hours of vile dreams—I'd wake up with my heart hammering, exhausted and desperate.

By way of unpleasant static in the background, the 'rents were still totally off-radar, and I found that I couldn't stop worrying about them. Jimmy, Lorna: Why why why no message, no contact? After crossing into Armenia, we spent two weeks stuck in Yerevan, while Rosko got one and a half fingers amputated and we jousted with four different national bureaucracies—German, Scottish, American, Armenian—over the delicate matter of being in the wrong country with no paperwork. I got one message from my parents there, just one, saying they were safely out of Iraq. Then nothing. Captured on the border by lethal jihadi wannabes and dragged back to a filthy bunker in Mosul or Raqqa? Captured by the Seraphim themselves in what was left of Turkey? Already killed for ticking the wrong box on the Supernatural Commitments form by some brand-new group with an acronym the West hadn't even heard of yet? I needed to *know*. The pinnacle of human achievement, the cherry on western civilization's five-thousand-layer cake, is that you can post a cat video from any yurt in Kazakhstan. But week after week Jimmy and Lorna sent nothing. *We're still alive*—that would have been nice. *We're safe*. Even: *We've been detained, but we're safe*. I could have settled for any of those. Nothing.

I couldn't contact Charlie Balakrishnan either. Sure, I'm a seventeen-year-old nobody and he's a busy international tycoon—a mover and shaker in the financial and industrial ionosphere whose daily worries no doubt range from the well-being and efficiency of thirty thousand employees on five continents to the new custom paint job on his backup Gulfstream. But when the director of his own fancy institute has disappeared, and his old friend Bill Calder ditto, and then he gets messages from me on his corporate email account saying, *Daniel and I were at Ararat*, and *I heard Julius Quinn's last words*, and *I tried to intervene in the Anabasis, and failed, and survived*, and *Bill and Mayo were there too, and Mayo spoke to me, but they died too*, and *I need to talk to you, please? Like, yesterday*, was it too much to expect that he would take a moment away from the company spreadsheets to snap his fingers and instruct the nearest PA/minion/lackey/aide to press "Call Back" on his gold-plated speakerphone?

Apparently it was too much to expect.

It was so irritating to be so irritated—with myself and everyone else. It was like having the worst PMS of my life, for weeks and weeks.

Can you imagine?

No, obviously not. Fair enough. So let me cut to the chase. With all that swirling around in my head, I have to get this one thing clear. Out in the open. Out of the way.

Are you truly ready? Good. So here it is: I decided to make things easier for myself by refusing even then, just as I refuse now, to feel even a tiny bit guilty about, you know.

That.

Kit was over at the Eislers' constantly, right from the start. She wanted to hear the stories and help look after you—which she was annoyingly good at—and she said she needed to get out of the apartment because her mother was acting "wa-wa."

"What do I mean, 'wa-wa'? I mean that she is like totally freaked, ever since you tell her about Mayo being on Ararat. Eyes is jumping around like two mice on hot plate. OK, so he was her boss, and instead of Mr. Smooth Science Guy, he is some kind of crazy. So I expect, you know, she is upset. But not like this. Fourteen-hour days is normal for my mother. Twenty hour, not so much. Probably thinks she can figure everything out single-handed. Understand what happened to Daniel. Explain Ararat. Explain what her boss was doing. Save whole world from creepy Architects if only she never sleeps."

"Sounds like someone else I know," Rosko said pointedly.

"Yah," she said, giving me a long stare. "Like Morag, who also is putting herself under too much stress, also getting, how is it, snapple?"

"Snappish," I snapped.

"My mother is all freaked because she is in middle of big something at her lab, and Institute's fancy mainframe computer is acting all screw-loose since a week at least, and her favorite student, who does all her coding and babysits the computer has, ka-pow, what you say, puff of smoke."

"Disappeared? That's the code geek she shared with Mayo, isn't it? Carl Bates?"

She nodded. "Is no big deal, I think, but my mother is like, total hysteria. Invites him to dinner, because she thinks he is lonely over the summer and needs a mother. He says, 'Yes, thank you for invitation, Professor, I'd love to come.' And I say to Natazscha, 'What you think we feed him, given you are worst cook in history of world?' This is true, actually. She makes Ukrainian stew with lentils, and smell is maximum bad, maximum, like you microwave old running socks. Whole apartment you can't breathe. And, lucky for that, he never shows up. I say to her, 'Good, relax, he probably forgot. Or he went on vacation or something.'"

Not wanting to deal with her mother's problems, Kit had plenty of incentive to hang with us at the Eislers—even though Rosko liked yanking her chain. "One thing I don't understand," he said. "Why is your mother's English so much better than yours? It's not like she's a Babbler."

"No, Rosko, she is not freak like you and Morag. But she studies English in school ten, fifteen years, and I study two years. Also, she is obsessive-competitive—"

"Compulsive."

"Whatever. Work maniac."

For me, having Kit around was wonderful. And also—how shall I put this?—really difficult. Because it meant that, on top of everything else, I was forced to put up with another, if possible even more painful layer of confusion and inner struggle.

Over and over, from the first time I saw her again, I said to myself: *No, Morag.*

No.

Be calm. Be sensible.

Bad bad bad even to think about this now.

You don't feel this way really. You only think you do.

I'd say things like that to myself while my back was turned to her, while maybe she fixed you a sandwich or played cards with you. (She was the one who discovered that you could still play, and enjoy, a game like Hearts.) I'd shuffle blindly through something on my screen, resisting and resisting the temptation to glance back at her.

Work, Morag. Work on Bill's notes about the Disks. Or the few bits of Shul-hura's Babylon tablets that you still haven't translated. Or why not email some random people who might have known Mayo?

Everyone goes on about your brain, so use it.

Then I'd glance back at her. And maybe her face would be at a new angle, or lit differently, or I'd be just in time to catch some characteristic gesture, like the way she always tilted her head slightly as she tucked a strand of hair behind her ear. And my heart would stop beating for a dangerously long interval.

Don't make a fool of yourself, Morag.

It's irrational. It's pathetic. It's ridiculous.

You have more important things to think about. The job is to understand what Mayo was doing on Ararat. In the hope of that helping you make sense of the Architects. In the hope of that making it easier to bring Daniel back.

A mission! A lifesaving mission! So put this silly, trivial, personal stuff aside. Emotions! Nothing but a bloody nuisance.

Who needs them?

It was right after one of these pathetic little autotherapy sessions that you gave me the picture of her.

Magnificent, it was. Uncanny.

The one positive thing those first weeks was that you'd begun to draw. It wasn't a skill you'd ever had, but you were visibly trying to teach yourself, on every scrap of paper you could find, like a frustrated mute seeking another line of communication. Old envelopes. The back of a foot-long Costco receipt. A yellow pad. Unintelligible squiggles at first, they morphed into thumbnail-sized kindergarten images: chairs that looked like a pile of sticks and faces that looked like potatoes. Then plausible houses emerged, and groups of stick figures. There was something that looked vaguely like a cave, with more figures, and you did that one many times, and though the features were hazy, the bodies gradually became more detailed, more accurate. Next you produced a larger, full-page outline of a woman's head; it was much more sophisticated, and though you left the face blank, I knew immediately that it was Iona.

"That's your mother, Daniel. Iona. She was trying to find out about the Mysteries when she—when she died. And you wanted to carry on that work."

"Yes," you said, but when I asked you about drawing the face, you looked away.

Then the drawing of Kit. It was on a totally different level again, like something a beginning art student had taken a week to complete. Head and shoulders, it was, with the head turned slightly. And the striking thing wasn't just that you'd drawn her face, but that you'd made it so real. With full eye contact.

I could easily have believed, and part of me wanted to believe, that in some sense this was a memory. Were you really dredging up the fact that once you'd had a thing for the green-eyed Russian girl, who you'd found so friendly and yet so oddly resistant to the Calder charm? But you didn't keep the drawing to yourself, and you didn't show it to her either. Instead, in private, you handed it to me. Presented it to me. Made a gift of it, with a formal gesture and a look that was hard for me not to read as amusement.

"For me, Daniel? Thank you. But why?"

"It's Kit."

"Yes, I can see that. You've done it so well, especially her eyes. She looks—she's so—it's a really good drawing. But why are you giving it to me?"

As if I didn't know! As if I didn't know that somehow you knew. By then, I'd already begun to see that your silences and absences hid a strangely sharpened intuition. You knew things it was surprising you knew. You knew things you couldn't possibly know.

I put the drawing away on the slatted IKEA utility shelf in the basement, under my collection of five identical black T-shirts. It would be safe there and not in anyone's way. I was grateful for it, and I made a genuine effort not to slip it out and stare at it more than four or five times an hour.

You know how Kit never seems to think about her appearance? Old jeans, no cosmetics, ponytail held in place with the blue rubber band from her mother's unread newspaper. So it was a mild surprise, a couple of mornings after you'd given me the sketch, when she reached into her day pack, pulled out a small hairbrush, and asked if I'd fix her hair.

I probably spent about half an hour just staring at the brush with my mouth open. It was an ordinary black plastic thing, five bucks at the drugstore, but it sort of amazed me, like I'd been offered the first-ever glimpse of a scientific instrument from another planet. *Whoa! In the depths of that secondhand Lands' End day pack, Kit carries around a hairbrush!* Fascinating! My whole concept of who she was shifted subtly at that moment. I don't mean it made her better or worse. It just made her someone who sometimes carried a hairbrush around, and I'd never thought of her like that before. It opened up a whole world of other possibilities. Delicious trivial secrets about her that were still out there by the dozen, waiting to be known. Maybe she loved Indian food? Or was allergic to cats? Or quite liked early Taylor Swift, but had never admitted it to anyone because it would fry her credibility as a fan of Russian punk? I had no idea! Whole continents to explore—

"Morag? Can you?"

"Sorry. What?"

"Brush my hair out. That's all. Do you mind?"

Mind? Was she kidding? I couldn't hold my hands steady. I couldn't breathe. I couldn't think, or string a sentence together. I was so afraid of my own feelings that I blurted something idiotic like *Your hair looks fine.* After which, naturally, I wanted to stab myself and crawl away to die, because now she would shrug, as if nothing in the world mattered much, and put the brush back in the bag, or worse, ignore me and turn to Rosko, and tell him a joke and ask him to do it instead, in which case I'd have to stand there and watch him do it, and feel horribly excluded, and on top of that feel ashamed of having such ridiculous feelings.

She didn't ask Rosko. Instead she took my hand, placed the brush in it, and gave me a look that made me feel like I was trapped in front of a heat lamp and might get blisters on my eyelids. So I brushed her hair. And it was a strange experience, because while I was doing it, the rest of the universe, including not just you and Rosko and the kitchen table, but all hundred billion galaxies, simply vanished, ceased to exist—evaporated and gone like a snowflake. Later, when she left, the universe showed up again, or enough of it did for me to watch from the kitchen window as she walked away up the street, trailing her fingers against the side of a yellow car. I felt violently, insanely, murderously jealous of the car. To get over the feeling—and maybe hide myself from the sheer embarrassment of having had it—I put my face in my hands and closed my eyes and took deep breaths, only to discover that I'd just perfumed my entire consciousness, every nook and corner of my mind, with the scent of her.

That's when I gave in. That's when I admitted to myself that for the first time in my life my emotions were not mine to control—had been, in fact, hijacked. It was thrilling. It was frightening too. And (how's this for irrational?) it managed to make me pissed off even at Kit. I didn't have the time for this. I was too preoccupied with Really Important Stuff, like saving you from a condition I didn't understand and saving the world from a threat I didn't understand or even believe in, but had to believe in because I'd seen it with my own eyes. Now, of all times, when I was trying to play the part of Morag Chen, Metaphysical Detective (Private Eye: Clients Include Daniel Calder and the Rest of the Human Race), how dare this tall, calm, kind, sane, funny, sensible, sarcastic goddess wander into my life and pick me up and pull me down without permission into this whirlpool of sentimental, self-indulgent longing? I had romance novels for this. *Captured by Love. Hunter's Heart. Tonight and Forever.* I can read one in an hour. I can scratch that obscure emotional itch without examining it too closely. I don't even mind that the narrator's always a thinking girl's nightmare, or that her dreamy stud-muffin of a savior is a spray-tanned chunk of lunk with a chiseled jaw, a Rolex collection, and the conversational skills of Washoe the chimp. Consume, toss aside, get on with other things. For years, that's been my technique for not admitting to myself that I'm a wee bit confused about certain feelings. My technique for coping with Lorna when she tells me one more time that it's a lonely life in an archaeological camp, but I'll meet a nice boy eventually.

Yekaterina Pavelevna Cerenkov. She was never meant for you, and it wasn't my fault that being pickled in testosterone prevented you from seeing it. So I want you to know this, D: as soon as I admitted to myself how I felt—and still without even the slightest shadow of a reason to think she was interested—I made a decision to expend zero emotional energy on feeling guilty about it.

OK?

Got all that, Daniel Calder? Not going to hate your "twin sister" for not being who you thought she was?

Good.

Now we have that sorted out, you can stop biting your nails and listen. Because, kiddo, it's story time. By the fireside. At whatever's left of your local library.

CHAPTER 2

THE FLAME OF KNOWLEDGE

After Ararat, after Quinn's death, you might have expected the Seraphim to deflate—a balloon without the helium. You might have thought that thousands of believers being fried where they stood would put off potential converts, or at least make them think twice. But it was just the opposite. The message of Julius Quinn had been confirmed, it seemed, and the new system of belief became an irresistible flood, carrying away Christians, Muslims, Hindus, don't-knows, and atheists without distinction. Millions of people who had been merely curious about the Seraphim—and who had also, perhaps, sorta-kinda believed in an afterlife (which is to say: they'd been told to believe it when they were children and had never given it a minute's further thought)—were finding to their own surprise that this time they really truly did believe it. The stairway to eternity! Complete with friendly Architects, like event volunteers in blaze-orange safety vests, waiting to give a hand up onto the first step! Amazing how many people wanted to give away everything they owned, and leave their families if necessary, and get in line.

The Seraphim were quiet, nonviolent revolutionaries: nice, ordinary people carrying their smiles door to door, where they fingered their narrow white scarves and spoke with calm confidence, like people who'd already seen the future and wanted only to share. They were polite about their infinitely large promises, not trying too hard to persuade but giving away copies of *Anabasis* ("complete with the new introduction") while proclaiming with great satisfaction the Coming of the End, the Beginning of Infinity, the Immanence of the Post-Human Eternity. Students with half-baked beards. Middle-aged ex–soccer dads in khakis. Retired people with walking sticks and neon-white dental implants, neither of which they'd need much longer because apparently the "unembodied" neither walk nor chew. Theirs was not a religion, they always reminded people: not a "mere faith." What Quinn had revealed, thanks to the Architects, they spoke of as if it was a brilliantly original but well-confirmed scientific theory. The deep truth at last about humanity's nature and destiny.

We hadn't been back in Seattle more than a week when I had my own doorstep encounter. A well-scrubbed, perky couple in their twenties, clipboard and all: they might have been going door to door for a local election. "Ascend!" they said. "Come with us, and we will ascend to the realm of the infinite!" It made me think of those freshly dead saints you get in baroque paintings—surrounded by a winged rugby scrum of angels, eyes rolled back as if Tasered by the Lord, being borne up into a cumulonimbus heaven. No thanks. I cut the conversation as short as I could, because I didn't want anyone putting two and two together. There were rumors, you see: rumors about a helicopter, which a survivor had seen escaping from the summit just before the eruption. Those people would have been oh, just *fascinated* to discover that Bill Calder's son, plus that Asian girl who helped with the Akkadian translations, had been aboard.

"Very interesting," I said, taking yet another copy of the familiar red book. "I'll be sure to read it."

"Please do. It will persuade you."

They seemed so horribly, horribly *nice*. Moony, earnest, harmless. I was careful to keep us both out of sight after that, and it was only partly because I didn't want us to draw attention from the Seraphim. On the streets of Seattle, like everywhere else, there were meetings, demonstrations, counterdemonstrations, demands for information, kicking and screaming. Ordinary life, like a layer of old paint, was beginning to blister and peel.

And then the burnings began in earnest.

When we'd left for Crete in search of your dad, a whole month or lifetime earlier, there had been, what, a couple of dozen cases of unsolved library fires around the world? It got some airtime, sure—a shockingly novel form of cultural terrorism, like the sledgehammering of antiquities in Iraq. (People said the same things about one as they had about the other. Being ignorant of their own history, they were filled with self-righteous amazement that a culture could believe it was a good thing to destroy knowledge and obliterate the past.) But the targeted institutions were small and scattered, and I remember feeling oddly comforted, as if the world had dodged a bullet, when the number of incidents didn't snowball.

This time, the number snowballed.

The first big story was a blaze at the Chester Beatty Library in Dublin—a modern building full of very old stuff. They lost "several dozen of the world's oldest surviving biblical and Islamic manuscripts, among other treasures." Two days later, it was the Wren Library at Trinity College, Cambridge: plenty of historic carved bookcases destroyed, but their first edition of Newton's *Principia* miraculously saved. The day after that, the Theological Hall at Strahov Monastery in Prague, another famous seventeenth-century library and described by one devastated bookworm as "the most physically beautiful library in the world," was totally gutted in the middle of the night. At which point some blogger did the digging and discovered many more recent fires (or attempted fires) around the world at other less-picturesque venues.

The timing was quite something: I'd been reading to you, and our latest bedtime story was Partridge's unpublished manuscript. *Burning the Books: What Really Happened at Alexandria.* I'd picked it up because I thought maybe, just maybe, talking to you about him and our misadventures in Rome might knock something loose inside you. No luck so far, but the book was a page-turner.

It starts with the headline stuff, the famous names, the human-interest clickbait. It's 48 BCE, and handsome Roman badass Gaius Julius Caesar is down in Egypt visiting beautiful Mesopotamian badass Cleopatra. The city she rules makes Glorious Rome look like Inverness on a wet Sunday in winter: it has the greatest roads, the greatest temples, the greatest festivals, the greatest public art of any city in the world. And the cultural crown jewel is the library, by far the most impressive ever. Gaius Julius's ships have rock-star parking in the harbor, right next to it. For the glam couple, it's a multipurpose trip: trade, diplomacy, cultural exchange, feasts and celebrations put on at great expense to impress the unwashed masses, and time left over to make the beast with two backs on a solid-gold bed in the palace.

While Jules and Cleo are lying there amid the damp silk sheets with silly grins on their faces, one of the Roman ships catches fire. Nearly burns the library down.

Oops. An embarrassing accident!

Or that's the official story. Partridge leaves you hanging at the end of the chapter, but you already know he doesn't believe it.

He jumps narratives at that point, gives you the history of the *saráf*, the shadowy organization with—like Seraphim—a name from the Hebrew for "burn." According to Derek P, the *saráf* were the ultimate fundamentalists: their mission was getting us back to the language of the gods by burning away all the corrupt, merely human knowledge. *Simplify simplify simplify*, that was their mantra, like all the other fundamentalists since. Save humanity from itself by cleansing the mind of impurities! Wipe away the fog of civilization! No need for any of it: we have the Answer Book right here!

He told us the *saráf* had a nickname; do you remember that? *The Fire Seekers.* Because of their taste for arson, but also because they were obsessed with the idea that the gods had first visited humanity at a volcano. And would return to us at a volcano.

But back to the smoke-choked harbor in Alexandria. Partridge says that Caesar's "accident" is, like the biblical version of Babel, another cover story. The flames didn't spread from the ship to the library. They spread from the library to the ship—a deliberately set fire that went out of control. Caesar (and Cleopatra, and the head librarian too) were *saráf.* Alexandria was their big project: the world's greatest-ever pile of manuscripts, preferably unique ones. Put in one place not to preserve them but to more efficiently destroy them.

The rest of his book piles up evidence that Alexandria was only the tip of the iceberg. Or should I say the tip of the volcano? There were big, important libraries at Nineveh and Pergamon. Ugarit and Knossos. Babylon and Nippur. Ebla. Constantinople. Ephesus. Stone buildings housing clay tablets. Or, in the later ones, papyrus scrolls. Not much combustible material, and their only sources of heat or light would have been half a dozen clay lamps running on animal fat. But when you look at the ruins? Inferno, every time. Listen to this, D.

I'm quoting him from memory, but that's OK, because my memory's a photocopier:

> *Imagine yourself arriving in a foreign country. You come to a broad valley, where felled trees, all that remains of a great forest, lie scattered across the land. As you watch, teams of people are busy collecting them, working together, stacking them carefully in the middle of the valley. A neat, symmetrical tower is forming. What is your theory? What are these people doing? One theory is that the stack of timbers is the beginning of a great building. A permanent structure, certainly; perhaps a monument to one of their gods.*
>
> *But there is another use for tall piles of timber.*
>
> *The evidence I have found is that the major libraries of the ancient world were created deliberately and lovingly indeed. One document boasts that at Ephesus they managed to accumulate unique copies of works in Phoenician, Coptic, Aramaic, and even whole languages for the existence of which no other evidence now survives, from as far away as India, Morocco, and the Ethiopian Highlands.*
>
> *These institutions were created by the saráf as sacrifices to the flame of purity. They were designed for the efficient destruction of knowledge, not its preservation.*
>
> *They were anti-libraries.*

Partridge was fond of irony: he called that chapter "The Flame of Knowledge."

"Seraphim," you said without hesitation, when we looked at the pictures from Strahov together. "Purification. Preparation."

You seemed a little obsessed: you even found an old atlas in the Eislers' shelves, a huge blue hardback with *WELTATLAS* in gold caps on the spine, and hunted for the sites, pointing them out to me and marking the pages. It was a surprise; it showed a level of understanding I hadn't thought you capable of and made me just a little more confident that *you*—all your normal mental abilities, along with your memories too, and that most obvious missing thing of all, your sense of self—had been obscured, not erased.

Rosko was dismissive of the fire stories, as if arguing with you—or arguing with me. "It's like terrorism," he said. "The proof that it works is that it terrorizes people right out of their common sense. My mother texts while driving. That makes her way, way more dangerous than any terrorist—but terrorism is always going to be a better story than a suburban mother with thumbs for brains. Burning libraries make a cool story too, but what's the big deal? It's cheap symbolism. Knowledge isn't under threat. It's not like they can burn down the Internet!"

You looked at him and tried to say something. "Manipulating—manipulating symbols. Numbers. They—if they—they can—" You stopped, frustrated, and stared into the distance, gripping the atlas so fiercely I thought the spine would rip.

"The Seraphim haven't even claimed responsibility," I pointed out. But they didn't need to. They left the question of their own involvement infuriatingly unspoken but plainly implied. One of their new leaders, an American named Zachary Ash, chose instead to release oracular statements about what must be done:

> *Revealing our true nature and our true destiny to ourselves requires that we focus on one sort of knowledge only: the language of Architects, which is the stairway to the liberation of the mind. Everything else is a distraction. Speak little. Forget*

your own history and culture and languages: they can be of no
use to you now. They are trash now. Leave them, and prepare.

It was odd—or, OK, so maybe it wasn't odd, and I'm prejudiced,
but it was interesting—that the established "faith leaders" were the ones
who came out swinging over this stuff. Not presidents and prime min-
isters. Not even scientists and scholars, for the most part. They seemed
stunned, frightened of the Seraphim's popularity and unable to lead. It
was the bishops and imams, the sadhus and the Panchen Lama, who
were prepared to call a spade a spade. They were the ones saying that the
Seraphim were dangerous, that they were misleading the vulnerable; it
was they who were mobilizing people to protect both their loved ones
and their heritages. Now, sure, if you want to be cynical—and you
know me: cynical is my default setting and no apologies—you could say
it was simply in the interests of the traditional faiths to point the finger
at their big new rival in the Hearts-and-Souls game. There's something
to that. But most of them truly were appalled, I mean totally gob-
smacked, by the idea that knowledge itself could be seen as the enemy.
God does not value the deliberate cultivation of ignorance—that was your
dad's old nemesis, Cardinal Gerhard Kirkmünde.

As the Catholic Church's head scholar, announcing new security
measures at the Vatican Library, he sounded totally plausible. But the
fires continued, horrifying one group of people as they energized and
enthused another. Kirkmünde again: *This terrible urge to purify has been*
with us since Plato. In the past it has found shelter within many religions,
including both Islam and Christianity; it also reemerged in new and ter-
rible forms among the Nazis, who claimed to be Catholics, and among
the Communists, who were atheists. Human beings and their cultures and
languages are diverse and complex—and an abhorrence for that fact has
been common in the scientific community too, for centuries. The desire of the
purifiers is to wipe everything clean, to get rid of all humanity's inadequacies

and problems at once, and to begin from the imagined simplicity of a fresh beginning.

Yes, Zachary Ash and the Seraphim said. *Precisely. But this time we are right. And the cost of not believing in purification will be that your mind is not adequately prepared. And the cost of that will be infinite.*

Inevitably, as the fire phenomenon spread, it got local. The main library in downtown Seattle was heavily damaged after a truck full of gasoline was left in its underground parking lot. Several city branches had minor fires, as did two of the smaller libraries on the university campus. You drew your own versions of each incident, over and over.

"What's so important about them, Daniel?" Kit said, leaning over me to get a better look.

Your response had a hint of Iona's voice again, and its precision and coherence made it sound as if you were quoting her. "People only lie if they need something," you said. "Gods also."

Kit leaned in closer. "What is he trying to tell us?"

She was wearing running shorts, and her feet were bare, and I noticed that the little toe on her left foot was slightly crooked. I checked the other one to be sure; no doubt about it—a tiny, insignificant asymmetry. Tell me something, D: How is it that you can be powerfully, powerfully attracted to someone, and when you notice something like that it makes them even more unbearably desirable than ever? Doesn't make sense, does it?

"Morag. Hello, Morag?"

I shrugged. Even if I'd known the answer to her question, right then I couldn't have formed the words.

CHAPTER 3

ALIENS AND EXTENDERS

The fires were unnerving, sure. But if you weren't Seraphim—if you hadn't already Accepted the Truth—what to make of Ararat was the really big question still on everyone's mind. The problem was that few people on the mountain had survived—they'd either died or become Mysteries, the fate you'd only partially escaped—so for the unbelievers, the undecided, and the global bazaar of talking heads, there wasn't much in the way of evidence. A scattering of contradictory eyewitness accounts, satellite imagery that proved nothing, some head-scratching seismographic data. Maybe that's why civilization didn't immediately fall apart: there were still sane and half-sane things for so-called experts to sit in front of the cameras and say. In place of immediate global panic, what we got in those first weeks was endless interviews with geologists, "international security consultants," priests, sociologists, and fortune-tellers. Also "futurists"—who turned out to be fortune-tellers too, except that they'd ditched the gypsy costumes and had better jargon. The televised chatter established one thing beyond doubt: being introduced as an "expert" didn't guarantee that you knew anything about anything—not even the extent of your own ignorance.

I watched it all—unable to tear myself away, like a witness to a road accident—and felt sorriest for the professional scientists, the sort of people who actually knew Schrödinger's equation from a hole in the ground. Most of them had a hard time being patient with Traditionals, because who needed God in a universe that the equations had already described down to the last quark and gluon? They were even more let's-be-frank about the Seraphim, who were surely just the latest and most successful in a long line of whacky cults with a death wish. Branch Davidians, Heaven's Gate, Order of the Solar Temple: you get the picture. But the laughter, or the smirking, had a hollowness to it this time.

The equation guys needed to explain Ararat—and, in the face of not being able to, they seemed torn between three instincts. Make up a story about the eruption that'll at least sound kinda sciency? Say nothing, for fear of being exposed later as an idiot? Or admit openly that you're stumped, speechless, up a creek without a hypothesis? Hard to choose: their polite, catty, ruthlessly competitive world was supposed to be full of disagreements about how best to make sense of existing stuff. Bird navigation—how the hell does it work? (Nobody knows!) Earth's billion gigatons of water—where did it come from? (Nobody knows!) Those swirly patterns in the Cosmic Microwave Background, like foam on the Mother of all Lattes—what do they mean? (Five different theories!) Those were the things serious scientists argued over. It was what you signed up for. New stuff wasn't supposed to show up this late in the game. New things certainly weren't supposed to sound like a bad tabloid headline. Any mention of Anabasis, and the Mysteries, and the unprecedented signature of the explosions, and you got the feeling that what the scientists wanted to say was *Put that away. It's not polite.*

A meteorite was ruled out almost immediately. Terrorists-gone-nuclear was clearly rubbish. One evening we sat on the couch—Kit and Rosko too; at least one part of my brain was grateful that Kit and

I were six feet apart, with you and Rosko in the middle—and watched a program in which they paraded some of the best muscle in physics. Professor A (Berkeley) said that the "Ararat event" was consistent with the earth undergoing a freak collision with a submicron black hole. Professor B (Caltech) and Professor C (Large Hadron Collider, Geneva) said that Professor A had his head up his singularity.

The Japanese astrophysicist Hideo Murakami was a Nobel contender. I'd heard of him before. Not yet canonized, not yet transformed into a Holy Man by a telephone call from Stockholm, but definitely a big name in the field of mathematically hairy exotica that might explain, you know, *Everything*. He had a pop-sci book, *The Memory of Time*—an obvious attempt to fund his retirement by pulling a Hawking—but his latest thing was a breezy *Scientific American* piece in which he claimed that Ararat might have been caused by (take a deep breath) "density anisotropies in the scalar field I call the Substrate." As if that wasn't enough, he went on to say that this Substrate could explain the whole universe, and even our capacity to experience the universe.

Should have paid attention to that. Didn't. I thought *Substrate* was kind of ridiculous, actually. It was like, hey, it turns out the universe is a parking lot; all we have to do is pickax our way through the tarmac and keep digging. Once we're down through the neutrino sand, the quantum clay, and the seven extra-peaty dimensions of string theory, we come at last to the Deep Underlying Reality at the Bottom of It All. Which is like, *gravel* or something.

Sorry. See how impatient I was becoming? I used to love all this haute speculation—the bright gas flares of exotic What-If, guttering brightly above the shale beds of everyday science. But it was too late for speculation. I wanted to know, preferably yesterday, WTF Was Actually Going On. And unfortunately there wasn't much to be said, or not much that didn't stink of the supernatural.

I think that's why some scientists went from muttering about quantum tunneling and energy gradients to saying that their money was on alien abduction. It was meant to be a joke. But the idea was given form, and a thin gloss of cred, by the announcement from the JPL in Pasadena that the Slipher Space Telescope had eyeballed an exceptionally Earth-like rock a mere handful of light years away.

Zeta Langley S-8A, they called it, and it seemed like good news at first because it fitted so neatly everyone's desperation for a second, untrashed home. It was the right size, the right mass, and slap in the middle of Goldilocks country. It had, if you believed everything you heard, a 310-day year, an oxygen-rich atmosphere, and average surface temperatures like San Diego in spring. Judging from the hysterical joy of the initial online commentary, there was even a faint scent of mown grass hiding in the ninth decimal place of the spectroscopic data. Then someone said the obvious and ruined the moment:

Oxygen-rich atmospheres don't come from nowhere. So maybe S-8A isn't a potential new home for us, because the oxygen means it's already home for someone else? What if the poor, abused Earth is about to become a second home? For, say, the Architects?

The idea was like static in the air when a storm's coming. OK, people argued: those reports we've been hearing about creatures dripping out of the sky above Ararat might be the mere raving of post-trauma religious hysterics (subtext: ha ha ha, what credulous rubes!), but the explosion was certainly real. And if it wasn't caused by "gods," what but an alien invasion could possibly be going on?

Cue the full 1950s panic-fi scenario, in grainy black and white. Beings with corny silver flight suits and eyes like moist American footballs are about to emerge from their aluminum pie plates directly onto the White House lawn! An inexperienced cop will wet his undies and pull the trigger! And one of the "visitors" will brush off the bullet like a fat dead fly and say, *Greetings, primitive monkey-creatures. You look so tender and juicy.*

I liked the discovery of S-8A. It cemented in my mind an essential division. One set of people thought the truth about the Architects was "up" there, in the Realm of the Eternal, while another thought it must be out there, among the stars. Kit expressed the idea just right, in her ungrammatical way. "Is always same, yah? When scary somethings happen, only we have the two ideas. Gods? Or aliens? So we have to decide which one. What you think, Morag?"

But the almost-unique privilege of having *seen* them left me with no idea what to think, and my only real clue—or hint at where I might find a clue—was the fact that Mayo had shown up on Ararat. Here was a man as belligerently, dismissively atheist as Bill Calder, a man professionally fascinated by the brain precisely on account of the fact that, quote, "We are our brains. And nothing else." So why'd he show up on Ararat, in his expensive street clothes, with millions of dollars' worth of scientific equipment, apparently trying to "measure" a religious ceremony?

Minutes before he died, he told me that he'd dismissed the whole Seraphim/Mysteries phenomenon—until Patagonia. Had he converted? I didn't believe that for a moment. Had he merely gone off his rocker with the sheer lust to harness an apparently limitless source of power? That would have been more in character, but I didn't believe that either. He'd known something. Been onto something. Seen farther into this than I'd seen.

That thought pissed me off in a major way, *naturellement*, but at least it pissed me off in a way that was motivating. If he knew something about the Architects, or had guessed something and was trying to figure it out, surely I could figure it out too? Natazscha had been one of his most senior colleagues at Charlie Balakrishnan's Institute for the Study of the Origin of Consciousness. So, despite her claiming to be too busy to eat, sleep, or talk, I got Kit to engineer a couple of brief conversations with her. Not helpful. "David's office is on the top floor of the Institute," she said, rubbing at the bags under her eyes. "I went up there as soon as I heard what happened in Turkey. I thought I ought to look around, because, well, you're right—the whole thing seems so odd. He had pretty much the whole floor to himself, and he was rather secretive. But there's nothing there. No notes, no telltale files or off-network laptops lying around with the truth inside. Sorry. Just lab equipment and a couple of empty spare offices. I can't imagine what he was up to."

There wasn't much on the Net, either, which was odd in itself. I assumed there'd be information on him all over the place, like blood on a slaughterhouse wall, given that he'd been a well-known researcher, churning out intellectually hip ideas while holding prestigious appointments at big universities. But it was like someone with time and tech at their disposal had performed a deep trawl and cleaned up.

Not much there, except the basic vertical career trajectory. Finishing high school at fifteen. An online degree at seventeen and two more by twenty-one. Right around the time he'd have met Iona, that famous first paper on brain emulation. ("Wetware to Software: Does Consciousness Count?"—not just clever, but a sucker for the cute pun.) Australian National University making him director of their brain science program about five minutes after that.

Rosko dug up an old interview full of superficial, let's-wow-the-masses answers to questions about brain science. (*Modern scanning technology can watch you in the act of thinking!*). And there was a politically incorrect bit, vintage Mayo, in which he seemed to be amusing himself by deliberately echoing Julius Quinn's theme—the purity and unity that would prepare us to become gods:

Interviewer: [Blah blah, preservation of minority cultures and languages.]

DMJ: "My friend Bill Calder, the linguist, is always going on about this issue of preserving cultural diversity. But why do we care about it so much? It's just sentiment! Wouldn't it be a good thing, actually, if all these minor languages and cultures died out?"

Interviewer: "I—I don't think I—"

DMJ: "Why not care about unity instead? War is caused by misunderstanding. Misunderstanding is caused by cultural differences. And what are culture differences but an infection caused by the virus of language? Sentimental people complain that the world is becoming more homogenous, but surely that's a good thing? If we all spoke the same language, and we all have the same cultural assumptions, perhaps we'd stop killing each other quite so much."

It reminded me of a line I'd seen in one of Derek Partridge's books: *The dream of total purity has proved seductive in every age. It is one of the engines of history.* And it turned out that Mayo was in the purity business in even deeper ways. At ANU, he got involved with a global network of people interested in prolonging life through technology. *Extenders*, they called themselves—or, more grandly, *transhumanists*, because they believed they were (to quote the man himself) *on the verge of a revolution in biotechnology that will accelerate our "evolution" a thousandfold, redefining us so quickly and so profoundly that within as little as one or two generations we can expect to become, in effect, a new species—as far advanced beyond* Homo sapiens *as we are now beyond our cousins the apes.*

The Extenders were a mix of high-caliber people in fundamental science, Silicon Valley übernerds, and bioengineers. Plus, on the fringe, a lot of people whose science training probably consisted of bingeing *Star Trek*. Their ambition wasn't to live forever, just to avoid dying for as long as possible. So they were all about radical diet retuning, advanced medical augmentation, megavitamins, micronutrients. Daily cocktails of modafinil and testosterone, served shaken over ice with a twist of serotonin. Discussion groups on cloned organs, whole-spine regeneration, and injectable nanobots—which, apparently, D, are going to live permanently in our bloodstreams, grazing on our middle-aged arterial plaque like trout controlling milfoil in a lake. There was a whole separate subculture of cryonics, too: they already had an old Nevada mine shaft, complete with geothermal juice, where for the right money they'd stuff you into a stainless-steel keg so you could spend as many decades as necessary hovering patiently at a few degrees above the floor of Kelvin's basement. A colleague of Mayo's had even organized a whole conference on advanced enzyme synthesis: apparently one of the big worries about returning from an icy vacation under Nevada was that getting you back to room temp might reduce your lovely, buff, alpha-specimen self to fifty kilos of ricotta.

Actually I wasn't so sure about the alpha-specimen part. As far as I could tell, the Extenders were almost exclusively rich older men with a personal terror of death. Reading their stuff, spittle-flecked with enthusiasm, gave me this vivid image of humanity's future: a couple of dozen palsied egomaniacs, cloned into thousands, forming a new superrace. They'd get smarter and smarter, and they'd be so pickled in Botox that each would live to be 130! Then 160! Or even worse! I have to say, it made the extinction of the species sound like a wise plan.

Perhaps Mayo was on Charlie Balakrishnan's radar even back then. Impossible to tell: there were big gaps in the résumé. I was expecting "Institute for the Study of the Origin of Consciousness" to leap out at me. Nope. And still nothing that would tell me why he'd ended up saying such very strange things to me just before Ararat turned him into a bacon snack.

A dead end. Literally. Though one more sentence he wrote at that stage grabbed me by the eyeballs and should have grabbed me more: *Once we have gone beyond individual diseases and solved the problem of the ageing process itself, the gateway to immortality will open in front of us.*

"Maybe you need to focus not so much on Mayo," Kit said to me one day, "and more on just spend good time with Daniel."

Was she implying that I didn't care enough about you? That was annoying! Was she implying that she could show me how to look after you better than I was doing already? That was probably true, and really annoying! Was the fact that I was annoyed evidence that I was feeling useless, and cornered, and defensive, and that in dealing with it I was showing all the cool maturity of a hypoglycemic toddler? That was seriously, seriously—

"You need to work more on helping him rebuild his memories," she said. "This is what I think."

I need to work more systematically on hugging you, I thought, and I was so annoyed by the complete impossibility of that ever happening that what I said, without thinking about it, was "You have any bright suggestions?"

I regretted "bright" as it fell out of my mouth. Just how much does life suck when you're half-mad with longing for someone, and they have no idea and never will, and you deal with that by insulting them?

"No, Morag," she said levelly. "I only have dim suggestion."

"I'm sorry. I'm sorry. I didn't—I'm tired. I didn't—"

"You said Iona liked photography, yes? So maybe find family photographs? Share them with Daniel. Maybe that helps?"

I swallowed my pride. "I'm really sorry. That's actually kind of brilliant. Maybe I should go back to the Calders' house and see what I find."

"Take him with you."

CHAPTER 4

NARAKAIN

Early that same evening I was alone in the house with you. You were absorbed in the atlas again, riffling through the pages as if hunting for something new. You seemed anxious, but at least you were doing your own thing. Maybe your abnormality was becoming normal to me; anyway I left you alone for half an hour and drifted onto the front porch. Feeling trapped, needing fresh air. I took my phone, which was a mistake, because it gave me time to catch up with the fact that they'd found an entire large village almost descrted in the High Atlas of central Morocco, with only children left behind. And that violent street battles had erupted in the favelas of Buenos Aires between Seraphim supporters trying to build a pyramid-like structure and other residents trying to stop them. And, from Japan, the big one: the Seraphim had taken over the Horyu-ji temple near Osaka, an explosion had destroyed the whole thing, and there were reports of darkness, "like an eclipse," and deafening voices, and "spirits of great beauty reaching down from the sky."

Honestly, I'd almost forgotten about you—staring into a peaches-and-cream sunset, with my mind as blank as I could make it—when I heard the Eislers' car pull up at the back of the house. Gabi and Rosko, back from the grocery store.

Footsteps on the steps up to the kitchen. A banging door. Then Gabi's voice: "Guten Abend! Anyone home? Hello, Daniel."

Then Rosko's voice: "Hi, Daniel. Where's—shit, what have you done?"

Then Gabi's again: "Oh no! Are you all right? Ach, look at the wall. Morag? Rosko, get a bandage and paper towels. In the kitchen. Morag, where are you?"

You were cross-legged on the floor, rocking back and forth, with a pair of scissors in your right hand and blood all over the other. It was cool in the house, but there was a sheen of sweat on your face. Gabi had dropped her shoulder bag and was on the floor beside you, kneeling in a litter of cut pages and irregular strips of white page border—the ruins of the atlas. She produced a wad of tissue and started inspecting the damage. "Iona," you were saying. "Iona."

"Oh, there you are," Gabi said when she saw me, as if I'd been absent without leave from a sentry box. "He must have cut himself doing this."

She pointed to the wall next to the TV, where you'd taped dozens and dozens of cut-out pieces of map, liberally smearing the wall wherever your wounded left hand went. Some of the pieces were easy to identify; others I had to kneel and squint at. New Zealand and Turkey (surprise, surprise). Ecuador. Alaska. Chile. Part of Antarctica. The Kamchatka Peninsula—you'd shown me a video about sea kayakers exploring that coast, with huge bears on the beaches and huge volcanoes behind. A chunk of East Africa. Iceland. There would have been something insane about it even without the blood. The maps were cut savagely, jaggedly, and attached to the wall at crazy angles. At least four long strips of tape held each piece of paper in place, and some of the strips were a couple of feet long.

You'd used a fat black marker to circle six of the map fragments, and you'd joined those six with lines, right across the wall: central Italy, central Mexico, Japan, Hawaii's Big Island, the island of Java, and Washington State, all connected up like bugs in a spider's web. And, just in case anyone didn't get the point, you'd used your very own red ink, fresh from your hand, to daub a list in three-inch caps right next to them:

VESUVIUS

POPOCATÉPETL

FUJI

MERAPI

MAUNA LOA

RAINIER

We'd already heard stories about Rainier by then—there were "unconfirmed reports," as the anchors liked to say, that groups of Seraphim were going up there to "sense" whether the mountain was suitable. Two groups had gone up from opposite sides at night, wearing nothing but street clothes. One person had died in a fall only just beyond the visitor center, three more died of hypothermia higher up, and a dozen who'd stayed with them had to be search-and-rescued. Were the Seraphim planning to stage an "event" there? (Since Ararat, "event" had come to mean something both enigmatic and specific.)

I was thinking about that, and still taking in what you'd done, when you surprised me with a word Gabi couldn't possibly have made sense of—a word I hadn't heard pronounced in seven years. "I'iwa." You even got the intonation just right, I noticed: the little pop of pressure on the first syllable, and the long, stressed middle sound liquefying into two: *Ih-iii-yi-wa.*

"I don't care about the atlas," Gabi said faintly, to no one in particular, touching her finger to the map of Washington State. She was talking for the sake of talking, completely spooked. "I gave it to Stefan years ago, for an anniversary. But nobody uses such things any more."

Rosko came back and started to clean you up. I put my hand on your arm, and you were trembling. "What is it, D? What do you know about the I'iwa?"

"I'i-who?" Rosko asked.

As if in answer, you reached forward and pulled down the six marked maps. Big flakes of paint came away with the tape like dead skin. Then from your lap you took a seventh fragment of map. It was different from the others—cut more carefully, emphasizing its bird shape, which I recognized instantly, even without the prompting of that half-forgotten, jungle-scented word.

"New Guinea," Rosko said. "But what's that?" He pointed to a neat question mark you'd drawn with a marker at the center of the island.

"What that is, Rosko, is weird. Daniel's marked an area called the Star Mountains. They're very remote. Almost uninhabited. It's where Jimmy and Lorna and I lived for a few months with the Tainu."

"That tribe you told me about?"

"Yes. A people whose entire culture revolved around protecting the ghosts of their ancestors so that the ghosts could go on protecting them from the gods. Their language is Tain'iwa—but the word *tain'iwa* can mean either 'the language we speak' or something more like 'the people who use words.' *I'iwa* is the opposite: it means 'the speechless people.' Or 'not-people.' Or 'ghost people.'"

Rosko looked again at the map. That's when we noticed that it was attached with a paper clip to a second piece of paper. I recognized that instantly too: it was a drawing of your parents' house.

Gabi had just finished cleaning up your hand and putting on a large Band-Aid. "Maybe we should have a doctor look at this," she said.

But I'd had enough of doctors' opinions about you. "No," I said. "He's fine. Come on, D. I'm taking you over to your parents' house.

We can look through Iona's stuff. Like Kit said—see if there's anything that'll help you."

"I really think it would be better if—" Gabi started, but I was running out of patience. I pulled you to your feet.

"Daniel has worse injuries that need fixing."

No drama, no one about. I let us in at the side entrance, tripped over a pair of your running shoes, and felt mildly surprised that the light switches did something as ordinary and predictable as turn the lights on. But it was dusty, and somehow unnaturally silent, and Iona and Bill haunted every inch of it.

I took you into the kitchen first, because it was always your favorite room and I hoped it would stir those memories Kit had talked about. Instead I found that my own memories were choking me. You, cooking mushroom risotto at that stove. You, kneading bread on that counter. Bill, opening a bottle of wine and pouring a glass for Iona at that table.

"Those cinnamon rolls you used to make, D. Do you remember? Insanely rich, with brown sugar and cinnamon and pecans, and about three pounds of butter. I loved those things, D! Do you think you could still—?"

But you held your hand up to cut me off, as if you needed to think or listen for something. You ran your fingertips over the cabinets, the magnetic knife rack, and the knobs on the stove.

"Here. They were. Here. But—it's—"

You stopped, with your head cocked. Then, as if coming to a decision, you walked out of the room and headed for the basement stairs.

"Where are we going?" I asked, which was a way of making conversation or not listening to the horrible silence, I suppose, because the answer was obvious. Iona's study. At the bottom step, you flipped the lights on. The house had looked normal, undisturbed, but when we stepped into her work area, I knew something was wrong. Every book and file had been stacked neatly on the floor. Derek Partridge's office in Rome all over again.

You stepped in gingerly among the piles and turned slowly, scanning the room. Two paces, and you were at the closet on the far side, pulling out typical basement-closet stuff: a coat; two plastic tubs, one for hats and one for gloves; an umbrella with a broken strut; old gallon paint cans, one with "Downstairs Bath" in black marker on the lid. Up top, at head height, there was a shelf with two brown cardboard boxes—"Spare Bulbs" and "Batteries." You looked at everything carefully, and then stood at the other end and reached up to touch, with your fingertips, a foot-wide space next to "Batteries."

"It's gone," you said.

After that you went into a controlled frenzy, talking loudly to yourself as you systematically ransacked the house. Drawers pulled out. Chairs overturned. Every cupboard and cabinet flung open. Bedrooms, attic, garage. Back to the kitchen. The words were an unintelligible mix of fragments, in both English and the "language" of the Architects:

> "They will know it."
> *"Ol-CHI-ma, dem-UK-tel—"*
> "The river into the cave—"
> "Calculating, calculating—"
> "So long ago—"
> "The volcano is a computer, a trap."

You frightened me: you seemed to be approaching some psychological cliff edge. But I didn't interfere, perhaps because I'd not seen you so purposeful, so motivated, and there was a sliver of hope in *motivated*. But eventually you'd looked everywhere, it seemed, and you had such a wild look that I tried to urge you to give it up and leave. You shook me off and went back to the basement.

It was on the floor, what you were looking for. It was leaning up against the baseboard at an odd angle as if thrown there, only three feet from the bottom of the basement stairs. An expensive old camera, big and clunky, the black metal casing scuffed from use. Iona's old Nikon. "She had this one when she came to us in New Guinea," I said. "It used to have a wide bright-orange strap. That flash of color through the trees was the first thing I saw when she arrived in our encampment."

"Iona," you said, nodding furiously. You held up the camera. "The I'iwa. The I'iwa were there. At the beginning."

The I'iwa were there. At the beginning. I knew what you were talking about. Or did I?

It was that summer of your first trip to Crete. You and Bill were in Heraklion, discovering that the Phaistos Disks were several thousand years older than they were supposed to be. Meanwhile Iona was globetrotting, because she was still building her company and hadn't yet made out like a bandit. But even then—so typical!—en route between important meetings in Oz and important meetings in China, she decided to take a week off and drop in on us. Because Lorna had a bee in her bonnet about the evolution of tool use, the family Chen were living in a bug-infested hut with a roof made of pandanus leaves, deep in the mountains, on the border between Indonesian West Papua and Papua New Guinea.

"Iona, pet," my mother said by shortwave radio, from a dripping front porch the size of a closet. "Ye're entirely welcome here, an' entirely mad. We're on a river that has nae even a name. It's a tributary o' the August, which is a tributary o' the Sepik. We're at least a twenty-mile hike from the nearest airstrip. An' the trails? Frankly, gurrl, even wi'out the leeches, an' the snakes, an' the certifiably insane wild pigs, the trails round here are an unmitigated feck'n bastard."

She must have known that news of danger, difficulty, or discomfort would only be an incentive. Sure enough: a few days later I was playing in a mud hole with some Tainu kids when I heard voices and saw a flash of orange through the trees, and the president and CEO of IONA Bioencryption Systems—Mom, to you—walked into camp with a big smile on her face. Two exhausted local boys, Willem and Yosep, were bobbing erratically in her wake, looking glassy-eyed, bewildered, shocked. No doubt they'd taken her for a typical *wait meri*—one of the feeble creatures who came in hordes, looking for the Garden of Eden, and discovered instead a kind of vertical tropical hell through which they needed to be carried after the first hundred yards. They probably took bets on how quickly Iona would pass out, then found themselves struggling to keep up. No one warned them they were guiding a world-class fitness nut who'd recently pioneered a new route on the south face of Aconcagua.

"That wasn't bad," she said in greeting, like someone returning to the house after a jog in the park. A camera—*that* camera, on the orange strap—was around her neck. She swung down her pack and handed me a mildly crushed packet of McVitie's dark chocolate digestive biscuits.

"Thank you thank you thank you, Auntie Iona! My favorite!"

"I know."

"And I haven't tasted chocolate in weeks!"

"Eat them all, Morag. They're good for your brain. And don't call me Auntie. It makes me feel old."

Iona also brought real sliced white bread. For dinner, we toasted it over a fire and ate it with canned baked beans. I introduced her to my new Tainu friends while babbling at her about their language and culture. And beliefs too—though I left their beliefs about the I'iwa for later, when we were alone, because I'd already worked out that merely saying the word bothered them.

"You're learning so much, Morag," she said. "But none of this sounds like archaeology."

"Morag has turned into our resident anthro," Jimmy said proudly. "What brought me and Lorna here was something else. Stories from downriver about the Tainu still using exceptionally primitive tools. We were already interested in comparing modern New Guinea tools—the sort of thing the locals were using before steel was introduced—with pre-metal tools in Europe. So we decided to trek up here and see what we could find."

"And?"

"Total wild goose chase," Lorna said. "Nothin' new here. Nothin' particularly interestin'. But there is a wee bit o' a puzzle. When we describe what we're lookin' for, instead o' sayin' that they've never heard o' anythin' like that, they get all sheepish an' want to change the subject. An' then they say, *Oh, um, we sometimes find odd things like that in the forest, but they're nothing to do with us.* It's like they're sayin', sure, tools like that exist here, but some other tribe is responsible, an' we don't want to talk about it."

"Did they show you any examples?"

"Morag," Jimmy said, turning to me. "This is your story."

So I told her about the Ghost People. Or I told her what I thought I understood about them.

"The Tainu believe that the spirits of their ancestors live in caves at the head of a valley west of here," I said. "I'iwa. The I'iwa almost never show themselves and never speak. They sometimes come out at night and hunt, but their purpose in life—or death—is to protect the living Tainu."

"From what?"

"The Tainu say that the I'iwa protect them from the anger of the 'volcano'—which stole the I'iwa's own language."

I used my fingers to put scare quotes around *volcano*.

"Hang on a minute," she said, turning to Jimmy. "You told me once that all the volcanoes here were at the western end of New Guinea."

"That's right," he said. "But according to Morag these guys keep insisting there's one right up the valley there where the I'iwa supposedly live. They say they've seen the smoke. It's nonsense, of course. Sorry, go on, Morag."

"The thing about the I'iwa," I said, "is that they don't like to be seen, and they're very good at not being seen."

"So how do the Tainu know they exist?"

"Some people claim to have spotted them. Not in the open, not standing there on the path. But glimpsed through the trees, maybe at dawn or twilight. And sometimes the I'iwa want to remind the Tainu that they're watching. So they leave signs. Broken plants or scratches on a tree."

"Or one o' these primitive stone tools," Lorna said. "An' the Tainu claim that sometimes sweet potatoes are stolen in the night, or that, even when no one from the tribe is out huntin', they'll hear a chicken or a pig bein' killed in the forest."

Iona asked a thousand questions. Did the Tainu think of the I'iwa as ghosts or spirits in the Western sense? Did they believe they lived forever—the immortal souls of the departed? Or, if they were dangerous, and stole things, and occasionally left stone tools behind, were they more like real creatures, with bodies? But then surely there would be more evidence of them? How could they be so elusive, so—

"Ghostly? I asked them that," I said.

"And?"

"I think the question annoyed them. Oma said to me, 'Agota ena I'iwa-ben, kopol okt indai. Okt'in, hawa filim waro'p aru.' Which means, or I thought it meant, 'They're ghosts. They're beyond our understanding. How can you expect us to know what they're like?'"

"A reasonable enough response."

"He also used a word from Tok Pisin, though—"

"That's the national creole, isn't it? I heard it in Port Moresby. But I thought people like the Tainu were too isolated to know it? Sorry, Morag, I interrupted."

"The Tainu know some Tok Pisin for the same reason some of them have vaguely Western-sounding names. There was a missionary here before us."

"A German Baptist," Lorna said. "Josef Kurtz. He taught them enough Tok Pisin to tell them Bible stories an' stuck around long enough to baptize some o' them. Sorry, Morag. Go on."

"The Tok Pisin word that Oma used to describe the I'iwa was *narakain*. That's literally 'another kind.' It means different people, another tribe—and it can mean 'not normal,' which from a tribal point of view is pretty much the same thing. But it's not the word I'd use for a ghost. We use ghost stories to scare ourselves, right? But what if the 'ghost' story was a way of covering up for an even scarier possibility? That the I'iwa were real."

"But in the end you have no evidence one way or the other?"

Jimmy said, "At first the Tainu said they'd found strange tools on the path. Only in one area, far up the valley near the waterfall. When I asked if they'd kept them, they said, *No, no, we must have lost them.* I could tell that was rubbish. The tools unnerved them in some way."

"Like Robinson Crusoe finding Man Friday's footprints in the sand?" Iona said.

"Yes. But instead of investigating, or 'losing' them, what they'd done was take the objects far into the forest and throw them into a river."

"Out of sight, out of mind?"

"Maybe. But I get the feeling it's something they think about all the time—they just don't like to. They believe these tools belong to the I'iwa. Their ancestors."

Ancestors. That's what I'd said to Jimmy and Lorna. *They're talking about their ancestors.* My mistake.

"I'm beginnin' to think they're makin' the whole thing up," Lorna said. "Foolin' outsiders but maybe even foolin' themselves. Maybe these 'tools' are the real ghosts. Thuss idea that they find physical evidence but always destroy it because it's bad luck; it's too bloody convenient. In which case we've been wastin' our time here."

"We're not wasting our time," I said crossly. "While you've been chasing ghost tools, *I've* learned Tain'iwa."

Aye, I know. A royal pain in the bum, I was. And I never appreciated how patient they were.

Iona was with us for less than a week before the gravitational pull of her other world, data tech, took her away again. "Got to get back to my negotiations," she said as she crouched on the ground helping me and one of the village girls sort through a pile of candlenuts. "The Harbin city government has built the world's largest server farm down an abandoned mine, complete with its own fourth-gen nuclear power source. It's already three-quarters built. I get to tell the local party boss that our DNA-based storage makes it obsolete; no point in ever turning it on. It's going to be tricky, finding a way to sound as if I'm offering an opportunity and not a career-ending embarrassment."

But on her last full day, fearless adventurer that she was, she left our encampment before dawn and went into the forest. "We don't go beyond the waterfall," the village chief had said. "The I'iwa will not permit it."

"It's a taboo," I explained, showing off my fluent command of anthro.

"I know," she said mildly. And then, when Jimmy and Lorna were out of earshot: "But the I'iwa aren't my ancestors. So perhaps the taboo doesn't apply to me? Don't worry, I'll be back by the afternoon!"

She wasn't. It was only long after dark, when we'd put in two hours of worrying and were trying to organize a search party among deeply unwilling Tainu, that she walked back into the encampment.

"Sorry."

"Is that so?" Lorna said, meaning *No, you aren't.* Iona looked pale, though: either exhausted or scared. But privacy's nonexistent among the Tainu, and we had to wait until later, when the four of us were briefly alone, to get the full story. She sounded like a kid admitting she's had a scary adventure in the wrong part of town.

"I went beyond the waterfall."

"Iona, lass," Lorna said. "We told you it wasn't wise, and we kinda dropped a few wee hints it might be dangerous too, so you goin' ahead an' doin' it anyway was totally a given. Please, tell us somethin' we couldn't have guessed."

"All right," she said. "I will. I was hot, so I waded into the pool beneath the falls to wash my face. I stood there for a while and sensed I was being watched. I kept seeing movement out of the corner of my eye."

"It could have been an animal," I said. "A wild pig."

"It could have been an animal, but it wasn't. Someone was trying to get me to notice them and follow them."

"And you did?" Jimmy asked.

"There's no way up except a steep path right next to the falls. I climbed about a hundred feet. At the top, right where the river pours out of a hole in the mountainside, there's a rock platform."

She used the end of a stick to scratch a diagram of what she was describing in the mud.

"In the center of the platform there's a round, flat rock, like a tabletop. I don't just mean roundish: it's unmistakably a worked object, not something natural. This was sitting in the middle of it."

She handed Jimmy an object the size of a fist. It was a flattish stone, shaped like a teardrop, with a round edge on one side; the other side had been knapped to a razor sharpness. He looked at it carefully, turning it over, and handed it to Lorna. She held it up, rotating it in her fingers, the way you might examine a monster diamond, and blew out a long breath before passing it to me. It was smooth and heavy. It seemed to fit into my hand as if it belonged there.

"That's a hand ax," Jimmy said. "It reminds me of things they've found in France, dating to forty, fifty thousand years ago. It isn't remotely like anything else from New Guinea. When Europeans arrived here in the 1930s they said, 'Stone Age people, Stone Age tools.' That was right, in so far as the locals didn't have metal. But local tools are 'like' that thing the way a bird's like a bat."

I must have yawned, because Lorna announced that it was time for me to go to bed. We were right in front of the hut the Tainu had allowed us to take over. Reluctantly I said good night. Before I went in, I turned back to look at the group of three adults.

"Doesn't make sense," Lorna was saying.

Iona stirred the fire. She was looking pale, drawn, and intensely serious. "Makes even less sense if it was made by ghosts," she said.

I went into the hut and lay down under the mosquito net. I don't know how long I stayed awake, but I must have drifted off while they were still talking.

You clutched the camera to your chest all the way back to the Eislers', where Rosko quickly confirmed that its battery was long dead. But there was a memory card inside. You plucked it from his hand and looked at it as if it was a holy relic.

"An old one," Rosko said. "Wrong size for my machine." But after rooting around in a boxful of cables, he came up with a charger for the camera battery and an adapter for the card. "Let's see what she left for us."

What she'd left was not much: the card was almost empty, and it gave us a frustratingly narrow window into your past—a dozen photos, all taken on a single not-bad spring day a couple of weeks before you, Rosko, and Iona left for Patagonia. Three weeks to the day—I did the math—before she died. The house. You in front of the house. Daffodils in almost bloom. A chestnut tree against the sky. You at the park, with a blurred jogger in the background. I wanted to linger over every frame, but you thumbed through them impatiently, your breathing short, and when you got to the end, you kept scrolling, as if you could magic more images into existence. At first I assumed you were looking for a picture of her, and of course there never are pictures of the photographer. But eventually you stopped. There were tears in your eyes—whether from grief, fear, or frustration, I couldn't tell.

"New Guinea," you said. "Photographs."

"Not on this card," Rosko said.

"There are photographs," you insisted.

"So where are they? And why do you want to see them?"

"Mayo."

"Mayo what?"

You looked down at the camera as if it was a wounded bird and hugged it to your chest again, as if either you could save it or it could save you. Then you said, in your own voice, something simple but perfectly clear.

"Mayo wants the answer. The I'iwa—"

That intonation again: it was amazing. As if you spoke the language.

"The I'iwa. They have the answer."

Rosko took the memory card and turned it over in his fingers again. "If there were more of these, with more photographs, Iona would have backed them up. They have to be online somewhere."

"Forget it," I said. "You know Iona—her company *owned* the encrypted storage business. And the big sell was that other people wouldn't even be able to find your files in the first place, much less decrypt them."

"Not the sort of woman whose password is *password*. You're right. So, if there are other photographs, we have to find the cards they were originally saved on."

You reached for the little blue square of plastic again.

"Yes," I said. "Or Daniel has to."

Chapter 5

Wortspiel?

The morning after we'd been to the house, there was a tap-tap on the screen door: your old semi-Goth pal, Ella Hardy. Standing on the porch with a brown paper package under one arm, she was looking good, in an Ella kind of way: ripped pink jeans over glitter-red Doc Martens; a *"Black Sabbath World Tour"* T-shirt; a studded gunmetal-gray fake leather biker jacket draped over her shoulders; Midnight Corpse eye shadow (guessing about the color there); and a radical new retro-seventies David Bowie 'do: short, spiky, and the dye color was, guessing again, Vomit at Sunrise.

I assumed the package was for the Eislers, so I went to put it on the counter behind me. You took it out of my hands.

"You need a break, Morag," Ella said.

"How can you tell?"

"Hon, I'm *looking* at you—that's how I can tell."

"Thanks."

"Like I said, you need a break. Looking after a—looking after Daniel must be tough."

"Daniel is fine," I said. Which was a lie. What I'd meant to say was *Looking after Daniel is fine.* That would have been a lie too. But I wasn't going to admit my fears to Ella, because I suspected her of thinking you were—as one of the doctors had been pleased with his own frankness for saying—*another of these hopeless cases.*

"The forecast says ultraclear skies at the end of the week. Astronomy club's going to haul out the telescopes and head east over the mountains. It'll mean a four-hour drive, staying up half the night, and camping. It's what you need, Morag. A total change of scene."

I thought of the pile of papers on the table in the basement, and the need to bug everyone I could think of about Jimmy and Lorna, the need to pick Natazscha's brain about Mayo, and half a dozen other things. Above all, I thought about my general, overwhelming sense that I must *work work work* at understanding what had happened to you. Solve the puzzle. Not a moment to lose.

"Like I said, I'm a wee bit busy."

"Have you ever even seen Messier 33? A supercute spiral galaxy. It's three million light years away, Morag! If you come with us, and let me show it to you, photons will fall into your eyes that set out before human beings came down from the trees. Speaking of supercute, is Rosko here? It was him I wanted to ask, honestly."

I bet it was.

"He's out. I'll tell him."

"Be sure to do that. Oh, and I was going to ask Kit Cerenkov. Would that be OK with you, Morag? You two seem to, I don't know, totally get along."

Had she seen right through me? I tried to sound as if she'd mentioned someone I was only hazily aware of, out at the periphery of my life, instead of the girl whose image and voice and scent had taken over my mind. "Kit Cerenkov. Sure, ask her. Why not?"

"Fun fun fun," she twinkled. Her boots twinkled too, catching the sunlight as she danced down the front steps.

△

You'd gone into the living room, ripped open the package, and were already wearing what we'd left behind in Yerevan: your dad's old jacket. You were perched on the arm of a chair, sketching furiously. This time the face emerged quickly and clearly: Bill, wearing that same jacket, as we'd seen him on Ararat. It was the best, clearest evidence yet that you *had memories*. That there might be a way back.

On the left arm of the jacket, where all the blood had been, the edge of the stain was still visible like an afterimage. A note, handwritten in blunt pencil, was lying on the floor by your feet. It was from Mack's cousin, Anahit Boghossian, whose tiny concrete apartment in Yerevan had been home while we got our paperwork sorted out.

> *Dear Morag, Rossko, Daniel, please excuse my English. You forget coat. Blood stain was still there, so I wash again through machine. Difficult times, but we are strong. With best wishes of you in America.—Anahit*

"That was nice of her," Rosko said when he got back, swinging a bike helmet.

"Yes," I said, and told him about Ella's invitation. "She likes you," I added.

He didn't bite. He kept looking straight at you, as if admiring the jacket. "Ella?" he said neutrally. "She seems nice. It'll be fun to get out of here for a night."

For the hundredth time I wondered about him. He wasn't gay. But you'd expressed the puzzle to me before: he was kind, smart, and gentle. A charmer. Good-looking despite the scars. A nice guy who made girls—some girls—visibly woozy. But he didn't notice, or want to notice. I didn't get it. And I didn't have time to think much about it, because Stefan Eisler came in with a phone to his ear.

"Yes. This is his father, yes. That's right. Mein Gott—wirklich? I was led to understand that you—they told me—I see. Danke. Ja, sicher, Professor. Zufällig ist sie gerade hier. Yes. Right here."

His eyes were wide. Which wasn't surprising, since I'd told him the whole story by then, Rome included.

"Sein Deutsch ist gar nicht schlecht," he said, and handed me the phone. "Ziemlich gut sogar. Besonders für einen toten Engländer."

Stefan was right. Good German, especially for a dead Englishman. And, once he'd switched to his native language, it was hard to get the dead Englishman to stop talking.

"Me? Oh no, not even slightly dead! They put a bullet in the ceiling, and another through my right arm. A third ricocheted off something and ended up in my upper right scapula. I was lucky with that one. But they must have decided that they hadn't been paid enough to risk a murder charge, because after that they resorted to the blunt end of the gun. Gagged me, trussed me up like a turkey, and tossed me into a ditch at the edge of a golf course. I never did like golf. When I'd managed to loosen the ropes, I crawled a hundred yards and collapsed in the middle of the eleventh green. Quite dramatic, utterly ballsed up someone's long putt, and an ambulance was there in minutes. At the hospital in Rome, they x-rayed me until I was medium rare. *Bleeding into the brain cavity,* they said, *concussion with intracranial swelling.* Oh, and *near death:* they kept saying that to each other in loud whispers. Exercising their national right to become overexcited while stating the obvious. So much more entertaining than the English—our preferred modus operandi is to be boring while understating the obvious. Naturally I was near death. Anyone my age lives every day with one foot in the long wooden box."

"So great to hear your voice, Professor Partridge. Are you still at the hospital?"

"Goodness no. I overheard one of them mentioning exploratory brain surgery. I expect they thought I was so far past my sell-by date that they might as well use me for practice. I worked out where they'd put my clothes, waited until the coast was clear, and scarpered like a thief in the night. Thanks for the help, *amici*! Sorry to rush, but so much to do, world to save! *Stammi bene!* In two shakes of a lamb's tail, I was on a plane back to Boston."

"Are you OK, Professor? Honestly?"

"Never better. The only lasting pain is that those louts in Rome got to my copy of the *Geographika*. Probably the last copy on Earth, might be one of the keys to what's happening now with the Architects, and it'd taken me years to track it down. I never even read the whole thing before they stole it."

That was when I grasped that Partridge knew *nothing*. Not that Bill was dead. Not that we had rescued his precious papyrus of the *Geographika* and then been responsible for its destruction. Not even that we'd been at Ararat.

We were on the phone for over an hour. Toward the end he went so quiet that I kept thinking the connection had dropped.

"Poor Bill. And poor Daniel. Oh dear, I am so sorry, Morag. I've seen the pictures of Ararat, just as everyone has. But I had no idea how well all this fits—which means it's every bit as bad as I feared."

I should have asked him what he meant by that. Instead I tried to lighten his mood, and mine, by telling him how glad I was to be getting out of town.

"Ooh, astronomy!" he exclaimed, bubbly and as easily distracted as a child. "Tell me more. Where is it you're going?"

⚠

Ella was supposed to pick us up early on Friday morning. Late into Thursday night, I read aloud to you from Shul-hura's Akkadian manuscripts. "He's a recovering fundamentalist without a support group," I said. "His problem is he believes in the Architects, but he's stopped believing what he's supposed to believe about them. Listen to this." And I read you one of the passages that intrigued me most, retranslating the cuneiform as I went:

> *Those who obey will ascend and become perfect. Freed from the body and freed from death—eternal. Or so we are told.*
>
> *It is wrong to ask questions. Questions only obscure our path to infinity. Or so we are told, and so we tell the people.*
>
> *The Architects have taken away our languages, and these old languages may not be used, on pain of death. Only a few of us retain the memory of them. So I write these questions, on pain of death: Do they want companions, or cattle? And how can we know?*

It was warm in the basement, airless, but as I read and talked, you lay on the camp cot fully clothed, jacket and all; you couldn't retain body heat, were always cold. Your eyes flicked from me to the book, then to the ceiling, then back again. Again I had the sense that you, like me, were trying to work something out, under stress, under time pressure. At some level, I knew you were taking in what I was saying and understanding it. You were hyperalert and even less able or willing to sleep than me.

I must have fallen asleep. That's how I came to be alone and drowning, in a rough sea at night, ten miles from Antikythera. A wave reared out of the dark and crashed over me. The water was warm and salty in the back of my throat. I spat, gulped air, and screamed your name. But I knew it was too late: you were already gone, already drowned. I tried to scream one more time, but the water rushed into my mouth as the weight of my clothes pulled me under.

I woke with my heart doing 180 and my clothes drenched in the saltwater of my own sweat. You were lying down, still fully clothed but apparently asleep at last. I crept out to the bathroom, threw up, got some water, and changed into dry things. It was five in the morning.

I peeped in through our curtain divide again, and I was about to drop the curtain back in place when your right hand strayed up to your heart, as if you'd just risen to your feet for "The Star-Spangled Banner." But your fingertips shifted, as if you were checking the breast pocket of the jacket.

"Daniel?"

Ten minutes later I'd woken Rosko, and the three of us were sitting at the kitchen table, hunched over an object the size of a phone, while Rosko used a set of jeweler's screwdrivers to loosen eight black screws that looked like mustard seeds.

He lifted off the top of the housing and held it up to the light. Someone had written the mathematical sign for "square root of two" on it in black permanent marker: "$\sqrt{2}$."

"This is brilliant," I whispered. "A breakthrough at last. I know this is going to clarify everything."

"Don't go all bipolar on me, Morag," he said. "One minute we're all doomed. The next minute we're all saved. It gets confusing. This is a hard drive from a laptop, and it's had a rough time. See the dent in this end? Pried out in a hurry, maybe with a knife. Broke the power connector."

"Can you fix it?"

"Power connector's a piece of cake. The memory itself, who knows? Laptop hard drives are crap to start with. This one's been in a Turkish crevasse, an Armenian washing machine, and the international mail system."

He picked up the soldering iron and a pair of tweezers. "Daniel, hold this end steady for me with your fingertips. That's right."

Complete silence. It was like observing heart surgery. When he was satisfied with the new contact, he used a magnifier to examine the whole drive.

"Daniel, do you know what this drive is? Whose it is? Where it's from?"

It was probably seventy degrees in the Eislers' kitchen, but you'd zipped the jacket all the way to your chin, as if not having the hard drive in the pocket made you even colder. "Numbers," you said, shaking your head.

"What numbers, Daniel?"

"Numbers."

"Why didn't you tell us about it before?"

You raised your eyebrows as if to say, *You didn't ask.*

"This must have been Bill's. Yes?"

But you shook your head. "Mayo."

"Scheisse. Bill must have gotten it from him, and it's been in that jacket pocket the whole time. Which means—"

Rosko sat back in his chair and looked at the ceiling.

"What?"

"Do you write '$\sqrt{2}$' on your own laptop's hard drive? No, because the drive's inside the laptop. So if this is from Mayo's machine, and Bill took it out, then Bill wrote this."

You were nodding. I couldn't tell whether you were saying *Yes, that's reasonable* or *Congrats, finally you got there.*

"And so this is a message to us from Bill," I said. "See any other damage?"

"See, no. Which doesn't mean a thing. But since I'm an optimist I'll give it a ten percent chance."

You reached out and stroked the top cover of the drive, the way you might stroke a small animal, letting one finger rest on the black symbols. It was as if you were saying, *Yes, this is my father's writing.*

"Mayo knew," you said. "Eighteen twelve. Eighteen twelve."

Rosko looked at you with a tolerant exasperation. "Daniel, my friend, this would be an excellent time to make sense. 1812 is a famous date, isn't it? The Battle of Waterloo or something?"

"Eighteen twelve," you repeated, more insistent this time, as if our hearing wasn't good.

"Not Waterloo," I said. "That was 1815. Wellington gets all the glory, but he'd have lost except that at the last minute von Blücher and the Prussians showed up—"

"Morag."

"What?"

"Stick to the point, Morag."

"Sorry. 1812. OK, yes, 1812 is—is—oh."

"What?"

"Eighteen twelve isn't a date. It's two numbers, eighteen and twelve. We're not talking battles. We're talking a horseshoe of twelve symbols containing a spiral of eighteen more. It's the structure of the Phaistos Disks. Daniel pointed it out to Bill. You were proud that you'd noticed what Bill missed, remember?"

There was a faint smile at the corner of your mouth.

"You do remember! Eighteen twelve." I turned to Rosko again. "It will work, won't it?"

He positioned the cover over the drive and started reinserting the tiny screws. "What's that idiom in English about betting the farm? Don't."

"It will work," you said. We both stopped and looked at you.

"It will work," you said again. "But—"

Rosko raised one eyebrow. "Thanks for that, Daniel." Then he held up the cover to me before starting to reattach it. "Root. Auf Deutsch heisst *root* 'Wurzel,' oder? Vielleicht ist das ein Wortspiel?"

"A pun?"

"Ja. Yes. Like: the *root* in '$\sqrt{2}$' is referring to the root of a plant, maybe. Or the root cause of something? The origin?"

We both thought about that. But *second root of a plant* and *second origin* didn't make sense.

"*Root* has only two meanings I can think of," I said. "It's a noun, like in *The tree has shallow roots* and *Money is the root of all evil*. And it's a verb, like in *The pig is rooting for food* and *He's rooting for his team*. There's nothing else, is there?"

"Root two," you said in a harsh whisper. "Root two." You'd turned pale, with small beads of sweat on your upper lip, and you were trembling with annoyance or frustration, as if this at least was vitally important. You took a sheet of printer paper, picked a stub of pencil from where you'd parked it behind your ear, and drew a simple thin line, like a degraded sine wave, that was clearly meant to be Ararat. Above that, a dark scribble that looked like nothing—except that I could tell right away it was meant to be the cloud from which the Architects had emerged. Then you mashed the pencil point down so hard that the point crumbled, and wrote a thick black "$\sqrt{2}$" inside the shape of the cone.

"Why Mayo was there," you said again, looking at us as if you simply couldn't understand how slow we were being. "Root two. Root. Two."

Or, language being a tricky thing, that's what I thought you said.

Rosko searched around in his box full of cables, found what he wanted, and hooked the drive up to my machine. Nothing happened. He raised his eyebrows in a resigned, told-you-so look, but unplugged it, poked at the connectors, and tried again. There was a faint, almost inaudible hum that stopped, started again, and made all our hearts skip a beat with a single high squeal, *eeeeeeeeeee*. It sounded like a pig falling off a cliff.

"Great. So much for that," I said.

"Patience, patience, patience." He took the entire housing off again and cleaned the inside with compressed air. Moving so slowly that I wanted to scream, he clipped two wires and resoldered them. Finally he was ready to try again. And, impossibly, it worked. The names of sixty-eight files—I could have guessed that number—unpacked themselves across the screen:

> *Phaistos_original_a.tiff*
> *Phaistos_original_b.tiff*
> *Phaistos_calder_01a.tiff*
> *Phaistos_calder_01b.tiff*
> *Phaistos_calder_02a.tiff* . . .

I couldn't speak, so I pointed to the first one. When Rosko opened it, what swam up onto the screen like a pizza was one side of the first Phaistos Disk—the one Bill took you to see at the museum in Heraklion.

"Now open this one," I said, picking another file at random near the end of the list. It was a Disk we'd never seen.

"Must be one of Cicero's souvenirs," Rosko said. "From the wreck."

"Then we have all thirty-four known Disks here."

He nodded. "Sixty-eight sides. Mayo must have had them, like he told you, and Bill managed to steal these images."

"I can unpick the puzzle now," I said. "I'm sure I can." I was trying for total confidence, which was way more than I felt; it didn't help that Rosko said nothing. I wanted to say, *What? What? Don't you believe me?* I settled instead for "The first thing is to not lose any of this."

"I can upload it all to—"

"No. Not the web. But make sure we have it safe. Save the files to something portable too. I should get down to work right away and—"

A door slammed, and I heard the beep of a car being locked. You were already standing at the window, as if you'd anticipated the noise. Rosko stood up and looked out over your shoulder. "It's Ella. Driving a huge new truck. Toyota Testosterone, Chevy MegaHeavy, something like that."

I looked out too. She had just climbed out and was adjusting a stretchy, horizontally striped black-and-white microskirt.

"She's got a thing for you, Rosko. You do know that, don't you?"

"Don't be ridiculous."

"I'm serious. The hots, totally."

He turned to the screen again. "This is a big job. Full manual count of the symbols, key in all the data, reconfigure the statistical app."

"I should stay here, then. Get started."

"Don't do that. You need the break. We both need the break. And it's a one-night thing—we'll be back here tomorrow. Soon enough."

"Bill looked for this material for ten years. Now I have it in my hands, and you want me to leave it?"

"For a few hours, yes. Come back to this rested."

There was a bang on the screen door. "You guys ready to roll?"

I went to let her in. "Hi, Ella. Killer skirt."

She used both hands to smooth it against her thighs, then adjusted her earrings, which were wooden *X* and *Y* Scrabble tiles. "I already picked up Kit for you." She was speaking to me, but looking past me at Rosko. "Are you coming or not?"

Picked up Kit for you. Was that merely an odd way to put it? A slip of the tongue? Or a carefully calibrated tease? Whatever: sure enough, Kit was stepping out of the truck on the far side of the street. She hadn't seen me. She was standing under a cherry tree, right hand on left shoulder, stretching. Above her, a solitary scrap of cloud was glowing pink in a clear sky.

We had a full set of Disk images. A real breakthrough at last? Now maybe I could get somewhere? The right thing to do, obviously, was blow off the trip and get down to work without delay. And part of me wanted nothing more than that.

Part of me. But we all live with little hints of schizophrenia, don't we? It was like two people squabbling inside my head. Left brain, right brain. Or sensible brain, insane brain.

The Disks!

The chance to get out of the Eislers' house and be around Kit!

The Disks!

The chance—

"We've not even thought about food, or what clothes to bring, or camping gear," Rosko said to Ella.

"Julia's bringing food for an army. I have spare camping gear. How long will it take you to find a sleeping bag, warm clothes, and a toothbrush?"

I took a long look at the image on the screen. When I looked at Ella again, she was using an antique silver compact to adjust her jet-black lipstick. I felt weak and stupid for doing the wrong thing.

"Five minutes," I said.

CHAPTER 6

FOOL FOR LOVE

It was an ordinary drive. A strange journey. A turning point.

For an hour, up into the mountains, we talked about everything and nothing. Ella seemed relaxed, even if she kept glancing sideways at Rosko. Rosko seemed no more troubled than usual and yawned frequently—friendly with Ella, but clueless about the attention he was getting. You were wary, twitchy, clutching Iona's camera and shivering under a blanket even though it was a warm day; you stared out of the window, your eyes wide, like you were suffering from a combination of the flu and acute agoraphobia. From time to time you'd mutter fragments of sentences, and you began to calm down only when I handed you sunglasses and your sketch pad. You spent a long time drawing an odd series of pictures. They were shaky because of the truck's movement, and each one was framed by a sketch of the back of a camera, as if you were drawing her viewpoint—magically recreating her missing shots. And sure enough: one of them, more elaborate and detailed than the others, showed a small clearing in a forest. It wasn't a generic scene, but a real place: when I looked closer, I could identify the species of nearly every tree and shrub. A memory. Only, not your memory, because it was a place you'd never been.

"What is you think of this new planet thing?" Kit was asking Ella.

"We're not going to see it—that's for sure. Wrong side of the sky."

"I mean, do you believe these stories about this is home to Architects or something?"

"Not a chance. If you look at the actual data, instead of the dip-wad journalism, for all we know S-8A could have sulfuric acid oceans. Or an atmosphere thinner than the Death Zone on Everest. Or enough gamma radiation to barbecue steel. Plus, it's thirty-five light years away. With anything like our technology, that's a round trip of three million years."

"Maybe the Architects have better rockets," Rosko said.

She shook her head. "If someone out there thinks thirty-five light years is no big deal, they're not using rockets. Warp drives, wormholes, teleportation, who knows? The point is, if you're commuting between stars, then you've invented something that makes the speed of light irrelevant. And if the speed of light's irrelevant, distance is irrelevant. Thirty-five light years or thirty-five million light years, what's the diff? They could have come here to show off their 'Einstein Was Wrong' tattoos from anywhere in the universe."

"Anywhere," you said, looking up from another sketch. "Or everywhere and nowhere."

"What does that mean, Daniel?" Ella asked. She sounded irritated, as if she was convinced that you were incapable of anything except the occasional eruption of nonsense. "What does 'everywhere and nowhere' even mean? They've got to come from somewhere, right?"

But you might as well have been speaking to yourself. "Everywhere and nowhere," you muttered to yourself; you were already busy drawing again.

We were all quiet as we came down out of the mountains into the gorge of the Columbia. Even for me, it was a comfortable quiet, for about half a minute. But I hadn't thought through the trip. I mean, I knew Kit would probably be there, but I'd never planned to spend two hours sitting inches away from her in the back seat of a truck, parted from her by nothing but a thin, invisible, increasingly potent, and maybe lethal wall of electrical current. She used a Swiss Army knife to take slices out of an apple and offered me one on the tip of the blade. "Thanks," I said, and discovered that my throat was so dry I could barely swallow. When she said a couple of ordinary, sensible things like "You want another slice?" or "Wow, look at wind farm over there" or "Tell me more about the Professor Partridge" I could only blush, stammer, and feel appalled that she looked and sounded so relaxed. I even got a curling paperback out of my bag—one she'd picked out for me, from one of those free libraries in the neighborhood (What did that mean, her giving me the book? Was it just a thoughtful, friendly gesture?)—and spent three minutes trying to read.

And another three at least pretending to try to read.

Fool for Love. That was the title. Go on, laugh if you want. Ha bloody ha.

Train of thought—train of inner argument—with eyes pointed in the general direction of the page:

> *Kit's relaxed because she knows how I feel. And she's OK with it, so it's not a big deal.*

> *Oh, get a grip, Morag. If she's guessed how you feel, then it's a big deal either way. She's relaxed because the thought of you*

being attracted to her has never, never entered her head, not even for a split second.

OK, you're probably right; I've been misreading the signals.

No! That's not the problem! The problem is there never have been any signals. None. You're . . . what do they call it? Confabulating. Making stuff up. Constructing the emotional reality you need to believe in because the real emotional reality—that she's not only not interested in you now, but never, ever could or will be—is too painful to think about. Am I right?

There's no need to rub it in.

There's plenty of need to rub it in. If you give away how you feel by some half-intended slip or look or gesture—which, let's face it, is becoming more probable by the second right now as you sit there having your smiling panic attack—she'll be horrified. Or maybe not horrified. Maybe she'll think it's funny. Interesting question there, Morag: Would you prefer to be an object of horror and loathing to the person you're obsessed with? Or are you going for ridicule instead? Monster or clown? You decide! Well, no, that's all part of the fun of being desperately, helplessly infatuated with someone, isn't it—you don't decide. You are powerless here, because she gets to decide in which of two different ways to make your life not worth living.

Should have stayed at the house, shouldn't I?

Yes, you should have.

Should have stayed hunched over the computer, doing the necessary, important, boring stuff on which lives may depend, and which I'm good at, instead of trying to have an emotional life, which I suck at?

You got it.

But now I'm stuck here in this truck with her. Right next to her. And I can't stand it, because all I want to do in the whole world is what I don't have and never, ever in my whole pathetic life will have the courage to do. Which is tell her. Be open, and clear, and look at her and tell her. Just say the words.

Cowardice will serve you well here, Morag. Don't do it.

Oh, shut up and sod off, will you? Just saying the words is all I want to do: "Kit, Kit. Listen to me. Listen, will you, for a minute? Because I know it sounds absurd, but I can't help it. I have to tell you. See, the thing is, well how can I put this, whenever I look at you, or hear you speak, or smell your hair, I have this overwhelming, um, this wonderful, oh, words are so useless! This exhilarating, but at the same time unbearable—"

I threw the book back into my bag as we crossed the Columbia. When we crested the long rise on the other side, with the great river gorge behind us and farmland opening up to the east, I turned to my left to check on you, then looked back over my shoulder at the view.

Anything to break the spell.

Anything to take my mind off my own mind.

I put my left arm up along the back of the seat, where there was plenty of room for it, because you were scrunched into the corner, leaning on the door. I pivoted around in the seat, making a conscious effort to focus on what I was seeing and not on what I was feeling, and it was only natural after a minute or so for my right hand to offer me a little balance by dropping into the space on my right side, onto the seat.

The boring tan-colored seat.

Only, Kit had kicked off her shoes, as she always does. And tucked her legs underneath her, as she always does. And so my open palm came to rest—

Not on the tan-colored seat, but—

Not on the tan-colored cloth seat, a dead, dumb material object made in a factory in Taiwan or Tennessee, which had neither feelings of its own nor any emotional significance for me, but—

—instead—

—*oh holy crap you're an idiot, Morag, an idiot*—

—across the smooth cream-colored arch of her naked foot.

Some absolute, hundred-proof madness surged up my arm and through my body and into my brain at that moment. There was an instinct in there, a strong one, to draw my hand away, to make things normal again, to take the world back a pace by offering a meaningless, polite apology, the way you do when you bang elbows with a stranger in a corridor. *Sorry! Invaded your personal space! Clumsy old me!* But the madness crushed that instinct; it was still there, a small terrified voice begging me to be sensible, to salvage things and get back to *before*. But I couldn't act on its instruction.

I stopped breathing, I swear, the moment our skin made contact.

The inside of my palm fit so neatly over the curve of her foot. It liked being there. It wanted to stay there. So it did—rebelling against the shrill cry of reason.

I could feel the warmth radiating from her skin.

There was a violent roaring in my ears, like static. There was also, at the same time, a silence as absolute as the spaces between the stars.

I was running out of air. My vision was blurring. And despite all that, a strange calm descended on me, because it was too late now. I'd made my terrible, awful, shame-inducing mistake. She *knew* now. There was no way to take back my hand's confession. I'd just have to wait for the world to fly apart and explode. Perhaps she would sit up, quietly remove her foot, and look out of the window with a blush of extreme discomfort on her cheek. Or perhaps instead she'd look at me in horror and say, *Fuck it is you are doing?*

And let's look on the dark side. (I was already looking on the dark side.) Perhaps she'd never speak to me again.

Hours passed. Whole monstrous endless seconds.

At the end of them, Kit's foot was still mysteriously there, under my hand. And then, in a development that I could see with my own eyes but not in the least make sense of, she took her own left hand, which was resting on her knee, and picked it up and opened the palm as if to look at it, and turned it over again, splaying the fingers wide. And shifted it in my direction. And put it down again, very slowly and delicately and deliberately, so that it covered mine.

And Ella was leaning over to whisper something to Rosko. And a horse looked up at us from a sunlit field. And Rosko was saying something to Ella in reply; I knew he was, because he'd turned in his seat up front and maybe glanced back at us—I wasn't sure of that, but I could see his lips moving, and oddly enough I couldn't hear a thing.

I closed my eyes. I was shaking. I took two long, deep breaths, and turned to look at Kit's hand, because it being there, on top of mine, was like a difficult theoretical proposition that I'd been told about by someone else and needed to confirm by collecting further evidence. Yes, no doubt about it: there it was. Kit's hand on mine. I'd never taken in how slim her fingers were, or how neatly she kept her nails, or the fact that the thin silver ring she wore on her little finger was pitted and worn.

When I summoned up enough courage to look at her, it was as if I'd never once before seen those beautiful, hypnotic green irises, chocolate-colored at the rim and flecked radially from the center with bright ocher and jade and chestnut. I could see nothing else: it was like they were planets, filling my whole visual field. I had to look down at our hands again, look up again, force myself to mentally back away from her eyes so that I could take in her whole expression.

She was looking at me steadily and seriously, but with a hint of a smile at the corners of her mouth. She continued to hold my gaze, rock solid, and as she did so she ran her thumb in a slow diagonal line across the back of my hand.

"I think I'm going to faint," I said.

"Is OK," she whispered. "Is OK."

All I could do was nod, and keep looking at her, and smile, and then stop smiling, and look down at our hands yet again. Then I touched the back of her hand with my other hand and maybe nodded some more and looked up at her and nodded again. I tried to smile again, too, I remember that, but the muscles in my face weren't working right. So instead I touched my fingertips to my own cheek, and then to hers.

From somewhere in the far distance someone was saying my name. It was Ella. "Morag," she said again. "Oy, Morag."

I glanced to the front and saw her looking back at me in the mirror. She was grinning from ear to ear, smug as a squirrel.

"What?"

"I don't want to give you relationship advice or anything, honey-buns. But if you sit like that much longer, you're going to get a wicked crick in the neck."

It was meant to be funny. It was funny—I could see that. So could Kit, who squeezed my hand, glanced at Ella too, and turned back to me with a huge, gorgeous, blinding megawatt smile.

I tried to smile back, but my face still wasn't cooperating. I got about halfway there. Then I burst into tears.

CHAPTER 7

HISTORY AND HOPE

That dry eastern rangeland was one of the places you'd always promised to show me, and you'd described it well, but its strangeness still came as a surprise, so breathtakingly different from the misty, tree-conquered coast. The land was open, undulating, and almost barren, with nothing but small angular rocks littered among the sagebrush. We could see snowy peaks, low and distant on the horizon. Occasionally the sagebrush gave way to plowed fields, cleared fields, fields furred emerald with new grass. Miles of this—and then, down a dirt farm road, we came over a small rise and saw a silhouette so unexpected that it might have been an alien spaceship. It was a lone boulder, tapered and rounded at the bottom so that it seemed to float a few inches above the ground. A lone boulder the size of a house.

"That's it," Ella said. "The Bretz Erratic. Five thousand tons of greenstone, brought here from hundreds of miles away by the Missoula Floods."

"I know," I said. I knew because you'd told me the story. The ice dam giving way at ancient Lake Missoula, fifteen thousand years ago. Walls of water two hundred feet tall roaring across the land, an unstoppable inland tsunami that carried giant icebergs with these monster rocks embedded in them. By then, the first Native Americans would have been scratching out a life here. I tried not to imagine, and couldn't stop imagining, how small doomed groups of them might have heard thunder one clear morning, and looked up in puzzlement, and watched as the eastern horizon glinted, flexed, and rushed forward to engulf them.

Ella pulled off the road next to the boulder. We parked so close to it that we missed the ageing dark-brown VW minibus that was lurking on the other side. But the figure I saw on the ridge—baggy clothes, lopsided stance, wild tufts of hair—was instantly recognizable.

"Oh my God, I don't believe it."

Kit followed my gaze. "Who is?"

"It's—I don't believe it. Wait here, OK?"

We locked eyes again for about half a second as I scrambled across her to the door.

"You are run away already?" she said, pouting theatrically. "Before even have kissed me?"

"Rain check?" I said. Then I ran across the field, stumbling on the uneven ground.

"Professor! How on earth—?"

It was Derek Partridge, beaming at me. "Ah. Good afternoon, Morag. A relief to know that I'm in the right place. Wonderful to see you."

"But you were in Boston when you called! You must have driven nonstop."

"I did pull over and nap once or twice. As for the driving, a scholar's job is to sit in a chair all day, and I've been doing that for decades. The same thing at fifty miles an hour is not much of a hardship. And, after our conversation at the beginning of the week, I had to see you. So"—he pointed to the Volkswagen—"I got Brunhilde an oil change and pointed her west."

"But—"

"Morag, please, *I know.* I'm a seventy-six-year-old wine-lover who's survived a brutal mugging and a week being prodded and condescended to by perky Italian medical experts who could have been my grandchildren. At the end of it all, I had to deal with the awful news you gave me when we spoke. And it follows that my decision to jump into my faithful old Kombinationskraftwagen and drive 2,904 miles just so that I can talk to you in person is incontrovertible proof of my senility. I humbly accept your judgment."

I stared at him.

"Wasn't that what to were going to say?"

"I wasn't going to say any of it."

"You are a true diplomat."

"No, I'm not. I say what I think. But I'm also big on subtle distinctions, and I don't think you're senile. I think you're a nutter."

He smiled indulgently, as if accepting that that was an improvement. There was something paradoxically strong in him, for a frail old man. That, or his connection to Bill Calder, or maybe his connection to you, made me lose it at that point. I flung my arms around him and nearly knocked him onto the grass. When he didn't fall over, I kissed him on both cheeks. He smelled of cheap shaving foam, and his skin was thinner than loo paper.

"I'm sorry," I said. "The first thing I should have said is I'm so glad that you're—that you're not dead. But I still don't understand why you came all this way."

"I came all this way because we're in trouble, Morag. Big trouble."

"We?" I looked around at the empty field with its handful of human figures.

"We, meaning all of us. *Homo sapiens.* History is repeating itself. I know a lot of history, and I'd rather it didn't."

"Are you talking about the Seraphim? Or the Architects?"

"Both, but the Seraphim are just enablers. The important point is that what's happening now is like a mirror of what happened at Thera and after, in the Bronze Age. The Architects were there then, and they did a huge amount of damage. But something scared them off. Now they've come back to finish their work."

"You believe the Architects are literally *gods*, don't you? The Mesopotamian gods, returning?"

His eyes twinkled mischievously. "Would that bother you very much?"

"Bill Calder taught me that calling something supernatural was the essence of unscientific thinking."

"Oh, Morag, my dear, you learned all Bill Calder's lessons well, and I'm going to miss him as much as you do," he said. "But *unscientific* is a bully word. People swing it around like a fat stick to intimidate people. To stop them thinking."

"Shouldn't we try to be clear about what's scientific and what isn't?"

"Indeed yes—and one of the dirty secrets of science is that scientists themselves often fail that test. Learn some of science's *history*, my dear! When I was growing up, well-known psychologists were telling parents that it was 'unscientific' to hug and comfort their children. That wasn't science! That was baseless, evidence-free drivel! But a white lab coat has such prestige in our culture that if you wear one and talk loudly enough, you can persuade people to believe any nonsense you dream up."

"Sure," I said, "but one example of bad science isn't a reason for believing the theology of ancient Mesopotamia."

"So let's just say that *the ancient gods have returned* is my working shorthand for a pattern that I see but don't understand. What they 'really' are, leave that aside for now." He picked a piece of lint from his sleeve, held it up to the light, and gently puffed it away. "The thing to focus on is that they visited us before and went away again—which is why half the world's religions are about begging the absent gods to come back. But leave that aside. Now the Architects are back. And they want what happened at Ararat to repeat, all over the world."

"So we have to prevent that," I said.

"It may already be too late to prevent it. The Seraphim have just declared six semiofficial 'areas of interest'—Epicenters, as they call them. Places where they're concentrating their resources for the next attempts at Anabasis."

"They're planning multiple Ararats?"

"Ararat had all sorts of historical significance for them, but it's in a remote area. Amazing that they got as many people to it as they did. These new Epicenters are all volcanoes in populated areas. Vesuvius in Italy. Popocatépetl in Mexico—"

"Holy shit. Sorry. Vesuvius. Popocatépetl. Fuji. Merapi. Mauna Loa. And Mount Rainier."

"You've heard about it too, then?"

"Daniel had, apparently." I told him about the atlas and your list on the wall; I left out the blood. "So this is like Shul-hura said about all the ancient worship at volcanoes—and all the pyramids and ziggurats, which were just models of the volcanoes, in effect. Places for the Architects to tune in?"

"I think so, yes."

"And then what?"

"More Anabasis, I assume. More Mysteries. And more power: they're getting stronger, you see. They're *feeding*, and—"

But he stopped there and looked around, like an old dog smelling the wind, and then waved his hand dismissively. "Now that we're together, Morag, in this beautiful place, let's save for later any more of these cheerful speculations about humanity's destruction. First things first: introduce me to your friends. And reintroduce me to Daniel—do you think he'll know me?"

"He doesn't even know me. Or I don't know that he does. He's only lucid from time to time, and the lucid bits don't always make a lot of sense either."

I walked him back to Ella's truck, where the three of you stood watching. "Look who came to join us," I said. "Rosko, this is—"

"Herr Professor," he said, all German and formal, putting out his hand. "Professor Partridge. Yes, I recognize you from your author photograph."

"Well well well, and you are Rosko Eisler. Der berühmte Bergsteiger!"

"Climber, yes. Not famous yet."

"Aber es ist mir eine Ehre, Sie kennenzulernen," Partridge replied, with a little bow. Such a charmer: *An honor to meet you*. It was flattery, but the real charm lay in the fact that he so obviously meant it.

"Danke," Rosko said. "Sie auch."

Partridge turned to Kit, and bowed slightly. "And you must be Natazscha Cerenkov's daughter. Yekaterina, isn't it?"

"Kit," she said, taking his hand. "Kit is easier. You recognize how?"

"Daniel's father once introduced me to your mother at a conference."

"I am looking like my mother?" She sounded horrified.

"Oh, there is a slight family resemblance," Partridge said delicately. "It must be your eyes."

"Good catch, Professor," Ella said.

It *was* kind of funny, I had to admit; I was glad to be turned toward her, so that Kit wouldn't see me smiling. "And this is Ella Hardy," I said. "Ella had the idea for the trip. You could say she's our resident astronomer."

I assumed that a crusty old Brit in a tweed sport coat and an over-painted teen in a microskirt and combat boots would disapprove of each other on sight. Instead, it was like long-lost friends.

"An astronomer? In that case, no doubt you have much to teach me. I see that's a Dobsonian telescope you're unpacking."

"Fifteen-inch f4.2."

"I'm going to make a wild guess that you're a deep-sky fan. Galaxies? Planetary nebulae?"

"The Cat's Eye's my favorite."

"Ah, yes! Dear old NGC 6543. Evidently we share the same refined aesthetic sensibilities! I shall look forward to the privilege of exploring the sky with you tonight. By the way, I do love those earrings."

I was about to introduce you last of all, but you'd stepped away from the truck to watch the dust trail as a convoy of other cars approached—your musician friend Julia Shubin, who had all the food, plus half a dozen others. You quietly absented yourself from those introductions too. It was only half an hour later that I managed to get the three of us—you, me, Partridge—away from the others. As the late afternoon light turned the fields from green to gold, we went for a long walk back along the farm road, Partridge propelling himself awkwardly but energetically with the help of a stick.

"Daniel, it's so good to see you again. Perhaps you won't remember me, but we've met several times before. Your father was my star student."

I didn't expect you to say anything. I was happy enough to see how clearly you were focused on him—how obviously you were listening. But you nodded, or perhaps I imagined you did, and you said your father's name.

"Bill Calder."

"Yes," Partridge said. "Bill was a remarkable person, as both your parents were. I'm very sorry."

He had the right instincts with you—kind of the way Kit did. Instead of pressing you to say more, he just chatted, as if it was a normal conversation, reminiscing to you about your parents. Gradually he came around to Bill's work on the Disks, and Iona's search for an answer about the Mysteries, and the way those both connected up with his own research on Thera and the Bronze Age. You didn't once take your eyes off him.

"I suppose I've always been fascinated with the idea that we might be thoroughly wrong about everything," he said. "That, with all our knowledge and our sophisticated theories, we might be missing something fundamental. And that seems to have become a bit more probable of late, what with one thing and another! You see, I think the Architects you met on Ararat were the same beings our ancestors worshiped at Thera. The same beings that Morag's Shul-hura worshiped, and then developed some doubts about worshiping. And the record seems to show that they were powerful—but that someone fought back."

"Too much knowledge," you said. "Babblers. Too many languages."

He looked at you for a long time, as if assessing something, and raked his hair into place with his mottled, lumpy old man's hands. Then he turned to me. "You only managed to read part of the *Geographika* before you two dropped it into the Mediterranean, am I right?"

"You're not going to forget that, are you?"

"No," he said mildly. "But no use crying over spilled milk, as my mother used to say. The point is, I did read the part about some Therans 'ascending' and others 'failing.'"

"Mysteries."

"Yes. But there was a brief mention of a third case." He looked at you and patted you on the shoulder. "A marginal case, where people lost all sense of their own identity, but acquired a holy reputation because they were seers, credited with knowledge of the gods. Knowledge of the future, even."

You'd been listening to every word. "There is no time," you said.

"Do you mean that we have to hurry, before the Architects come back? I couldn't agree more about that."

"They will return," you said. "They're already returning. Infinite and hungry." And with that you shrugged, as if talking to us was useless, and walked ahead down the slope through the dry bunchgrass to the campsite.

"A bit epigrammatic," Partridge said. "But he's more articulate than I expected."

"That was pretty much the most he's said since Ararat."

"You're right—he knows something, and he's trying to communicate it. He may not even know what it is he knows, but it's in there. Keep listening to him."

"I think—" I said. I couldn't believe I was actually going to say it, but Partridge had kind of a knack for making me feel that anything I said would be OK. "The Architects got to Iona. But I think he—"

"Yes?"

"After she died in Patagonia, he kept hearing her voice. He said it was like she was urgently trying to tell him something. And I think, at Ararat—"

"He succeeded in communicating with her in some way? As if she, or some part of her, had continued to exist?"

I couldn't say anything. I just looked at him.

"Well, my dear, you have an open mind as well as a quick one. That's a good thing. They don't always go together."

It was a clear evening, and the air temperature dropped sharply as the sun set. When a breeze came up, everyone reached for hats and jackets—or everyone except Partridge, who just stood there, oblivious, in the same thin white shirt and shabby brown corduroy jacket.

He had his stick hooked over one arm. A thin lock of hair moved back and forth across the front of his scalp like a weather vane. He was still as a statue. Then, without warning, he raised the stick like a sword, turned slowly as if about to defend himself from attack, and pointed it at a star on the horizon.

"Fiery orange dot, low in the southeast. Ella?"

"That's Antares rising."

"Indeed yes. An unstable red supergiant a thousand times the diameter of the sun. Getting near the end of its life, just like me. Though, due to lack of mass, I am relatively unlikely to explode. Oh, what I wouldn't give to be around when Antares goes pop!"

"Any chance that'll happen this evening?" Rosko asked.

He shook his head. "Sometime in the next half million years, maybe."

"Oh. I was wondering if it'd be worth staying up all night, in case."

Ella turned from examining the telescope. "If you're willing to stay up all night, Rosko, so am I. Who knows? We might get lucky."

Kit was standing next to me, pressed up against me, twining her fingers in and out of mine. "I think Rosko maybe not so smart about this?" she whispered. "Maybe Ella have to bite his ear before he is getting hint?"

I still hadn't heard from Jimmy and Lorna. I still didn't know what the Architects were, when they were going to come back, or whether I needed to understand what they'd done to you—where you'd *been*—in order to get you back. But we'd retrieved the images of the Disks, which I was convinced would lead me to a breakthrough. And now, for the first time in my life, I'd found someone to be with who knew instinctively, better even than you, how to allow me to be *me*.

Amazing to relate, D, but Kit just *wasn't interested* in the fact that I speak a dozen languages and have a photographic memory and a six-sigma IQ. She'd seen through all that, seen right through to the neurotic mess underneath, and for some strange reason liked it, felt comfortable with it, was even attracted to it. She'd unbuttoned my whole persona, peeled it off, and underneath—

Sorry. Time to switch metaphors. Shoes! I felt like someone who'd spent her whole life in shoes that never quite fit, and she'd thrown my shoes away and handed me a pair that did. It was so thrilling to be wholly, uncomplicatedly *me* for the first time in my life; so thrilling that it was easy to pretend there was nothing wrong with the world. Nothing I can't do now! The Architects are toast! Daniel's as good as cured!

It's amazing what the hormonal equivalent of being drunk as a skunk can do to a girl's judgment.

"I feel stronger now," I said to her later, as we lay in a spare tent that Ella had discreetly made available. "I feel as if I can cope with anything now. It's like I can see a path forward. Like there's a ray of hope."

Such a cliché, that, *ray of hope*. But I have to tell you: it was a super-nice feeling while it lasted.

PART II:
ZONE OF MIRACLES

Chapter 8

God's Monsters

The day started well. I'll give it that.

I woke up early, feeling newly energized and hopeful. *Get back to Seattle ASAP,* I thought. *Get back to the Disks, and I can kill three birds with one stone.* Bill had said we could translate the language of the Disks if only we had enough text for his software to work with. Now we did have enough—which meant I was going to succeed him as the world's most famous linguist *and* reveal the six-thousand-year-old secret of the Architects *and* find a way to cure you of whatever they had done to you.

Time for work!

Except that no one else in the campsite was up. Nothing but a grunt of mild annoyance from Kit. Silence from most of the tents. Snoring and boy-funk when I stuck my head in the one you were sharing with Rosko. And when people did emerge from their burrows, an hour or more later, they stretched and yawned, and wanted to take forever cooking breakfast burritos, and then noticed how good the sun felt and started throwing a Frisbee around. As the day grew more perfect, the vacation mood got more and more annoying—especially when Kit, of all people, said to Rosko that I was in "some kind of mood, whatever," and the two of them took you for a two-hour walk.

At least it was a chance to get Partridge back on track. "What did you mean, history repeating itself?" I said, pulling up an old folding deck chair at the side of his van. He handed me a mug of undrinkable instant coffee.

"Gods, spirits, aliens. It doesn't matter what you call them, because they're probably beyond our understanding anyway. But they want us, they need us, and it's bad news. Ararat was just the start. With every new Ararat, they will get stronger and harder to stop. They made us what we are, and you and I need to understand them if we're going to help defeat them. This isn't just about helping Daniel."

"I know," I said. "But Daniel is one of our best hopes for understanding them. So I have to focus on him too."

I wanted to pour the coffee onto the grass, but he kept looking right at me. "You've heard of this Murakami fellow? Japanese physicist? Higher mathematics was never my strong suit, but he's interesting. The first person to ask exactly where all that explosive energy is coming from, and the first person to point out that conservation requires an equal amount of energy to be going somewhere else. The idea that consciousness itself could be a hidden aspect of physical reality is absurd, of course, and it doesn't make a whit of sense according to our existing physics. But then I seem to recall that '$E = mc^2$' was a bit of a shocker once. Maybe the man's onto something."

At last the three of you returned, and it was time to go. "Rosko," I said. "You want to ride with Ella again, don't you? Thought so. Good."

"Uh, aren't you coming with us?"

"We'll keep Professor Partridge company. That all right with you, Professor?"

"Certainly."

"Kit, you mind being with Daniel in the back?"

She stuck out her bottom lip, for about a tenth of a second. "I do you deal. I sit with Daniel in back, then you let me call you Majka."

"What?"

"Majka. Is your new nickname. I invent."

"When? Why?"

"When I invent is five minutes ago. Why is because proper Russian nickname for Morag is Moragashka, and is too big the mouthful. Majka is better."

"What's wrong with Morag?"

"Nothing! But I want special name for you, yah? Name which is for me only. And I choose, if you like, Majka."

She said it slowly, drawing out the first syllable and then doing some complicated Russian thing with her tongue on the second: *MAH-dz'j-ka*. It made me feel like someone had removed the bones from my knees. "You can call me anything you want," I said.

Finally, on the road! I had just enough time to untwist Brunhilde's antique nonretractable seat belt, get settled in, and—pop. In the middle of nowhere, less than half a mile into a four-hour drive, a flat tire. And the spare was damaged. Which meant Ella had to drive Partridge to a town forty miles away to get a replacement.

It was still a nice day: as Ella helped her new astronomy buddy change the tire, herds of fat little clouds were grazing picturesquely eastward through columns of sunlight under a sky the color of old denim. But it was already late afternoon, and the weather was changing. Big fists of wind were pounding the roadside grass. An ominous gray band had risen on the western horizon.

Brunhilde could manage only forty miles an hour against the gusts, but she got up to sixty on the long downhill to the Columbia River—or sixty was my best guess, given that the red pointer behind the speedometer's cracked glass was jerking around between forty and eighty like a limbo dancer on acid. Partridge was in a good mood. "I love to drive," he said, as he failed to slow down on a tight, steep curve, ignoring the fact that Brunhilde, riding high on her skinny tires, had museum-quality brakes and was thirty years short of an air bag. I forced a smile and hung on tight to the little plastic hand-strap.

Your drawings were becoming quicker, more economical, and more disturbing. One, featuring a man in flames on top of a volcano, could have been Mayo, or maybe your father, impossible to tell. Another showed me in water, clearly struggling. But as we made our labored progress toward Seattle, you began a long series of drawings—twenty at least—of flames coming out of large buildings; you kept showing them to Kit, or to me, bringing them to our attention.

"You are thinking about the libraries, yah?" Kit said. "We have no Internet for whole day; I wonder if there is new stories."

I reached for my phone, only to discover I'd slung it in a bag that was now strapped to Brunhilde's roof. Kit must have been reading my mind. "I am having nothing," she said, shading her screen with one hand. "Maybe because mountains. Maybe because phone is cheap old piece of bullshit."

I considered trying to explain why *bullshit* wasn't the right word. *A phone can't be bullshit, Kit. That's a quality of what someone says, not of a thing. Rosko told me there's a philosopher who wrote a whole book about it. Apparently his main point is that bullshit is*

Maybe not. Instead I reached for the dashboard radio, only to discover that there wasn't one. A metal bracket was bolted to the underside of the dash. A bundle of wires poked out of it.

"Sorry," Partridge said. "The radio broke about ten years ago, and I never replaced it."

"You drive three thousand miles without music?" Kit said, sounding horrified.

"Not quite. I know vast amounts of Italian opera by heart, so I sing to myself. Very badly, but—" he patted the dashboard—"I have a forgiving audience."

In the silence that followed, while I waited for Partridge to burst into an aria, you reached forward and put another drawing in my lap. Partridge glanced at it out of the corner of his eye.

"You've a talent there, Daniel. It looks frighteningly real."

"What do you make of this?" I asked him. "The libraries—is this what you meant when you said, 'History is repeating itself'?"

Before answering, he negotiated the rest of the downhill run and swung onto the long, low bridge over the Columbia. The wind was even stronger in the gorge, pushing whitecaps upriver against the current. Brunhilde drifted, loped, and staggered, an exhausted marathon runner nearing the finish line.

"Just putting the jigsaw together in the best way I can, Morag. All my decades of research, plus your discovery of Shul-hura's alternative Babel story, plus what we found in the *Geographika*. The disappearances. The rise of the Seraphim. And Ararat, of course. My guess is that the library fires in the ancient world started for the same reason they're starting now: the Architects put into a few influential heads the idea that we needed to *back out of* human culture, so to speak. Destroy all records! Destroy the very languages! Wipe the slate clean! If the *Geographika* is anything to go by, the whole of Theran civilization was devoted to that project. They were obsessed with being worthy of the ultimate privilege—immortality. Anabasis was the end of life, in both senses of the term, and that required the right kind of purification. After Thera was destroyed, every culture in the region became divided between believers and rebels, so you had an almost permanent state of region-wide civil war. The Architects encouraged it and took what they could get. That's the Bronze Age Collapse—a mopping-up operation."

He was talking to all three of us at once, and he'd twisted around in his seat, only one hand loosely on the wheel. "Watch out for bicycle!"

Kit shouted. He swerved hard, narrowly missing a startled-looking couple on a tandem bike, and carried on as if nothing had happened.

I wanted him to say more about the Architects. I wanted him to get beyond his hippie-dippie "ancient gods" talk and say what he truly believed about them. Instead he started talking about his hospital stay.

"They did all those X-rays in Rome because they were worried that I had a skull fracture. The brain is soft tissue, so it doesn't show, and what you get is a picture of your own empty skull. Rather alarming! But you know how the brain looks, don't you, the two hemispheres? Like a walnut."

"I am thinking, like two pieces of bread dough put in bowl that's too small," Kit said. "Like, God made two brains for each person, but put both into same skull. And not enough space, so they kind of squish."

"That's a good image," Partridge said. "And there might even be something to it. Bill Calder and I were fans of a theory called bicameralism. Two chambers in the brain, like two chambers in Congress. The idea is that the two hemispheres of the brain really did act like two separate brains for most of our history."

"I think that work as well as snake with the two heads," she said.

"If the two halves were equals, yes. But the bicameral theory says our hemispheres were more like master and slave. Most people think humans became conscious over a long period of time, slowly rising from the mental level of the lower animals, then dogs, then apes, to where we are now. But the bicameral theory says that the big mental differences between animals and humans came much more recently. Back in the early Bronze Age, five or six thousand years ago, nobody had anything like our sense of individuality, personal agency or choice, free will. All anyone had was voices in the head. Inner gods, telling them what to do."

"So," Kit said. "This theory saying we are *not conscious* before then? That sounds crazy. We were, like, what? Robots? Zombies?"

"Not quite. The idea is that back in the time before written language, we were not individuals in the way we now understand the idea. Not self-aware."

"I don't see how there could be any evidence for that," I said.

"That, Morag, is because you share the modern prejudice that all evidence is scientific evidence. The big source for the bicameral theory isn't lab data—it's ancient literature. We think we know what it's like to be human, so we project what we're like back onto these people who lived thousands of years ago. But when you read Egyptian theological writings, or Hittite funereal urns, or early Greek poetry—"

"Yah, sure," Kit said. "Funeral urns especially. All the time."

"—you meet human beings with an inner life that's profoundly odd. They had only a primitive, half-formed sense of *self*. They didn't even think of themselves as individuals, really, as beings with choices. They just listened for commands and obeyed them. Or tried not to and found it didn't make any difference to the outcome. They called it *fate*."

"They were hearing voices?"

"Perhaps. But the bicameral theory says the voices were really the dominant left hemisphere talking to the subservient right hemisphere. The gods were inside us."

"Is good thing we don't have to be slaves of voices in the head now."

"Oh, but we are, Kit, we are. You think your *self*, the real you, is like the captain on the bridge of a ship, yes? Someone who sits in a big leather chair, three inches behind your eyes, watching and steering? But think of the internal struggles we all have, all the time. Laziness. Fear. Temptation. Why? Why these internal, deeply painful and emotional struggles? If we're each only one person, ask yourself a simple question: Who's doing the struggling? It takes two to wrestle. I say, Kit, could you pass me some more of that tea?"

He'd made her caretaker of his family-sized thermos, a quart or two of milky Assam stewed to the color of cheap leather. While I tried to digest the possibility that every single human being on the planet was schizophrenic, she poured a couple of inches into the plastic lid and passed it forward. He took both hands off the wheel and reached back to accept it, then blew across the top, holding it up to eye level and peering at the steam. As I was about to shout a warning, he put three fingertips back on the wheel, leaned forward, and slurped noisily. At that exact moment Brunhilde was hip-checked by a big gust of air as Ella's truck blew past us, doing eighty. Ella gave us a smile and a finger wave as we shot two feet over the white line toward the barrier wall. Completely unperturbed, Partridge steered us back into the lane, raising his cup to return the greeting. A tsunami of tea crested over the lip of the cup and splashed onto his brown corduroy pants.

"Well, bugger," he said cheerfully, looking down at the damage. "The only clean pair I've got too. I get clumsier and clumsier. Old age shouldn't be allowed. I suppose that's part of the Seraphim's appeal, eh? The traditional faiths don't like the body because it's so distractingly beautiful when it's young. The Seraphim don't like the body because it gets old and breaks down. They both think the body gets in the way of immortality."

He slurped the remains of the tea.

"But I wonder: Is *not* having a body such a good idea? The Architects are disembodied, but like the Greek gods, they keep interfering with us. Why? Why do they still need us so badly? Sorry, what were we talking about?"

"Bicameral two loaves of bread thing," Kit said. "You are saying the Architects made us that way? So this is like, creationism? My mother is geneticist, you know. I warn you, if you say that she is having like a total cow."

"Oh, I don't think they *created* us. I find evolutionary science entirely persuasive on that point. My guess is, they showed up at a certain point in our development and saw our species as *promising*—for their purposes. You know: going in the right direction, but in need of a push."

"They redesign us, you mean?"

"We do it to other species routinely. Ancient Mexicans, for example: they discovered a completely useless plant called teosinte; in next to no time, they used selective breeding to turn it into corn."

"So we are like that? We are domesticated species, you are saying?"

"Well, I don't think the Architects are *farming* us—you know, the hungry-alien hypothesis. Though in another sense that is what they're doing; it's just that they're not interested in our *bodies*. The crop was, and is, consciousness. For reasons that remain unclear, they seem to want our feelings, our memories, our experiences."

"But don't you think the Bronze Age Collapse is evidence that something went wrong with the plan?" I said. "That they couldn't fully control what they created?"

"Frankenstein!" Kit said.

I thought maybe she'd noticed an especially ugly driver in the next lane. It seemed kind of a mean thing to say. But there was no other car nearby.

"What are you talking about, Kit?"

"God creates Adam, right? Out of clay or something, and puts in spark of life. Zap."

"Close enough," I said. "According to Genesis, God made us out of dust and breathed our souls into us through our nostrils."

"OK, God breathing up the nose is good enough, I guess, if he cleaned teeth recently. Maybe he didn't—that could explain a lot. Anyway, we do *Frankenstein* in school, in Russian. You have read of course?"

"Never," I admitted.

"You amaze me, Majka. I am thinking you know everything, have read everything, and then you are total know-nothing about somethings you should know all about. Almost you are sometimes like normal person!"

"Thank you."

"No, is good. Too perfect is pain in the butt. So. Mary Shelley writes this book when she is nineteen or something. Our teacher, big fat Siberian guy, very intense, he says, kids, this is the original science-fiction story, and the plot is so ultraspecial, so completely wow, that it is pretty much only plot anyone ever uses again. Clever scientist makes creature, robot, android. Scientist loves his creature, it is his creation, he is proud like father with baby. But creature is not just a baby. It grows up, is powerful, gets own ideas, wants freedom. Scientist is super-scared now, like crap-in-trouser scared, and thinks maybe he has to kill this thing he created because it is too dangerous. Has big moral thing, what do you say—"

"Dilemma."

"Big moral dilemma, yes, like, do I have to kill my own child? But while he's sharpening knife maybe, and thinking about this, creature says, no way, José, hasta la vista, baby. Kills scientist, escapes. Crazy terrified stupid mob, big fight. Blam blam, end of creature. Or, creature kills mob, escapes again, end of civilization. In which case, last shot is maybe scientist's daughter lying in ruins, and we think she is dead, but her hand twitches, big cliché, now we know she will be hero in sequel."

"Or else the last shot is the creature crying because everyone is dead, even its own father, and now it's lonely," Partridge said. "Which suggests it was more human than the humans who tried to destroy it."

"Yah. I think that maybe is Mary Shelley's point. But now think of Bible again, and Architects again. In Genesis story, who is it makes creatures out of mud—"

"Dust."

"Stop interrupting, Majka. Who makes creatures, and breathes life into them through nostrils? God, yah? So God is original Victor Frankenstein, and we are original monster. God brings us to life, is happy he succeeded. Like, wow, look how cute! But we are too much clever, too much independent, so we start to grow up and want to disobey. Eve and Adam in garden, all woman's fault of course, blah blah, give me break, and God is now crazy angry. You are saying Architects tried to make us the way they want, and make us obedient, but they failed. Same story also, yes?"

"What are you saying?" I asked.

"Architects want obedient slave, but they need also clever, thinking slave. Self-conscious slave, because it is our minds they want. And this is problem, because clever slave does not want to be slave. Clever slave is nothing but trouble, like duh. I think clever slave found out how to invent its own languages, which was like, mental jailbreak. Freedom from their influence. Why the Architects are not predicting this? Maybe they also should have read the book."

All that time you'd been sketching furiously, page after page. More jungle scenes. Your parents' house. Ararat. A waterfall. Rows and rows of symbols that looked sort of like the ones on the Disks but weren't. A group of what looked like bald cavemen in front of a cave, holding spears. Now that you had our attention, you began to rip the drawings out and deposit one in my lap, one in Kit's, one in Derek's even—and then another and another. All the ones you handed to us were variations on the same theme: a building in flames.

One of them included a mark in the corner that I couldn't make sense of at first. It was just three lines: two of them almost vertical and leaning against each other, with a third forming a loop near the top.

The Space Needle.

"You are trying tell us something, Daniel?" Kit asked.

"Natazscha," you said to her. "Natazscha."

"What about her?"

"She's—she's OK."

All three of us turned to look at you, Partridge included. At the same moment Kit's phone dinged. "Shits," she said. *Sheets.* "My mother is text. Library on campus burn this morning."

"Which one?" But I was looking at your first sketch again, and I knew. Should have got it right away. The page was nearly all flame, the building nearly all consumed, but the shape behind the flames was clear. "It's Odegaard, isn't it?"

"Odor Guard?" Partridge asked. "That sounds like a brand of deodorant."

"O-de-gaard. It's the main undergraduate library. Right next to the Institute."

Kit's phone rang. After a conversation in Russian so rapid-fire I couldn't follow it, she said, "She is OK. Working in lab all night of course, like, why would person need to sleep? Says she was taking nap under desk this morning when library goes up, like whoosh. Big big fire."

"ISOC is right next door—is she all right?"

"I think so—"

"Good," I said. I ought to have meant *Good, I'm glad she's safe,* but the truth was, I meant *Good, we don't have to waste time dealing with that, and we can stick to plan A, which is getting straight back to the Eislers' house and the Disks.*

"But she says to come straight there, quick as possible."

I wanted to scream. Another delay? I looked out into the gathering dark and thought about the Disk images sitting on the computer at the Eislers' house. I had no interest in rubbernecking at a fire scene.

"Why?" I said. "What's the point?" The obvious answer—that making sure she was OK was the nice thing to do, at least if you weren't an emotionally challenged language nerd fixated on your own issues—seemed to hang in the air between us. For a moment I thought from Kit's silence that I'd seriously hurt her feelings. But she was texting again.

"She say, she has been working on something she wants to show us, and now she is worried they will close down the whole campus before she can get us in."

"All right," I said, trying hard to keep the exasperation out of my voice. "You'd better tell Ella to meet us there." I turned around in my seat to look at her, and squeezed her hand, trying to make up. "Are *you* OK?"

"Da. Yes. Maybe."

"Seraphim," you said, to no one in particular.

At least Kit hadn't lost her sense of humor. She looked at you and lifted one eyebrow. "Burning down university library, you mean? Girl Scouts, I don't think."

Despite the new urgency, Brunhilde slowed to forty or less as we climbed back among the peaks of the Cascades, and her engine sounded like a sewing machine being drowned in a bucket. Partridge spoke to her in an affectionate mess of English and German. "Come on, old girl. You can do it. Es ist nicht so schlimm. Nur ein paar kleine Berge. Sea to shining sea and all that. Wir sind fast da." And to me: "Her first time on the West Coast! I don't think she thought she'd ever live to see it."

We staggered to the top of the pass just as it began to rain. Amid the rusting remains of the old ski resort, an abandoned chair lift was swinging in the wind. You turned and looked intently at it.

"Iona," you said, and stabbed your finger at the glass, almost as if you'd spotted her on the empty brown slopes.

"Aye, she taught you to ski here, didn't she? When you were little. You told me about it."

"Iona Maclean." You looked away and dropped your hand into your lap as if you'd made a mistake. "She's not here."

"No."

"She's here," you said, picking up one of the sketches. And the tone of your voice was edging toward hers again. "Waterfall. Tall and thin. Beautiful solitude."

"This is the waterfall in New Guinea," I said. "Isn't it? The one at the edge of the Tainu's territory, where Iona went looking for the I'iwa?"

"She's alone. But—but not alone."

"You know what this is about, Majka?" Kit asked.

"I think Daniel is somehow channeling Iona's memories from when she visited us in New Guinea."

"Maybe Iona just tells him about it," Kit said.

It was a reasonable explanation, almost. But the voice and the sketches made it all too perfect for that. I remembered Rosko philosophizing: How could memory even work, if tasting a lemon was an experience so completely different from *remembering* tasting a lemon? And I thought, no, you weren't remembering something Iona had said about her experience. You were *experiencing her experience*.

"At the waterfall," you said. "Being watched."

As we crossed the floating bridge over Lake Washington, there was just enough light in the west for a pillar of smoke to be visible, gray on gray, above the University District. It reminded me of Ararat. Natazscha had told Kit to meet us at the north end of the university campus, but we got stuck behind a bus at the freeway ramp, and the streets into the University District were gridlocked. The sidewalks were nearly as bad: serious faces picked out by the headlights under wet hoods and umbrellas. Partridge opened his window to wipe the mirror, and the sour-sweet aroma of charred building flooded in, as if a cook had set fire to a batch of caramels and put out the flames with vinegar.

We stop-started our way around to the north side of campus and came into quieter side streets full of shuttered fraternities. Natazscha was waiting by her car as promised, and Rosko was already with her. No sign of Ella. After waving and circling the block twice, Partridge gave up looking for a space and simply stopped next to her.

"Delighted to meet you again, Professor Cerenkov. That's right, yes. Amsterdam, about five years ago—Bill introduced us. Look, I've got Morag and Daniel and your delightful daughter here. But I can't find anywhere to park, so I'm going to hand them over and find my hotel, if that's all right? I think I can find my way. Best of luck. I'll be in touch tomorrow, shall I?"

Natazscha opened her mouth as if to protest, but then seemed to give up, unable to make the effort. As I climbed out, I was shocked by the way she looked—the word *deranged* came to mind. She was in her usual high-fashion outfit: an old jacket that didn't fit and that she hadn't bothered to zip, despite the rain, over a vaguely peach-colored house dress. No big deal. But her hair was greasy, the dress crumpled and stained, and there was a big smudge of soot on one cheek. With her moon face and cheap, wet, scuff-toed flats, she looked less like an A-list scientist than a Russian peasant, setting out to sell the last half kilo of potatoes on some godforsaken street corner in Chelyabinsk.

"I wanted him to join us," she said as Brunhilde's brake lights receded into the rain. "What I've been doing in the lab, he—" Then she gave up again, her shoulders slumped. I wondered when she'd last slept. Not for a long time.

"You have not been home since get here yesterday?" Kit asked.

She didn't so much shake her head as twitch it sideways, as if she was being bothered by a wasp. "I was working. I raised the alarm and got out of the Institute as soon as the fire started, but it was already going hard before the firefighters arrived. The police questioned me for a long time, but I didn't see anything. When they let me go, I went back to my office."

"Went back into the Institute?" Kit asked. "You crazy?"

"Some of our windows cracked in the heat. Then the fire became so intense that it created an up-current between the buildings. It sucked the broken glass right out of the frames. The firefighters were overwhelmed at that point, so I took a couple of fire extinguishers and went over everything from the inside. Around dawn I was worried that they'd turn their hoses in through the gaps just in case and get water everywhere. So I ripped out some paneling and boarded up the damaged windows myself."

She showed us a purple thumbnail. "Hammer."

"Where's Ella?" I asked Rosko.

He looked at his toes. "Dropped me off," he said tersely, then raised his eyes and gave me a look that said *don't ask.*

Kit asked. Or rather, guessed. "Argument, yes?"

"Sort of."

"She is so frustrated with you for not getting message, lots of hints and no response, so pretty much puts tongue in your ear. And you tell her you're not interested. Which hurts her feelings, sure."

He didn't say anything, and he didn't have to. "Yekaterina," Natazscha said. "This is not the time. Come on. Let's get this done."

Police were stationed by a barrier at the north entrance, waving people away. But it was hard to seal the campus thoroughly; only twenty yards farther on, under the cover of an illegally parked truck, we dodged through a hedge and were in. We skirted the edge of a parking lot opposite the Burke Museum and followed the avenue of maples that runs downhill toward the war memorial. The big trees loomed and billowed above us like the ruined umbrellas of giants. Patches of gravel-colored sky showed through the branches. No light here except some old ornamental fixtures, hexagonal glass crowns throwing down feeble rings of bile-colored light. Even so, we stuck to the dark gulfs in between.

There was a strange peacefulness there: no one around, and little sound except the wind, the distant traffic, and the muffled, too-distant-to-catch sound of an amplified voice.

About halfway to the Institute we crossed a driveway near the great prow of the law school. Natazscha was leading, with you and me next, and Rosko and Kit behind us. There was no one else around. But, as you stepped up onto the curb on that side, you flinched violently and darted a look to your right.

It was as if you'd been startled by a noise—and there, a full second after you reacted, it was. Rustling. Like someone trying to extract a sandwich from a paper bag. Then silence. And then a deafening, ragged, multipitch squeal, like tearing sheet metal.

The squeal froze us all to the spot. It was so shocking, so out of place, for a moment I thought I'd imagined it.

After a second squeal, even more piercing than the first, two fat raccoons fell squabbling from a branch. They landed ten feet away and stared back at us as if amazed, rigid on the tips of their toes. They shifted their heads slightly, in unison: left, right, down, up. Sniffing, thinking, sampling the wind. When they'd seen enough, smelled enough, they wailed at each other again, turned their backs, and lumbered away under the cover of a rhododendron.

"Scheisse," Rosko said, and blew out a long breath. "Now I have to get online and order a new set of heart valves."

The timing of your reaction, which I'd thrust out of my mind for a second, came back to me then in all its oddness. What was going on with you? Way better hearing, all of a sudden? That would be a nice simple theory, wouldn't it, and Bill always said you should go for the simple theory first. But after some of the things you'd said, and what Partridge had said about seers, I'd become tempted by the nutty theory, the impossible theory, which was that you'd known the sound was going to happen before it happened.

Down the slope from the law school, George Washington stood high on his plinth at the university's west entrance. He was directly between us and the fire scene at the library: silhouetted against a flood of yellow emergency lights, he looked like a miserable commuter waiting for the last bus home. To his left, the gray outline of the Institute hid all but a corner of the library.

There were police cars and fire trucks everywhere, and a truck from a TV station, and a line of people holding up their phones. Half a dozen officers were manhandling railings and herding the gawkers back toward the street.

When the library came into view, I was amazed that so much damage could have been done. I mean, a four-story 1960s brick-and-concrete book-fortress: somehow you didn't imagine it could burn at all, but it had been reduced to an eyeless, soot-blackened skull. At one end, where a wall had collapsed, a hook-and-ladder crew was playing a hose over a bird's nest of steel beams. An ambulance crew lounged and waited. Yellow crime scene tape was wrapped around the whole area, including the Institute.

"This way," Natazscha said, but you contradicted her sharply—"No!"—and led us back around the other side, toward the university's brick central square.

"Seraphim."

And sure enough, there was a crowd the police seemed to be watching but dared not disperse. Five or six hundred people were ranged across the square in neat rows, like toy soldiers, facing the burned shell. Heads uncovered and oblivious to the rain, they each wore the thin white scarf. And every one of them held their hands up in front, as you had on Ararat, as if raising an invisible offering.

And they chanted together:

Op-JOL-ye
Xum-IL-bek
Dal-PA-min

Voh-CHAL-voh
Rem-YE-lut
Kee-HAN-dja

You began to nod and join in. With Kit's help I started to drag you away, back toward the Institute, hoping we'd be out of earshot there, but you held back, looking over your shoulder, not wanting to leave. Following your gaze, I saw that a solitary man with a megaphone standing on a wall was directing the chant from one side. He raised his arm, and they pivoted as one to face the other way—southeast, down the slope, toward where the outline of Mount Rainier was supposed to make the campus picture perfect on a clear enough day.

"Tahoma," you said.

"Tahoma, Daniel, yes," Natazscha said. "That's the original Native American name. You climbed it with Rosko. And Iona."

Even though it was invisible under a sixty-mile blanket of darkness and rain, you stared as if you could see it and made the gesture you'd made after Ararat: reaching out with your palm stretched wide, as if trying to pick it up off the sky.

Over the crackle of a police radio we heard the man with the megaphone speaking. It was the voice we'd heard before, still distorted, and we leaned forward, held ourselves tense, trying to make out the words.

"The world must burn," he said. "All the languages and cultures of the world must burn in order for us to be cleansed. Only then will we know the true fire. Only then will we be ready. *Aka-PEL-ten, jat-AM-rok, or-OM-aku.*"

Six hundred voices answered him. It was only a drone, really, like a church service heard from outside the building, but they were repeating it: "Only then will we know the true fire. *Aka-PEL-ten, jat-AM-rok, or-OM-aku.*"

A deep voice behind us made me jump. "Campus is closed. I need you to leave the area, please."

Two police officers, a man and a woman. I wanted to start an argument and point out that they didn't seem to need the Seraphim to leave. Luckily Natazscha had more sense. "Oh, I'm so sorry," she said, the picture of meekness. "I work here, you see, and I was talking to one of your colleagues. My daughter and her friends came to pick me up. We were just leaving."

It wasn't a very good lie, but if either of them wondered how the daughter and friends had got onto campus, they didn't say so. "Go on, then," the woman said in a kindly voice.

Natazscha led us back in the direction of the car, then took a detour into a stand of dripping trees. We waited there until the officers had moved on.

"Let's try that again," she said.

CHAPTER 9

FOXQ3

"Quickly," Natazscha said.

The rain hadn't let up, and the wind had risen to a roar. ISOC's blank rear wall gave us some protection, plus it was in shadow. But as soon as we followed her around the corner of the building, we were hit in the face by a huge wet squall—and the firefighters' lights. She scurried along with her shoulder almost touching the wet brick and stopped at a side door. The whole building had been encircled in yellow tape, like a gift; where the tape ran across the door, she seized it angrily and pulled with both hands until the plastic stretched and separated.

"I feel as if I'm breaking into my own lab," she said.

"You are," Rosko offered helpfully, detaching one end of the broken tape from where the wind had blown it across his shoulder.

She took out an ID card and waved it in front of a black plastic scanner. Nothing happened. She wiped the card on her dress and tried again. Nothing.

Where we stood, we were completely exposed. Down toward the library, or what was left of it, I could see a line of four backhoes parked at the edge of a collapsed wall. They looked like a line of dead bees, pinned to a board in a museum collection. Two figures were standing by one of them. Ants. It was impossible to tell if they were looking our way.

Natazscha tried the card reader a third time, and a fourth. "Maybe the university security already resets the locks?" Kit said. My thought exactly, and I spared a split second to savor how wonderful it felt that Kit sometimes had my thoughts exactly. But we were wrong. Fifth time lucky: when Natazscha held the card steady for a few seconds, a green light winked and the latch clacked. When she'd opened the door, I took your hand and steered you inside.

"He's here," you said. "He's here."

"Who's here, D?" But you shook your head and frowned, like a swimmer with water in your ears. Like you were picking up a faint signal but couldn't hear the message.

Rosko turned to close the door behind us. He didn't need to: with a sound like a plane coming in to land, a strong gust came along the outside wall and almost ripped the handle from his grip. The metal door was sucked back into its frame by the negative pressure.

With the noise abruptly turned off, the silence inside was oppressive. I had a feeling of being sealed in, as if we were a rescue team in a sci-fi movie, closing the air lock after arriving at a mysteriously abandoned moon base. Deep synthesizer music would have been appropriate. Maybe with a tremor in it, and a tinkling four-note piano line in the background, to foreshadow the creepy surprise lying in wait.

"Don't turn any lights on," Natazscha said. We didn't need to: ISOC's thoughtful, limitless-budget designers had installed soft green emergency lighting at floor level; it made the place seem like an underwater cave, but it was plenty to see by. As my eyes adjusted, I also became aware of a gauzy bride's veil of white light in the direction of the main entrance. Silently we moved toward it. When we emerged into the big polished foyer, we saw that the light was coming from the hundreds of tiny LEDs they'd used to tastefully backlight Charlie Balakrishnan's famous founding quotation:

INSTITUTE FOR THE STUDY OF THE ORIGIN OF CONSCIOUSNESS

BACTERIA ARE NOT CONSCIOUS. BUT WE ARE, AND WE EVOLVED FROM THEM. SO WHEN . . . ? WHERE . . . ? WHAT . . . ?

Et cetera.

"Excellent questions," Rosko said. "Charlie B's a deep thinker. What's the relationship between the lurching heap of stuff we call a body and the mystery spark that makes it lurch? Soul, psyche. Mind, spirit. Geist, atman. What is it?"

"I think that was the issue until Darwin," Natazscha said. "Since 1859, the question has been different. Not what the mind is, but when did it show up? Hence the name."

It was a funny moment. I'd always thought that unraveling the mystery of consciousness by unraveling *where it came from* was a super-cool project, ever since your dad first told me about it, and I didn't mind which version of the question people asked so long as they were asking it. Plus, Darwin was one of my heroes. But a seed of doubt that I couldn't quite name had taken root in me. Perhaps it was reading Shul-hura. Perhaps it was seeing the Architects and having to live with the brute fact of their existence. But something had shifted in me. We'd had a century and a half of like-wowsa, OMG progress in evolutionary theory, genetics, molecular bio, cell bio, computational modeling, and cognitive psych. We knew about protein folding, glial cells, and mirror neurons. We had CAT and PET and fMRI. And how much better did we understand *consciousness*? Roll the drums! Crank up the spotlights! Whisk the magician's handkerchief off the top hat, and look—it's a stone-dead bunny rabbit. The science blogs are full to choking with smi-ley, clueless, upbeat crap about Vast Strides in Neuroscience. Meanwhile the truth, which no one wants to admit, is that when it comes to the mind, we don't have a single effing ghost of a freaking clue.

What if that's because we're on completely the wrong track?

What if Mayo knew that?

My train of thought was interrupted by a squall hitting the glass front doors, sending rivulets of water scurrying down the panes, and we heard the wind again, barely, like someone moving wooden barrels in the distance.

"Is it right that Balakrishnan builds this place after he comes to Seattle to do business with Iona?" Kit asked.

Natazscha nodded. "Daniel's mother's company had a data-encryption contract with BalakInd in Delhi. But they discovered all sorts of mutual interests in mathematics, information theory, that kind of thing. Come on. This way."

Two flights up, we emerged directly into the second-floor lab, though *lab* didn't seem the right word—it felt more like the break room at a nerdboy start-up. Dartboard, game controllers. A discarded trans-parent snack wrapper that probably once contained a vending-machine Danish. On the floor, the bleached, crushed shells of long-dead lattes.

"Mathematicians," Natazscha said apologetically, as if that explained the trash. "Maynard Jones called them Iona's Boys. Because they're all boys, and half of them used to work for her."

Behind the big glass security door at the north end was ISOC's malfunctioning brain—sixteen matte-black monoliths arranged in two rows. Each unit was two feet thick by four wide by eight tall. They didn't look like machines. They looked like something carved from blocks of obsidian eons ago to impress or appease the inscrutable silent gods. Some wit had taped up a sign next to the door: "Office of Mr. Turing."

"It's named after the British guy who came up with the idea that fundamentally, everything is computable," Rosko said to Kit.

Kit rolled her eyes. "I know who is this Alan Turing. I am B-plus student, Rosko Eisler, but this is not implying I am total know-nothing, yes? We do about him in history class. Super-amazing Second World War code breaker, defeats Nazis single-handed, blah blah. Then commits suicide when they find out he is picking up men in the pub."

"It's an incredible machine," he said. "One of the fastest in the world. Isn't that right, Natazscha?"

"Oo-oh," Kit said, peering in through the glass and drawing out her lack of enthusiasm into two long syllables. "Big black boxes. Possibly I faint with excitement. But is not so powerful right now?"

"No," Natazscha said "Rosko's right, in theory. But it's been acting up for two weeks, and now it's completely out."

The "Mr. Turing" label seemed all wrong to me. He'd been an über-misfit, a passionate, quirky human genius, and his disciples here, with their bright ideas and bad diets, had made the mistake of memorializing him in this silent, soulless reasoning machine—the thing he'd predicted, not the thing he'd been. Natazscha had said that with Mayo's eager involvement, they were working on brain-body interaction and "virtual awareness." Were they trying to make computational systems that came ever closer to the quirks and capabilities of a funny, passionate, awkward human genius? Or did they, like some of the Extenders, think that human beings—Turing and themselves included—were a kludge? A halfway house? A wet computer, slapped together badly by brute Darwinian forces and, like a leaky old house, ripe for improvement?

"You said this was mainly for Mayo's benefit?" Rosko asked.

"David's blue-sky project was using it, along with the muon scanner upstairs, to create a full digital model of at least some parts of the brain.

He said he wanted to capture consciousness 'like a mouse in a trap.' Which struck me as a rather unpleasant way of putting it."

He pawed the glass. "Can you get me in?"

The answer was no. Even after repeated polishing and swiping on the polyester house dress, her card wouldn't open Mr. Turing's door.

△

The third floor had all the lab gear you'd expect—sinks, emergency eyewash stations, fume hoods. Natazscha pointed out each piece of equipment as we passed like it was a member of her personal team. "Magnetometer. Atomic force microscope. Nano-balance. Gyroscope. Cesium-fountain atomic clock."

The scanner stood in its own bay, next to Natazscha's office door, on which an overburdened metal sign was etched with the words "Professor Natazscha P. Cerenkov, Human Genetics & Epigenetics, Hominin Paleoanthropology, Paleolinguistics."

"This way," she said, hurrying us past. She sat down at a desk next to the scanner, motioned for me to sit in what looked like an upscale dentist's chair, and clipped a heart-rate monitor to my finger.

"I can't do much without the main computer," she said. "But I can run enough of this off my local drive to show you how it works and what I discovered."

"You are being like this is big secret," Kit said.

Natazscha ignored her to focus on the machine, fiddling with the dials and muttering in Russian. Silent as a feather, a gleaming ceramic helmet on a telescopic arm descended from the ceiling above me.

"Looks like robot's skull from a comic book, yah?" Kit said. She was right. It was head shaped, but the simple, slightly curved geometry made it look menacingly alien—like something that might be puzzled by its own awareness, puzzled by its own origin, and not sure whether it's an organism or a machine. Rosko voiced my thoughts:

"Balakrishnan's rivet-jockeys thought they were just making a medical tool," he said. "But you can kind of tell they were raised on *Star Wars*. Trust the Force, Luke."

"Yah," Kit said. "Or maybe just trust paycheck."

"I don't think an actor would be very happy wearing this," Natazscha said. "The interior is tungsten, which has the same density as gold, and it weighs fifty kilos." Her fingers attacked the keyboard. The sound was like rain on the fly of a tent. The helmet descended over my head and I heard, or felt, a low hum somewhere around my temples.

"Hold still, Morag. Your head is moving too much."

"Sorry."

"I have noticed, she does this head bobble thing when she is worrying," Kit said. "Right now, she worrying all the time." Kit had kicked off her bright-yellow running flats and was sitting with you on a small love seat, her long hair swept forward over one shoulder and her long legs tucked neatly beneath her. She'd hooked her arm through yours and put her head against your shoulder, which, ridiculously, I found annoying. But then she caught my eye, and something about her expression melted the emotion. It was like, *It's OK. I'm here. You can rely on me.* She slowly pursed her lips into the most delicate suggestion of a kiss, and it was such a perfectly judged gesture that my heart started to thrash around like a fish on a hook.

"What was that, Morag?" Natazscha said, peering in surprise at a readout.

Emotions! So embarrassing!

Um, well, Natazscha, it's like this. Your daughter showed me an intimate sign of affection, and I wasn't expecting it, or not right at that moment, so I felt a rush of embarrassment, but also at the same time this intense, warm-as-a-bath, overwhelming happiness. And embarrassment that I could so easily be made so happy, along with annoyance at being so easily manipulated, and puzzlement because I wasn't sure whether I was annoyed at being manipulated by Kit, or only annoyed at being manipulated by my own emotions about her, and oh, by the way, is that a clear distinction in the first place? And I felt a strong desire to reach out and touch her, but let's not go there, because you're her mother and this is embarrassing enough already. I was hesitant about returning Kit's gesture, so I didn't, which made me feel bad. And I could tell that I was blushing, and I was annoyed at being unable to control these unconscious somatic responses, which is stupid because, as you of all people must know, you can't control a mechanism that was installed in the brain stem a hundred million years before the rest of the human cauliflower even evolved. I also thought—for a while, maybe an hour or two, or maybe seventeen thousandths of a second, it's hard to say—about the strangeness of having all those good but confused feelings in the midst of all my other current feelings of anxiety, dislocation, stress, guilt, fear, and—

"Nothing," I said. "I'm fine."

Kit smirked.

I stuck my tongue out at her.

"Look at this," Natazscha said. A big wall monitor came to life, with a blue-gray image of a brain in the middle of it. The image shimmered and twitched: it was a short video loop, in which waves of colored highlighting drifted and sparked. Beneath, like a caption, there was a long succession of codon triplets—a gene sequence:

TAA AAC TGC TGG AAA AGT
AGT CTT CTC TTC TGT CTG
CTT TAG ATT ACA AAA CTA
TCA CAA ACA TAC AGT GTG
AGA CAA GCC AGA ACA TAC

"That's me?"

"Not yet. This is only a standard case, for comparison. A typical brain, which for these purposes means someone with no speech or language abnormalities but also no special talents. Not a Babbler."

"You?"

"No. Carl Bates."

Rosko pointed to the screen again. "What's the DNA stuff underneath the image?"

"Segments from chromosome 7 in a gene known as FOXP2."

"The language gene," I said. "Isn't that what they call it?"

"We know FOXP2 has something to do with language, but it's more complicated than that." She tapped a key. The image on the screen slid neatly to one side, and a second image came up, with its own block of codons. "This is the brain of a man in London. His family is famous in the research literature. They share a rare defect in FOXP2, and although they have normal general intelligence, they can't produce or understand words in a normal way. So here's what I've worked out. Babblers appear to have an even more radically mutated FOXP2. It generates an entirely different protein, which I've called FOXQ3. And the effect of FOXQ3 on the brain architecture is dramatically novel."

The faint hum around my temples cut out, both images on the screen slid to the left, and a third appeared on the screen.

"Me at last?"

"You at last."

The first two images disappeared, and the third one expanded to fill the whole screen. The visualization was amazing. My brain! My everything! My own personal zone of miracles! It was luminous blue gray on the monitor, like spotlit smoke, with a shifting overlay of green, red, and electric turquoise. Natazscha zoomed in toward a point near the center, and it was as if we were falling into the image, accelerating down through cloud layers of neurons: space-troopers fearlessly navigating a dense, mysterious nebula. But eventually we reached a layer of tissue that was solid, palpable, with an infinitely fine grain to its surface. She guided an arrow onto the image and brought it to rest in an area that looked like flakes of pastry.

"This is low resolution compared with what we can do. But we're now inside your right-side hippocampus. See how it's larger here, at this side, than in Carl's scan? This tiny ribbed patch, just a couple of cubic millimeters, is where all those extra languages of yours get stored and processed."

"Is beautiful," Kit breathed, silkily.

"Thanks," I murmured, trying not to move. "It's the first time you've mentioned liking my right-side hippocampus."

"Never showed it to me before. Shy girl you are. But is like, yah, sure, dead sexy."

"It's part of the limbic system," Natazscha said loudly, as if that would prevent her or anyone else in the room from noticing that the word *sexy* had been spoken. "Limbic system. Important in memory. The point is, I think FOXQ3 is what makes people Babblers. And, while Derek Partridge and your ancient friend Shul-hura are busy convincing you that language and full consciousness showed up all in a rush seven thousand years ago at Thera, I've been working for years on evidence that the Neanderthals had full speech at least forty thousand years earlier."

"That would mean Professor Partridge's theory—that this all begins with Thera—can't be true," Rosko said.

"Derek is fixated on Thera and the Bronze Age, and I agree with him that something strange happened in that period. But *Homo sapiens* having language, and ten million other species not having it, *that's* the real puzzle. The answer has to go deeper than the Bronze Age."

"I don't see why language is such a big deal," I said, and reeled off all the usual pop-sci about animal cognition. "It's just a continuum, isn't it? From fish to crows to dogs to us? Gorillas do sign language. Chimps trick one another. That thing about vervet monkeys have one warning call for *snake* and a different one for *eagle*. Elephants checking their bald spots in the mirror."

Natazscha wasn't impressed. "Misses the point, Morag. Not a single one of those species can compete verbally with a human two-year-old."

"So you're saying animals are stupid. What does that have to do with Partridge?"

"I'm not saying animals are stupid. The point is not that they can't master language, but that they don't *need* to. For millions of years, before we came along and started exterminating them, chimpanzees were hugely successful at being chimpanzees. Without ever using language. So why do we have it? Most people just don't grasp how incredibly strange it is that language ever showed up."

"Every species is different."

She shook her head. "Having language isn't like having spotted fur or sharp teeth."

"I don't see why is big difference," Kit said.

"Imagine you're doing research on rain-forest frogs," Natazscha said. "Some species are bigger or more brightly colored than others, or have extra toes or poisonous skin. You've spent years classifying those differences, sorting out order and family and genus and species, the familiar Linnaean dance. Then one day you come into a clearing and discover a species of frog that's, I don't know, *good at playing chess*. Language is like that. We're so used to it that we can't see what a fantastical thing it is. It breaks all the rules. It should not exist. Everything about us is driven by evolution: when the creationists say that natural selection can't explain the eye, they're just advertising how little biology they know. But language truly is an evolutionary puzzle. It doesn't make sense. It's a superpower. Where did it come from?"

"Gift from God," Kit said. "According to Babel story."

"Aha, but Morag's friend Shul-hura says that's backward, doesn't he? According to him, God didn't turn one language into many to prevent us from communicating. We were already speaking many languages, and doing just fine with them, at the point when the Architects arrived.

Where did those original languages come from? There has to be a much older origin."

"But," Rosko said, "I thought you only had to go back to the Neanderthals for the vocal tract to be the wrong shape for speech?"

"And also Neanderthals is too stupid," Kit said.

"Yekaterina, you never listen to anything I say. We like to say that early hominins like *Homo erectus* must have been much less intelligent than we are, because they had smaller brains. But we also want to say that the Neanderthals were too primitive for language, even though their brains were *bigger* than ours. Apparently we're so clever that we don't even have to be consistent. As for their vocal equipment, the jury is still out. But that debate may be irrelevant. Language doesn't have to be spoken."

"I don't understand," Rosko said. "What else could it be?"

"FOXP2 helps the brain's centers of perception communicate with the larynx. But in monkeys it helps those same areas connect with the parts of the brain that control the hands. Have you never seen someone gesturing even though they're talking on the telephone? Have you never seen two people having a conversation in ASL?"

"You're saying our ancestors could have had sign language before they had speech?" I said.

"For all we know, complete languages could have preceded any *spoken* language by tens of thousands of years. Who knows? But I haven't told you the most important part yet. Everyone in the field's been looking at FOXP2 as the human norm. So, either you have FOXP2 and you're fine, or you have a damaged version and that's a terrible disability. The existence of Babblers made me think: What if FOXP2, the norm for our species, is the disability? Maybe FOXP2 is the signature of a terrible handicap in our evolutionary history, like losing the ability to fly or something. And then there would be a reason why we lost it."

"What are you getting at?" I asked.

"We have complete genomes now for several hundred early Paleolithic humans, a dozen Neanderthals, three Denisovans, and one of the Red Deer Cave people. As far as I can tell, not one of them has FOXP2; they all have FOXQ3. If that's right, then you and the other Babblers aren't a new evolutionary development. You're a remnant of the old 'normal.' The rest of us—me, Kit, and more than ninety-nine-point-nine percent of the species—are profoundly mentally disabled."

Kit rolled her eyes ostentatiously. "That makes me feel great. Before I am just not good at languages, or maybe dumb. Now I get to be 'mentally disabled.' Thanks, Matushka."

"I don't think Natazscha meant—" I said.

"Yah, Majka, she did meant. And is so totally not fair. You guys, you don't know what is like. Me, I work hard two years at English, also French, is difficult. Stay up late, give myself headache. But I have wrong gene, so I can't do it, and I get also like crapshit grades."

"Two things," Rosko said. "First, your mother isn't a Babbler, and as I've said before she speaks way better English than you do—"

"Because she study longer."

"Because I went to Soviet schools," Natazscha said. "If you didn't get it right, they screamed at you and humiliated you and called you a capitalist dog. And if that didn't work, they beat you, which is very effective."

"And the second thing is," Rosko said, "it's either *crap* or *shit*. You have to say one or the other. *Crapshit* is not a word."

"You think you own the English language or something just because you speak it so good, Rosko Eisler? Crapshit crapshit crapshit! There, see? Word used all time, in fact. Is common. Especially with angry young Russian womens. What I am saying, Natazscha works for years to learn English, and I work hard also, but you Babblers pick up new language like *pah*." She clicked her fingers explosively. "Is not fair. Is actually crapshit."

"Natazscha," I said, "when would the genetic change have happened? From FOXQ3 being dominant, to what's normal now?"

"A long time ago. Fifty thousand years? Eighty? Which puts it right at the beginning of the so-called Great Leap Forward. When the first cave art and deliberate burials show up, the first evidence of music and religious ritual, all that sort of thing."

She pushed a button, and the tungsten helmet floated back to its spot on the ceiling, silent and weightless as before. I shook my head from side to side several times. I felt a strong need to make sure it was still attached.

"I'd like to scan Daniel," she said. It was only then that we realized you'd walked away.

Kit jumped up and went out to the main lab. "The stairs," she said, pointing. "There."

You were almost at the top. Natazscha called out to you. "Daniel. Come down. There's nothing up there. Just another lab and Mayo's office."

"You're wrong," you said, and kept going.

CHAPTER 10

√2

At the top of the final flight there was a small landing. It had enough room for a potted palm, fake but plausible, and one of those random space-filler armchairs that you can tell no one's ever sat in. The landing had one door, opposite the armchair, with a metal touch pad instead of the card reader we'd seen on the other doors. Natazscha punched in a code, swung the door open, and flicked on some lights. The air smelled sour, like uncollected trash.

You'd never been up there before, had you? Not to the fourth floor? Situation normal, as far as I could make out. They'd had public tours of the building and all, part of the university's PR machine. Docents in their purple shirts waxing lyrical to their flocks of visitors about how ISOC was "bringing cutting-edge cognitive science to bear on the nature of the human self." But even Rosko had never been up here; he said the fourth floor always got waved off. "Nothing interesting. The director's office. Some conference rooms. That's all."

Nothing interesting. Carl Bates was one of those docents, and he certainly knew that was a big fat lie, oh goodness, yes.

It was an almost windowless space, a copy of the spaces below. Office doors in blond wood alternated with lab benches around the outside. The sinks looked too clean to have been used. The only experimental setup, in the same position as the scanner downstairs, was on an L-shaped arrangement of tables at the far end. You walked right over to it and examined it with a jeweler's attention, extravagantly intense, stroking each component as if to verify that it was real.

"What is?" Kit asked Natazscha.

"This is a laser. Probably a quantum computation experiment. It was one of the things Maynard Jones admitted to having a personal interest in."

"Wow," Rosko breathed.

"Wow because why?" Kit was making fun of him. Or indulging him. Or both.

"Because, Kit, if you could get a quantum computer to work, it would make that fancy machine downstairs look like an abacus. The logical architecture is based on qubits instead of bits, and they use a quantum superposition of—"

Kit held up the palms of her hands. "Totally enough. I believe everything you say."

"It's only theoretical, in any case," Rosko said, annoyed that she'd cut him off.

One wall near the laser was taken up by a huge glass board. From six feet away, the surface looked clean. Up close we could see a ghostly forest of half-erased mathematical symbols, a handwritten text so dense it reminded me of Shul-hura's cuneiform. You came and stood in front of the board with me; we were like two children in a fairy tale who've discovered the witch's cottage.

"This angled bracket notation is familiar," Rosko said. "Quantum mechanics?"

Natazscha peered at it. "Yes. This looks like a calculation of the Bekenstein bound. A measure of information density."

"Information can have a density?" Kit said. I was thinking the same thing, but being distracted by a bell going off deep in my memory.

"It's a kind of absolute limit on how complex something can be. Which apparently is a big thing in artificial intelligence."

"Now I remember why that sounds so familiar," I said. "Iona. Back when she was a lowly math student, before she set up her data-encryption company, the title of her thesis was 'Minds, Machines, and the Information-Density Limit.' Lorna told me she'd been working on how much information you could possibly store in one place—and how excited she was when she met an Australian bloke who was trying to calculate the information capacity of a human brain. According to Lorna they spent their first date talking about whether space-time is ten- or eleven-dimensional."

Natazscha pointed to a door in the middle of the opposite wall. The sign said, "David Maynard Jones, Director." It led to a space that was almost empty, with cleaned-out bookshelves, no extra furniture except a big metal cabinet full of office supplies, and a bare metal slab for a desk. On the desk there was a single unused yellow pad, aligned with the desk's corner, and one of those old-fashioned multiline desk phones. I opened the desk drawers (empty), opened the cabinet (boxes of Post-it notes and pens, Scotch tape, more yellow pads), then closed the cabinet and walked slowly around the whole space.

When I turned back to you, you'd opened the cabinet again and you were rocking on your heels in front of it. You waved your hands, groaned, and lunged in with both arms, raking out the contents onto the floor. At the back of one shelf, at head height, there was a stack of half a dozen small cardboard boxes. You reached in and tugged out the lowest one. The boxes on top spilled sideways, then out, sending paper, toner cartridges, and paper clips all over the floor.

The box you were holding was the size of a large book. It had "Amazon Prime" on the side. You took it to Mayo's desk, ripped off the strip of packing tape that was holding it closed, and slid it over to me.

"What is it, D?" I said, but you just looked at me, so I unfolded the cardboard flaps. And the first item I saw, lying on top, was instantly familiar: Iona's orange camera strap. The color had faded from neon to pastel, and up close the webbing was frayed and thin. It was like a memory of the real thing: a signal from a past that I knew was real but couldn't quite believe. Beneath it was Iona's *Anabasis*, with her handwriting in pencil on almost every page. Beneath that, a sheaf of handwritten notes. Several old envelopes that had once contained handwritten letters, all empty. A few printed-out emails. Web clippings about the original disappearances.

"This is what you were looking for in Iona's study," I said to you. "Mayo, or someone working for him, must have taken them."

"Oh my goodness," Natazscha said. "This was hidden in plain sight. I'd already looked through that stuff."

You picked up the camera strap by one end, and it unfolded. A transparent pouch with six square pockets was clipped to one side of it. Each of the pockets contained a square blue memory card. You picked one of them out and held it up between your thumb and forefinger, nodding. You spoke quietly, as if to yourself, but I heard: "I'iwa. I'iwa."

"So this is good, yah?" Kit said. She was sitting cross-legged in the middle of Mayo's desk. "We have what Daniel is looking for, maybe. He needs to get home and look at this. You need to get home and look at Disks. Also is after midnight, and we need to leave, because this place giving me bad feeling."

She jumped down and went back out to the main lab area. I passed my eyes over Mayo's office and the lab area one more time, willing them to yield up some new fragment of information, but there was nothing. By the time I came out, Rosko and Natazscha were already at the top of the stairs. But you'd stopped, clutching the box in front of a door I hadn't paid any attention to, and you were shaking.

"What is *m-e-c-h*—metch?" Kit said.

"Mech": that's what the sign said. Natazscha sounded impatient and barely glanced back in her direction. "It's short for *mechanical.* Air-conditioning, plumbing, that sort of thing. Come on. I want us out of here."

"Strange though, yes?" Kit said, rattling the handle. "Big fancy computer is locked up, maybe I understand. But why plumbing door is only other one locked?"

You made a strange whimpering sound in the back of your throat and seemed to reach for the door and back away from it at the same time. The hairs on the back of my neck went all porcupine. Shoving Kit out of the way, I started pushing at the door. But there was nothing. It didn't even rattle. It looked and sounded like I was pushing on a section of wall.

"Useless," Kit said. "Get out of way."

I did as I was told. Aye, I know. She looks like she never ate a diner breakfast in her life, but she's also not a bad athlete. She backed up all the way to the wall, put her head down, and began to run as if launching off sprinters' blocks. She only had room for four or five short, chopping steps, but she picked up an amazing amount of speed. Then she turned gracefully sideways, lifting her feet at the last moment, and allowed her entire body weight to collide with the door, right next to the handle.

A section of the frame disintegrated, but she bounced off and landed sprawled on the floor.

"Crapshit. I maybe break shoulder or something."

I was stepping forward to check on her when you walked over to the door. The indecision had broken—your movements had a fluidity and purpose to them. After examining the damaged frame, you stepped back a pace and stood upright with Iona's cardboard box in one hand. You looked like a soldier on parade. And then you raised one knee, screamed "No!" at a deafening volume, and let fly with a precise, powerful kick. Your heel connected with the wood an inch above the handle. The door emitted a single yelp, as if you'd stepped on the paw of a dog, and exploded inward.

Kit was fine. Rubbing her shoulder, she was the first to go through. I had a good view of her face, illuminated by a soft artificial glow, as she turned to her left.

In the movie version of the moment she would have cried out. Or maybe gasped and made a melodramatic gesture of some kind. But real horror is different. For barely a heartbeat, nothing, and then she folded sharply at the waist, like someone who'd been punched. She collapsed forward onto her knees, face pointed at the tasteful, putty-colored, polished concrete floor, and threw up.

Afterward, it was tempting to think I'd had a premonition about what Kit would find in that room. But when I stepped inside—one hand on her hair, trying to comfort her, and one hand flying to my nose and mouth against the twin stench of vomit and rot—the light was so low that I took longer than she had to make sense of the scene.

My first impression: *Room. Dark. Light at the other end.*

My second impression: *There isn't any mech in here.*

It was a small, plain room, maybe ten by twelve. A computer cart in one corner had an open laptop on it. There was a big main desk covered in books and papers.

An office, then. A poky windowless side office, perfect for a lowly grad student. And behind the desk there was a person observing us—or not—from a chair.

The chair was identical to the complicated, hi-tech number we'd used downstairs. The white helmet, ditto. A big monitor, on an armature at head height, was angled toward the helmet and was giving off enough cold blue light to pick out the claws clutching the arms of the chair, the big Velcro strap holding the chest in place across a yellow-on-purple Minnesota Vikings T-shirt, and the grotesque white Kabuki mask that had once been a face.

Carl Bates.

He was seated, or strapped in, under the scanner helmet. It was still poised over his head, but his body had twisted forward and sideways against the strap, so that his head was half out of the scanner, tilted awkwardly toward us, one ear visible. It looked as if he'd been frozen solid while struggling to get up.

His skin was stretched tight as a balloon across the bones of his skull. His lips, scored by deep vertical cracks, looked like segmented earthworms. The eyes stared at us, imploring, but they were as dry as dust-coated marbles and so prominent it seemed they might fall from their sockets and shatter.

Kit staggered to her feet. Trying to get away from the sight, she more or less collided with her mother in the doorway. Natazscha pushed past me, threw the main light switch, and rushed to kneel beside the figure at the desk.

"Oh God, no. Carl, Carl. Oh God, no."

She grabbed his wrist, checking for a pulse that she must have known wasn't there. Then, with a delicate, tender gesture she pushed a strand of hair back from his forehead. It stayed put for a moment before falling again.

"A boy from Minnesota who was homesick for flat land and bright winters," she said, talking quickly, as if only words could protect her from the full power of what she was seeing. "Good at his work. A magician with code. He was supposed to be doing his doctorate in computer science, but he helped me out with a project and then started following

Maynard Jones around like a puppy hoping for a treat. The last few months, he was spending nearly all his time here at ISOC. Look at the face. Dehydration. And the way his back is arched. That's renal failure."

A big, empty IV bag hung from a metal stand next to the chair. She looked around on the floor and picked up the loose end of a transparent tube. A curl of medical tape was attached to it.

"See how there are two bags? This one was a cocktail of anesthetics. Propofol and pentobarbital, I expect. Perhaps alfentanil. Those drugs are lethal if the dose isn't right. The large bag was probably saline, but it looks like it wasn't connected properly. As if he tried to set this whole thing up himself."

Behind him there was another, smaller glass board, blank except for two lines written in black marker near the middle:

THERE IS NO GHOST: THEREFORE $\sqrt{1} = \Theta$

THE MACHINE IS THE GHOST: THEREFORE $\sqrt{2} = \infty$

Kit was outside, spitting into one of the lab sinks. When she came back she stood on the threshold amid the splinters of wood, dabbing absently at her lips with her sleeve, her eyes wide and her face the color of a bleached sheet. Then she reached out and touched my shoulder.

"Sorry for puke."

I put my arm around her and glanced behind her to a window. "I don't get what this means, but we need to get out of here."

"I get it, Majka," she said. She pointed to the board. "Is obvious now, yah?"

"It is?"

"Sure it is. Root symbol was on Bill's hard drive, and root symbol is again here. But *root* is a pun, like Rosko said. *Wortspiel*, yah?"

Rosko was standing just an arm's length from Bates, fingering the keys on the laptop. "We already got that far," he said dismissively. His tone annoyed me—partly because he was saying that Kit couldn't possibly have thought of anything he and I hadn't already thought of, and partly because I was uncomfortable with the fact that I kind of thought that too.

"Yah," she said coolly. "You already got that far. But maybe fantastic Eisler brain have not got far enough."

That made him look up.

"Pun is not like you are saying. Not like root of a number is one thing, and root of plant is another. What this means is the line on a map that tells you where to go. *R-o-u-t-e.* How to get someplace."

He must have known she was right, but he still sounded grudging. "If it means 'second route'—alternative way—then route to where?"

She rolled her eyes and tapped at her forehead. "You guys is supposed to be the smart ones, yes? With me is always like, nice girl, blond hair, nice face: obvious not much happening up the stairs."

I wanted to protest, but she was on a roll. "What is it Seraphim are offering people? What they give that is so popular? Same thing what religions always offer. Power? No. Money? No. Extra serving of ice cream? I don't think. They are offering the one thing everyone wants even more than power and money and ice cream. *Not to die.*"

"Heaven," I said. "The infinite."

"Yah. Join Seraphim. Believe everything Quinn says. Learn language of Architects. Then, boom. Leave body behind, and become like a god, blah blah. Well, so that is Route One to immortality. That is what Seraphim is selling. Actually, if Professor Partridge not crazy, that is what Architects is selling, through the Seraphim. And Mayo doesn't believe in it, because he is like Bill. He think supernatural is all flip-flap."

"Flimflam."

"The word he used was 'bollocks,'" Rosko said, not looking up from the laptop.

"That is for sure correct. Religion, he say, it is total, one hundred percent bollockses. Science is only true knowledge and such. And that is what this means. '√ı' means the old route to immortality, through religion and God. Or through the Seraphim and their Architects, which is like new version of old story. Is all Route One."

"But," Rosko said, "the circle with the line through it is the Greek letter theta. What does that have to do with anything? It means half a dozen different things in math and physics, but—"

"People write theta as shorthand for *theory*," Natazscha said.

"You guys," Kit said. "I think sometimes you know everything, sometimes maybe nothing. We do class on ancient Greeks. Teacher goes on about Plato, trial of Socrates, blah blah. Theta is shorthand there too, but not for *theory*. Athenians, they used it for verdict in a trial. Is first letter of the word *thanatos*. *Thanatos* means 'death.'"

"Kit, this is brilliant," I said. "You're saying that the Seraphim think Route One leads to infinity, but Carl thinks that's all an illusion; trusting the Architects only leads to death. But, on the other hand—"

"Maybe Mayo, he decides medical advances are not good enough for him," Kit said. "You can clone new kidney. Fix brain damage maybe. Put new lenses in eye, new valves in heart. But that is like Professor Partridge replacing rusty exhaust pipe on his van. Mayo, he not wants only to keep his body going. He wants to do like religion—say goodbye to body, be free of it, and become mind only. So. He gets interested in mapping the brain, so he can upload it, and *va-voom*! Who needs religion if you can have immortality from science?"

"Route Two," Natazscha said, nodding approvingly. I got the impression she was making a parental note to stop radically underestimating her daughter. "Carl must have wanted to show that it was possible and decided to impress Maynard Jones by making himself the guinea pig."

"What pig?"

"Guinea pig. It means he used himself as an experimental animal."

"Yah. Science not so nice to experiment animals."

Rosko was still at the laptop—looking at Kit, then at me, with a dark expression I couldn't read. What was he thinking? Annoyed that Kit had beaten him to a puzzle's solution—or only annoyed with himself for not handling the fact more gracefully? Jealous of her closeness to me—or of my closeness to her? I didn't quite buy any of those. But there was something going on with him that I hadn't worked out. When our eyes met, he quickly looked down at the screen again.

"There's a work log," he said. "The mainframe shut down at 19:33 yesterday."

"But Carl did not die yesterday," Natazscha said. "He must have been here like this, I don't know. A week, at least."

"How long did it take to run that scan you did on Morag? Three minutes?"

"That's typical for a small area, if you don't need the highest resolution. Why?"

"What's the longest single scan you've ever run?"

"Forty or fifty minutes. That was to generate an overview of the whole neocortex. Maynard Jones did it on himself. He said he didn't want anyone taking the risk."

"Which is silly," I said. "The muon scanner's not like an X-ray. It uses ambient radiation, right? So it's no riskier than when you take a photograph."

The screen in front of Rosko was dark, except for a few rows of data near the top in plain white Arial. He looked at Carl, at me, then at Natazscha.

"What is it?" she asked.

"Why would Carl strap himself into a chair, hook up a half gallon of happy drugs, and set up a scan of his own brain where the run parameter is"—he looked more closely at the readout—"ten days?"

The question hung weightless for a second in the still, foul air of that little room. Then Natazscha said, with a sudden decisiveness, "I want you all out of here. Now. I'll have to report this immediately, and I don't want any of you involved. Come on."

We shut the splintered door behind us, even though it wouldn't close all the way, and went back down the main stairs to the third floor, then the second. We had reached the messy domain of the mathematicians again when we heard a voice coming up from the lobby.

"Hello. Hello? Is anyone in here?"

"Politsiya," she hissed. "Police." Backing up, she put a finger to her lips and gestured for us to follow her across to the other side. Down a short side corridor, past Mr. Turing, there was a fire escape. A flashlight beam played up the stairwell behind us. I heard the crackle of a handheld radio and the words *backup* and *Institute*.

I didn't dare look back—it was the child's instinct that if you can't see, you can't be seen. Seconds later we were in a concrete delivery bay at the rear of the building. There was a truck-sized roll-up metal door—locked, and in any case it would have made too much noise. Next to it, hidden behind a pile of empty boxes, there was a regular exit door—also closed. It was only a dead bolt, though, and it slid back with a single squeak.

The rain had almost stopped, but the walkways were slick black leather. We were so busy working out how to get away from the building without being seen that we turned a corner and nearly ran straight into a dozen Seraphim.

They were standing motionless, staring up through the veil of floodlit moisture toward the wreck of the library. The late-night shift? All of us had the same instinct, which was to put our heads down, ignore them, and keep moving. All of us except you.

"*Dze-OK—Dze-OK—*" you said, as if greeting them.

"Daniel, what are you—?"

"*Dze-OK-ma. Ok—Ok-ZU-qe. N'd—*"

"D, come on. Let's go."

"Dz e-OK-ma. Ok-ZU-qe. N'd-UL-gor. Da-NOM-hut. Kul-MIN-ya. Ek-EP-su. Ep-GE-ret."

They were fascinated. Enchanted. But also torn between the desire to pursue you, to find out who you were, and the desire not to be distracted from the ruin of the library. Rosko grabbed you by the shoulder and started to pull you away. Two of them came forward, their arms out; it could have been a greeting or a threat.

"We make a run for it?" Rosko muttered.

"No," Natazscha said. "That'll only draw attention to us. To Daniel."

"Dze-OK-ma. Ok-ZU-qe. N'd-UL-gor. Da-NOM-hut—"

I looked up. Someone was flicking on the main lights on ISOC's second floor. Luckily it distracted the Seraphim as well: they looked up, then turned to their comrades as if to get advice. Rosko and I took you by the arms, and we walked away quickly, back up the slope in the direction of Natazscha's car. When I risked a glance back, the whole group of Seraphim were looking at us and pointing.

I reached for your hand and squeezed—for my comfort, not yours.

"We're getting you two out of here," Rosko said.

"But the Disks—" I pleaded.

"We'll get everything," he said, "and go somewhere nice and quiet, where you and Daniel can rest."

"I don't want to rest. I don't have time to—"

"Majka," Kit said. "Majka. We'll go get the files. Rosko is right. Get out of here is better. Daniel rests, I look after, you work on Disks. OK?"

PART III:

AN ALTERNATIVE TO GOD

CHAPTER 11

ROAMING

It was a good idea, in theory: a few days away from accidental Seraphim encounters, and Seraphim marches, and burning libraries, and the sheer horror of discovering Carl Bates. I hadn't wanted to leave the city, but Rosko and Kit ganged up with Natazscha: it would be good for me; it would be better still for you. When we'd all had not-enough sleep, and met the next morning in Natazscha's postage-stamp kitchen, even Derek Partridge joined the cheerleading team. Wouldn't it be good for Rosko and I to have peace and quiet! Really put our heads together on this big, urgent puzzle! He said "urgent" at least three times. It was kind of obvious he wanted to come too.

In retrospect, I was swayed by the fact that I was carrying around in my head such a clear picture of what the words *oceanfront cabin in the Pacific Northwest* were supposed to mean. The picture was brightly lit and squeaky perfect. It had Scandinavian armchairs in primary colors, a wood-burning stove, and someone else's collection of beach glass arranged prettily on the window ledge in the hypermodern kitchen. I only had to squint a little to get sunny weather too, and piles of books on a pale maple floor, and you—the old, pre-Ararat you—pulling fresh bread out of the oven while Kit and I lounged and cuddled in one of those armchairs.

Oh well.

"A poky little cabin belonging to some friends of my parents," that was what Rosko had said; I should have listened harder to "poky," and maybe done more of a Sherlock when I saw the rust-stained key on its length of frayed string. A Realtor would have called it "ripe for renewal," or "filled with possibility"; an honest one would have said it was a scab on the skin of the land, a teardown, fit only for scraping off with a bulldozer and, as they say in the burial service, committing to the deep. On second thoughts, it looked like it had been coughed up by the deep: marooned on a sand-blasted bluff above the Strait of Juan de Fuca, it could have been the weathered wreck of a boat, washed in on the last storm surge along with the inevitable plus-sized driftwood, Japanese fishing floats, and seal carcasses picked eyeless by the gulls. The exterior cedar planks were like muddy fur. The front door was stuck shut—and, as if mocking us, wouldn't shut again without a struggle once it was open. The kitchen had mold, mouse drop-pings, and dishes still in the sink from the last user. There was lethal-looking wiring leading from a rooftop solar panel to a stack of car batteries, which ran half a dozen forty-watt light bulbs, two electric baseboard heaters, and a dorm fridge that wheezed and stank like a dying cat. There was no Internet and no landline, and the cell reception was terrible to nonexistent. At the back, the "sun shower" was a stone-cold outdoor dribble coming from a plastic barrel, with privacy-lite on two sides thanks to some blackberry bushes; on the north side, you got to show off everything you had to the whales, the wind, and the binoculars of passing tanker captains.

And it wasn't just in the shower that you felt unprotected. That big, muscular arm of the North Pacific frightened me even when I was safe inside. Too much water. Should have thought of that.

As soon as we'd arrived and wrestled our way inside, I hated it. I suspected you'd hate it more. But I was so ready to tackle Bill's old problem at last—the secret of the Disks—that I ignored you all that first day, trusting that the others would do their magic and look after you. I knew I'd have to get Rosko helping me soon enough, but we couldn't run software on the images without a lot of plain looking and list-making, so I worked furiously on that. I had to get an accurate count of the symbols and the way they were grouped: pure manual tedium, but I didn't mind; when I was done, we could feed the digitized essence of Theran civilization into the software Bill had written for the purpose. I worked hard, long into the evening, willing those ancient symbols to cough up the nugget of meaning that Bill had always wanted to find in them. And I didn't have to feel too guilty; even Kit and Rosko didn't have to do much to entertain you. You were like me, I suppose: too intent on Iona's photographs to notice the cabin much, or notice us.

By the next morning I had some preliminary data counts. With nothing but PB&Js and about three pots of Stefan's Expensively Organic, Small-Batch, Shade-Massaged French Roast to sustain us, Rosko and I attacked the problem together. While I checked my lists and sat hunched over the sixty-eight glossy prints, trying to see if I'd missed anything, he tweaked the software.

"It can translate, you hope?" Kit asked.

"I wish," I said. "All this can do is sniff out the underlying structure of the language. It's designed to look for clues the way any linguist would. Where are the word breaks? What are the short words and how do they repeat? Are there prefixes and suffixes? Are there any proper names?"

"That was crucial when Champollion worked out the Rosetta stone," Rosko said.

"And if it works like you hope?"

"Then, in theory, Morag can work out how to translate it."

He didn't sound enthusiastic or hopeful. "Then I'll translate it," I said, "and we'll know what the Architects said—and maybe even know what the Babbler priests like Shul-hura did to escape their influence."

You'd been Bill's sidekick on the project since the age of ten, and I hoped you'd be as excited as me about what we were doing. Instead you were irritable from the start. You kept getting up, sitting down, biting your nails, looking out the window. I sensed that you didn't even want to be in the room with us. Your irritation irritated me, at the beginning, and then it began to alarm me. You began to tense and relax like someone with cramps; you made low, guttural sounds that sounded like "no" or "you can't." Your cheeks were hollow; the way you looked at me was hollow; again I had the sense that you were trying to communicate with me from inside a locked box.

For several hours I managed to distract and calm you by getting you to help. "Count these," I said, pointing to a particular symbol. "I need the total number of repetitions on these six sheets." I wasn't expecting that you could do it, but you did. A cliché from the autism spectrum: a repetitive, logical task was something you could become absorbed in and do accurately. And fast.

"Fifty-three."

"Good. That's what I got. Now I want you to count how many instances of the walking woman?"

"Thirty-eight."

"Fabulous. You're going to be a big help."

You weren't, though, not much. We went on like that through another dozen or more symbols, but it was annoying you, as if you were being forced to perform a trick and you weren't interested. Eventually you sighed, bit your knuckles like you were trying to prevent yourself from crying, and walked out of the room.

There was a long, long way to go at that point. I checked on you briefly—slumped into an armchair in the living room; staring vacantly into the middle distance—and dug into the task at double speed.

I was wired, frantic, poised between an almost romantic elation and an ominous sense of defeat. I couldn't know what the software would tell us, if anything, but my mind whirred with the possibilities, with what a thrill it would be if some pattern magically emerged telling me, I don't know, that all the groups with the stick symbol in last place were nouns. Or something. It would be the light at the end of the tunnel. Bill had spent the last seven years of his life trying to translate those Disks. "I feel like a child outside a locked candy store," he'd said to me. "I feel the way Kober and Ventris must have felt, spending decades hammering on the door of Linear B, knowing there was a whole civilization in there."

As I finished sections of the visual count, Rosko transcribed them to a digital key and sounded a note of skepticism as he loaded that into the software. "Tell me again how this is going to work," he said, between flurries of typing. "According to Bill, this was just an ancient language. According to you, it's the language of the Architects, the language they gave to the Therans—"

"Or imposed on them."

"Or imposed, sure. So if we can read the Disks, it'll be like, what? Discovering the Ten Commandments?"

"What the Architects said is something we won't know until we know, Rosko."

"So how do we know it will help?"

I didn't have an answer, only hope. "Just run the software, will you?"

"Getting there. I need five more minutes. And more coffee."

When I got the pot from the kitchen, I noticed that it was already evening. I turned on some lights, poured the muddy dregs into his mug, handed Rosko his coffee, and sat next to you on the floor, holding your unresponsive hand, as five minutes turned into an hour. Rosko loaded data and steered Bill's program through a series of trial runs, validation tests, and adjustments, all the while muttering "Scheisse" and "das könnte klappen" and then "Scheisse" again under his breath. Screen after screen filled with data, which resolved into colored patterns. More data, more adjustments, more patterns. It was like Bill himself was a presence inside the machine, sorting, hunting, comparing, and combining.

"How long?"

"This is just the chew-and-swallow phase," he said. "If we had the ISOC machine, it'd already be done with that, and the whole process would take another five minutes, max. On this, I don't even know. Hours, for sure."

We sat and stared at the screen for a while, even though it was pointless, as if we wanted to show the electrons tearing around in the CPU that we were there for them, and cheering them on, and really cared. Then Kit announced proudly that she'd made macaroni and cheese. She'd managed to get the amount of milk wrong, even though it was the kind in a box with only three instructions, but we made grateful noises and ate, and afterward I even surprised myself by sleeping.

I woke before dawn, shivering. The cabin was far too cold, and at first I was annoyed to be, yet again, the first person awake. But I went eagerly to the kitchen, hoping that Rosko's machine would show me something useful. No such luck—the software was still chewing away at its task, like an old man working on a stale bagel. I was itching for what it could tell us, and stood there with my arms wrapped around myself and my feet numb while I watched it for half a minute; a progress indicator in one corner of the screen rewarded me by shifting from 87.03 percent to 87.04 percent. Then I felt a breeze on my face, and when I found the front door hanging open, my half-awake brain went into melodrama mode: *Daniel's wandered off! Daniel's wandered to the beach and drowned! Daniel's been kidnapped in the night by the Seraphim!* But you were sitting on the front step in the gray early light, once again bent over the glow from Iona's camera.

We found six memory cards in Mayo's office. Each one had a tiny white label, filled out with dates in her handwriting. They were a miniature record of your life, your past, and even the past that preceded your past. You'd been inserting one after another, then cycling back through them again, as if determined to drink in every last detail of every image. Bill, absurdly young, leaning against a taxi in New York. Jimmy and Lorna, lounging on an emerald hillside in China. When I came out and sat down beside you, you were looking at a series that featured you and me as babies in Scotland, with Iona and Lorna being Proud Mums in scarves, green wellies, and comically dated hair.

Any of the shots that included Jimmy or Lorna made my breathing ragged. I still had no confirmation of where they were, or whether they were safe or even alive. Seeing the photographs of them should have make me feel better, but instead I thought of the rituals you perform— *One last look, shall we?*—when you go through someone's things after they die.

"What I want you to do," I said, putting my arm around your shoulder and trying to sound matter-of-fact and practical, "what I want you to do is see if you can identify each of the shots. Think about where they were taken, who was behind the camera, what else happened that day. Yes? There's a story here, your story. Try to remember it and bring it back. Everything that's nested around these pictures. Why were you there? What happened afterward? Were you happy? Anything."

Anything. I sounded desperate even to myself; I hoped you weren't picking up on that part. At some level, at least, you knew what I was asking you to do, that much was clear. And, spookily, you could look at what appeared to be junk snapshots and say "Lorna Ainslie," which meant you knew it was from before they married, or "Glasgow," which—since it was Jimmy in front of a parked car—I couldn't imagine how you knew. So it went: "Bill Calder. Boston." "Iona. She's happy."

It took a long time, because you examined each image in painstaking detail, clicking up to the highest magnification, poring over each one. I heard a pot being rattled in the kitchen, but ignored it. You came to another picture with you in it—aged about five this time—and I stopped you. "That's *you*, Daniel. You. Do you understand that?"

No, you didn't. "Child," you said. "Iona's." It was like you were learning about the life of someone else. You couldn't see *you*—or else there was no *you* there to do the seeing. The few photographs where you couldn't identify a person, or a place, you never even said *I don't know what this is*. The word *I* had slipped through your mind's fingers.

The light had changed, almost an hour had passed, and I became aware of Rosko and Kit standing behind us with mugs of tea. I hadn't even heard them get up. "What you make of it, Rosko?" Kit asked. I couldn't tell whether she was trying to help or subtly hinting that I should at least let them help.

"I've told Morag before," he said. "I was there. And I don't mean there at Ararat, there on the mountain. I mean, up there. With the Architects, while they were taking him. It only lasted a few moments, but—"

The words stopped as I turned back to look at him, but his hands carried on, making loops and shapes in the air as if gestures could succeed where language failed. I waited.

"I can only describe it by analogy. It felt like getting to a gate and being refused admission and watching Daniel step through the gate. Which probably makes it sound like the gates of heaven, but that's not what I mean. It was like he passed through a barrier and was gone, and I couldn't follow. By the way, the software just hung up at eighty-nine percent and shut down. I'm going to have to debug it and start again."

"Shit!" I screamed the word, as loud as I could; if I'd had anything in my hands, I'd have broken it. Something about the intensity of my frustration must have reached through to you, because you actually put the camera down for a moment and turned and hugged me. "Can't we go get a faster machine from somewhere?" I said over your shoulder.

"I was thinking that too," Rosko said. "But I just looked at the error file, and I don't think it's the machine. It's the software itself: there's something about this data set that it's not set up to handle. Give me time."

"We don't have time."

I suppose that wasn't very helpful. He threw a *you-deal-with-her* glance at Kit, and went back inside.

We did OK, sort of, for a day or two after that, but it wasn't easy. We were like settlers, cast ashore in an unforgiving land—no phone service, no Net, and fifteen miles to the nearest grocery store: serious priva-tion—so we tried extra hard to be nice to each other and succeeded some of the time. Rosko worked and worked at the keyboard, Kit gave him neck massages, and I stuck with you and tried not to bug him. Kit and Rosko found my focus on you and the photographs irritating, as if I was encouraging you in an unhealthy obsession, but they were polite about it. Rosko was irritated (but equally polite) when Kit attacked the kitchen like one of hell's Furies, and, once it was clean, proudly made us a string of bad meals based on overcooked spaghetti, freeze-dried chili, and undercooked rice. Meanwhile Kit and I became irritated with Rosko as he grew more and more uncommunicative. He kept promising to be done "soon," and during occasional breaks would wander off on his own to stare at the ocean.

"Are you OK?" I asked him when he had just returned. His hair was wild, his eyes distant.

"Me? Fine. Tired, that's all."

"Sure. Tired of not telling anyone else what you're thinking." The truth was, he'd been way more unsettled by his experience at Ararat than he'd ever let on, and had never really said much about what that experience was. Seraphim-curious now? Secretly half-convinced that "ascending to the Eternal" might be a good thing? I could have believed that.

I was feeling my own growing claustrophobia; after Kit made some not-bad curried-chicken sandwiches and we'd eaten them in a tense, uneasy silence, it was a relief when she got up from the table and said, "I need a walk too. On the beach, but with all of us together. Come on. Let's check out one more time that place for cell you found."

Rosko's moody wandering had had one useful effect: he'd discovered a rocky point where it was possible to hold a phone in the air like a catcher's mitt and catch maybe one bar. Canada lay across the strait like a gray battleship; YOU ARE NOW ROAMING INTERNATIONALLY, the messages said. Which was funny, almost: I'd spent my whole life roaming internationally, and here I was stuck like dried food to the rim of the United States. Never mind: this time, at last, we each got something. For Kit, several rambling messages from Natazscha about dealing with Carl's body and the police. For Rosko, updates from his parents about nothing in particular. And for me, a frustrating fragment of the message I'd been waiting for all these weeks:

ACROSS THE BORDER WITH THE OTHERS. TRYING TO GET FARTHER SOUTH, BUT WE CAN ONLY MOVE AT NIGHT. WE HOPE TO REACH

Border? Others? And hope to reach where? No idea—my attempts to reply got me no response beyond Unavailable and System Error.

We came down off the point and did another two or three miles along the beach—me and Rosko separately, you being gently pulled along by Kit's hand. For an hour, none of us spoke. There were whitecaps on the strait like pills of wool on an old sweater. Lines of waves were coming in toward us at an angle to the beach, and the visibility was down to a mile or so: a bleak scene, with the surrounding world rubbed away. Eventually Rosko stopped to skim stones, and Kit stood a few paces back, her arm linked through yours, watching. There was a chill in the wind that made me want to keep moving, but I stood even farther back and didn't say anything.

"Daniel," Kit said, "you keep looking at the photographs from Iona in New Guinea. Why is? What happens in New Guinea?"

"He wasn't even there," I said. But she was right. You had the old Nikon in your hands even there on the beach, and at every spare moment you were shuffling through the images, as if the screen on the back was a window into a world you were trying to revisit. You'd linger over a shot, zoom in, and peer at the little screen as if examining every last pixel. Then you'd stare for five minutes at a blurred blowup of a stick, or someone's knee, or a patch of mud. Thousands of images, stretching across ten years or more—but it was that one trip you kept coming back to, even though you'd been in Crete with Bill at the time.

It wasn't getting any easier for me to look at pictures involving Jimmy and Lorna, and changing the subject was tempting. But for better or worse, you seemed to be forcing me to turn over my memories, and I knew that might help you to recover your own. I moved down to the water and tried, without success, to skim a stone.

"You need lower angle," Kit said. Standing next to Rosko, she showed me how it was done. They competed for a couple of minutes. Five skips! Eight! Ten! She pushed him and laughed—which made him smile for the first time in a while—and I felt a pinch of jealousy about even that. Here was something easy, ordinary, and normal, something they were good at and could relax into doing together—and I (trying again) just didn't have the knack.

Stupid, stupid, stupid emotions. But Kit canceled them, thankfully, by grabbing my wrists and kissing me. "Daniel can't tell me about the trip, Majka," she said. "You tell."

So I did: everything from Lorna's interest in the emergence of the first tools to trekking into the deep wilderness of the border territory and "discovering" the Tainu.

"They were, what you say, uncontacted? Until then?"

"Not quite. They'd traded with the lowland tribes in the Sepik River valley. And they'd already been 'discovered' by one other Westerner, a Baptist missionary named Kurtz. He'd taught them Tok Pisin along with his Bible stories and even baptized some of them. That's why the kids I played with had names like Abel, Moses, and Natalis."

"But this Kurtz, he already is gone when you show up—why?"

"Far as I could reconstruct, they kicked him out in disgust after he admitted that the 'Jisas Kraist' he kept talking about was someone he'd never met. You have to understand, for them it was like someone says, *My chief is bigger and stronger than your chief*, and they say, *So where is he?*, and you say, *Oh, he's coming*, and then later you admit that he died two thousand years ago. It must've sounded like a bad joke."

"But why they put up with crazy Chen family?"

"I don't know. Because they didn't know what to make of us? Because they were frightened of us too? They were certainly frightened of Lorna."

"Frightened of your mother?" Rosko asked incredulously. "I know she swears like a trucker, but that's hard to believe."

"Aye, but they'd only ever seen one other Caucasian, and white freckled skin with strawberry-blond hair totally gave them the creeps. What broke the ice, what made it possible to win their trust, was my being able to pick up their language."

"You must have been the first outsider to use it," Rosko said.

"Kurtz must have tried. But Tain'iwa makes even Navajo look easy. All I know is, they were amazed by the idea that they could teach me their language. The idea that someone could go from not speaking to speaking was new to them, and they got a huge kick out of discovering they could teach me. They kept saying that by giving me Tain'iwa they were *ola-apan gok'iwa geswet ar-apan*—bringing me back from the dead."

"You're the only non-native speaker of Tain'iwa in the world, then?"

"Oxip'den di-amou, exip'den ki-amah."

"Bless you."

"It means 'That which we think, so you will think.' *If we teach you our language, we can communicate our ideas to you.* Or maybe *feelings* is the right word."

I was still holding the stone I'd picked up, so I leaned down and flipped it toward the water. It skipped twice, came to a halt, and seemed to pause for thought before going under. It reminded me of the boat at Antikythera, and I shuddered. Then I turned round and noticed that you were kneeling in the sand with a stick and had drawn a neat, perfect outline map of New Guinea. It even showed the Indonesian border, and the course of the Sepik River. With a decisive thrust, you placed the stick in the sand like a flagpole, right in the Tainu's territory.

"The volcano," you said. "Here." Which was curious: the fact that the Tainu had insisted there was a volcano at the center of their territory—in a place where any geologist could have told you that was impossible—wasn't a detail I recalled sharing with you.

"It's a good map," Rosko said. "By the way, Morag, how did you find out about the I'iwa? The Ghost People?"

"Well—"

Somewhere in the corner on my awareness there was a droning noise, like a low-flying plane. We were all looking down at your map. The drone grew closer. I was in the act of looking around for a plane when Kit grabbed my arm and screamed.

"Majka, look out!"

Too late.

Time did stop, briefly, just long enough for my mother to put her head round the door of my consciousness and say, *Morag, gurrl, I told ye, never stand wi' your back to the water; sneaker waves, is what it's called, aye, they come outta nowhere.*

Maybe it was the long-delayed wake of a ship. Maybe it was just an unusual wave. But it was big—and as I watched it narrowed and reared higher still, like a cartoon cobra, a glossy gray tongue of muscle. I was aware of Kit at my side, holding my arm in both hands: she barely even got splashed. Rosko was two or three feet away, and barely a drop of water reached him. The cobra narrowed, reared, and lunged forward, hitting me at chest height, but the frothing cap surged right over my head, and I felt the cold invade my clothes—and my sinuses—even before I was slammed back onto the beach.

Afterward I knew I'd never been in any real danger, because Kit never let go. All the undertow did was drag half a kilo of sand into my clothes. I was still in the final backwash of the wave—vaguely thinking to myself, *Feelings, we were talking about feelings*—when, with a show of strength I thought you were no longer capable of, you waded in, scooped me up in your arms, and carried me up the beach to dry ground.

It was a long walk back to the cabin, and the shower was freezing misery. But it was followed by a dry towel, a clean bathrobe, and

Rosko being a sweetie: he brought me an oversized mug of cocoa, with marshmallows floating on top, and looked shyly at me as if anxious to see whether the gesture was acceptable. While I sat there sipping it, you sketched me. I looked so pathetically sorry for myself that after I'd seen it—and Rosko reminded me that we'd been talking about the I'iwa—I made a conscious effort to sit up straight and put more light into my voice.

"I found out about the I'iwa because Kurtz and my mother were both pale-skinned freaks who didn't speak Tain'iwa."

"The Tainu thought the missionary and your mother were ghosts?"

"Not literally. But they didn't have any other category in which to make sense of them, and white people already fit into their world view in a way they weren't jumping up and down to share. Maybe it was a taboo about mentioning their ancestors: that's common. They'd gesture up-valley with a shudder, and refuse to look in that direction, as if they were saying, *That's where the ghosts live, not a place you ever want to go; let's change the subject.* I only found out more when one of the women died."

"She become ghost?" Kit said.

"Not that I saw. But the Tainu do a strange thing with their dead. OK, so every culture does strange things with the dead. We don't like dead bodies, and we want to get rid of them—we want to get rid of the very idea of death—so we dress our corpses in fancy clothes and stick them six feet under. Or burn them. The Tainu do the opposite. They place the dead person in a sitting position, on a sort of wooden deck chair, and smoke it whole over a fire—"

"Then they eat corpse, are you going to tell me? Excuse me, I throw up. Sorry. Is becoming a habit."

I have to admit, I was getting a small kick out of teasing Kit by grossing her out. "No, no. They do end up looking like extra-large beef jerky with teeth, but the point of smoking them is to preserve them—to keep them around."

"And then what?"

"They're placed on cliffs overlooking the valleys. And they just sit there, for months or even years, scaring away the tribe's enemies."

"Would be scaring the shitless of me," Kit said.

"The thing is, the Tainu made it clear that this dead woman, who had to be smoked for over a week, was still a real person. *Embok dilu Tain'iwa* is what they said—still part of the language community of the Tainu. At least until the flesh has rotted away."

"And the I'iwa?" Rosko asked. "Is that the next stage, after the body's gone?"

"That was my guess too, at first, because the Tainu said they were pale, and didn't speak, and were hard to see. In a culture full of witch-craft and sorcery, being worried about something like that didn't seem strange, so 'ghosts' was the natural way to think of it. Though the I'iwa coming out at night to hunt pigs and steal sweet potatoes, that was odd."

"So you began to think they might not be ancestors but a really, genuinely uncontacted tribe? Who paint their bodies with clay or something?"

"Crossed my mind. A tribe near Goroka does that."

Speaking of ghosts, you'd been so silent that I'd almost forgot-ten you were there. But your reaction to what I'd said about the I'iwa reminded me to refocus. Your breath had quickened, and your eyes were flaring as if you were having a panic attack. You had the camera in your hands, of course, and in seconds you found a shot we'd looked at before: me with Jimmy and Lorna and our guides, standing on a chalky path in front of the tentacle roots of a pandanus tree.

"Who are these two?" Rosko asked. "Guides? But she's a child."

The sight of those two faces made me ache, almost as much as I was aching for Jimmy and Lorna. I'd missed them and thought about them and wondered about them ever since we left New Guinea. "Friends," I said. "Good friends. This is Oma, the old headman, and his daughter, Isbet. *Homer* and *Elizabeth*, Josef Kurtz would have said. She was the same age as me."

"You say he give Christian names," Kit said. "But Homer is Greek poet, yah?"

"Homer was a blind storyteller. Oma was a good storyteller too, and he was going blind. He had cataracts."

"He can't have been much of a guide, then."

"They were a team. Oma had a staggering mental map of the Tainu's territory, like he could remember every path and gully for miles around. But he was learning to rely on Isbet's eyes. Between the two of them, they could safely take you anywhere."

You produced the New Guinea map you'd torn from the Eislers' atlas.

"That's right, Daniel," Kit said. "New Guinea." And to me: "He is trying to tell us something about this."

"No shit," I said—and immediately hated myself for sounding so dismissive.

What *were* you trying to tell us? That you remembered me talking about New Guinea and the I'iwa? That seeing the pictures from there reminded you of Iona, and made you miss her? That you now knew something about what she believed, and were trying to tell me what it was? I had no idea. Your dad used to say, *For any finite body of evidence, there are always infinitely many consistent theories.* Great.

"Talk to me, Daniel," I said. "Talk to me, somehow. What is it you're thinking?" But you only looked at me with what seemed, more than ever, to be a combination of frustration and pity. So I turned angrily to Rosko, who'd just walked out of the room and come back in again. "What about you? Why don't you talk to me, Eisler? You, who's been busy not saying what you really think ever since Ararat?"

Boy, I was becoming unpleasant. I was so angry that I managed the whole diatribe before I realized that he was holding his damned silly laptop with its screwed-up software in his hands.

He had every right to be angry right back at me. But his expression was one I couldn't read. Exhaustion? Puzzlement? Affection, even? Pity?

"It's finished," he said, holding up the machine. "One hundred percent. And I'm prepared to talk now."

CHAPTER 12

WHAT RAVEN DID

"Morag," he said, "I did try to tell you what I thought, right at the beginning, but you didn't want to listen. I've been trying to accept that. I've even been trying to persuade myself that maybe I was wrong and you were right. But Ararat—"

"Yes?"

"Ararat was so strange, so far outside of anything else in my experience, that it's almost impossible to put into words. But that doesn't mean it isn't a clear picture in my mind. They took Daniel. Whatever happens to people afterward—'up there,' I mean, in the realm of the Whatever—the Architects take the conscious experiences stored in our minds as their raw material. Do they install our memories in their own minds? Do they just consume them like cookies? I don't know. But they take them, and they took Daniel's. Sure, he's not a complete Mystery—in other words, the process was interrupted, and they didn't take everything. That's why he has some language left, plus these random obsessions like Iona, and the fires, and New Guinea. Those things make it look to you like he's got some important clue to communicate. But there's no reason to think that. They're fragments, like pieces of a dream. Or the things shamans say when they're five miles high on peyote."

Kit could probably see that I was about to boil over. I was—I felt completely betrayed. To change the subject, she jerked her head toward the computer. "What about this? Famous Disks you and Majka are wanting to understand. Anything?"

"That's the other piece of bad news. The other part I've been suspecting, but not quite admitting to myself. Morag, you said a long time ago that you doubted Bill's analysis."

"What about it?"

"You said he'd never looked beyond the assumption that it was an ancient language, something *spoken* by the ancient Minoans or the Therans. And maybe he was wrong; maybe it wasn't a language, but something else."

All that was true, but I was feeling too resentful, too angry about his pessimism, to even nod.

"Well," he said, "the statistical analysis shows—it shows—" He stopped again, blew out a long breath, and looked at you. Then he closed the laptop. "Let me tell you a story."

◭

"They brought me to ISOC because I was a Babbler," he said. "Just like you are, Morag. When I first got there, the linguists were interested in assessing my learning speed. So they gave me the toughest language they could think of, then checked me out under the scanner twice a week."

"What they throw at you?" Kit asked. "Something Asian, I am betting. Vietnamese?"

"Good guess. They started with Korean, and that resulted in at least one published research paper on the growth of my neural kudzu under learning stress. But even Korean was too easy for the ISOC sadists. They found an old Canadian First Nations guy from way up the coast. Albert. I never did get a last name. He spoke Nuxalk—*Nu-haug-wlk*. It's a language on the verge of extinction from a valley in British Columbia. A totally alien set of phonemes, and some of the words have no vowels, which makes it impossible even to say how many syllables they have. It might as well be a language from another planet."

I was determined not to participate in the conversation, and I'd snuck over to your chair and was hugging you, my face pressed against your chest, unsure which of us was comforting which. But I was listening to every word.

"Albert spent a lot of time just explaining their culture," he said. "Teaching me their myths and stories. Which are really interesting. *Tl'alhi-na. Tsut-kw'its'ik t'ax. Qwaxw, way. Ays-kwtutuu tx, Tl'upana, stl'aps uulh-tx. Tsqm-na. Tsut-kw'its-ik t'ax. Tcaliitsim-kw tx.*"

The sound of the words was harsh but fluid, like rocks in fast, shallow water.

"What's the translation?"

"That's from a story about Raven and Cormorant. They go halibut-fishing together in a canoe. Cormorant is good at fishing, so he catches plenty, but he's also trusting, naive, not too bright. When Raven catches nothing, he decides to steal all Cormorant's fish. The way Albert told it, you're set up to hope Raven will be forced to apologize, or else he'll be found out and suffer some kind of punishment when they return to their village, and poor Cormorant will get his fish back. But apparently the Nuxalk aren't big on Disney endings."

He slowly repeated the Nuxalk phrases again, reveling in the strangeness of the sound. "That line is what happens right after Raven steals the fish. 'Come here, Raven said to Cormorant, and open your mouth. So Cormorant went to him and opened his mouth. And Raven cut out his tongue.'"

"Yuck," Kit said.

"Yeah. Raven commits a crime—and then gets away with it by making it impossible for Cormorant to tell people what really happened. A simple moral. If you don't want people to know what you're really up to, silence your victims."

"What does this have to do with the code?" I asked.

"Like I was saying, Bill was all about the Phaistos Disks being an undiscovered language—the next Sumerian or Linear A. But you started to have doubts."

"So?"

"I'm convinced now that you were right. All these ancient sources talk about how humans were given language by the gods, right? And then had it taken away? But I always wondered: What if that's just a bad analogy? Being a geek, I thought, maybe what the gods did wasn't so much give us a language as install an operating system."

"This idea is surely the total geek, Rosko," Kit said. "Architects installing software in our minds?"

"Bill's software can identify over a thousand languages, and if you feed in something else, it can say, OK, this is more like Croatian than Bosnian, or it's more like Mixtec than Zapotec. But it had a coughing fit because the data from the Disks doesn't have a structure like any language, and that's because it isn't a language. It's math. Something to do with a complex function based on huge prime numbers, I think— which is kind of like the encryption that runs the Internet, actually."

"Kind of like the encryption that runs the Internet," I echoed, trying to keep my voice level. "But it was written down on clay tablets by a bunch of Babbler priests living in a small isolated civilization on the flanks of a volcano, a thousand years before the Sumerians worked out enough cuneiform to keep track of their fucking goats?"

"That's what I'm saying. And, if it's really based on prime factorization, it's beyond the reach of any computing power we have. This little laptop, it had some trouble there, but after I straightened out the code, it managed to identify, you know, the shape of the building. But now that we know what that building is, we also know there's no possibility of breaking in, not even with the ISOC machine. Not with all the computers in the world."

"Hard for believe," Kit said, "that we were programmed."

"People found it hard to believe that the earth goes round the sun. Or that the continents float on lakes of liquid rock. Or that we're descended from fish. But it's still true."

"So you're saying what?" I asked. "That it's hopeless? That this just confirms what you've secretly suspected ever since Ararat? Which is that we should just give up?"

He turned away to look out of the window, which seemed like answer enough. But you jumped up and kicked the table. "No," you said. "No!" You were shaking, and sweating, and crushing the New Guinea map in your hands.

I should have tried to comfort you. But I was so angry and frightened and so in need of air that I grabbed Kit by the hand, pulled her outside, and spent twenty minutes sobbing into her shoulder.

Part of falling in love was being amazed by how well Kit could understand me, could intuitively just get it, could know who I was and put up even with the annoying parts without the need for endless backfilling, explaining, and apologizing. (Litmus test for a healthy relationship, D, try it out sometime: if you keep having to say "What did you mean by that?" you're screwed.) But another part of falling in love was greedily expecting her to understand me perfectly, and side with me in everything, and being crushed when she failed the test. The sense that Rosko had betrayed me—that he'd known we couldn't help you, or learn any more about the Architects that would make any difference—was bad enough in itself. But it was almost worse to grasp that she pretty much agreed with him, that all her care for me was just kind of pity for the deluded, and that all her care for you, her obvious affection for you, was like the attitude of a nurse while hanging around waiting for her terminal dementia patient to die.

I didn't just think all that: I said it too. Which was a mistake. And I said it angrily, which was a bigger mistake. At that point she ran out of calm and bit my head off, and the word *bitch* got used, by one or the other of us.

OK, OK: probably, realistically, she didn't bite my head off, but she was annoyed with me (I wonder why!) and she didn't hide it. Or did hide it, but not well enough. The end result was I felt like she'd bitten my head off, but suspected I might be overreacting. At which exact point, natch, she said dismissively, "You're overreacting." She also said, "Don't be a whiner, Morag." She even managed to make me feel guilty by saying it was immature of me not to put aside my own obsessions and focus on "just taking more proper care of Daniel." *More proper:* as if what I was doing didn't come up to her standards and therefore didn't quite count.

Arguments are like flash fires—they spread so quickly that afterward, you can't describe the order in which things took flame. But somehow I managed to use a particularly self-pitying tone to bring up Jimmy and Lorna.

I know, I know, Kit lost her father to booze. And she had that offhand, irritable-practical, slightly distant relationship with Natazscha, which I couldn't decide whether to admire or feel sorry for. But her reaction made me conscious of how deeply she didn't see that aspect of me, didn't have the capacity to imagine what it was like for me, to grow up traveling the world with my parents, for their life to have been my life, for them to have been my closest friends, for them to be *missing*.

Being in love makes you so, so stupid!

Did I say that already? Sorry.

You don't understand me. You're not even listening. You can't imagine what it was like to be blah blah blah. Or how it's been for me, not knowing blah blah blah. It's easy for you because et cetera, et cetera, et cetera.

High-drama relationship clichés, tumbling out of my mouth one after another. Embarrassed by myself? You have no idea. I thought, *This is not even me, the way Daniel is not Daniel.* The end of it wasn't even me feeling annoyed, wasn't even me feeling alienated from her, or having the satisfaction of feeling wronged because she threw a pot of boiling tea at me. No. A pot of boiling tea would have been easy. Instead, she just said, "I'm going for a walk." Rosko came out and joined her, and the only thing she threw at me as the two of them headed toward the beach was a look. A coolly offended, *fuck-you-too* look that burned and burned and burned.

A short unpleasant visit inside my head:

I'm crazier about her than she is about me. In which case, it's only a matter of time before she gets tired of me. Maybe she's already tired of me. Maybe I should wear clothes that are less boring. Or do an Ella and go for a radically different hairstyle. Or just become, overnight, a completely different person. A more interesting, more empathetic, more attractive person. A better person. Because what have I done? What I've done is announce that I'm too self-absorbed to have even noticed or cared about any of the things that in fact I've been noticing half to death, the things I care about more than I know how to say, like how kind she is, and good with you, and funny, and how every time I look at her I feel like a helpless minor asteroid being caught in the gravitational field of a star—and—and—and if she leaves me now, if just as this has got started she changes her mind because I'm such an emotional idiot, I can't survive that. It'll crush me. Maybe it's already too late. Maybe I'm so bad at this that I've already done the damage. Maybe—

I know, because I read about it: this is stuff that some people spend 90 percent of their lives on. But I'd never felt the reality of it before, never understood that love and longing and uncertainty and need could be such an exhausting, all-body workout. Never guessed just how much of me could be taken over by this trivial, everyday agony.

No doubt Kit was complaining to Rosko about how Majka was impossible / was losing it / was, frankly, just between you and me, Rosko, the selfish-centered painfulness in butt, yah? So I tried to distract myself by talking to you and managed to talk only about whether you thought I was selfish or not. You'd have called me on that, once. Not now. So I stared out of the window, stirred some chili, checked the time every thirty seconds, and stared out of the window some more.

When Kit had been gone for forty-nine and a half minutes—during which a thousand years passed, and I burned a pan of corn bread—I filled the kettle. It was white with a floral pattern and rust spots showing through the coating; the stopper in the spout had one of those whistles that responds to the steam pressure with a noise like a mezzo-soprano being strangled.

"You want a cup of something?"

"Yes."

O-kay. You were looking at your hands, not at me, so I couldn't tell whether the "yes" was, hallelujah, a direct answer to my question. That would have been a first, but maybe you were thinking of something else.

"A cup of what? Regular tea? Peppermint? Ginger?"

You opened your mouth again, paused, and then flinched, the way you'd done before the raccoons came out of that tree on campus. It set my neck tingling. A threat? Had someone found us? Many things were interfering with my ability to believe I was still rational. One was the memory of being nearly kidnapped by that gorilla of a guy near your parents' house. It was there all the time, in the background, like having something sticky on my hands that I couldn't wash off.

You got up slowly and stood at the window. I squeezed your hand. For once, you squeezed in response, but the way you did it was unsatisfying, mechanical—as if you'd had the gesture described to you but not explained. As if Rosko and Kit were right about you.

"What? What did you hear?" There was nothing out there except some wind-whipped grass and the flat gray strait.

Ten or fifteen seconds passed. I was on the point of saying, *No, D, it's nothing*, when the top of Rosko's head, then Kit's, rose into view as they climbed the beach path. Part of me was relieved that it wasn't scary strangers. Knowing that Kit was coming back to the cabin, a larger part of me was occupied with all the cruel things, or the merely final and irrevocable things, she might say. But most of me was preoccupied with something else. I thought of the raccoons outside the lab; of all the times you'd spoken confidently about things that hadn't yet happened; of you saying, "There's no time"; of what Partridge had said about "seers."

"You can see the future, can't you?" I said. "You're turning into what all the religions claim to have. A seer. A prophet. One of the special people who get glimpses through the smoke?"

You just looked at me. Just looked—but it was a look that seemed to brim over with meaning: the very opposite of blank, your eyes had frustration and sympathy in them—as if I was the one suffering an enigmatic mental deficiency, and you were the one trying and trying to help me toward understanding.

"What am I supposed to think, D? I want to laugh at this. I want to say it's totally unscientific. Mumbo jumbo. Seeing into the future is an absurd idea, impossible. Even more impossible than ancient gods installing software in our heads. What the hell am I supposed to think?"

Rosko, coming back in, had overheard me. "You should give yourself a break," he said, putting down a big pair of marine binoculars and kicking off his shoes. "Even the physicists don't know what to think. Half of them say the future can affect the past, and the other half say time's an illusion. That aside, the whole house of cards is glued together with three big theories—relativity and quantum mechanics, which contradict each other, and string theory, which is mathematically beautiful junk. As for consciousness, it's reality's dick: too embarrassing to mention."

"Thanks for that, Rosko."

Kit came over and took the kettle from under my hand. "Works better if you turn on the flame," she said. Her voice was neutral. I tried to hunt for clues in her expression, but I couldn't focus because I was distracted by her hair, which had been darkened slightly by the damp. It was tucked into the upturned collar of her jacket. I'd never seen it like that before, and it made me ache, fiercely, all over. I looked down at the kettle again.

"She is like you," she said, turning to Rosko. "Too much the thinking." Hearing her refer to me in the third person was agony; I knew, in that moment, that it was over. "And now she have something more to think about."

She was holding out my phone. At arm's length. I couldn't even meet her eyes this time. "Forgot I had it still in pocket," she said. "Pocket goes ping. Then ping. Then also third time ping. Somebody must like you."

Some body. That's how she said it. In a sane mood I could've taken it for gentle irony, a joke, a sign that she was looking for a way back to safe ground. But naturally I jumped to the opposite conclusion: she was rubbing salt into my self-inflicted wound. She was mocking me. She was cruelly expressing surprise that anyone could like me—never mind her.

"Thank you," I said miserably, taking the phone.

I should have said, *I'm sorry.* I should have said, *Please be careful, because right now I'm constructed entirely out of eggshells.* Instead I just looked down at the black rectangle and read the screen.

It said WELCOME TO CANADA. Then it changed to OUT OF SERVICE AREA. But the three messages were still there.

The first one was from Partridge. I skimmed it, not much interested; it seemed like pleasant chatter that I didn't need to pay attention to:

I'm sorry you had to push off in such a hurry, but I do understand. Another riot here, in the middle of downtown: I got a ringside seat from my hotel and it wasn't a pretty sight. You'll well out of it. Thanks for the copies of all your notes—I'm working on them. Meanwhile, up at the university, the Seraphim are trying to prevent them from even clearing up the library site, and Natazscha has been questioned at length by men in dark suits. All minor stuff compared to what's happening in places like Japan of course, which, having discovered the joys of sectarian violence, is starting to look more and more like the Middle East. But I fear we are not far behind.

I'm still convinced that the Disks and the Bronze Age Collapse are where our answer lies—that's when the Architects gave us language, or took away our other languages. Perhaps you could get somewhere with the Disks if they get the computer at the Institute for the study of the origin of consciousness working again? But I don't think that's going to happen soon. I've had dinner with Natazscha twice, incidentally. Wonderful woman! But she's quite dismissive of my idea that this business all got going during the Bronze Age. She thinks language and a full sense of the self emerged much earlier—Cro-Magnon art, Neanderthal burial practices, that sort of thing. So, while I'm fixated on the Theran

CIVILIZATION, WHICH GOT GOING SEVEN THOUSAND YEARS
AGO, SHE THINKS THE BIG STUFF HAPPENED MUCH FUR-
THER BACK. I CAN'T BELIEVE SHE'S RIGHT, BUT THEN I'M
NOT SURE WHAT TO BELIEVE.

DID YOU HEAR THE STORY FROM NEW ZEALAND ABOUT
SOME OF THE MISSING FROM THE RUAPEHU INCIDENT COM-
ING BACK? FASCINATING! SOME SAY IT'S ALL HOKUM, OTHERS
SAY IT'S PROOF OF REINCARNATION, AND A THIRD SAY IT
PROVES THEY WERE ABDUCTED BY ALIENS. SO MANY THEO-
RIES! DO GET PLENTY OF REST AND FRESH AIR.

The second message was what I'd been imagining and waiting for
all these weeks:

DEAREST, DEAREST MORAG: LONG STORY, BUT WE ARE SAFE.
TRULY SAFE, THIS TIME, AND HOME SOON. MADE IT TO
JORDAN YESTERDAY. NOW ON OUR WAY TO AMMAN. MORE
IF/WHEN I CAN. HOPE YOU ARE SAFE AND WELL, AND I JUST
WISH I KNEW FOR SURE THAT YOU'RE GETTING THIS. LOVE
LOVE LOVE FROM LORNA X LORNA X LORNA X AND JIMMY
X JIMMY X JIMMY X

The third message was the least expected. The one I'd more or less
given up on:

MY DEAR MORAG, I AM SO VERY SORRY THAT I DID NOT
GET BACK TO YOU. ALAS, BEING IN A MEDICALLY INDUCED
COMA HAS PLAYED HAVOC WITH THE SOCIAL NICETIES. I
AM STILL UNABLE TO TRAVEL, BUT I HOPE THAT I CAN PRE-
VAIL UPON YOU TO VISIT ME. COME AT ONCE, IF YOU CAN.

I WANT TO TALK TO YOU ABOUT MAYNARD JONES. AND I
HAVE SOMETHING REMARKABLE TO SHOW YOU. WITH SIN-
CEREST RESPECT, AKSHAY "CHARLIE" BALAKRISHNAN.

There was contact information underneath Balakrishnan's message,
but I didn't read it. Rosko did.

"Hawaii? He wants you to go to Hawaii? I thought he lived in New
Delhi."

"Kona is Hawaii," Kit said. "I think that guy maybe lives
everywhere."

"I'm not going," I said. "I can't leave Daniel now."

I'd been holding your hand, and you tugged on it. "You will go,"
you said. It sounded almost like a recommendation, almost like a command, but it was neither. It was a statement of fact: you knew that I'd
go, and you were telling me so.

Kit put her hand on my other arm and squeezed gently, which
made me feel like a starving person being offered a grape. I was craving
her touch, craving reassurance, craving, honestly, the chance to put
my face on her shoulder again and not move for an hour. But was she
offering a gesture of reconciliation? Or an attempt to be kind about
not offering one?

"Majka," she said, "You have been trying to find out about Mayo,
yes, because you think he knew something about the Architects that
you don't know? His Route Two is about using ISOC to emulate whole
brain, upload consciousness to cloud or something, digital immortality, blah blah. But he finds it not working so good, something missing.
You still don't know what. Maybe Rosko is right. Maybe Architects are
just beyond us, like we are cat trying to do calculus. But maybe not.
Balakrishnan founded ISOC. He hired Mayo, was Mayo's boss. Also a
friend of Iona, yes? So talk to him. And if he is too sick to come here,
then of course you go."

Majka. That meant something, right? If she was still seriously pissed off, she'd have called me Morag.

Shut up. Shut up. Focus.

I took a deep breath and tried to sound normal. It didn't work: my voice came out squeaky, needy.

"We can all go."

"No, Majka. Daniel, he cannot travel now, I think. Too much change already. Look at him—he lose ten kilo. And you need to do this, not us. We stay here, look after him, no problem. You think me and Rosko can't look after him?"

"No, I don't think that."

"Good, so no excuse."

Rosko was trying to make up to me. "The Big Island's one of the Seraphim's so-called Epicenters," he said. "Mauna Kea and Mauna Loa—huge volcanoes. Maybe you'll find something out about that. What they're really planning."

I sat down heavily on one of the kitchen chairs and managed to avoid saying, *But you think it'll all be pointless.*

"Come on, Morag," he said. "It's six hours there, six back, no big deal. Maybe you'll only be gone a day or two. You'll be back before Jimmy and Lorna even get here."

The thought of leaving you was unbearable. It was even harder now that I sensed that Kit and Rosko, for all their compassion, had so little hope you'd recover.

And honestly—honestly—the thought of leaving Kit was even more unbearable.

Crapshit.

If I'd had the courage to say that, instead of just think it, maybe she'd have smiled.

CHAPTER 13

ILDAVAN

We'd heard that a lot of Seraphim were visiting Hawaii or even moving there. Still, it was a shock that some airlines had put on extra flights, and more of a shock I still couldn't get a seat. When I dug up a cheap last-minute deal—Kona via Honolulu via LA—it was ten and a half hours including the two layovers; I hesitated for all of five minutes, and when I looked again it had evaporated. Eventually, after an hour of hitting refresh, I snagged the last seat on a direct flight from SeaTac to Kona.

It was an oddly private, subdued crowd on my plane. Three or four people were wearing the white Seraphim scarf, but I assumed (because of the clothes, and despite their reserved manner) that everyone else was a tourist, flying to the middle of the Pacific for the usual ritual: extra-deep sunburn; rip-off drinks made from canned pineapple juice with grain alcohol; Cambodian-sweatshop hula souvenirs. But no, these ordinary American couples and singles and buddy groups weren't about to become beach lobsters. They were new acolytes, converts to the Word of Quinn, going eagerly for initiation at (as they were calling it) the First Epicenter.

An affable-looking granddad with stained teeth and a hearing aid was in the aisle ahead of me after we landed. He'd put on a "Know It Is True" baseball cap. In the little open-air terminal he seemed to be on his own, lower lip trembling as he fiddled with his belt, so I went over and risked talking to him. Why had they traveled all the way to Kona from what was already an Epicenter, the Pacific Northwest?

"Tahoma's not ready!" he said, and stared at me with watery eyes as if he'd said the most obvious thing in the world. "Tahoma—that's Mount Rainier, you know—it won't be ready for a while yet! As a matter of fact—" He looked around, confused, as if he'd dropped something. "As a matter of fact, Mauna Loa isn't ready either. But it will be! Soon! This is the one we're going to focus on first, d'you see? The best chance we have of getting onto the stairway. I'm hoping to meet Mr. Quinn himself! And of course there will be time to meet everyone who's ever been born, because where we're going there'll be no end to time! Are you practicing?"

Practicing?

I didn't know whether he meant it like *Are you a practicing Catholic?* or like *Have you done your piano practice?* Or both.

"Oh yes," I said. "Practicing. All the time." Then I pointed up at the sign for the women's bathroom. "Sorry, got to go!"

"Practicing your chants!" he called after me. "Simplifying your mind. *Ut-QOR-met, bir-ARD-ku, rem-EP-zi, tav-AU—*"

I didn't need to use the bathroom. But I went in, throwing an apologetic smile over my shoulder, and dithered at the sink, hoping he wouldn't be there to continue the conversation when I came out. While I stood there, pretending to clean my nails, I thought about you—thought about how torn I was, because my brain wanted to meet Balakrishnan but my heart wanted to get on the next plane back— and then I found myself eavesdropping on a conversation between two dressed-up-nice suburban mom types who'd just come out of their stalls. As they washed their hands and adjusted their makeup, they were talking about how wonderful it was "to have truly given everything up at last"—excluding the mascara, apparently—and how they'd heard "totally *amazing*" things about "the arena they're building up there on the mountain." When I emerged, Grandpa had drifted over to join a gathering of fifty or sixty people around a huge Samoan woman in an orange muumuu who was standing precariously on a chair. She smiled too much and said "Aloha" too loudly. It looked like she was distributing the traditional leis, but they weren't leis. They were cheap acrylic knockoffs of the white scarf, complete with the broken golden triangle.

I'd been told a driver would be there for me. For some reason *driver* conjured up a skinny, sandy-haired guy with freckles and a cheap blue uniform, so I wasn't prepared for the muscular Hawaiian dude with "Chen" on his signboard. He looked like a Special Forces soldier on a fashion shoot, with a fresh white shirt showing off his pecs. More tousled, less neat, and he could've had a career doing romance novel covers.

"Ms. Chen? Welcome to the Big Island. My name is Kai Kaiulani. I work for Mr. Smith."

"Yes. I was told about the 'Mr. Smith' bit. I'm really here to see—"

He held up a finger. "Mr. Smith, in public. His compound is a short drive from here. Follow me, please."

Outside the terminal and away from the jet-fuel fumes, the sun was blazing and the tropical air smelled wonderful, but soon I was enveloped in chilled air in the back of a white SUV the size of an aircraft carrier. I waited until Kai had threaded us around twenty or thirty tour buses, then tried to draw him into conversation. Not much luck. When I asked about the Seraphim, nothing. In response to "So you're

Mr. Smith's driver?" I only got "I'm his head of security. I also do all his travel arrangements an' dat."

An' dat. For homework on the flight—or to distract myself from being suspended helpless in a beer can over several thousand miles of water—I'd watched a bunch of videos on Hawaiian pidgin. I was gearing up for the usual experience: getting it all wrong, being laughed at and corrected, then getting it. But Kai had the accent without the language. He dropped words here and there, played loose with verb forms, said *an' dat* and *togedda*. But that was it. Maybe he was speaking Mainland for my benefit—or did it every day for his employer.

"Not much travel lately," I said. No response. "Tell me about his health." No response, followed after a long pause by "Can't comment on dat. We be there in a few. Relax. Enjoy the view."

The road followed the coast, but we crested a small rise and saw the Pacific spread out to the horizon like a pale-blue rug, with darker lines running in parallel as if someone had prepared for my arrival by running a vacuum over it.

Kai checked his mirrors constantly. Once, he pulled off the road, waited twenty seconds, and made a U-turn; then he drove half a mile back toward the airport and made another U-turn. Twice, he took detours that seemed to make no sense. I shot off a quick message to Kit, and another to the number Lorna had used, and rewatched for the five hundredth time a ten-second clip of Kit blowing me a kiss. (Her lips barely moved, as if the whole gesture was an afterthought. The power was all in the eyes—in the way they held mine and didn't move.)

"So," I said, "the Seraphim are more active here than I thought. What are they doing?"

He couched his reply in such a way that I couldn't tell whether he was quoting Seraphim propaganda or simply saying what he thought. "Mauna Loa is a sacred mountain. Like all volcanoes! It's a good point of contact with the Architects. A place where maybe more people can, uh, go up. Experience Anabasis."

I thought of something Partridge had said. "Have you heard the stories about people experiencing Anabasis and then, um, showing up again?"

"Seraphim not supposed to believe that. Reincarnation, that's other religions. Quinn said we don't need the body no more."

"But some of the relatives have claimed—"

"I know."

"You—" I didn't know why I'd started to ask, but I blundered on. "What do you think?"

In the mirror his gaze was hard, unreadable. "I'm not paid to have opinions about eternity, Ms. Chen. That is Mr. Smith's department." He drawled *Smith's*, as if making fun of his own precautions. "This is a volcanic chain of islands. Hawaiians have worshipped the snow goddess Poli'ahu and the fire goddess Pele for over a thousand years. Poli'ahu lives on Mauna Kea, which is a few feet taller. Pele lives on Mauna Loa, which is the biggest volcano anywhere in the world. Hawaiian people have lived with liquid fire from the beginning. So Julius Quinn is popular. His ideas are popular."

I wondered if, in a thousand years of human habitation, it was just fire and lava that had amazed the Polynesians into belief. Or had some of them, deep in the unwritten past, seen something more specific?

The founder and CEO of BalakInd was richer than some medium-sized countries, so I'd pictured a trophy oceanfront villa: white columns that might be Ionian or might be Doric, reflecting pools, all the square footage and domestic warmth of a hotel. The usual billionaire crap. That's what the rich were like, wasn't it? Needy. Sad. Desperate to show off. Excluding Iona, of course, who was way too nice and way too interesting to care about showing off. I knew she and Balakrishnan had liked each other, but it hadn't occurred to me that they'd be alike in that too until we turned inland off the highway into an ordinary suburban neighborhood. There was a sense of the ocean, not a view of it. Kids were on bikes in the street with their red flip-flops up on the handlebars. The houses themselves were small, ranch style, with carports shading stacks of beach gear and well-used Toyota pickups.

We made several turns before drawing up in front of a gate next to a palm tree. Kai slid his window down and spoke his name slowly, formally, into a little metal grille, like he was about to order a burger and fries: "Kai Kaiulani."

Voice recognition, I assumed. After a short pause, as if digesting, the speaker emitted a satisfied plink. Another pause, then an Indian woman's voice filled the car—silky, sophisticated, and formal, with a diplomat's cold politeness.

"You have with you Mr. Smith's guest, I see."

"Yes, Mrs. Chaudry."

He must have seen me in the mirror, craning my neck and looking puzzled; he pointed out a security camera artfully concealed on the far side of the palm tree.

"You were not followed?"

"I was not." He rolled his eyes.

"I suppose you had better bring her in, then," the voice said, with what sounded like regret.

The gate hummed open. We drove through onto a short gravel driveway. I could admire Balakrishnan for wanting to live modestly, but this wooden bungalow, on a residential street and surrounded by other small houses, didn't make sense.

"Stay in the car," Kai said, and I got my explanation quickly enough. He watched in the mirror as the gate swung closed behind us. When it clicked shut, there was an answering click from in front of us, and a section of the garden wall—or what I'd taken for the garden wall, complete with blood-red hibiscus vines—began to move. It was a concealed second gate. Across a strip of grass, it gave access to the house beyond.

"He owns all these properties," Kai explained, using a finger to draw a loop around the perimeter. "Security, housekeeper, some of his business employees, a guest house. He uses this one in the middle. It has no access directly from the street."

The second house was bigger than the first, but only because it had two stories. There was a Japanese rock garden, and beyond that a manicured lawn. Two Indian children, ten or twelve years old, were standing barefoot on the grass. They wore bright pastel shorts and T-shirts. A sister and her slightly younger brother, for sure. They seemed to be playing a game.

"Wait here, please," Kai said as I got out of the car. He took my bag and disappeared around the side of the building.

Everything was calm, relaxed, and beautiful—in a way it was hard not to find annoying. I thought of you again, of how downright ill you were, and of all the time I'd already spent getting nowhere. I wanted to *hurry*. Instead I was in a sunny garden in Hawaii, watching two children playing.

The girl held a soccer ball. The boy stood a few feet away with his hands out, as if expecting her to throw it. Instead, she tapped it to her forehead three times and turned her body slowly through three-quarters of a turn, so that she was facing me. She cast her big brown eyes in my direction but ignored me. Lowering the ball to waist height, she used her fingers to rotate it, also three-quarters of a turn, in the opposite direction. Then she turned back to the boy, touched the ball to her forehead again, and threw it to him, saying something that sounded like "Jataka-jélup."

"Akan-jata-kipólnet," he said, twirling the ball expertly in one hand. A shrill, piping voice—he was younger than I'd thought. His head bobbed in what seemed like a random combination of nods and shakes.

"Hello," the girl said, turning to me and bowing slightly. "Let me permit me to introduce you to yourself. You are the famous Morag Chen."

I decided not to react to *famous*. Maybe it was a joke. There was something grown-up about her manner—or something calculated to make fun of grown-ups. "I'm Morag," I said. "Yes." And, going along with the game: "I'm very pleased to meet me."

"This is my brother, Sunil."

"Nice to meet you too, Sunil," I said to the boy. "How does your sister know so much about me?"

"Because you're famous," he said. "She already told you that. Also because you're expected. Uncle Akshay told us how excited he was to meet you at last. The three most important facts about you are that you're a Babbler, like us, that you translated the tablets your parents found at Babylon, which says the Architects lied to us, and that you want to cure your brother."

"Your brother, Daniel, who became a Mystery," the girl continued, as if completing the same sentence. "Which means he probably won't be cured and will die soon. Because that's what Mysteries do."

"My brother isn't a Mystery," I said, sounding more defensive than I'd intended, "and he's not going to die."

I half-expected her to challenge me, but she continued as if I hadn't spoken. "Uncle Akshay wants to help you. But you'd better hurry. He's very sick, and they can't cure him, so he's going to die soon too."

She spoke of it flatly, with the special indifference about death that only children can manage. Sunil continued brightly: "Oh well. No one can live forever. Everyone has to die eventually! Unless they become Seraphim of course. Seraphim live forever!"

"Do you think so?"

"No," the girl said. "He's joking."

As if to underline that, he grinned wickedly and spoke in a mocking singsong, like a kid might say "na-na, na-na, boo-boo": *"Em-DA-chol.*

Ul-KO-vok. Ret-YEM-an. Ar-QA-het!" It was a quotation from Quinn's *Anabasis*—minus the usual reverence.

"I'll take that for a no," I said.

"Actually we're not sure what we think." Her eyes sparkled. "But we *think* that what we think is what we *think* you think."

"Or," Sunil added, "we think we think what Uncle Akshay says he thinks you think."

"O-kay," I said. "Before I get lost, tell me, what is it that Uncle Akshay thinks I think?"

The girl took over again, speaking rapidly. "He thinks you think the Architects enslaved us thousands of years ago. He thinks you think they needed the Babblers but couldn't control them."

"I'm fascinated by all these ideas of mine," I said. "Tell me, what do I think the Babblers did back then?"

"You think they became the priests, at first. The translators of what the Architects wanted us to do."

"Messengers of the gods, then."

"Yes. Leading people to the Architects. Telling them that obedience meant eternal life and disobedience meant death. But the Babblers were a paradox."

She said *paradox* slowly, importantly, obviously proud of using it. "Why a paradox?" I asked.

"Because the skills that made the Babblers good at persuading other people were also the skills that made some of them doubt what they were saying to the people. And made them safer from the Architects themselves."

"Wow," I said, trying to keep the tone light. "That's right. You seem to know everything about me!"

"That's not true," Sunil said. "We don't know what you had for breakfast this morning."

"Toast with butter and marmalade. The very best Scottish marmalade, imported from Dundee, with big chunks of peel in it. Americans don't really understand marmalade. But it was wasted. I burned the toast. I was distracted."

"I do know one other thing about you," Sunil said. "I know you're still wondering what my sister's name is."

"You're right, I am. Without knowing her name, how can I introduce her to herself?"

"Her name is Vandana," he said. And they both chanted at once, "Vandana Vandana Vandana!"

"I see. Sunil and his sister Vandana Vandana Vandana. I'm sorry I interrupted your game."

"It's not a game," the girl said, and made a wriggling movement, as if shaking off a bug. Sunil giggled, and said, "Tamjen-ékul-ókamem."

"It's a language," she said. "That's what we do, you know. Invent languages."

"I don't understand."

"We're Babblers, like you. But most Babblers only learn foreign languages. We invented one of our own when we were still babies. It's called Ildavan. That's what we speak most of the time. Since then we've invented five more."

"The other ones are Ilnu, Andu, Andanil, Vasadin, and Slaa," the boy said proudly. "Their names are all made up from our names. The more we speak, the more invincible we are! The one we were using just now is Slaa. Every sentence in Slaa is a single word."

"Brilliant," I said, convinced that they were having a joke at my expense. "Can you say something to me in Ildavan? I'll give you a test, if you like."

"Yes please!" Sunil said. "We love tests!"

I went over to Vandana and spoke with my hand cupped to her ear. She nodded, frowned, and then stood still, like a nervous primary school kid about to give a presentation to her class. I stepped back and waited, feeling the sun on my face and the smell of the sea. The house stood behind me—blue gray, featureless, the essence of ordinary—and

I wondered whether I was supposed to just walk in. Someone moved in a downstairs room, and I had the sense I was being watched.

Vandana still hadn't said anything. She wrinkled her nose, squinted, and adjusted her hair. Her brother was looking straight at her with his eyes narrowed, all concentration. She looked up at the sky, then at me, then at the ground. She twisted her fingers together fiercely, as if desperately trying to wash something invisible from her hands, and moaned, and her whole body seemed to vibrate and shiver with tension. It was like witnessing intense embarrassment, but the twitching motions and the noises suggested Tourette's. When she stopped, she stood awkwardly, with one foot held sideways, biting her lip.

"Well," I said, trying to be sympathetic, "I'm not understanding much Ildavan so far. But that's all right. Maybe later."

"You're not understanding it," Sunil said, "because you don't know it."

"What I mean is, Vandana didn't say anything yet."

He rolled his eyes at me with the frank rudeness only children can get away with—the expression said, roughly, *I didn't expect you to be such a moron.* Then he repeated what I'd said privately to his sister, complete with a merciless, over-the-top parody of my accent: "What you said to her was 'Tell yer brothah ah flew all the weh from Seatt-ul jess tuh see Mustur Bulu-krush-nun. And thut the vulue of pai es approwk-su-mutleh three point one fower one faive naine.'"

Vandana put a hand to her face and snorted with delight. I was about to ask how they'd done it. But a tiny gray-haired Indian woman had come out onto the front step and was waiting.

Fifty? Sixty? Seventy? I couldn't tell. Her sari was a rich green silk threaded with gold, as if the silkworms had been raised on a diet of pure money. She didn't smile or give the impression that she'd ever had much practice smiling.

"Ah, Miss Chen, yes," she said, looking me up and down. "Welcome." There was more regret than welcome in her voice, as if she wanted to convey simultaneously the idea that my appearance disappointed her and that she was too well-bred to say so. And I detected a hint of condescension in *Miss*, or I thought I did—almost as if she'd called me *child*.

"You must be Mrs. Chaudry."

She rolled her head to one side, then the other, a very Indian gesture I'd seen before. It might have meant *Perhaps*, or *Yes*, or *Follow me and don't waste my time with chitchat*. On the front step, I turned back to say good-bye to the children, but they were engrossed in their language "game."

As we stepped inside, I glimpsed a younger woman in a nurse's uniform through an interior doorway. Mrs. Chaudry took me down a short corridor to an elevator.

"This way please. Mr. Balakrishnan is waiting for you on the lanai."

"Don't you mean Mr. Smith?" I was trying to get a rise out of her, without success.

"Mr. Balakrishnan is very frail. He insists on seeing you, but he will not be able to talk for long."

It meant *I will not permit you to talk for long.*

"What does he—?"

"No doubt he will explain everything."

One floor up, when the door slid open, she made no move to get out. "Please go. This is where Mr. Balakrishnan works. As I said, you will find him out on the lanai, through the door to your right."

It may have been an ordinary house, but I was standing in a surprisingly grand space, a study or gallery that took up the entire floor. Cello music that I couldn't identify—Bach?—was flooding in, loud, from invisible speakers. A half wall with a teak bookcase partially blocked the view down the room, but I could see that the far end was dominated by a huge desk, and an arrangement of soft chairs in pale leather around a fireplace. Although it was a summer afternoon in the tropics, small blue-and-yellow flames were blooming there like crocuses.

Above the desk there was a large, colorful abstract painting. Some hunch or other told me it was by someone famous, and not a reproduction, and therefore worth a million dollars per square foot. But the biggest, most striking piece of art in the room was definitely a reproduction. The original wouldn't have fit in the house—and the Louvre wouldn't have let it go, not even for Balakrishnan's money.

An old friend, you might say. Do you remember, D? No, of course you don't remember being in Paris with us in January. You probably don't even remember the fog, or the ice-bound fountains, or having bowls of hot chocolate in Montmartre, with those pastries called *cravates* that you always chose because they were the biggest. I don't suppose you remember being taken to the Louvre by Lorna either, but we saw this with her. We stood together, you and I, staring up at the five-meter original, while she told us the story.

"Look at the big bad laddie wi' the stone beard, boys an' girls. Gilgamesh! His mother was human, but his da' was a demon, a *lilu*, an' that means the wee bairn was a demigod. Aye, yet another one, Morag, like the kings o' Java, an' the Chinese emperors, an' Zeus's whole family o' brats an' troublemakers. Not to mention Jesus, o' course, an' enough characters in Hinduism to fill a bloody football stadium. *Hemitheos*, that's the Latin. Half god. Like superheroes, isn't it, special powers an' all. And the idea's been all over human civilization like a rash since, oh, a very long time before anyone thought o' Superman. Gorgeous muscles, don't you think? Gilgamesh was one o' the first. He's special for another reason too. The Sumerians kept very good records—bunch o' bureaucrats, frankly. According to their official list, he reigned as king in the Sumerian city o' Uruk for 126 years. Not a bad innings, ye'd think. But he wasn't satisfied wi' that. Och no. He was right miffed about not bein' a true immortal, see? He wanted the whole package. To be a god. To never, ever die."

It's epic, the statue, but comical too: the great hero's arm is clamped casually around the neck of a lion, and the lion hangs helpless against his thigh, struggling feebly on its last breath—it has all the scale, power, and dignity of a rabbit. *An interesting choice of decor,* I thought, *for Balakrishnan.* And that was before I'd met him.

When I stepped between Gilgamesh and the bookcase, I could see the whole room for the first time. Down one wall there were big picture windows with a view of Mauna Loa—though the mountain's so gently sloped that it looked like a low, distant ridge. On the other wall, opposite the windows, a sliding glass door, partly open, led out to a lanai. To the left of the door there was a big glass-fronted cabinet.

The cabinet held four rows of small round objects, above a large mechanical device that glittered and moved. I knew at once what the round objects were. I'd never seen the mechanical device before, but I knew what that was too.

CHAPTER 14

IMMORTALITY MAN

I stood just a few feet from the door onto the lanai. There was a sliver of a view over low rooftops toward the ocean. Part of a wheelchair was visible, and a bony hand on the armrest.

Silence.

I walked softly to the door. The lanai was five or six feet deep and maybe twelve feet long with a metal railing. At one end there were two cloth-covered outdoor chairs and a glass-topped table; at the other end, in the wheelchair, a man was sleeping under a heavy tartan blanket. Only his face and the hand were visible. The wheelchair, the awkward angle of the head, the sunken features—it was like that last picture of Hawking. I've seen photos of Charlie B. Who hasn't? But it was difficult to connect this shrunken figure to the global dealmaker in ten-thousand-dollar suits. He was so still, he could have been dead already, until a fly buzzed his face and he shifted slightly.

Mr. Balakrish—

I didn't say it. His name was on the tip of my tongue, but I changed my mind and went back to the glass display case. It was eight feet high, ten feet long, and two deep. The top half held all thirty-four of the Phaistos Disks in four rows: eight along the top, then nine, then eight, then nine again—the pattern reminded me of the alternating rows of stars on the American flag. The lower half was taken up by a moving, glittering network of cylinders, dials, gears, and levers; they looked like the inner guts of a monstrous clock in a Victorian inventor's dream. Some of the parts were silvery metal. Some were made from clear plastic, so that you could see the parts behind.

Several hundred gear wheels—but it took my eyes only a moment to pick through all that dense mechanical choreography and find the bit you and I both knew so well. The thing that had wowed the archaeologists and historians—*an analog computer a thousand years ahead of its time*, according to Derek P—was tucked into a corner near the front, and it was revealed here, in this grand reconstruction, as nothing more than a minor servomechanism. The much larger machine into which it fit, the real Antikythera Mechanism, also had the delicate intricacy of an old chronometer, but the size of it reminded me of farm machinery.

Obvious: the divers who'd attacked you in Crete—working for Mayo?—had found the whole thing. Or found enough of it to reconstruct the whole thing. And Balakrishnan had worked out that it wasn't just a calendar device or an eclipse predictor but a computer designed to decode the Disks. You could see the symbols etched on some of the wheels, dozens of them legible and dozens more eroded into enigma by time.

Click, click, click: it was going through the combinations. Or trying to. When I'd asked Rosko about the numbers involved, he'd said, "The cable lock on my bike has four digits, with ten numerals each. That's ten thousand possible combinations. Imagine a lock with as many possible combinations as—uh—look, there are 10^{80} protons in the observable universe. One followed by eighty zeroes. If every single one of those protons was a universe in itself, there'd be 10^{160} protons in all those universes. With me so far?"

"Sure, Rosko. Every proton in the universe is a universe. No problem."

"OK. Well, more than that."

The desk by the fireplace was made from a dark exotic hardwood, inlaid in an abstract pattern with other exotic hardwoods, but other than that it was a lot like Mayo's desk at ISOC. It looked barely used, and there was nothing on it except a single folder under a paperweight. The folder was dark red and had "BalakInd Corporation" in gold letters on the cover.

I should have gone straight out to the lanai, but I couldn't resist sitting in the chair and running my hands over the polished surface. It was like a metaphor of my own ignorance. What did I know about Balakrishnan? About as much as I knew about Mayo. Almost nothing.

One of the drawers had been left open; my hands were picking through its contents before I'd even thought about it. Pens and mints. More folders. Thick, creamy, old-fashioned personal writing paper, with nothing but "A. Balakrishnan" at the top of each sheet. More mints.

The fire was right at my back, and I started to sweat as I took out one of the folders. There was nothing in it but spreadsheets filled with big-money numbers. My phone buzzed in my pocket. I reached to turn it off, then saw it was Kit. The sound was off, so all I got was her face, her lips silently moving, her eyes unsmiling. Her expression had the unmistakable look of—

OK, so on second thoughts it wasn't unmistakable. A whole ragbag of different interpretations sprang into my mind and started throwing punches at each other. Stressed out by Rosko? Mildly fed up because she burned the lunch again? Generally bored due to still being stuck in the cabin? Anxious about your mental state? Anxious about my safety and/or mental state? Conflicted and guilt-ridden because she was unsure how to communicate while temporarily withholding from me (with, oh, the best possible motives!) the information that she's decided this relationship might be, let's face it, shall we, Morag, a huge mistake?

No idea.

Too many ideas.

My thumb fluttered over the sound icon, but it wasn't the best moment. Besides, if I did contact her, I might have a hard time finding the sweet spot between sounding not-quite-believably casual—*Aye, the flight was no problem. Everything's fine. How are you guys doing?*—and sounding not-quite-bearably needy:

I love you. Missing you is like being stabbed in the heart over and over with a rusty screwdriver. I can't bear to be without you, and it absolutely pisses me off that I don't have the strength of mind to stop thinking about you even when I need to stop thinking about you. Seeing your face makes it better. And worse. At the same time. I feel like an addict, and it turns out that addiction is a total blast (brilliant insight here: that must be why addiction is so, you know, addictive!—never thought of that before). A total blast, right up to the moment when someone takes the goodies away and you go into withdrawal and discover that withdrawal is a creature straight out of the pit of hell, and, when it gets its claws into you, you'd rather die than breathe. Which is how I feel now, and oh, by the way, on top of all that or beneath all that or mixed right in with it, there's thinking about Daniel and what if I fail and—

Luckily, all that took only a fraction of a second in real time. And it was interrupted soon enough by Sensible Morag:

Stop it. You're pathetic. Just do yourself a favor and stop it right now. Switch off the emotions, and shut up, and concentrate.

I took one more second to look at her face. OK, five. Then I tore my eyes away and switched off the screen. But I still had the phone in one hand and the BalakInd folder in the other when Sunil's voice floated up from the garden, high and lilting and insistent: "Ok-díjen-yat-éjen. Dor-bi-mílok. Omdalu-kájanit."

His sister responded in a slow drawl. I couldn't understand a word—"Oón-ováy-ara-jékdikar"—but it was perfectly clear that she was asserting her big-sister superiority by dismissing whatever it was he'd just said.

Balakrishnan must have woken up and heard them too, because the next voice was his, calling down to them. An unsteady voice. An old voice: "Sunil-énembit? Gárakom?"

Sunil again: "Akshaylam-íngeteth? Lam-gójemek!"

I fumbled the phone and dropped it on the desk—during a pause in the music, of course. It clattered on the wood, dropped to the floor, and exploded noisily into three pieces. Phone, cover, battery. Angry with my own incompetence, I failed to suppress the instinct to say "Fuck" really loudly. As I scooped up the debris and stuffed it back into a pocket, I heard the scrape of a chair or table from outside.

"Ms. Chen, is that you at last? This way! This way! I'm out here in the sunshine, warming my brittle bones. So glad you could come."

Gled: a hint of upper-crust British. I wondered when the Ahmedabad slum boy had taken time out from business to fake that up.

"Right here," I said brightly. "Just arrived." I crossed half the space between desk and door, but I'd left the drawer open. In two strides I was back behind the desk. Something made me pick up the paperweight.

The folder underneath was the same as the ones in the drawer—except for the additional notation in black marker pen: *DMJ*.

I was still standing behind the desk, with the paperweight in one hand and my fingers around the folder, when I heard Balakrishnan's voice again.

"Ah. It looks as if you found what you're looking for."

I had the impression that, out of old-fashioned habit, he'd forced himself to get up. He'd slid the door open so quietly that I never heard it, and with the help of a rubber-tipped walking stick, he was propped in the opening. His hair was still dark and thick, with a smudge of gray at the temples, but his skin had gone gray too, his eyes bulged, and his neck was too thin for his shirt—over which, despite the temperature, he wore a blue V-necked sweater. I thought of Derek Partridge. But the two men weren't just ethnically different. Derek was an old man driven by a high-voltage current. Charlie Balakrishnan was a decade younger, at least, but Sunil's casually brutal assessment was right. "Uncle Akshay" was very, very sick.

"I hoped you might be captivated by this," he said, gesturing with his eyes toward the mechanism in the cabinet. "But I see you've found something more interesting."

I put the paperweight down. "If you hoped we could use this to re-create the language of the Architects, you're out of luck," I said. I told him about our work at the cabin. "Rosko thinks the Disks represent a trapdoor function—a mathematical problem even our best modern computers will gag on."

"Beautiful, though, isn't it?" he said mildly, putting a hand against the glass cabinet. "And I have a sentimental attachment to the idea that this was designed by Archimedes of Syracuse himself, and since he may have had the highest IQ of anyone in history, I'd wager that he knew what he was up against. Still, Rosko's pessimistic assessment may be right: not enough firepower then, and perhaps not enough even now. Let's sit outside. Bring that file with you."

It was still in my hand. "I'm sorry," I said, as I followed him out into the sunshine. "I shouldn't have looked at it. I shouldn't have been in here. It's just that I need answers. And I—"

"No apology necessary, Ms. Chen. You need answers, because you want to save your brother—"

"How did you—?"

"You forget that Natazscha Cerenkov is my employee. You need answers because your brother's mind has been stolen from you by strange forces that you don't understand; you want to understand those forces so that you can bring him back, and you think I might be able to help. Which perhaps I can, and that indeed is why I asked you to come all this way. But of course you don't know whether to trust me."

With painful slowness, and my hand steadying one elbow, he eased himself back into the wheelchair. I put the folder down on the table next to him. Bluntness seemed like the best strategy. "You're right. I don't know whether to trust you. If I did, I wouldn't be behaving like a house thief."

I stood with my back against the railing. He steepled his fingers and looked up at me. His eyes were amazing: haunted by sickness, but at the same time sparkling, friendly, mischievous.

"As Socrates observes, knowing how ignorant you are is the first step toward wisdom. So. If you don't have reason to trust me, don't. I hired Maynard Jones, and I certainly thought I could trust him. Apparently not. We all make mistakes."

"Maybe that's a good place to start," I said. "He took the Disks from Crete, right? He must have been watching Bill Calder for a long time, waiting for an opportunity to pounce. But one of the last things Bill said before he died was that Mayo had sent the Antikythera Disks to you in India."

"I've always been a magpie," he said apologetically. "Easily distracted by shiny things. At my house in Delhi I have superb collections of everything from Renaissance maps to Japanese art deco movie posters. But undeciphered texts are my real passion. I own the Dorabella cipher, the Rohonc Codex, and whole rooms full of writing in Olmec, Rongorongo, and the Indus Valley script. And one of my most prized possessions is the Voynich Manuscript, for which I paid Yale University a positively absurd sum. I don't regret a penny of it."

He stopped to breathe, aware that he still hadn't answered me.

"The thing is, I had the Disks diverted here because, at the point when they came under my control, I'd just found out that I would be stuck in Hawaii for some time."

"Stuck in Hawaii? That's an odd thing to say."

"I have not been taking surfing lessons, I assure you. I've spent most of the time deeply unconscious in an oxygen tent at a clinic I set up in Honolulu. Please take a seat; you're making me feel impolite. And let's have some tea, shall we?"

Let's have some tea. It was like God saying "Let there be light": the instant he said the words, Mrs. Chaudry emerged onto the balcony with a wheeled silver trolley. On it there was a carved wooden tray that looked Indian, a fancy tea service in blue china that looked English, and a plate of tiny white sandwiches that looked as if they'd been cut with a laser.

Mrs. Chaudry poured silently for both of us, threw me another disapproving look, and left. "You met Sunil and Vandana?" he asked when she'd gone. "Her grandchildren. Very interesting. The only case we know of in which both parents are Babblers too."

When he picked up the delicate china cup, the sun shone right through it onto the tea. I took a sip of mine: it was scented with cardamom.

"I am honored to meet you at last, Morag Chen," he said. "Your reputation precedes you, of course, along with the Akkadian translations.

Outstanding. But the reason I wanted to meet you is not to shower praise on a fellow Babbler or quiz you about the relevance of Shul-hura's 'alternative Babel' to our current situation. My purpose, rather, is to acknowledge that you and I are facing the same puzzle. The difference being that I have been busy trying to save myself, while your concern is for someone else."

"For Daniel, yes, but it's much bigger than that," I said. "I can only help Daniel if I understand what the Architects did—but they're a threat to everyone. And one of the few leads I have is the thought that Maynard Jones was on Ararat because he knew something about them—and that you can help me find out what it was."

He considered that for a long time. "The Architects are real, you say. I haven't seen them, but I'm inclined to believe you. A funny word, though, *real*. Isn't it? You and I and this table are real. Easy cases. But gravity is real too, and the past, and the number three—and now we find ourselves in very deep water indeed. Are you enjoying the tea?"

I nodded. "Cardamom's one of my favorite spices." I was about to say, *Daniel loved to use the whole pods in curries*, but I kept the thought to myself: I didn't like the idea that I was falling into the habit of referring to your likes and dislikes in the past tense.

"The *flavor* of cardamom is real, wouldn't you think?"

"Sure," I said.

"No less real than the chemical compounds that underlie it! Yet the chemicals are basic, textbook science, and the flavor itself, the experience that the chemicals generate, is an enigma utterly beyond the grasp of science."

"Hence ISOC."

"Yes. And no. I'm afraid I was never entirely honest about the real motive behind my little Institute."

(I had to admire the sheer scale of Balakrishnan's ambitions. You pony up a hundred million and change, to build an organization dedicated to discovering the meaning of life—and it's *my little Institute*.)

"Let me take you back a few years. Most people get very interested in not dying when they grow old. Somewhat unusually, I've been obsessed with the thought ever since I was a child. Daniel watched his mother die from a fall in Patagonia, when he was seventeen. I watched my mother die from a burst appendix, in a squalid tin shack on the Sabarmati River, when I was seven. After that, my lifelong insomnia began. I'd spend entire nights wide awake in a state of the most pure, most refined terror, thinking, *Death is there, waiting! Tomorrow, or next week, or seventy years from now, death will be there. No escaping it: one day, sooner or later, I will be extinguished forever.*"

"And then you discovered a group of people who were terrified of death, like you, but determined to do something about it. The Extenders. Who were interested in pushing death back as far as humanly possible."

"Just so. And when I discovered that I was not merely mortal in the ordinary way, but likely to die well before my time, I began to make myself something of a guinea pig for their ideas. Special ultrahigh vitamin diet. Cloned muscle grafts. Nerve-fiber reconstruction. Daily blood plasma nanofiltering. Replacement joints, of course. All that sort of thing. I had a cancer scare too, and half my esophagus is straight off a 3-D printer."

He stroked a finger down one side of his throat. A scar was just visible among the wrinkles. There was a thin film of sweat on his cheeks.

"May I ask what you—um—?"

"I am the proud owner of a rare and thoroughly fatal blood disease. Its cause is four different faulty genes, all doing their mischief together like an evil string quartet. The probability of getting all four mutations in a single genome is about one in a billion. Something akin to winning the lottery four days in a row."

"They diagnosed it here?"

"Only tracked down the exact genetic villains. The diagnosis came many years ago, so I've known this time bomb was ticking nearly all my adult life."

"And you've just undergone a new round of treatment?"

"A new round of hopeful experimentation, I'd call it. It involved keeping me in a medically induced coma while they did clever things to my spinal fluid and bone marrow. A last-ditch attempt to buy me more time by slowing down the collapse of my cellular machinery. That's what the Extenders are all about. Buying time. Unfortunately this round of experimentation was, um, not successful."

The uncharacteristic pause, the little *um* at the end of the sentence, said it all. He was letting me know that he'd accepted defeat, that he was dying, like everyone dies, and that there was nothing more he and all his money could do about it. It struck me then why Iona had liked him. Hugely ambitious, aye, maybe even self-absorbed in his concern about his own mortality. But he was aware of his own flaws, didn't try to hide them, and, even though he'd barely admitted the fact even to himself, he was really driven by something larger than his own survival: before the end, he wanted to *understand*.

"I'm sorry," I said, conscious that it was a pathetically inadequate response. But the word made him flinch, and I got the impression that he thought there was something distasteful about the idea of wasting time on being sorry *for him*. He started waving his arms around. He was trying to get up again. I helped him stand. When he was leaning against the railing, I stayed close, worried that he might tumble headlong into the garden.

"Thank you, my dear. I absolutely hate sitting down, and these days I do very little else. What was I going to say? Oh yes. David Maynard Jones was interested in all the Extender technology too. That's why I knew him. But the thing that really excited me about him, and made me put him in charge of ISOC, was discovering that he was already a step ahead of those people. Why buy yourself an extra ten or twenty years? Because it's good in itself. But there's a much bigger prize. An infinitely bigger prize: living long enough to see the day when it's possible to stop repairing the body and simply leave it behind. David saw that the body's just a vehicle. The Extenders are obsessed with the vehicle. But the fundamental goal is preserving its cargo."

He raised his walking stick and used it to tap his forehead.

"Consciousness," I said.

"Not needing a body any more than God needs a body! A newer, more reliable way to immortality! According to religion, consciousness was the flickering of your immortal soul—the thing that survives death. Just at the point in my life when I was despairing of all that, and was hoping at best to die at a ripe old age instead of far too young, David came to me and persuaded me that there was something else. 'Mr. Balakrishnan,' he said—very formal: I could tell he was about to ask for money—'Mr. Balakrishnan, we're close to a technological tipping point. Science fiction is about to be science fact. Soon, we won't need to repair the physical medium in which the mind resides. We'll be able to save the conscious mind as code—as software. Who needs God to check you in at the Cloud Hotel when you can build a cloud all of your own?'"

"And you agreed? You accepted that?"

He tried to laugh; it came out as a wheeze. "I believed what I needed to believe. Naturally I wanted to know whether we were five years out from his goal or fifty—whether I personally had any hope of getting there. He said, oh, ten years or less, and I chose to believe that too. In retrospect, it was an absurd figure—it was like being told as a boy that soon we'd have atomic cars—but I didn't want to think about the possibility of failure. And he was very persuasive. Emulating the whole brain would be just like taking a photograph. There were some technical obstacles, certainly, because it would be a photograph with a fifty-yottabyte file size. I confess that I nodded sagely and had to look up *yottabyte* afterward. I was too giddy with joy to be skeptical. I said, 'David, if this works, you'll go down in history as the man who invented the very thing we've all been looking for. Something better even than wealth, or youth, or excellent cheekbones. Infinity. Eternity.

An alternative to God.' I think it was in that very conversation that he came up with the idea that it was Route Two against the old Route One."

I picked up my teacup, then put it down again. I could see Sunil gesturing to his sister. "I never did quite believe that ISOC existed just so that you could scratch some personal philosophical itch," I said. "The origin of consciousness? I mean, I get why it's a puzzle. But it seems a bit abstract."

"On the contrary, it's the most practical and urgent of all questions. Especially for those of us who assume that one day we are in fact going to die. I knew the medical interventions would fail me in the end. The only way I could hope to stay alive in the long term was by digging deeper. Investigating what 'being alive' means. The biologists think that's a question about cell regeneration, genetic damage, and the length of your telomeres. It isn't. The question of what being alive means, for a human being, is inextricably bound up with the philosopher's question about consciousness. Can *that* survive without a body? Or does it depend absolutely on the failing brain? If consciousness could be separated from the brain, then I had a chance. ISOC was a Hail Mary pass, as I believe they say in American football."

"I'm not good at sports metaphors."

"Seconds left on the clock and nothing to lose. Might as well throw a long ball and pray."

"But something changed Mayo's mind. Something, or someone, made him take seriously the idea that the whole technological approach, the whole concept of 'Route Two,' was missing something. That there was more to it than just bytes?"

"Yes."

"Mr. Balakrishnan—"

"Charlie, please. I've been Charlie ever since discovering that so few people in the West can get *Akshay* right. They say *Ash-kay*, which sounds like *ashtray*, and I have never smoked." He grinned, showing off his pink gums, and made a rippling gesture with his long, delicate fingers.

"Charlie, then." I felt uncomfortable saying it: he was too old, too rich, and too sick to be *Charlie*. "Look, I don't have much time—"

Too late, I realized how bad that sounded. He was the one who didn't have time. But he just smiled.

"Morag, don't feel sorry for me. If you do, you don't understand. Let me tell you something very important. People want to live for a long time, and then at some point they think, oh, if only it could be forever! Sounds good, doesn't it, 'eternal life'? I made the same mistake, but I've changed my mind. I have Gilgamesh standing in there as a reminder and a warning. People think they want eternity only because they haven't thought about what the word truly means. Eternity isn't just a long time! It's a place beyond time. The annihilation of time. And when you understand that, you come to see that eternal life is much, much more frightening than death."

As he gave this little speech, your voice dinned in my head, and I thought that perhaps I'd glimpsed your meaning at last: not a call to action so much as a description of a place you'd seen: *There's no time. No time.*

"So why did you get me out here?" I asked. "What do you know about why the world's top researcher into Route Two became interested in new religions and their gods? And why do you care?"

"Why I care is easy to answer," he said. "I'm very fond of Sunil and Vandana. In fact, I think of them as my own grandchildren. And they represent for me all the other children in the world—the future of the human race. I don't want them and their futures destroyed. As for the question about Maynard Jones—"

"That will be enough," Mrs. Chaudry said. She had appeared silently again—as if by magic again—and her tone had the sharp finality she might have used to corral her grandchildren. I was being dismissed, and she probably had a point: Balakrishnan looked as if he'd reached a whole new level of exhaustion, and he did nothing to stop me leaving. "Take the folder," he said. "There are a couple of things you may find relevant to your question, and we can talk about them tomorrow, perhaps. I do hope you're comfortable in the guest house. Mrs. Chaudry will be delighted to provide you with anything you need."

The name *Mrs. Chaudry* didn't seem to belong in the same sentence with the word *delighted*. I picked up the folder. As she was escorting me out, he called after me, "Get Kai to show you the volcano. Can't be on the Big Island and miss Mauna Loa. Especially since the Seraphim seem to want the Architects to blow it up."

He was like Kit—I couldn't tell when he was joking.

CHAPTER 15

IONA'S THESIS

At the guesthouse, invisible hands had laid out a meal for me. The choice made me want to cry: cold salmon, potatoes with chives, and a salad of green beans with preserved lemon—a combination almost identical to one you'd once prepared for me. I couldn't bring myself to eat it and put the whole thing in the fridge. There I found the only concession to Hawaii, a single perfect mango laid out on a dark-red china plate with a paring knife next to it. I smelled it, picked up the knife, and took it to the table. Then I changed my mind and had a glass of water for dinner. Pathetic.

There were messages from Kit that I should have responded to. But there was something about the way they said nothing and everything: anxious bulletins filled with trivia, telling me indirectly about every up and down, mainly down, of your emotional state. You kept saying fragments of things she didn't understand. You were drawing dozens of things at whirlwind speed. Your hands were steady when you drew but trembled violently when you held a cup.

She wanted me back ASAP; that was clear. Which would have been nice to know, if I'd had any sense that the emotion had something to do with *us*. But she didn't say, or seem to imply, anything about *us*. Her tone suggested that ordinary facts (like her being sorta kinda interested in me maybe; like me being as helplessly in love with her as a novice swimmer in a rip current) were subjects too trivial to worry about now.

Some of what she said was about Rosko too, and I had to read between those lines as well. Words like *polite* and *helpful*, even *kind*, said loudly that I wasn't getting the whole picture.

I had another delicious glass of water, and opened the *DMJ* folder. A single sheet, attached to the inside front cover with a paperclip, had just a few lines at the top in a hasty scribble that must have been Mayo's:

> THE SERAPHIM WANT TO FOCUS ON KEY VOLCANOES IN POPULATED AREAS: VESUVIUS, POPOCATÉPETL, FUJI, RAINIER, ETC. MAKES SENSE, I SUPPOSE—INCREASE THE NUMBERS, INCREASE THE POWER. GOD HELP US, AS PEOPLE LIKE TO SAY, BUT THESE "GODS" ARE HELPING THEMSELVES TO US. CLEVER IONA FOR FIGURING OUT WHAT THEY ARE AND GIVING ME A GLIMMER OF HOPE THAT THERE'S AN ESCAPE ROUTE. BUT HOW HOW HOW DID THEY DO IT, IONA? I SUPPOSE YOU DIDN'T KNOW.

It sounded like one magician talking to another about a rival's best trick—an impression reinforced when I saw, penciled faintly in the margin, the words *Iona's thesis*. But I didn't pay much attention to the added words at first, because I thought it must be an obscure reference to, you know, her *academic thesis*, the stuff about information density that she'd ditched when she started her company.

Most of what followed was a letdown. A careful log of each "Mystery" incident. Ordinary information about Quinn and the Seraphim. A short summary of all Derek's work on Thera and the Bronze Age Collapse. Notes about Bill, going back years, and about Iona, going back even further. Notes about me too, after the Babylon discovery. I read those extra carefully, out of vanity probably, but they only told me what I already knew: at some point, Mayo had become passionately interested in the Phaistos Disks and Shul-hura's alternative Babel story.

Near the end I found a long, unpublished paper by Mayo that definitely fell into the *Show All This Technical Crap to Rosko* category. It was all tricked out with footnotes and a bibliography, like something waiting to be submitted to a research journal—but *PERSONAL FOR A. B.* was printed on the title page, as if he'd put it together exclusively for his paymaster. I only skimmed: there were pages and pages on the Bekenstein bound, scanner technology, and the need for both a working quantum computer "and fundamental breakthroughs in the efficiency of the algorithms we're using, before real emulation can get off the ground." The title was interesting, though—it pretty much summed up what ISOC was truly about, and what Carl Bates had been trying to do when he died in that little room on the top floor: Uploading the Soul: Problems and Prospects in the Technology of Human Immortality. No mention of the Seraphim. No hint that Mayo had started to have fundamental doubts about his scientific approach; it struck me as a stereotypical "further research needed; more money, please" kind of document. But at three different points that same phrase, *Iona's thesis*, had been written in the margin.

No question, the last page in the file was last because Charlie B had placed it there. For dramatic effect. It echoed the first piece in Mayo's writing: another single piece of white printer paper, but this time covered densely on both sides with Iona's tiny script, as precise and uniform as a ten-point font:

DREAMS—GOOD AND BAD. ALSO A REVELATION?

THE GOOD DREAMS ARE ALL ABOUT NEW GUINEA. I WAKE UP JUST WANTING TO GET ON A PLANE AND GO THERE. WHY IS A PLACE I VISITED ONCE, BRIEFLY, MURMURING TO ME SO URGENTLY?

THE BAD DREAMS ARE ABOUT THE DISAPPEARANCES. THE BOLIVIAN WOMEN: NEVER MET THEM, BUT IN THE DREAMS WE'VE WALKED A HUNDRED MILES ACROSS THE ALTIPLANO TOGETHER, SISTERS IN ADVERSITY AND HOPE. WE PASS AROUND OUR BRIGHT-RED COPIES OF *ANABASIS*, AS IF IT'S BETTER TO HAVE TOUCHED MANY COPIES THAN JUST ONE. THERE'S AN ATMOSPHERE OF ENERGY AND JOY AS WE REMIND EACH OTHER OF THE INFINITE ADVEN-TURE AHEAD. THEN I COME TO MY SENSES: THEY'RE WRONG; THEY'RE BEING SEDUCED; THEY'RE WALKING TO THEIR DEATHS! I HAVE ALL BILL'S LANGUAGES, SO I BEG THEM TO LISTEN IN ENGLISH, THEN SPANISH, THEN QUECHUA. BUT THEY CAN ONLY RESPOND UNCOMPRE-HENDINGLY IN THE ONE LANGUAGE THAT'S LEFT TO THEM, THE LANGUAGE OF THE ARCHITECTS. IT SOUNDS INHUMAN, MACHINE-LIKE. THEY THEMSELVES ARE NO LONGER HUMAN.

WHEN I WAKE UP, I FIND MYSELF THINKING ABOUT THE GROWING INFLUENCE OF THE SERAPHIM. BUT ALSO ABOUT DMJ AND HIS "DIGITAL IMMORTALITY." AS IF, INSTEAD

OF BEING SEPARATE EXPRESSIONS OF THE SAME DESPERATE HOPE, THEY'RE CONNECTED. AND THUS THE REVELATION.

I FEEL LIKE EINSTEIN: IT ALL FITS SO NEATLY THAT THE THEORY HAS TO BE RIGHT.

AND IF IT IS? WE'RE FINISHED.

It continued on the other side:

JULIUS ENCOUNTERS "ARCHITECTS" WHILE CLIMBING IN MEXICO. HIS VANISHED FRIENDS HAVE BEEN "TAKEN UP," HAVE EXPERIENCED "ANABASIS," HE SAYS, AND HE HAS BEEN GIVEN THE TASK OF A SECOND MOSES, BRINGING THE WORD OF THE ARCHITECTS DOWN TO HUMANITY. AND THE MESSAGE IS THAT WE CAN BE SAVED, CAN BECOME INFINITE LIKE THEM, IF ONLY WE PREPARE OUR MINDS. I COULD ALMOST DISMISS IT—EXCEPT FOR THE WAY SO MANY PEOPLE DON'T DISMISS IT: HIS HYPNOTIC PERSUASIVENESS IS ITS OWN KIND OF EVIDENCE.

POOR DAVID: IN LOVE WITH ME, AND DESPERATE TO IMPRESS, AND THUS UNABLE TO KEEP HIS MOUTH SHUT ABOUT $\sqrt{2}$. "THE VERGE OF IMMORTALITY!" HE SAID TO ME. "IT WILL BE THE MOST DELICATE SURGERY EVER UNDERTAKEN—USING SCALPELS MADE FROM CODE TO CUT AROUND THE MIND AND REMOVE IT FROM THE BODY."

I DON'T THINK YOU'RE EVEN WARM, DAVID, THAT'S MY GUESS. BUT LISTEN TO ME. SUPPOSE $\sqrt{2}$ REALLY IS POSSIBLE.

Suppose a route to something beyond the human—beyond the physical—isn't just a mad techie dream but a thing we could pull off one day?

Surely, in that case

In that case what?

I was exhausted suddenly, and even decided to be practical and sensible and resist the temptation to check for more messages before I went to bed. My determination lasted just long enough for me to pull a brush across my teeth.

He not sleep, not eat, lose the weight even more also. I don't know where energy come from. Says your name a lot.

I swear you, he has gone through every single picture fifty times. He is like puzzled, frustrated, growling—looking for something but cannot find.

"In that case what? It just ends at the end of the page. There has to be more."

I waved Iona's note at Balakrishnan. He looked two shades paler than the day before and was coughing ominously. "Iona's 'thesis' must be about the relationship between Route One and Route Two," he said. "Between the religious, be-nice-to-the-gods path to eternity and David's shinier, more modern vehicle."

"You don't happen to have page two?"

"I assure you, Morag, I'd happily swap the Voynich Manuscript for it, and throw in my Mughal ceramics collection too. Truthfully, I'd give up every single thing I own. I believe Iona knew something essential. She may even have tried to discuss it with Bill, only to have him dismiss it, and then she turned to her old boyfriend, who she thought would be more receptive. She shared with him some insight about the Architects that linked them to David's own research on consciousness. His ISOC work on Route Two had been a sort of intellectual hobby, driven only by my money, my curiosity, and my obsession with not dying. But I suspect this note was why he started looking for the answer to Route Two in the very heart of Route One."

"You must have some idea what the link could have been."

"I'm not sure how much use my speculation—"

"Tell me."

"Iona didn't believe in any particular religion. But, like most religious people, she thought the world was made from two fundamentally different kinds of stuff. Matter and mind. Matter and spirit. Things that take up time and space, and things that are immaterial, and immortal, and don't take up time or space."

"Rosko's talked about that. From that French guy. Descartes?"

"Yes, but the idea is much older than that. It goes all the way back to the distinction between a material world and the immaterial God who creates it. Descartes was just trying to ask the scientific question: *Where* is the soul? There's a little thing like a pencil eraser in the middle of your brain, the pineal gland. He said that's where your soul lives. Like a puff of smoke in a bottle!"

"The ghost in the machine."

"Yes. Most modern scientists think that's rubbish, of course. How can you and I be *bodies*, located in time and space, but carry around inside us a thing that isn't located in time and space?"

"But Iona was holding out for the ghost?"

"I was with Iona and Bill when David gave them the VIP tour of the Institute, just after it was built. He showed us the mainframe and said its capacity was comparable to the human brain's, which, after all, was nothing but a 'marvelously compact computer.' Iona wasn't impressed. She said to him, 'Your new toy is very fine, David. But when all's said and done, it's just the Arnold Schwarzenegger of filing cabinets. Lots and lots of memory—but you're forgetting that that's only a metaphor. However good your software is, you will never, ever, be able to give this machine *memories*.'"

I'd put Iona's note on the table between us. He picked it up and held it the way a priest would hold a holy wafer. "I don't know what this means," he admitted, "and my cellular clock has run out, so I probably never will. But I think David changed his mind very quickly. Around the time of Iona's death, he must have become convinced that the Architects were real, that they were a real threat to our existence, and that in fact he could pull off Route Two only by first understanding them."

Balakrishnan seemed to weaken even more after that second conversation, and Mrs. Chaudry began to ration access to him even more fiercely. We talked in the chairs next to his fireplace, and over a frugal meal of bread and salad in a tiny dining room below his study, and while I wheeled him around the garden—but I was never with him again for more than twenty minutes.

In the intervals, I was kept sane by Kai's willingness to play tour guide. He taught me some of Hawaii's geography, history, culture, and language. He took me to his favorite beachfront shack and introduced me to that high point of Hawaiian cuisine, a roadside "plate lunch." He even drove me and the kids down a rutted road to Kealakekua Bay so that I could see the spot where the locals had said a brutal good-bye to Captain Cook.

"Cook was haole," he said. "It means 'foreigner,' but also 'pale skin.' When he first arrive here, the locals are all celebrating Makahiki, which is the festival of the god Lono. At first, they think he is Lono. Then he tries to go away, and he's driven back by a storm, and they figure, maybe he's not Lono. So, right here in this bay, they steal his whaleboat. Big fight, boom boom, and they prove Cook is not Lono by swinging a war club at the back of his head. See guys, definitely dead! Definitely not a god! His crew buried him at sea, right out there in the bay."

Apparently that was the sanitized version. While Vandana waded and Kai kept an eye on her, Sunil and I walked to the end of a concrete jetty and watched pods of impossibly bright parrot fish pass among the rocks ten feet down. "It didn't really happen like that," Sunil said.

"What didn't?"

"The Hawaiians killing Captain Cook."

"You mean they didn't kill him?"

"I mean it was nastier than that," he said with relish. "They cut him up and ate bits of him. Then they cut all the meat off his bones and kept the bones in a box."

"So they didn't bury him at sea?" I said.

"The sailors only managed to collect bits and pieces. I think they buried those."

I looked down into the water again and almost jumped back when I saw a big, dark shape looming up from below. It was nothing but cloud shadow. But I quickly walked back to join Kai and Vandana.

When I said something about burying Cook in shallow water, Kai laughed. "This island is really three volcanoes, right? Mauna Kea in the north. Mauna Loa, which is most of the island. And Kilauea in the southeast, which is growing the island as it erupts into the sea. Here on this beach, we're halfway up Mauna Loa. Water just out there, where they bury him? Deep ocean—two, three miles deep."

The thought that we were standing on the sloping tip of a rock, in the middle of a bathtub three miles deep, was appalling. "Can you take us to see whatever it is the Seraphim are building farther up?" I said to Kai. "An arena or something?"

"I was planning to show you that," he said. "Quite a sight. We have to drive to the south side of the island to see it, though."

An hour later, and a couple of thousand feet higher, I learned why Sunil and Vandana took me so seriously.

"We're your biggest fans," Sunil piped from the back seat, as the road rose over the south flank of the mountain.

"Fans?" The whole idea was so ridiculous, I had to suppress a laugh. "What do you think I am, a movie star?"

"There are millions and millions of movie stars," Vandana said contemptuously. "Hundreds, at least. But there are only two famous Babblers. William Calder and Morag Chen. Uncle Akshay's told us all about you. Babel. Shul-hura. We even started teaching ourselves Akkadian."

"But then we got bored and decided to make up more of our own languages instead," Sunil said.

They chattered on for a few more minutes, then fell silent as we passed a heavily guarded gate. There were serious-looking men with guns, and two signboards showing the Seraphim triangle and the famous image of Quinn. Beyond the gate, a dirt road lead north, upslope.

"Summit's still twenty miles that way," Kai said, as we crested a rise. "Twenty miles and eleven thousand feet. You can't get any closer unless you have two spare days and a backpack."

Again I was struck by how totally different it was from Ararat. When Mack had landed that helicopter, the mountain dominated the skyline from twenty miles away like a barn in a field. But Mauna Loa was so much bigger, so much more gently sloped, that it hardly looked like a mountain. It wasn't an object in the landscape, because we were already on it; it was the landscape.

"The Seraphim put together a bunch of land deals around here," Kai explained. "They're very, very rich, plus, they're in the police, in the state bureaucracy, everywhere, so they get away with everything. They control this area now. There's plenty of opposition, you'll see. But—"

He trailed off as we arrived at a viewpoint, where he parked on the road verge behind a small swarm of cars and tour buses. One of the buses had a banner on the side with a painting representing the mountain as the goddess Pele and the bus-length slogan: "Mauna Loa Is Sacred." People were milling about with banners:

THIS IS OUR LAND
NO CONSTRUCTION
SERAPHIM GO HOME.

A big pair of military-looking binoculars was set up on a stand near a makeshift fence, neatly blocking the view of a sign that said, "No Entry: Private." Sunil and Vandana charmed their way to the front of a queue, and Vandana stepped onto a box so that she could see. I joined the back of the line; when she turned around and I asked what she'd seen, all she'd say was "We've seen it before. But it's twice as big now."

"Totally amazing," the woman in the airport bathroom had said. She was right. It wasn't just the scale, but the fact that it looked so different from any other structure I could think of. Alien. A silvery arc of what looked like metal had been extended out horizontally from the middle slopes. When you thought about the scale of the mountain, and the fact that you were looking at something twenty miles away, it had to be huge.

"Bleachers," Kai explained. "Bleachers in reverse. So that you get a view up the mountain, instead of down. There's already space for two or three hundred thousand people, and they're not pau yet."

Not finished. If Ararat was five thousand people, and— "Are they planning an event here? At a particular date?"

"Not that they sayin'."

"But aren't people afraid of what might happen?"

He looked away. "It like climate change. A few people take it serious from beginning. Most people take a long time. When something is too big like this, sure, you get guys with signs, but most people can't take it in. It still like, nobody believes it happenin'."

"According to my calculations," Vandana said, "and math *is* my very best subject after French, Spanish, Hawaiian, and Urdu—"

"Stop boasting," Sunil said, and he made a big production out of yawning.

"Stop interrupting. According to my calculations, the Big Island will be completely destroyed. Just like Thera. And the tsunamis will drown every city from Yokohama, which is in Japan—"

"We know that."

"—to Valparaíso, which is in Chile."

Sunil ran in a tight circle around us with his arms straight out like airplane wings. "I'm a tsunami," he roared. "A really big one. Rrrrrrrr."

"So what's your next step?" Balakrishnan said, when I saw him briefly that evening. I didn't know the answer, and said good night to him awkwardly, but the answer was handed to me half an hour later by Kit. Two messages, only a few hours apart:

YESTERDAY, RAIN IN ROOF. THIS NIGHT, RAT IN SHOWER. ROSKO IN BAD MOOD. DANIEL IN REALLY BAD MOOD. IS ENOUGH. MY MOTHER PICKING US UP.

And, back in Seattle:

Majka you will come home now, please? Daniel
found what he was looking for. He is frantic crazy.
He draw giant map of New Guinea and other stuff
with big Sharpie all over kitchen wall. Gabi tells
my mother, "that boy should be in psychiatric hospital." Also Seraphim is everywhere. They come to
Eisler house three times, like they smell him. I am
frightened for him. Now. Please.

Found what he was looking for? It was really Kit herself who'd
found what you were looking for, though she didn't have the chance
to tell me the details until later. You'd fallen asleep on the couch, and
then woken crying and struggling; trying to calm you, she'd talked you
through the idea that there was something you couldn't find. For want
of any other ideas, she suggested looking through all Iona's things, item
by item, including every page of that well-scribbled copy of *Anabasis*
we'd found in the box at the Institute. A miniature white envelope was
acting as a bookmark at page 104, where a single sentence was heavily
underlined. I'd read that sentence before; like about half the book, it
was famous:

> *You will come to a point at which the need for language falls
> away, and only your mind, in tune at last with its origin, can
> communicate directly with the Architects.*

Kit said you grabbed the envelope out of her fingers before she'd
had a chance to open it. "This. Here. I'iwa," you said. The envelope
contained one more memory card; the picture that you'd been looking
for, hour after hour and day after day, you found in less than a minute.

There were two photographs, one ordinary and one not. She'd
attached them to another message:

Look at first picture, then look at second. Use a big screen. Daniel says: "This is it. This is I'iwa."

Minutes later she sent a fourth message: ten riveting seconds of video. The first two seconds were Kit herself in close-up, her hand trembling as she said, "Majka, listen. Daniel have something to say. Listen, OK?"

The shot veered away. I got a blurred panorama of her mother's clutter—a table with dirty dishes, books stacked on a chair, an overstuffed grocery bag next to an open box of cereal on the floor. Then the wall on which you'd scrawled the map. The lens steadied as it found you, sitting cross-legged on the floor near the cereal with your back against a doorjamb. You looked at the camera. Looked at me. You were as thin as a corpse, but there was something familiar in your eyes that I hadn't seen since before Ararat.

"Morag," you said. "Go back. Find the I'iwa."

There was a break in the video stream, and when you came back, you were making a repetitive gesture, a sort of jerky pointing motion toward your own head. "The answer," you said, and "Eye. Eye. Eye."

What about your eye?

You trailed off for a moment and looked away, struggling, breathless. Then you looked toward the camera again, and this time you clutched at the front of your shirt as if you were trying to rip it off. There was something close to panic in your eyes, as if you were pleading with me to understand.

"Eye. Eye."

At last I did understand. Such a flood of hope! Such a small word!

"I."

What the photographs revealed, I could easily have kept to myself, but some powerful instinct told me to share them with my gracious, ailing host. Maybe it was just knowing that the sheer strangeness of it would thrill him? It was eleven when I got Kai on the house phone. With obvious reluctance, he woke up Mrs. Chaudry, who reacted to my request—that she wake her employer so that I could show him some photographs—with an absolute, flat, unconditional refusal.

I asked politely a second time: useless. Then I argued with her, also politely: equally useless. Plan C was to get angry and rude. Instant success.

He was wearing a long robe of red silk. Mrs. Chaudry wheeled him into the study ahead of me and parked him by the fire, which was already on. Then she provided more tea—ginger, this time, with buttery Scottish shortbread, which Balakrishnan didn't touch. When she'd retreated, I explained Kit's message, and told him I needed to leave first thing in the morning. Then I explained about Daniel and the photographs.

He waved his hands over a sensor, and the expensive-looking painting over the fireplace ("Kandinsky. An original. Rather fine, isn't it?") slid silently out of the way. A screen was recessed into the wall behind it.

"This is to do with Iona's trip to New Guinea? She told me all about it once."

"I don't think Iona told anyone all about it," I said.

The first photograph uploaded, and the surface of the screen changed from black to an almost completely even green. "This is New Guinea," I said. "In the Star Mountains, right on the border, just north of the area where we stayed with the Tainu."

"Nothing but trees," Balakrishnan said.

"Almost nothing." I pointed out the thin brown line of a path, crossing the frame from lower right to upper left, and, like ants on a lawn, five figures standing next to the path near the middle of the shot. I magnified that area.

"This is me with my friends Oma and Isbet. Plus two other Tainu men who came with us."

Oma, Isbet, and I had our arms around each other's shoulders, probably at my insistence—there was a faked casualness about it, and they looked uncomfortable in a way I'm sure I hadn't noticed at the time. The other two Tainu men were standing to one side, in their tanket-leaf skirts, their hands held up as if they didn't know what to do with them, eyes avoiding the camera. They looked a whole lot more uncomfortable.

"I assume Iona was the photographer?" Balakrishnan said.

"Yes. She took this from quite a distance. I still remember her shouting out, 'Let me get one more. Smile, everyone!' Like we were a family at the beach."

"These Tainu men weren't in a smiling mood."

"We'd already come farther than they wanted to. This was the point on the path where they basically refused to go on. See how the path becomes less distinct at the upper left? That's because you're higher up the slope there, but you're also looking fifty, a hundred yards farther back into the forest."

I panned up the path, then zoomed in tighter and tighter on the trees just above it, at the extreme corner of the frame. The image became pure green, pure mottled green, then a mere quilt of green and greenish-brown pixels.

"We're looking at a spot that's maybe a hundredth of the whole image. Now I'm going to switch to the second image, and do the same thing. OK? So we're looking at the same spot in the far background, above the path, but a few seconds later."

Click. Click.

Green. Mottled green. And—

Click click click.

The same patch. The same magnification. Only it wasn't the same. I switched between them, then switched again. "Now you see it. Now you don't. Now you see it—

"Stop. Are we on the maximum magnification?"

"Yes. And no doubt Rosko's been messing around to make it as sharp as possible."

"This is—oh my goodness."

Oh my goodness was right. Where the hell does something like that come from, in the middle of an uninhabited tropical forest? How do you explain a shift in the pixels that wasn't there a few seconds earlier, that you want to say is a trick of the light, a bug on the lens, or a leaf catching the sun, but so very clearly isn't?

"It's a hand, isn't it?" Balakrishnan said. "A hand, curled round the side of a tree trunk, as if someone is hiding. A very broad hand. And above it here—it's—there's no doubt, is there?"

No. Three-quarters hidden by the same trunk, but no doubt: the sliver of a ghost-pale face. And, when we looked further, hunting pixel by pixel, in the far background we saw equally undeniable hints of at least two more pale figures, almost hidden in the trees.

"So you were being watched," he said. "Apparently, you were being watched by a previously unknown tribe of albinos in the middle of the New Guinea Highlands. That seems, well, rather surprising. But why does Daniel care about this?"

"I can only find out by going back there."

Let me be clear about something with you here, D. What I wanted was to go back to you—and, yes, go back to Kit. But I was afraid of going back too: I was worried that if I did, I'd have to argue about what I was doing with Natazscha. Or Gabi and Stefan. Or Kit.

And—

This is hard to say, but going back to you felt like taking up a burden I needed to be without. You were still hard to communicate with. Maybe you were recovering, as I'd been trying so hard to believe, or maybe you weren't and never would, as Rosko thought—or maybe you were on the brink of dying. In any case, it was surely me, brilliant me, who was destined to find the solution and save you? Morag Chen: Little Miss Superbrain. I was the one who could always solve every puzzle, and I wanted to come back to you *after* I'd triumphantly solved this one. Besides, I was the expert: I knew New Guinea. The idea that you, or the knowledge you carried, hidden within you, were an essential part of the solution—I'd let the idea float through my mind only to suppress it.

So what I said to Charlie B was *I'm going, and I'm going alone.* And he was the one who shook his head. He was the one who stayed up, late into the night and clearly exhausted, talking me out of myself. He repeated himself a lot, but only because I was being thick.

"Daniel should be there with you."

"Why?"

"Because"—giving me this look of a father talking patiently to a slow-witted child—"because Daniel needs you, and you need him. And you need real support too, someone to help you through this."

"It'd be better if I go alone."

"I don't think so. I think it would be better still, actually, if Ms. Cerenkov is part of this too."

"Kit?"

"Yes."

"No. No—and anyway, then I'd have to go back to Seattle first."

"Rubbish. You've already told me that Ms. Cerenkov—Kit—is very good with Daniel. I think *brilliant* was the word you used. And you clearly trust her judgment in practical things, and—"

"And?"

"And you are obviously"—there was a millisecond pause—"obviously very fond of her."

"She's a good friend," I said, not managing to not sound defensive.

"A good friend. Yes, Morag. I'm sure she is."

Am I really that bloody transparent? That's what I want to know. And also, while we're at it, how did he manage to say it so completely straight, while managing so clearly to mean, with equal sincerity, two things at once?

"Go to New Guinea," he said. "We can ask Kit to bring Daniel to you. Bring your German friend too, if you like. Rosko, the one who was at ISOC. Kai can arrange everything."

"Natazscha won't allow Kit to come. And I nearly got Rosko killed on Ararat, so his parents certainly won't allow him to come."

"I've known Natazscha Cerenkov for a long time, Morag. She'll allow it, I think, with a little persuasion. Maybe she'll even join the party!"

It was pointless to argue—clearly Balakrishnan always got his way. "That's a lot of flights," I said. "How are you going to pay for it all?"

There was something good about being able to amuse him. His had the knack of being able to laugh with just his eyes. "I am being rather extravagant, now you mention it," he said. "My accountants will probably suggest that I raise the cash by selling Gilgamesh. But I don't think that will be necessary."

Half an hour later I was back at the guest house, lying in the dark, trying to shut down my brain enough to sleep. Fat chance. When my phone rang, it was after midnight. Since I was already awake, I decided to be cool about it.

"Hello, Kai. Did you get something arranged, then?"

It wasn't Kai—and, when I processed who it was, I thought I'd die of happiness.

"Morag? Morag? I canna believe I got through at last. Ye gods, it's been too long. Is that really you, gurrl?"

Chapter 16

Telefomin Ples Balus

The line was so bad at first that I was missing every other word, and what I could make out sounded like she was shouting at me from a mile away through a sandstorm. But her unique way of speaking—Bill had called it her "Slightly Scary, Don't Mess with Me, Inverness Hand-to-Hand-Science-Combat Voice"—was instantly recognizable. I loved it more than any other voice in the world, period. And I'd started to think I might never hear it again.

"I'm callin' from Amman, Morag. Amman, in Jordan. Jimmy an' I are OK. Are you OK?"

I knew where Amman was on a map. But I'd never been there, so my imagination had to invent the place she was calling from. Time difference: er, eleven or twelve hours, so it was the middle of the day there. She would be calling from the Scottish consulate, maybe, a shabby, generic office with a window overlooking a shabby, generic Middle Eastern street. Which meant what? Dusty trucks. A man with a big mustache, in baggy white clothes and a white cap, selling figs from a cart. Young women looking stylish in bright embroidered hijabs, and others, age unknown, hidden under the hoods of their black abayas. Clichés. Where she was, it probably didn't look anything like that. But I couldn't believe she was really alive without picturing her.

She was telling me they'd had what sounded like "a weeping pig denture" in the desert. I was missing stuff, and I was desperate not to miss stuff; having not heard from her in so long—given what had happened in the interval, it seemed more like years than weeks—I found myself trembling, panicked at the thought of the connection being dropped. It's amazing how eloquently poor sound quality can say *other side of the world*.

"Say it again. I couldn't hear you."

"A wee bit of an adventure."

I got out of bed and stood at an open window. The ocean was in that direction, but all I could see was a palm tree, rendered ghostly silver by one of the island's astronomer-friendly streetlights. I tried to make my mind stretch past the palm tree to the beach, and from there out across the thousands of miles of Pacific to China, Tibet, and beyond. The phone line made a new noise, like rain in a drainpipe, and I willed it, begged it not to go dead. The noise stopped. Silence. But then her voice came back loud and clear.

"—an' we still have a few bureaucratic heads to knock together. But once the paperwork hassles are sorted, we should be back in Seattle in a jiff. A week, love, tops."

Not knowing how long the clear connection would last, I launched into a machine-gun rapid, hypercondensed explanation of Ararat, and Bill, and the minor fact that I was in Hawaii as a guest of Charlie Balakrishnan. I didn't say anything about you, not yet: too complicated.

"My," she said drily when I was pausing for breath. "You must be doin' a'right if ye can still talk at three hundred words a minute. But when will you be back? I want to see you, right now!"

I took a second, deeper breath. "There's so much to explain. Too much to explain. But the important thing is, I'm not going back to Seattle. I can't. I'm leaving tomorrow, I mean later today, for Telefomin."

"Telefomin? Are ye kiddin' me, Morag, or has the line gone funny again?"

"Not kidding. Trust me, please. I want to see you too. Both of you. But yes, really, I'm going. Can you—"

It was a ridiculous thing to ask.

"Can you forget Seattle and meet me there instead? Telefomin *ples balus?*"

Ples balus. I'd been lazy about keeping up my fluency in New Guinea's national language, Tok Pisin, but as soon as I tried to get across to Lorna that I was going back there—and as soon as I thought of the amazing idea that soon, once again, she and Jimmy and I might be there together—I reverted instinctively to it. Just picturing the people, the humidity, and the mad-green topography had dropped me straight back into that strange, joyfully bastard language, in which "oldest child" is *nambawan pikinini* and "not working properly" is *bagarap.*

Telefomin is where our work with the Tainu began—a remote mountain station, right in the center of the island, an outpost even by Papuan standards. A short hike from the source of the Sepik River, it's nothing but a straggle of low houses in a flat valley, ringed by green mountains, connected with the world by *ples balus.*

It means "place for bird." So it also means "place for plane"—airfield. But in Telefomin, like so many places in New Guinea, the "airfield" was nothing but a strip of roughly level grass. A couple of times a week, people would stand on its fringe and wait patiently for an hour or three; eventually, a de Havilland Twin Otter would thrum down out of the clouds like an angry white duck, waddle to a halt, and disgorge sacks of rice, boxes of soap, and spare parts for *bagarap* Toyota Land Cruisers.

Lorna loved New Guinea, but she clearly thought I was nuts. "Telefomin! No, Morag, that's silly. It's thousands o' miles in the wrong direction. Which isn't even the point. The point is we're caught up wi' all the news about Ararat. And wi' Bill gone, your father an' I have a responsibility to Daniel as well. We absolutely must—"

"You don't understand—"

Snap, crackle.

"You don't understand. Daniel is—"

I don't know what it was—the relief of hearing her voice, the fear of being cut off at any second, frustration because we were already lurching into a practical disagreement that she took it for granted she'd win—but my own voice was strangled; I was on the verge of crying.

"Are ye still there?" she asked.

"I'm here. Mumma, please. Listen to me."

Mumma! The word just slipped out. I'd last called her *Mumma* just over ten years ago, on the afternoon of my seventh birthday. It was then, standing with our ankles in the North Sea, that we decided "child" was a category I didn't fit very well, and we'd do better to start treating each other as equals.

Mumma. I remember everything from that birthday. As if it's more real than real—as if someone went into my memory files and upped the color-saturation setting. Not just the fact that they'd taken me to Edinburgh for the museums and sights. Not just that Jimmy said it was too hot for town, and we should drive out to the beach at Aberlady and go fossil-hunting instead. No: I remember the smell of the car and the smell of the wind, the cries of each particular gull, the hot dry sand on the path and the cold damp sand below the tide line. I remember the exact feel of the broken silver zipper on the pink anorak Lorna hadn't wanted to buy for me because it was "a wee bit girlie"—the pink anorak I'd then demanded, because what was supposed to be so wrong with "girlie"? And I remembered both Jimmy's voice saying, *If you find a dinosaur, I'll buy you an ice cream,* and the infinitesimally grainy texture of the vanilla soft-serve that he did buy, even though I found only a trilobite.

"Mumma! Look!"

The trilobite was a good clean specimen, almost as long as my thumb.

"Mumma, no one has touched this in millions of years!"

As she came over, her crinkly red hair was all over the place in the wind, her hands gritty from digging and sifting. She nodded appreciatively.

"No human bein' has ever touched it, Morag. Not once, until now. Thuss poor little bugger got buried in the sand a hundred million years ago. Opposable thumbs weren't even a twinkle in evolution's eye back then—our ancestors still looked like rats, probably. So ye're the first."

"The first ever? The first ever ever ever, in the whole history of the universe?"

"Feels good, aye?"

It felt better than good: it was the best birthday present I ever had. Not the fossil itself, so much as the thrill of reaching down that far into the well of the past.

I decided I'd become an adult that day, so I started calling them Jimmy and Lorna. They rolled their eyes at first, then got used to it. But I was still a child, in some ways even a normal one. Passionate, but careless: for years afterward, I kept the trilobite in an old jewelry box, in a nest of tissue paper, and got it out to examine under a magnifier from time to time; then, unaccountably, I lost it.

At least now I'd found my mother again.

"Mumma, listen to me. I know it sounds crazy, but it's what we have to do. Daniel is—Daniel is—"

"Daniel is what, gurrl?"

"They tried to take him on Ararat. Rosko rescued him, but he's—not well. He's lost a lot of weight, and—"

"Where is he?"

"In Seattle still, with Rosko Eisler and—look, the point is, I think he learned something on Ararat, about what's really going on, but now he can't communicate."

"Oh, Morag, I'm so sorry. You're saying he's a Mystery?"

"No! It's not that simple." I tried to describe how you were: the fragments of speech, the drawings, the sense that you were like a man with his arms bound, trying to reach out.

And your voice. I didn't want to say it, not even to Lorna. Especially not to Lorna. "It's almost as if Iona is communicating through him. Or, I don't know, a fragment of her is buried inside him. Like, she told him something. After she was dead. I'm sorry. I know none of this makes any sense."

It was annoying that the static had gone, because over the clear line, she could hear me sobbing.

Her voice came back much softer. "Morag, Morag. Ye've had a really rough time, haven't ye? We were worried about ye o' course, but we had no idea. I'm sorry, love. I'm sorry we've not been there."

That made me feel weepier and more emotional than ever. I felt too tired to be interested in persuading her to come to New Guinea or anywhere else—I just wanted her to be with me. And boss me about. And not mind when I did the opposite of whatever she told me to do.

I forced myself to sound calmer: "Tell me something," I said. "While you were in Iraq, or wherever, did you and Jimmy speak to anyone who'd actually been at Ararat? Or hear any stories about people undergoing Anabasis and disappearing, and then showing up again?"

"Oh aye. Lots of whisperin' about that around Mosul. An' we met a Kurdish woman, Seraphim up to the ears, who insisted that she'd converted because her son had returned. He'd been right there in the middle o' the eruption, she claimed. Ka-boom. An' then a week later he came back to find her an' tell her all about partyin' with the Architects. *Reincarnation*, naturally some of them's usin' that word, though it pisses off the Traditionals an' doesn't fit in with what Quinn said either."

"Did you believe her?"

"O' course not. It's pretty thin stuff, isn't it, if ye think about it? I mean, if Jimmy disappeared an' then came back a week later with a glassy stare an' a cockamamie story about dying an' comin' back to life, I'd ask him what the hell he'd been smokin'. Why do ye ask?"

"Because Daniel predicted it, that's all."

"Predicted people would come back? Really?"

But the line fizzed ominously again, and it was all too complicated, so I changed the subject. She'd already evaded a couple of questions about what had happened to them in Iraq. "Are you both OK to travel?"

"Oh aye, we're absolutely fine."

If she'd said *We're fine*, I'd have believed her; I could tell from *absolutely* that she was lying. "OK, so tell me. What really happened to you? Come on, tell me the truth."

"Och, not so much. We were rounded up near Erbil by a Sunni group. They were goin' to give us the chop. Thought we were Seraphim, see, an' the Seraphim are polytheists, an' if there's one thing the jihadi boys can't stand, it's a polytheist. Jimmy managed to persuade them we were Christians, because that was the next most plausible thing. We spent a while chained up in an abandoned American barracks. Jimmy speakin' some Arabic came in way handy, aye. Made friends wi' one o' the guards, a nice village boy who brought us extra bread an' then looked the other way while we escaped."

"Then you just got on bicycles and headed for the border, or what?"

"No, escapin' was the easy part. We had to hide in the desert. Plenty o' experience with that, luckily. Jimmy saved us from dyin' o' thirst by making a solar still out o' a rock, an oil can, an' half a fertilizer bag."

"And you got to Jordan, and you're OK now?" I repeated. "Are you sure?"

She didn't answer my question. "Morag, what about Daniel?"

"I was getting to that. Charlie Balakrishnan's arranging for Daniel to come directly to Telefomin from Seattle. He'll be flying with um, a friend. Kit."

"Kit?"

"Yes."

"That wouldn't be Natazscha Cerenkov's daughter?"

"That's right."

"Really? Yekaterina is 'Kit.' An' she's not a friend, she's 'um-a-friend'? Well, well, well, Morag, yer full o' surprises. I don't recall ye having um-a-friend before."

"She's—she's—it's—"

I had no idea what to say. For about ten dozen reasons, I didn't even know what I wanted to say. What was the important bit here? I tried out various things in my mind. *I'm gay*: no, that got it all wrong, because it sounded like *I'm a socialist* or something, and I didn't "identify as gay" any more than straight people "identify as straight"—I just happened to be madly in love with one particular person, and that person happened to be Kit. *I've never felt like this about anyone in my whole life*: OK, so that was true, but it was too gushy to say to my mother. *It's all so new*: true, vague, a cliché. *It's already over*: probably true, hard to say without whining. *It feels like my heart is trying to strangle itself.* I trailed off into silence.

"Fancy a mother not noticin' a thing like that," Lorna said. And then she saved my blushes by returning to our earlier conversation. "Telefomin—my goodness. Such a long time. All right, all right. Ye're mad, is all I can say, an' Jimmy'll say I'm mad to have agreed. I know exactly what he'll say: *Single most crackbrained scheme she's ever dreamed up.* We'll get there as soon as we can."

Balakrishnan insisted on being wheeled down to the garden to see me off. Sunil and Vandana were supposed to be there too, but they hadn't shown up and Kai was standing by the SUV, looking at his fat black diver's watch.

"Mrs. Chaudry," Balakrishnan said, "are those little rascals coming or not?"

Before she had a chance to answer, I heard a gate bang shut and flip-flops slapping on the path at the side of the house. Sunil came around the corner at full speed with his sister just behind him.

"Morag-ákulan!"

"Morag-ínjaia!"

"Hi, guys," I said. I didn't even ask what their greeting meant, because they were too full of questions. Had Uncle Akshay and worked out what the Seraphim were doing in Hawaii? Had we worked out how to make him live forever? They wanted to teach me Ildavan—which was a big special privilege, because it was really their secret language, but they thought I'd understand, and not go teaching it to just anyone—so when was I coming back? And where was I going?

Kai opened the passenger door and coughed. I was flying commercial—first class, in compensation for none of BalakInd's planes being immediately available, but I still had to make the plane.

"I'm going to New Guinea," I said. "A big island north of Australia."

"I know," Sunil trilled importantly. "They have more languages there than anywhere else in world."

"Yes. And I'm going there to look for a tribe of people who supposedly don't speak any language and who guard a volcano that doesn't exist."

When I was seated in the back of the SUV again, and the garden wall was magically sliding out of the way, I looked back. Sunil bounced a soccer ball on one knee, oblivious. Balakrishnan watched me steadily, as if willing me to succeed. Vandana gave her shoulders an almost imperceptible shake. I slid the window down and leaned out.

"What did that mean?"

Her eyes creased in an impish smile. "Let's see. A good translation might be, um—" She counted ostentatiously on her fingers, as if to remind me of all the possibilities they'd invented. "*Jékamekt?* Or *kq'ud'zuq?* Or *obia oniatat o'oa?* Or maybe *thutheg cham phe amphai?*"

"I get it," I said. "But what did all *those* mean, Vandana? In English."

It was Balakrishnan who answered the question. "They mean 'good luck,' Morag."

It was the last thing he said to me. A few weeks later he was dead. And it wasn't even his faulty genes that killed him.

PART IV:
GHOSTS

CHAPTER 17

FISCHER'S KINGDOM

Dragged halfway around the world in the wrong direction, normal parents would have demanded a detailed justification, footnotes and all. But then normal parents take for granted all that stuff about adolescent brains being only half-baked and therefore crap at everything, especially risk assessment, so they also take for granted that their kids are screw-ups, and probably engaged right now in some idiotic, life-threatening mistake, of a kind the parents themselves would never have made, not ever, no way, not in a million years. (And, you know, let's not mention that story about the stash, the party, and the motorbike.)

Luckily for me, Jimmy and Lorna had never been within a light year of normal, and their default parenting position was always that I must be doing what I'm doing for a reason, and that they'd find out the reason eventually. So when they showed up in New Guinea only half a day after I did—"Lorna put the fear of God into the visa people," Jimmy explained proudly—they demanded nothing from me. We used up hours and hours just hugging, crying, laughing, and exchanging details. Over hot tea and a really bad meal at what passes in Telefol country for a restaurant, all Jimmy said by way of probing was "This is wonderful. Wonderful. But I still don't really get why we're here. Tell me about Daniel again, and why you think this has something to do with the Tainu."

If I'd played coy, if I'd said, "Wait and see," they'd have done just that. (Freaks. Call the parent police.) But it seemed unfair to make them wait.

"I don't know why," I said, "but Daniel clearly thinks the I'iwa hold the key to what I've been looking for. And they're not a legend. They exist."

When I described the two photographs, Lorna's response was not what I expected.

"Sod it," she said, turning to Jimmy. "We should've listened, aye?"

"What do you mean?" I asked. "Iona told you she'd seen them, and you didn't tell me?"

Jimmy put his hand on my arm. "There was nothing much to tell, not at the time. Not much to tell later, if it comes to that. But that last evening she was with us—"

"When she came back from the waterfall?"

"Yes. You were just a child. She didn't want to frighten you. So she kept two details to herself until after you'd turned in for the night. Those two details were, well, they were an interesting story. But frankly we thought she was imagining things. You remember the hand ax she found?"

Of course I did. "Just like the rumors you'd heard. Tools that were very primitive, like something from the Paleolithic."

"She told us that just as she picked it up, she heard a noise, and she turned in time to see a figure in the trees behind her."

"She *saw* the I'iwa?"

"A figure in the trees, that's all. Holding a spear, she thought. The thing she kept repeating was 'Lorna, Jimmy, listen: it was dark there, under the trees. I could only see it because it was white. And there are no short, naked white people in this part of the world.' Talk about seeing a ghost! Of course we said, 'Must have been a trick of the light, Iona; you're very tired, Iona,' all that sort of thing. But she wouldn't buy it."

"You didn't investigate?"

"Oma an' Isbet took us as far as they'd go," Lorna said.

"What about the ax?"

"Disappeared. An' we probably couldn't have dated it anyway. A wooden arrow or ax handle, bingo—but wi' no organic material, ye have no decaying isotopes." She shrugged. "The ax was a puzzler. But we never saw another one, an' it was just very hard to believe Iona's story."

"Time to put on the hiking boots," Jimmy said.

But not so fast.

As we wandered around that afternoon, reminiscing about our work there and taking in the familiar smell of the place, we bumped into an old friend, a Telefol woman named Fula.

"The town's changed," she said. "Do you remember how it was? More missinari than local people. Seventh-Day Adventist. Pentecostal. Catholic—"

"Evangelical Lutheran," Lorna continued. "Australian Church o' Christ the Savior. Tasmanian Church o' Jesus the Nazarene. Aye. I always wondered if gettin' saved by two different missions meant the first one wasn't valid."

Fula smiled thinly. "Everything different now. A few of the old missions still here. But Seraphim is big thing now. Danish man, Johannes Fischer, is chief. Some people he make believe in these Architects. Most of us, we are like the old missinari. Frightened of him."

"We should talk to him," Jimmy said. "But what do you mean, *chief*?"

"He get the government in Port Moresby to make him district commissioner for whole area." She trailed her hand through the air, taking in everything around us and ending with our objective in the northwest. "You want to go up there again? Into Star Mountains? You have to get his permission."

△

You and Kit arrived the next morning, while we were waiting to see Fischer. Natazscha and Rosko weren't with you. Kit ran across the grass from the little plane, dragging you by the hand, kissed me all over my face right in front of Jimmy and Lorna, and then pulled you toward us for a three-way hug.

"Hi, Jimmy and Lorna," she said breathlessly, breaking free to hug them both too. "Is so good to see you, and I am really great to be here! One of Mr. Balakrishnan's company planes took me and Daniel whole way to the capital. Port—"

"Moresby," Lorna said.

"Yah, Port Moresby. My mother, she refuse to come. She also does not want me to come, actually, but then I overhear long conversation she has with Charlie Balakrishnan, and I think he uses, like, ten-liter bottle of charm. She goes all blushes and eyelids batting—yes, Mr. Balakrishnan, no, Mr. Balakrishnan—and she say to me, OK, OK, you can take Daniel out there, you can visit with Morag. Excuse me, did I mention I am crazy about your daughter? But I guess you guess that? Anyway, Natazscha says me, yah, you can take Daniel, and make sure everyone is fine, and then immediately, Yekaterina, you must—"

She raised one finger, and swept it in an arc back toward Seattle.

I was horrified. And confused—still trying to take in the kisses, still trying to backtrack to that phrase *crazy about your daughter*. I actually grabbed her by the arm to slow her down. "You're going to leave again? You're going to fly straight back?"

"Majka, let me finish. There was Seraphim marches all over, last couple days. Seattle also, and many of them turning into riot. Is like, religious war not in Syria or something but middle of downtown, outside the Nordstrom. Natazscha is frightened things are falling apart, and she thinks I will be safer with her. Or thinks she will be safer with me. Both of which is like, total crapshit—"

"But you're not—you're not—?"

She held my face in both hands. "Majka, take fifteen deep breaths, OK? Of course not. You are very dumb sometimes for smart person. I stay here with you, and Daniel, until this thing is finished. My mother will be fine. If she is angry, I'm sorry, but she can frankly stuff everything."

"What about Rosko?"

"Rosko is complicated."

"He's angry with me for being angry with him? Or he's just given up?"

But she shook her head. "He's fine," she said quickly, as if dismissing the subject. "Gabi basically forbid him to come." She obviously wasn't telling me everything, but at that moment you managed to change the subject for her by handing me a drawing. The gesture reminded me of when you'd given me the one of Kit—which I was carrying, carefully folded, in my pocket. But this was one of the bald cavemen you'd drawn before—a single figure, face not visible, crouched over a fire. I more or less ignored it, I'm afraid.

"Thanks, D. How are you? You're skinnier than a measuring tape."

"He not eating, not sleeping, just pacing and muttering all the time," Kit said. "I say to him, Daniel, you eat, because if you die of starvation, Majka is killing me. But he doesn't listen."

You actually smiled at that: just a hint, but it was there. You pointed to the drawing in my hand. "This is the place," you said.

We picked up the bags and walked the half mile back to the little "house" Jimmy and Lorna had rented. We'd all gone inside, except you, and I could tell that Kit was marveling silently at the sheer unlikeliness of calling this two-room, tin-roofed shack a "house." Maybe because she'd noticed the almost total lack of furniture, she suggested we sit outside—and you'd already perched in the middle of the rough-cut front steps, with your sketch pad spread across your knees. The four of us gathered around you.

As with the photographs, there were two images in the double-page spread you showed us. The left side was an expanded, minutely precise copy of that corner detail from Iona's photograph, complete with the tantalizing, almost-hidden hand and face. On the other side, you'd done another copy, but edited. Around the edge of the drawing, every leaf was identical, but the section of tree trunk in the middle had gone, as if digitally removed, revealing the figure behind. I recognized it immediately as a more detailed version of the "caveman" you'd just presented to me. It was almost naked, but wearing a sort of gray skirt that looked as if it might be leather. And it was deeply strange. Not just bald but hairless, it had a squat body; a square, oddly proportioned face; and unnaturally large eyes. A big tattoo on its chest was immediately familiar: a shape like a stretched animal skin, almost identical to one of the Phaistos symbols.

"Daniel's good at drawin'," Lorna said. She was stating a fact—I'd shown her the picture of Kit. "Good at drawin' accurately—so what does it mean, that thuss is in such a strange style? These are like cartoons. The proportions are all wrong."

"I'iwa," you said. A thick blue binder filled with paper was next to you on the step. I thought it was sketch paper at first. It was two or three hundred pages of printed numbers.

"These are from Rosko's work with Bill's software," I said. "What he was doing in the cabin. Did he give them to you?"

You just looked at me, without saying a word, but the answer was so clear that I felt as if you'd spoken: *He didn't give them to me. I took them.*

"Why do you need these, D? What are they for?"

Again you didn't say anything, but again I felt I knew what you were thinking—maybe I was picking up on the way you were holding them, like a priest with an offering. Anyway, if I was right, it was the weirdest thought: *A gift. For the I'iwa.*

Lorna was still looking at the picture. "Daniel," she said, "when did ye see this?"

"Iona. Iona saw."

"Tell me somethin'," she said slowly. "Can ye *see* yer mother? In yer head? Can ye hear her voice?"

No response. I interrupted. "Daniel thinks about Iona all the time. But he doesn't know she was his mother, because he doesn't know who he is himself. He literally doesn't know that he's Daniel Calder."

"I don't think that's true," Kit said. "Not now. Daniel? He—"

"Quiet, both o' ye," Lorna said. She'd crouched down next to you and put a hand on your arm. You lowered the binder onto your knees. "Do ye remember bein' here, Daniel? Before?"

You hesitated, as if you knew what you wanted to say but couldn't come up with the words. Then you gave a sharp nod.

"But he *wasn't* here, ever," I protested. As if Lorna didn't know that.

"Hush, gurrl. What did ye see, Daniel? At the waterfall?"

"This," you said. "This."

"All right, Daniel," Jimmy said. "The I'iwa are real. Let's accept that. Why does it matter? I'm all for an expedition. But why do we need so badly to find them?"

You looked at him, and down at the paper, and with the tip of a finger you traced a triangle on the top sheet. "They know."

The story we'd decided to tell Johannes Fischer to keep him off our backs was that Jimmy and Lorna were just innocent academic fact-grubbers, eager to continue their earlier work on tool evolution. "Part o' a larger anthropological study o' how they're manufactured," Lorna mouthed to us, practicing. It wasn't super-plausible, given that they hadn't been in New Guinea for seven years, but that wasn't the problem. The problem was Fischer being Seraphim; the Seraphim thought, as fundamentalists do, that only the future can possibly matter.

He'd set up office in one of the recently abandoned mission buildings, a green-painted one-story house that had a veranda running around three sides. He made us wait around for a long time for our appointment, clearly a tactic designed to make us feel as unimportant as possible. Eventually we were granted an interview. Or Jimmy was. Kit looked after you and your sketch pad under a tree while the other three of us hung around his door, making ourselves as conspicuous as possible.

The man who emerged was fortyish, with short gray hair and irises made from little round pucks of glacier ice. In his khakis and neatly pressed white shirt, he could have been a manager for an international aid organization—Doctors Without Borders, maybe—or for one of the giant mines at Ok Tedi or Grasberg or Porgera.

He ignored Lorna and me, ushering Jimmy into his office. He had the door almost closed when Lorna got her foot in it.

"Seein' as how we've all been waitin' out here for such a long, long time," she said with a steely, dangerous brightness, "it only seems fair that we should all get to chat for a nice long time. D'ye not think?"

I admired the attitude. It didn't help much. He ignored both of us.

"And what are you doing here, Mr. Chen?"

"We're archaeologists."

"Is that so? I didn't think there was an abundance of temple ruins to be uncovered around here. It's not the Upper Nile or the Yucatán. And I have to inform you that sadly, the kind of work you are doing is wasted time now. The past is past. We stand on the verge of a profound transformation, and our need for this very planet—never mind our need for artifacts left behind in the ground by people who are long since dead—is coming to an end. Sorry to be so harsh. But better for you to recognize the truth sooner rather than later, don't you think?"

He was teasing, in both senses of the word. Making fun—and trying to extract more information.

"We've spent a long time studying the development of tools," Jimmy said, ignoring what he'd said and making the work sound as scholarly, boring, and harmless as possible. "Mesolithic versus Neolithic, Europe versus Asia, stuff like that."

"Ah. Tools, really?" And after a brief pause: "You don't know anything about the Tainu, by any chance?"

Lorna gave Fischer a well-crafted blank look. "Tay-what?"

He continued to address Jimmy. "Many years ago, one of the missionaries, a German Baptist named Kurtz, made first contact with a remote seminomadic group called the Tainu. They kicked him out after a while, and he went on to do other work. But I was told that recently he caught up with the Tainu again, got them to settle in a permanent village, and built them a church. Such a pity that dedicated, devoted people can be so wrong about everything! But I digress. The Baptist mission here hadn't heard from him in months at the point when I arrived. And here's the exciting part from our point of view. The mission looked through his belongings. Which wasn't hard, because everything he owned was in one string bag on a nail over his bed. But the bag contained hundreds of pages of note about the Tainu's beliefs. Two things caught our attention. They speak of a secret volcano, in a location where no volcano can possibly exist. And the site of this 'volcano' is protected by ghost-ancestors in the forest who have either lost the capacity for speech or choose not to speak. In view of what Julius Quinn tells us in *Anabasis*, we found that combination of myths fascinating. Perhaps you've heard of that linguist—Caldwell or something—whose big thing is that all myths have to come from somewhere?"

"Calder, I think that was his name," Lorna said cautiously. "So would ye—would the Seraphim, I mean—be lookin' for this tribe now?"

Fischer condescended to address her at last. "I was sent here to pursue a general strategy of poking around, you might say: finding out what areas are going to be the most fertile recruiting grounds for us. There are Seraphim spreading out in all directions through this country, as they are indeed all over the world. And just a week ago I was lucky enough to meet with a group of Seraphim volunteers who traveled here specially because they have a lot of expertise in languages and a specific interest in exerting our benign influence in the Tainu area."

I should have asked him more about that and then shut up and listened. But I was angry. "Benign? You think the Seraphim's influence is benign? How's it benign if every person who 'ascends' and every Mystery who fails to fully 'ascend' is simply being dragged to an early death? What if your Julius Quinn is wrong? What if Shul-hura in Babylon is right, and the 'dimension of the eternal' is just a lunch counter at which the Architects are the customers and human minds are the dish of the day?"

He smiled broadly. "Julius Quinn is not wrong. Of course there are risks involved in Anabasis, and some people go before they are ready. But the reward for success is real. Think of what that means! Think of what the word *infinity* really means!"

"I'm thinking of the Mysteries," I said. I glanced outside, and then pretended I hadn't. Mentioning the Mysteries brought back to me the fear that still hadn't gone away: that, despite the hints that your condition was improving, you were still in danger. "They're dying. Everywhere they're dying."

He shifted in his chair—there might have been a small shrug of indifference; it was hard to tell—and stared out the window as if he wasn't willing to talk about it further. I could see you and Kit under the tree and hoped he couldn't.

"The Seraphim are experiencing unprecedented success all over the world," he said. "But we've concentrated most of our resources on a few places where interaction with the Architects seems easiest."

"The Epicenters," I said. "Fuji. Mauna Loa. Rainier."

"We don't know why volcanoes are important. Julius Quinn believed it was a cultural memory of our first encounters with the Architects. The matter of language is clearer, though. People who have only one language are more susceptible to the language of the Architects themselves; their minds are already tuned closer to the right frequency, so to speak. The Epicenters are just our top picks, as you might say, because our biggest successes since Ararat have been in places with a single dominant language and population centers close to volcanoes."

"You expect to, what, entice the Architects back at those places?"

"Not entice. They are coming. Our purpose is simply to pave the way. Make the transition as effective as possible."

"So the Epicenters will be like Ararat."

He smiled. "A month at most to the next great Anabasis. And after that things will progress, oh, very quickly. Ararat was a village of the saved. The Epicenters will be cities of the saved."

"The explosions, though. If you gather hundreds of thousands of people—"

"The planning is for over half a million at Mauna Loa."

"Then—"

I was trying to imagine—trying not to imagine—a Thera-sized eruption in the middle of the Pacific, when Jimmy interrupted. "New Guinea doesn't fit, though, does it?"

"It's a special case. Highly volcanic, but also the biggest hot spots for linguistic diversity on the planet. In Papua New Guinea alone, there are 839 languages by our latest count, and a thousand or more before

European contact. That's my specialty—I'm a Babbler, if you know that term."

Jimmy nodded. "I've heard of it."

"Something isn't working well here. We've been meeting with a powerful resistance, as if something is actively interfering with our work. And, as I said, there's the curious myth about the volcano. So our people wanted me to investigate. Then a volunteer group showed up. Funny that they should be Australian, by the way. Poor things: down there, they don't have a single active volcano in an area twenty times the size of Japan! But we're been having some little success even there."

"Ye have?" Lorna said.

"Tut tut, not keeping up with the news."

"We've been a tad busy."

"Well then, an uplifting story I have for you." He emphasized *uplifting*. A preacher's pun: Anabasis was uplifting people into the Eternal. He picked up a tablet and found a news clip from an Australian TV station.

"A couple of days ago, this was."

Standing in bright sun, in a parking area, an earnest local TV reporter with too-obvious blue contacts was doing everything he could to ramp up the drama. He talked loud, held his shiny face close to the lens, and bounced on the balls of his feet like a boxer, as if maybe he was about to left hook the camera.

"For those of you who aren't familiar with it," he said, "and frankly, almost no one is familiar with Great Basalt Wall National Park, the word *park* is a bit of a misnomer."

Pa-AH-k, he said. *Miz-NOE-mah*. The accent was thicker and rougher than Mayo's.

"The Toomba lava flow is a unique geological feature." *FAI-cha.* "Four hundred square kilometers of exposed basalt from an eruption thirteen thousand years ago. It's probably the most isolated and inhospitable piece of public land anywhere in Australia. Or even the world. There's no public access, no roads, no nothing. Police are still collecting evidence, but there seems to be no doubt that this extraordinary event is related to Seraphim activity. Here in Townsville, we spoke to Kenny Kenner, who owns the Waverider Board Shop. Kenny, I understand you heard the explosion? Even though we're, what, a hundred and fifty k from there?"

The camera panned out to reveal a shop with a giant surfboard over the door. Kenny, standing proudly underneath it, was a middle-aged surfer, the hair around his bald spot a tiara of blonded spikes. He wasn't wearing a shirt, and his tan was so overdone that the belly hanging out over his peach-colored shorts looked like a well-oiled kangaroo-skin handbag. He scratched it affectionately.

"Yeah, mate, like I said. Massive crash of thunder out of a clear blue sky. I thought, crikey, it's the end of the world."

The reporter finished the picture with a couple of human-interest details I could have done without. All seventy-two of the people they'd found were from the same little mining town, Charters Towers. There was a separate list of missing, all of them children, and there was evidence that they had been there, but had wandered off. Any chance that they could have survived out there alone was being dismissed out of hand. As for the adult victims, the forensics people had said that at least a dozen of them were still alive when the dingoes arrived.

He didn't offer more detail on that, but the implication was clear. Most of the seventy-two had died outright, but some had not gone all the way. They had turned into Mysteries. Robbed of the will to move, they had just stood there, helpless and passive and waiting. Were Mysteries just mental blanks, empty husks? Or were they still capable

of suffering? Nobody knew. Nobody wanted to know, because it didn't
bear thinking about.

Fischer positively beamed at us: the whole incident was "very encouraging," he said, "because it just goes to show that the word of Julius Quinn
is spreading more rapidly than we could have imagined!"

"Oh aye, a great success," Lorna said grimly. "Seventy-two down,
seven an' a half billion to go, is it?"

But he didn't catch her tone, or pretended not to. "What a time to
be alive, don't you think? To witness the very end of mere humanity,
and the very beginning of something so much greater!"

Twenty minutes later we were back outside, fuming. "Smooth
bastard," Lorna said. Fischer was indeed now the sole administrative
authority for the area—he'd even showed us his certificates from the
national government in Port Moresby—and he didn't want us out in
the field, "not under any circumstances, because it might interfere with
our people's more important work."

But we discovered soon enough that he had less control over the
local situation than he thought. One "Seraphim," at least, had done an
excellent job of misleading him.

You and Kit were still under the tree where we'd left you. A loud giggle
erupted from a couple of local kids you seemed to be entertaining. You'd
presented them with a picture of themselves: a caricature, funny but
sweet, with big heads and exaggerated features. They smiled, thanked
you, and were turning to go, but you held up your hand in a *stop* gesture
and began riffling through your sketch pad. You held up a picture to
them, and their expressions became serious.

"Lukluk save?" you said.

I was amazed. Not just that you'd asked a coherent question, but that you'd done it in Tok Pisin, which you'd had no opportunity to learn. Where had it come from? The phrases I'd taught to Iona? You were struggling with them, but they were there:

"Lukluk—lukluk save dispela man?" *Do you recognize this man?*

The kids nodded furiously. "Yes," one of them said, pointing to the office. "Tokim dispela man."

"L—L—Longtaim bifo?" *A long time ago?*

"One week, maybe. He missinari, ask for Tainu."

We still hadn't seen the drawing, and you didn't seem to recognize its significance, judging from how casually you handed it to Kit. Lorna looked at the sketch over Kit's shoulder, and her jaw fell open.

"Jes' wait a minute, Daniel. Isn't that—isn't that—? Och no. Ye've got to be feck'n kiddin' me. Morag, I thought ye said—"

"Let me see."

Such a subtle business, drawing a face! Capturing not just the shape but the *look*. And this was one of your best, maybe even better than the one of Kit. Not just no mistaking who it was, but a sense that he was there, looking back at me.

"That's impossible, D," I said. "I'm telling you right now. It can't be. It can't be. That's just impossible."

You'd leaned back against the tree, as if exhausted, and the kids were moving away. I quickly called them back.

"Dispela man missinari? Tru? Bringim Jisas Kraist stori?"

They shook their heads. "Missinari bringim haus wokim stori."

I didn't understand until one of them made a roof shape with her arms. It still took me a moment to process, because every word and phrase in Tok Pisin means about ten different things. *Haus wokim* meant "builder." But it also meant "architect." Now it meant "Architect" as well.

"I'd say our clever Mr. Fischer has been bamboozled," Jimmy said. "And suddenly I don't care so much about getting his permission for anything."

⚎

An hour later, Fula had found us a local man with a four-by-four and a hole in his wallet. He made a big fuss about not wanting to get in trouble with Fischer. Then he said he could take us to the end of the most westerly road and demanded an outrageous fee. Jimmy haggled to no effect and agreed, and then the man said we'd need five gallons of diesel, which wasn't included.

So as not to raise any eyebrows, we walked out of town and climbed into his machine only after we were well out of sight. Then, for fifty miles that felt like five hundred, we bashed around in the back seats like slugs in a fisherman's bait box.

"Road in New Guinea is always like this?" Kit asked.

"Always." I wanted to sound like the experienced traveler, unruffled by anything, but even I was alarmed. Even I, as the wheels clawed at yet another crumbling edge, kept thinking about hurtling upside down into a ravine.

"What's the deal with Rosko?" I said, more to distract myself that anything. "Really?"

"Nothing. Not nothing, but nothing. We have kind of an argument I guess. I tell you later." She threw me a look that meant either *I don't want to talk about this* or *I don't want to talk about this in front of your parents.* She was saved from saying anything else as we slithered to a halt at a tree trunk, which had been dragged across the way to mark the road's end.

"You can leave us here," Jimmy said, peering at an old map. "I know where we are, more or less."

The driver got out and gestured at himself, at Jimmy, and then at a path through the trees beyond the downed trunk. "No rot, no rot, no rot," he said with a toothless grin. It was a double pun, not a repetition. The word *rot* meant both "road" and "choice": he was saying, *I don't have a choice, because this is the end of the road. And you don't have a choice either, because here, at the end of the road, there's only one way to go.*

After he drove away, leaving us in a gray cloud of flies and fumes, we hiked for three more hours on an easy path through a valley. At the end of the valley, the mountains began to loom clear and steep ahead of us in a green wall. As the afternoon light softened, we scrambled up a rise, five hundred feet maybe, onto a small, hidden plateau.

And smelled wood smoke.

Chapter 18

Oma's Dream

The first thing we saw was a clearing the size of a football pitch. Or do I mean soccer field—or football field? Anyway, a young woman about my age was seated on the ground near the edge of it, pounding at something with a rock. I could tell from her flat profile and exceptionally dark skin that she was Tainu. She had typical Tainu hair as well, a black mop cut into a bowl shape, similar to what I'd often seen in the Amazon, but with a long thin braid on the left side that had feathers woven into it.

The traditional Tainu covering, the same for men and women, was a short skirt made from the waxy, dagger-like, greenish-purple leaves of the tanket plant. This girl, like more and more tribal people, was wearing old clothes from the Western charity pile: a red cotton soccer shirt with the number "8" on the back, filthy running shorts that had once been blue. The missionary influence: *Dress modestly, like a European, or an Australian, or an American, in items made by Bangladeshi slave labor! So much better to do that than dress the way you've always dressed, using renewable local materials, and risk offending God with a buttock or a nipple.*

I mean, how stupid can you—

Sorry, sorry. Must have fewer opinions. Must stick to the point.

At least the string *bilum* bag on her back, in which a baby lay sleeping, was traditional. So was the work: between her knees she held a three-foot length of sago palm, cut open and formed into a trough. Slowly but steadily she raised and lowered the rock, pounding the starchy insides of the plant into a pulp.

I hadn't spoken Tain'iwa for years, so I rehearsed in my head how to say, *Excuse me, but I'm looking for a man called Oma.* Having thought it out, I hesitated, because Oma could be dead and referring to a dead man was the worst possible way to begin a conversation—you could speak of a dead man only after being introduced to the subject by his relatives. Before I had a chance to speak, she turned to look at us and opened her mouth in frightened surprise. But almost immediately her expression changed again.

"Morrrg?" she said. "Morrrg ekaba? Emakol diwo kim dawa. Em bivek, awa su bisu!" *Is it you? I can't believe it. You came back!*

It took me a moment to process, but when I recognized her, all the happy memories of being a kid up in those mountains came flooding back like it was yesterday. This was the little girl who, as much as anyone, had taught me Tain'iwa, and put up with my strange stupidity about local plants and animals, and enjoyed my crazy stories (which, like all the Tainu, she'd assumed were mainly inventions) about a wider world. I was so surprised to see an adult version of that same face that I only just managed to avoid saying something really dumb like *Wow, Isbet, I didn't recognize you. You've grown up.* Instead, I said in Tain-iwa, *Yes, Isbet, it's me. So wonderful to see you again! Are you well? Look, my parents are here too.* After the Tainu greeting—not cheek to cheek, but forehead pressed hard to the left shoulder—I introduced you as my friend. Brother would have been way too confusing to explain.

Whose is the baby? I asked in Tain'iwa.

"Ewa'o," she said casually. *Mine.*

Oh yes. Isbet was seventeen, like me. But seventeen was thirty here. *Wonderful! That's, uh, wonderful. And your husband?* I said.

A dismissive gesture with her hand: a twist of the wrist with the fingers splayed. It might have meant *Who knows? Who cares?* But then she made a sort of low mewing sound: "Me'iy'ih. Me'iy'ih."

I'd made the mistake I'd just avoided a minute earlier.

Me'iy'ih meant "he's not." But what it really meant was "he's dead." No reason given, both because it was something Tainu never talked about, and paradoxically because it was too ordinary. Poor nutrition, no antibiotics, frequent fighting, and frequent hunting accidents. Jimmy'd calculated that the average life expectancy for a male Tainu was thirty-nine years. I tried not to think about the fact that the baby's father was probably already well-preserved and doing scarecrow duty.

She showed us around the village. Most of the women were planting taro farther down the valley, she said, and the men were out hunting. The few women and children who were around rose and scattered like birds as they saw us, though I could tell they were watching from the tree line. The absence of people gave the village an even more desolate, abandoned feel. It was nothing more than a dozen sagging huts scattered through the clearing: not so different from the way they'd lived for countless thousands of years before, except that then they'd moved and rebuilt every month or so. Like so many before him, Kurtz had worked to settle them in this one place, so that the work of civilizing them, and saving their souls, would be easier, but the only physical sign of it was more trash, more mud, and more decay.

She took us through a stringy patch of tobacco plants to one of the larger huts on the edge of the clearing. "Wewa ina ge'je," she said, and translated by pointing to each of us in turn and putting her head sideways on her hands as if they were a pillow. We ducked under the dripping grass lintel and stepped inside. It was the church—a shabby wooden building the size of a suburban living room. A glass bottle stood on a folding table at one end. There were no chairs or benches, just bare beaten earth under an apologetic sprinkling of grass. Despite my months of living with the Tainu before, it was hard to imagine sleeping in this sad, mold-infested space.

"Ogme deg etwi'u balam?" I said. *Where is the man who built this?*

She was matter-of-fact about it: *missinari* had been here *longtaim*, after persuading them to stay in one place so that God could find them more easily. Did she mean the one who had found her tribe years before and tried then to convert them to *Jisas Kraist stori*, and given so many of the villagers, like Isbet herself, new names? Yes, the same man. And when he came back, she said, and persuaded them to settle, he also told them they must forget about their forest gods: the forest gods were not real.

So they were all Christian now?

She shrugged. She was repeating what she was supposed to say.

Why wasn't *missinari* there? I asked. Because they didn't believe in his god?

That wasn't it, she said. The trouble was he'd insisted that the I'iwa and their volcano weren't real either—but the Tainu wouldn't give up those two beliefs. So Kurtz had demanded they show him, and they had said if he went there, he would be killed. And he became angry, and said that he would prove there was no volcano, no I'iwa.

"Epe din ba'ooten madanu, warai da kem-kem pewanat."

He marched off to the waterfall and didn't come back.

Marched: she made him sound like a petulant boy playing soldiers.

We were interrupted by the sound of the men returning. Oma came first, wearing the traditional Tainu leaf skirt, plus several elaborate necklaces and a beard interlaced with small pink flowers. The long leaves bounced as he walked.

"Blind," you said.

Yes. You'd noticed it first, but even from a distance I could see that his eyes were the same milk white as his hair. But he didn't walk like a blind person. He strolled into the clearing confidently and turned toward us as if sensing our presence. Two younger men walked half a step behind him on either side like bodyguards. They were dressed the same, except that one of them was wearing a knee-length lilac skirt under the tanket leaves. I recognized them as grown versions of Willem and Yosep, the two boys who had brought Iona to our encampment. Yosep had a long bow over his shoulder, and the bamboo fiber cord dug into his chest. He also carried two bags that looked as if they contained dinner. Cuscus, as it turned out. Later that evening, Kit looked glumly at the hunk of half-raw fatty meat in her hand and said it was "cutest, most helpless-looking animal I am ever eating."

A Papuan hunting dog came out from behind the group and bounded over the grass toward us. It was the size of a big terrier, but it had the inquisitive, pointed face and triangular ears of a fox. Its coat was a dull gold, with matching white flashes on muzzle and tail. A couple of feet from Isbet, it stopped and rose on its hind legs, making a strangely articulate sound—*wrark?*—as it demanded to be noticed.

"Ga'iwa jam'eyep," she said. It was Tain'iwa for *dog*, but literally it meant *bad voice, good nose*. Which was right: they could track prey at speed, even in total darkness, but instead of barking they went in for a cracked wail. *Singing dog* was the optimistic term the lowlanders used.

The way you looked at the dog, and then at me, made me wonder: Did you remember how I'd pined for one? Did you remember how, living on the road with Jimmy and Lorna, any real pet was out of the question, and I made do with an ever-changing menagerie of caterpillars, beetles, snakes, and frogs? Well, Dog, as I named it, seemed to adopt me immediately. "Hello, Dog," I said, crouching down so that my eyes were on its level. "I probably knew your parents. Nice to meet you." It looked at me with its head to one side, as if carefully taking the measure of my voice. Then it sniffed both my hands, my arms, my feet, my face, my hair, and, aye, of course, it was a dog, so it had to maneuver around and check out my bum too. Satisfied, it sat down next to me with its eyes on me, as if awaiting instruction.

"That's about the most intelligent-looking animal I've ever seen," Jimmy said, and I translated for Isbet.

"Lopsom ikel dala," she said. "Mesomom kavi dala." *It looks intelligent because it is intelligent.* She ran over to her father, chattering with excitement.

"Morrrg wayu! Utmen Lona wayu! Utmen Gimmi!"

His eyebrows went up and he smiled, opening out his hands in a gesture that needed no translating. He was polite to Kit and very formally polite to Jimmy and Lorna, as befitted older people who were my parents. His reaction to you was very different, though. He seemed frightened of your presence at first, but afterward I came to see that he was not so much frightened as shocked—not quite prepared to believe what I was saying about you. He held you by the shoulders for a long time, repeating your name many times until he got the pronunciation right and touching your face with his fingertips as if to memorize it. Your reaction was almost as strange: instead of resisting his touch, you leaned into it, accepting it, and murmuring encouragement in a language that of course he couldn't understand.

"We need you, Oma," you said. "We need you. Your blind eyes will lead us." Then you reached into your sketch pad and handed Isbet the drawing you'd made outside Johannes Fischer's office. She gripped the sides of the sheet so hard that I thought it would tear and started talking very quickly.

Five men, she said. *This one and four more. With guns. They went beyond, to the waterfall. We told them not to go. My father said, we exist only to protect the I'iwa, and they exist only to protect us, and they don't like to be seen. He said, you must not go. He said, if you find the volcano, they will kill you. But their leader, the one with the ruined face, said, the volcano is what we are looking for.*

I asked her what she meant by "ruined face." *Him,* she said, pointing at the drawing. *His face is*—it was something that frightened or disgusted her. She made frantic clawing gestures all over her head, but she couldn't explain.

I wanted to take up what you had started—the tricky task of persuading them to guide us when I knew they wouldn't want to. As I fumbled for a way to explain myself, Oma pointed his white blind eyes at me and interrupted me with a long, complicated stream of Tain'iwa. He spoke in a singsong whisper, and it was hard to follow; I kept up with him only because I'd heard some of it before, and because he gestured so eloquently with his big, knobby, callused hands:

Our land is shaped like a ring, he said. *It encircles the valley of the I'iwa, and the place of smoke, which lies at the center of the ring. We do not go to the center, because the I'iwa will protect us only if they are left alone. So for generation after generation, the purpose of our life has been to circle endlessly. Always staying close, and always watching for outsiders, but never getting too close.*

It sounded like the refusal we'd heard before. He stopped, apparently too embarrassed to go on, and began to clean some mud from under a fingernail. I was wondering what other strategy I could use to persuade him, when he continued.

We did not want to stop circling the I'iwa. And we did want to stop Kurtz from looking for them. But he was angry with us, and determined, and I was frightened and weak. He never came back. Then the Seraphim came, the five men as Isbet said. We wanted to stop them too, but they had guns and we were frightened. We showed them to the waterfall because they said they would kill us if we didn't, but we felt bad about that. It was betraying the I'iwa.

"So you won't take us?" I said it in English, without thinking, but I didn't get a chance to translate, because he still wasn't finished.

I had dreams, Morrrg. Dreams about you returning with a tall thin man who was your brother but did not look like you.

He put his hand out and grabbed you hard around the arm.

This man. In my dreams, he went to the I'iwa also, and found the volcano. And in the dream it was right for him to go, and to take you with him to the I'iwa, because the I'iwa wanted him, and needed him, and helped him.

He broke off and spoke to Isbet in a low whisper.

"Esumek ku, tem timal ka," she said to me. "I'iwa-nok." *My father says we will go with you.*

I could tell Oma didn't want to go; his dream had simply persuaded him that it was the right thing to take a risk in order to help Daniel.

"Will you be frightened?" I asked.

We will go with you, she repeated, managing to sound brave and decisive without answering the question. As it happened, though, going to the I'iwa wasn't quite Oma's or Isbet's decision to make.

CHAPTER 19

A DEAD MAN WITH A RUINED FACE

A damp night in the abandoned church. Jimmy and Lorna were snoring in minutes, and Kit soon after, but you sat in a corner, fidgeting and not even pretending to sleep. I lay half-awake until a snake fell from the rafters onto my sleeping bag; after that, I lay fully awake. By dawn we were huddled outside around a fire I'd made—lots of smoke, no detectable heat. Then Jimmy came out and put together a delicious breakfast of cold purple snot, otherwise known as taro. Lorna and Kit emerged, both rubbing their arms and looking as if they needed to try the whole sleep thing again in a real bed. "I love New Guinea," Lorna said. "But either I'm gettin' old or I'd forgotten how amazingly uncomfortable it is."

You ate a few bites, once again looking faintly puzzled by the idea of eating, or the idea of flavor, then got up and started pacing the perimeter of the village, wringing your hands and peering into the forest. As the sun came up over the trees, light began to leak across the clearing like pale floodwater. It was a peaceful scene, but not one I had the heart to enjoy much; I felt as anxious as you looked, and I was losing an argument.

"We should leave this morning," I said, brandishing one of your drawings. "Daniel needs to find the I'iwa, that's clear. What are we waiting for?"

"Is too dangerous," Kit said, ganging up with Jimmy and Lorna. "Kurtz is disappeared, and this group of Seraphim not returned? We need more information."

You'd drifted back to us, and you were standing behind her. "He's back," you said. "He will take us." Not a contribution to the discussion; again, a bare statement of fact.

"Who's back?" Lorna asked.

You turned away and looked toward the trees, raising one arm and pointing west at trees that were already bright yellow in the first direct sunlight. Dog sniffed at you, made a querying *wuuh* sound as if to say *Are you sure?* and loped away to stand there with its tail in the air. After staring into the undergrowth for a few seconds it began a high, quavering howl that contained three or four cracked notes at once, *aaa-rrrr-ooo-uuu-rrrr*, like a malfunctioning ambulance siren. The effect on the Tainu was certainly like a siren. Several of the younger men appeared from nowhere and ran over to a spot just behind where Dog was standing. When they raised their bows, there was a flash of white at the points of the arrows.

"Bone tips," I said. I'd hardly ever seen them, but Oma had once explained them to me, in a disturbingly offhand way: you could hunt wild pigs and cuscus and tree kangaroos using hardened bamboo, but a bone arrowhead was more difficult to make and was reserved for the special task of killing people. Groups of women and children had been gathering around other fires, but the women knew what the bone arrow tips meant too, and they were backing the children away to the far margin of the clearing on the other side of the village, readying themselves to melt into the forest. Everything became still, like a painting. Even Dog managed to continue its eerie tune without visibly moving.

There was a crackling tension in the air, but it went on for a minute, then two, then three, and I began to think it was a false alarm. You knelt down beside Dog as if to whisper something; it gave an affronted *ooo-uuh* and fell silent. You stood again and turned to face the trees.

There was a crash-crash-crash in the undergrowth.

More silence.

Crash-crash-crash.

More silence.

And then a figure staggered into the clearing, swinging a black stick from side to side, low down, like a crude machete. A figure straight out of a horror movie.

Kurtz? That was what I thought.

The camo gear was caked with mud. Most of him was caked with mud. A fist-sized crust of dried blood was visible on his abdomen, under the open front of his shirt. Then he turned toward us.

Ruined face was right. His left eye was gone. His left ear looked like a fried mushroom, thick and shriveled and black. And the whole left side of his head was a crusted plain of red scar tissue. It looked like the throat of a lizard. Like a handbag shredded by a knife. Like a nineteenth-century astronomer's map of Mars.

The deformities, or injuries, were ghoulish and frightening. But the scariest thing of all was his surviving eye. It fixed on me, fiercely. Then it jumped around all over the landscape before fixing on me again. It looked like a small enraged animal in a trap. It was full of an energy and a desperation bordering on madness.

"Dru," I shouted to the men. "Ena i'bek'em." *No. Don't fire your arrows.*

The Tainu men weren't inclined to take my advice about how to protect their village. You were directly in front of them, but the arrows stayed notched, the strings taut. You shook your head, apparently fearless, and walked over to him. The bone tips of the arrows tracked you both as you came toward us.

The "stick" he'd been using to bushwhack through the undergrowth wasn't a stick. It was a fancy, modern, high-end military carbine. It seemed like an odd piece of gear for a missionary. And it wasn't until he spoke that I realized my mistake.

He looked so strange, so radically different, that I expected him to sound different—an insane cackle maybe, or a gravelly drawl suitable for someone back from the dead. The damage to his face had given him a lisp, but the accent was unchanged: educated Oz, rubbed smooth like a stone by large American universities. And, despite the derelict look and the mad eye, there was something instantly recognizable about his tone.

"Hello, Morag," he said. "What an excellent surprise. I wondered if you'd catch up with me eventually, and I have to say it's most fortunate that you have. Daniel too, eh, and Yekaterina Cerenkov? You must be Jimmy and Lorna Chen, the archaeologists? Mother not here, Yekaterina? A pity. Knowing her research, she'd especially enjoy hearing of my adventures."

David Maynard Jones. A dead man with a ruined face.

"So, ye really are alive," Lorna said. "Well, I'll be damned."

He turned around to slough off a small backpack; it had what looked like a hiking pole sticking up out of it. The carbine, now held correctly, remained in his hand. "Yes, as a matter of fact, you will be damned," he said. "No one but the Babblers have any chance of surviving what the Architects have in store for us. But I'm getting ahead of myself. First things first. I've been lost in the mountains with not much but this fancy fire-stick and the clothes on my back, and I've had nothing to eat in the last two days except some river snails, a giant rat that I more or less blew to pieces, and one impressively large tarantula. Could I trouble you for some real food?"

Jimmy handed him sago bread, a water bottle, and half a roasted breadfruit. He put the gun on the ground, squatting just outside our circle, and chewed hungrily for a while. Three mosquitoes landed on his forehead in a line and began to swell pinkly, like fat men at a bar, but either he didn't notice or he was beyond caring. I wanted to say something profound, but all I could manage was "How the *hell* did you do it?"

"*Hell* is right, Morag, I assure you. How did I survive the eruption? I'll tell you: in the space of an hour, I used up several lifetimes of the purest, highest-quality luck. Bill Calder didn't have so much of it. A pity, that. I thought I'd make him my partner, that he'd be intelligent enough to understand what I was offering him and what failure would mean. 'Bill,' I said, 'we're not talking about a better life, or some trivial advances in knowledge. We're talking about zero versus infinity. Eternity in the dark versus eternity in the light.' But he didn't get it. Or didn't believe it."

"Or he did get it," Lorna said, "but he didn't want ye to be in control of that knowledge."

Mayo didn't even turn her way; he continued talking to me as if no one else was there.

"Bill died when we fell into the crevasse. I was stuck on a ledge just below the lip. His body was twenty feet below me, like a broken doll. Head smashed open. All those high-quality brains spilled out like—well, never mind the details. I managed to wedge myself into a crack in the ice and get out. But the bloody helicopter was just taking off."

You nodded, as if agreeing with his description. "Angry. Certain death. Immortality taken away."

He put his head to one side and looked at you, puzzled and fascinated by what you'd said. Me too. But he continued with the story:

"It was hidden in the smoke, and I ran toward the sound. But the lava flow was barring my way. Actually, the lava was hidden in the smoke too, and I came within a split second of running directly into it. Instead I ran into a wall of thousand-degree air. It didn't feel like heat. It felt as if someone had come along with a sharp knife and sliced off one side of my body. Another two seconds, and I'd've lit up like a lamp wick, burned alive without the lava even touching me. But I managed to turn and throw myself in the opposite direction. I was blinded by the heat, stumbling across the snow, and miraculously I fell down what must have been a thousand-foot snow chute. Also miraculously, I avoided breaking my legs or colliding headfirst with anything. And then there was a delay before the big energy transfer and the main eruption, and even with bad burns and one eye gone I managed to get far enough away. Which wouldn't have helped, except that I was on the north side, and the eruption was focused in the opposite direction. Even so I ended up wading for miles through thigh-deep ash and nearly choked to death."

"Several lifetimes of luck," Jimmy echoed. "But your mission to discover the truth about the Seraphim was a failure."

"The Seraphim are lemmings, following their leaders over a cliff. Just like so many people down the ages before them. Seems obvious to me—if someone says, 'God has your best interests at heart, so do what he says,' isn't just a little skepticism warranted? Sure, anyone who can successfully pretend to be a god must have some tricks up their sleeve. But then the next question is, what are those tricks, how do they work, and how do I steal them? My goal wasn't to understand what happens to the Seraphim. It was to understand how the Architects became Architects."

"But why did you even believe they existed?" I asked. "Before Ararat, I mean. Why, if the Seraphim were just another religion, did you think their 'gods' were worth investigating?"

He looked at me, smirking, as if he was enjoying not telling me. As if waiting for me to beg, or say something more. Out of frustration, I did.

"I already know it was something Iona said. I've seen your notes. *Iona's thesis*, you called it?"

He popped a hunk of breadfruit into his mouth and sat looking at us each in turn, but again it was me his eye settled on. I had the sense that Jimmy, Lorna, and Kit were mere specimens to him, irrelevances. You puzzled and interested him, as you had never done before: with the sole exception of Iona, he'd looked down on people who weren't Babblers. But I was the one whose attention he wanted now; I could tell he was sizing up whether I ought to know, or whether he was ready to tell me. I wanted to urge him to go on, but you distracted us both, digging with your fingernails in the soil and breathing like you'd just finished a marathon. You cleared an area the size of a dinner plate, and your eyes were darting back and forth between me and the ground.

You smoothed the broken soil, then took a stick and scratched a semicircular arc like a bowl, and wrote "$\sqrt{1}$" at one end of the arc and "$\sqrt{2}$" at the other. Mayo looked at you with renewed curiosity. "Not as slow as I thought, your brother. Either that, or he is slow but he learned something awfully special up on Ararat. Meaning of life, right there. Meaning of life and meaning of death."

Lorna pointed to his chest. "Ye'd do well to get that cleaned up, I'd say. Yer not goin' to discover the secret of life an' death if ye die o' gangrene poisonin'."

He pulled open one side of his shirt to show us the wound. "That, Dr. Chen, is something far more remarkable than it looks. But don't worry. Antibiotics were one thing I did have with me. I'm not going to die."

"How did it happen, then?"

He pulled the "hiking pole" from the backpack and passed it to me. The Tainu men behind us gasped and started whispering to each other.

It was a short wooden spear. The shaft was thick and uneven, made from a roughly cleaned branch. But the tip, lashed to the branch with a piece of vine, was a sliver of knapped stone so elegant and symmetrical that it looked like something produced on a machine. Each of the three sides was a long, slightly concave triangle. Each long side was razor sharp. The point was like a needle.

"This was thrown at me from thirty feet away, aimed at my heart. I twisted sideways at the last moment, so it only took a chunk out of me."

"That's completely unlike anything local," Jimmy said.

Mayo grinned and got to his feet again. "Oh, but it is local. Way more local than these people." He indicated the men behind us.

"I'iwa," you said.

"I'iwa. They ambushed us as we were making our way out of what I absolutely guarantee is the strangest cave system in the world."

He paused, scratching himself, and grinned at us. The grin was lopsided because of the scar tissue. It made him look even more demonic.

"Bill Calder was a bright bloke," he said, "but he had an underdeveloped imagination. He'd grown up on stories about ancient languages, so naturally he thought he'd found another one, and his big ambition was to unlock it. A footnote in the history books! I suppose that's a cheap sort of immortality, isn't it? Not so bad, if it's all you can afford."

I wanted to throw a rock at him for talking about Bill's ambitions, and mine, in that way. To keep myself quiet, I dug my fingernails into my arm—and then realized it was Kit's arm. She detached my fingers, then held on to them.

"And you lot, you're bright too, but you also lack imagination, because your wildest idea about the I'iwa is that if they're not ghosts, they must be another 'lost tribe.' How exciting that would be—thought we'd found the last of those a long time back. The Hagahai, the Fayu, the Liawep, then the Tainu. But no, here's one more 'primitive' group left for us to prod, and document, and open up to the tender mercies of the religious fundamentalists and the mining companies. What fun! But, oh dear, oh dear, reality is so very far ahead of you."

"Just tell us," Jimmy said. "Who are they?"

"Well, the first thing is, the I'iwa are cave dwellers. And, as that derogatory Victorian term *caveman* might suggest, their material culture is so poor, so primitive, that it makes the Tainu here look like a bunch of upper-class Sydney wine-sniffers. But what you're going to have to get your pretty little heads around is that these 'cave' people were studying mathematics when we were still hitting each other over the head with clubs. And they've built something in stone that can only be described as a computer. And with it, they—"

He stood up, as if changing his mind about something, and shouldered the backpack again. "Come on. There's no time to waste. And since I found the entrance partly by accident and don't know how I got back here, we'll need the chief and his daughter to guide us. I know, I know, they won't want to. So just tell them to get over it, because they're going to die otherwise."

He turned and smiled at me conspiratorially, as if sharing a secret. "Actually they're going to die in any case. Everyone is. Apart from us."

"Us?"

"The Babblers, Morag. You see, I think the I'iwa have provided what you might call a digital life raft. A means of resistance and escape. Just for the carriers of FOXQ3. With their help, our fragment of humanity will be able to survive what's coming."

"You're mad," I said. "And you don't need to threaten Oma and Isbet. They already agreed to go."

"They did? How interesting."

"Oma wants to help Daniel."

You'd got up and stood next to him. Strange—you'd come to seem so fragile, but it was as if you were visibly growing in strength and purpose now; of course you were several inches taller than him anyway, and you leaned in close, dominating him. "There's no time."

I thought of what Balakrishnan had said: *A place beyond time. The annihilation of time.* But Mayo wasn't thinking of that. "If what that so-called district commissioner told me is true," Mayo said, "you're dead straight about that, Danny-boy. When those Epicenters are ready, it's going to be Thera all over again, except it'll be our civilization getting toasted. If you want to beat the Architects—and gain what they've gained, which is *everything*—you'll have to trust me and work with me."

He was replying to you, but looking at me, so he didn't see you watching him as he spoke. You gave an infinitesimal shake of your head, just a sideways twitch, and mouthed again, as if speaking to yourself: "No time."

Kit stood up next to you and almost spat at Mayo. "Pah! You are saying there is big Architect language secret that even Archimedes cannot work out, Bill Calder cannot work out, and Morag cannot work out. But now you are saying, some hairy guys in cave with spears did it? They have big stone abacus? Or maybe they are like, guardians of giant alien supercomputer? This is I think good idea for comic book story. But also totally crapshit."

I admired her for instinctively not believing a word Mayo said and for having the guts to say so. But I thought, *Isn't this basically what Rosko said?*

Lorna hadn't moved. She was staring into what remained of the fire, coaxing smoke out of it with a stick. "Frankly, David Maynard Jones," she said, "I have to agree wi' Kit. *Crapshit* is the very word I was lookin' for."

I had to smile. No idea how she did it, but with that one repeated word—overlaid with a passable imitation of Kit's accent—she'd managed to tell me that our relationship was OK, that she was completely fine with it. I guess if I'd been a normal teen, it wouldn't have mattered what my mother thought; it mattered. Hugely.

Mayo was scrabbling in his back pocket. He pulled out a filthy sheet of paper. "You don't trust me, Dr. Chen. Which is only reasonable. Besides, all the good evidence is a long, tough hike from here. But you might want to take a look at this."

The piece of paper was mainly stains and mud, but a rough pencil sketch was still visible. He passed it to Lorna.

"I have seen wonders," he said. "Wonders! This is a drawing I did of what we can call, if you like, the Calendar Wall. Actually this is a very rough sketch of one corner of the wall—the whole thing is as long as a football field, and each symbol, well, there are tens of thousands of them."

"Why 'Calendar Wall'?" she asked, squinting at the page. "Moon phases or somethin'?"

"Suns, actually. Every winter solstice the I'iwa have ever seen."

"How many?"

"The Theran civilization on Crete first encountered the Architects seven thousand years ago, am I right, Morag?"

"That's when the earliest Disks date from."

"And the Architects made the best of a bad job by destroying them—or taking them all up to heaven, if you like—in the Thera eruption, which was thirty-six centuries ago—"

"Right."

"And then, as Professor Partridge says, they cleaned up the resulting mess in the Bronze Age Collapse over the following few centuries?"

"Assuming we buy the supernatural stuff," Jimmy said, "what could any of that have to do with some uncontacted tribal people in New Guinea?"

"History. Is. Repeating. Itself," you said. You were quoting Partridge—there was even a hint of his accent.

"Yes, Daniel. History is repeating itself. And you think that's true because what happened at Thera is happening again now. But Thera was already history repeating itself. The I'iwa encountered the Architects too, you see, and had their own period of belief followed by their own period of rebellion. But not seven thousand years ago. Oh no."

"How many?" Lorna repeated. "How many suns?"

"Our history books are missing a zero, Dr. Chen. Not seven thousand. Seventy thousand. And the I'iwa have been in these mountains, carefully hiding themselves and some other remarkable things, for most of that time."

"That's rubbish," Jimmy said. "Humans first migrated to Australia forty or fifty thousand years ago. At the most. And they didn't get to New Guinea until well after that. If you're trying to tell us a small albino tribe has been living up there in a cave for sixty thousand years, you're hallucinating."

Mayo pulled open his shirt again. "I wasn't hallucinating the spear, was I? No more than Iona Maclean was. As for the dates for human migration, you're right. But I can give you a better date: fifty-three thousand, to be exact. And I know that because the I'iwa themselves appear to have recorded the event. You see, the I'iwa were already here by then."

"What *are* you talking about?"

"Call it the Stone Age Collapse, if you like. Maybe Partridge could write a book about it. As many as a dozen different human species were wiped out, as the Architects intended. The Neanderthals were almost wiped out, and they went extinct not much later. The Denisovans likewise. Then there's *Homo floresiensis*—the hobbits."

"The so-called hobbits survived on the island of Flores until ten or twelve thousand years ago," Jimmy said. "Or a lot more recently than that, if you take local legends seriously. The villagers on Flores were talking about the little hairy people who lived in the forest, the *ebu gogo*, until only a century ago."

"I know," Mayo said. "A remnant population of *Homo floresiensis*. They would have been the very last surviving part of a huge, multispecies experiment—the true, original Babel, at which the Architects were trying to cook up just the recipe they needed—"

"So my mother was right," Kit whispered.

"—except that the *ebu gogo* have been upstaged. You see, the I'iwa are very much alive today. Right up there in these mountains. And they're not *Homo sapiens* either."

Chapter 20

Off the Map

As we made for the edge of the clearing, Isbet was still carrying her baby in the *bilum* bag. He was a boy, but he didn't seem to have a name yet. I couldn't believe she was planning to bring him with us on so dangerous an adventure—but what other option did she have? At the edge of the village, I found out: as if by invisible signal, a woman near Oma's age came out of a hut. She was wearing a shapeless, stained cotton dress. Not Isbet's mother—she had died years ago, before we even came to the Tainu. This woman had a lined, tragic face, and barely looked at us. She exchanged a few words with Oma, then unshouldered a bag almost identical to Isbet's. They swapped. The new bag was full of food.

"Dolon ka'unaret," Isbet said as we moved on. It meant *husband-mother*.

The path Oma chose was almost flat, to begin with. Oma and Isbet were at the front, with you an eager pace behind, almost stepping on their heels. Kit and I followed you, a few yards back. Dog didn't have a place in the line; it moved so much faster than the humans that it kept disappearing ahead of Oma, only to show up mysteriously behind you, or by my side, before vanishing into the trees again.

Jimmy and Lorna were behind us—and falling farther behind, with Mayo prodding them along from the back, so Kit and I had a small bubble of privacy. One of the many things on my mind was what she'd said, or not said, about Rosko; about half a dozen times, I opened my mouth to ask her about it then didn't. Instead I made small talk about New Guinea—history, tribes, languages, oh, Kit, look at this cool flower. She put up with it for a while and then flashed me a look that said, *What are you really thinking about?*

"You said you had an argument with Rosko. But not an argument."

"Yes."

I counted our paces while she failed to say anything else: ten, fifteen, twenty.

"And you keep putting off telling me anything else."

"Sorry."

Ten, fifteen, twenty.

"Difficult to know how to say," she said. "But I try. When we are all together, Rosko is easy, yah? Relaxed kind of guy, nice guy, no drama, maybe a little, what do you say, difficult for read?"

"Hard to read. Go on."

"I feel awkward from him before, but is much worse after you leave for Hawaii. I was kind of glad I had to take Daniel back to Seattle. I couldn't make him out. I thought he—"

Ten. Fifteen. Twenty.

"I knew it is something about attraction. Romance. Sex. I think, maybe he is confused. Or maybe even he is attracted to Daniel—but I know that's not right. So, what? He is into me? Like Daniel was—kind of hanging around me like puppy and stupid straight boy so not getting it? But I don't think this either. Then we get back to Seattle, and guess what but Ella is there waiting with too much the cosmetics and tongue hanging out, and poor Rosko not maybe making best choices. He has thing with her."

"That sounds like a terrible idea for both of them."

"Only lasts maybe twenty-four hours, but yah, sure—she is crying in my lap, and angry, and he won't talk. You know I don't maybe like Ella so much, but I say to him, hey, Rosko, you have totally hurt her feelings, what the hell is this?"

"Typical boy," I said. "He doesn't know what he wants, so he gives up trying to work it out and goes for the first available distraction."

"No. Is not that, Majka. He knows exactly what he wants. He gets involved with Ella to try to distract himself from person he wants, because thinking about the person he does want, and can't have, is driving him crazy."

"Who, Kit? I can't think of anyone else he's ever seemed remotely—"

"You know what? Rosko is good-looking I guess, but he says to me, 'I feel that I know what it's like to be a very ugly person. There's only one person I ever felt mentally and emotionally in tune with, only one person I ever really wanted to, you know, *be* with. And that person looks right through me. That person has never even imagined seeing me the way I want to be seen, and never will.' So of course I say, Rosko, you can't know that. And he says, yes, Kit, I can. It's just something I have to accept and put up with."

"Who, Kit? Spit it out."

She stopped in the middle of the path and looked at me with a strange kind of compassion, as if she pitied me for not understanding. Jimmy and Lorna were just a few paces behind us.

"You, Majka. You. He said, 'I dream about her all the time.' Then he started crying. I never saw him cry before. And he can't stop apologizing to me, because he thinks I will be angry."

Lorna stopped because we were standing in the way. "Ye best close yer mouth, or you'll be gettin' mozzie bites on yer tongue," she said.

"What's the big surprise?"

"Oh, nothing."

"Aye, nothin', Morag, sure. Yer jawbone is trailin' in the mud, an' if it's nothin', I'm Joan of Arc. Never mind. None o' my beeswax, aye?"

"Keep moving," Mayo said.

⚠

The first climb came after that. Only a couple of hundred feet, but then we lost fifty, gained another two hundred, lost another hundred. It shouldn't have seemed difficult, but it was midmorning and the humidity was already extraordinary.

"My blood's thinned," Jimmy said at a water stop. "I'd forgotten how exhausting this is."

"After what you go through in Iraq?" Kit said. "Should be resting in hotel, not hiking in wild place."

"We'll be fine, Kit."

Fine? I wasn't confident that they'd survive even the next uphill slope. They'd gone back to Iraq looking fit for forty-five, but their ordeal in the desert had aged them both by decades. Just getting to the Tainu village had left them looking drained, and I felt stupid and guilty for involving them in this. Pure selfishness—I'd wanted to see them and hadn't been prepared to wait any longer. So here they were, sweating their way up a forest trail, and if that wasn't enough guilt for one morning, I was also wasting a lot of energy trying to suppress the idea that I was pissed off with them for slowing us down.

We entered denser vegetation, and the muffled green gloom became suffocating. All of us, except Oma and Isbet, had clothes soaked through with sweat. You, at least, were tireless: skin and bone, maybe, but I could see all that old mountain-man-rugged-dude energy surging back into you, as if you were too intent on the task to be aware of physical discomfort. Meanwhile Oma and Isbet, barefoot and scarcely clothed, didn't have a drop of sweat on their bodies, and they kept walking placidly, never varying their pace, as if no effort was involved. When Oma did stop, it was as if he'd turned to stone: he stood slightly knock-kneed, his toes splayed in the mud, his empty, big-knuckled hands held out at his sides as if weighing something invisible, and the only motion was an almost imperceptible waving of his fingertips, like kelp in a current. Sometimes he'd raise one hand, vaguely indicating a direction. Then Isbet would say a few words to him, words that often didn't make sense to me even though I could translate them: *shallow now; it's darker on the left side; long scratches high up.* Or she'd give a rapid-fire list of five, eight, ten plant names. She was painting word-pictures for him. Most of his replies were a single word, or a grunt, or he'd simply touch her arm. Then he'd pick a direction, grab Isbet by the hand or elbow, and launch himself uphill in some new direction.

Toward the end of the morning, in the worst of the heat, the path narrowed and turned even more steeply uphill. We climbed almost continually for two hours until we were working our way along a scree line at the bottom of a cliff. Out of the corner of my eye, I thought I saw people looking down at us from above; I made the connection just as I heard Kit's sharp intake of breath.

"Dolon te akim, biu!" Isbet said, smiling cheerfully. *Here is my husband, the third one along.* She raised her hand toward the row of seated figures, greeting him. I wondered whether he could offer us any protection.

We dropped a thousand feet to a soup-green river, forded the river, and gained more elevation than we'd lost in an especially brutal path on the other side. In some places we had to pull ourselves up using whatever loose roots or other handholds we could find.

"Uket minai'a bek?" Isbet said at last. *This is where we were before. Remember?*

I recognized the place too. "She's right," I said to Kit. "They had a temporary camp we stayed at, just over there. We're only an hour from the waterfall now."

"Yes," Lorna said. And threw up.

"You all right?"

"Fine, fine. Feelin' dizzy is all."

I wanted to believe her. But the afternoon was worse than the morning by far. More climbing. Clouds of sweat bees. Not a breath of wind. And heat that just kept building and building. She threw up again.

"Emdem. Jaa amt eyam, ipol enatak," Isbet said to me. Which meant, roughly: *Don't worry. Soon the world will rain, and then its coolness will enter us.*

"Kam apa ipol, otala re em," I said. *We will welcome the rain into us.*

Welcome turned out to be optimistic.

The waterfall was spectacular. Part of an underground river system, it unraveled like a bolt of white silk and plunged one hundred feet from a tall slab of limestone to where we stood. The area directly beneath it boiled and growled through a series of pools, but there were shallow areas even I didn't mind standing in, and the falling water was a natural air conditioner. Jimmy, Lorna, and Kit stood near me, knee deep, splashing their faces and enjoying the relief from the heat.

I tried to enjoy the moment. But Mayo was standing dangerously close to the place where the water came down, muttering fiercely to himself, and Oma and Isbet had huddled together by a tree about as far from the water as they could get, looking tense and deep in conversation. I watched them, wondering what they were saying.

Kit plucked my sleeve. "Daniel," she said, and pointed toward the cliff path. You'd already started up it, and were almost halfway to the top. You looked back, hanging on to a small tree, clearly impatient for us to follow.

"Come on," she said. I waved to the others and hurried after her.

By the time we got to the top, you were standing—like a statue on its plinth—in the middle of the rounded rock that Iona had described to us when she returned, pale and frightened, from her solo hike. Even though she'd told us it was strange, there was still something shocking about it. Not just round, but perfectly round; not just smooth, but with a surface as flawless as paper. Maybe three feet across and a foot thick with a subtly tapered edge, it looked like a piece of abstract modern art turned out on a lathe.

"She said the ax was here," Jimmy shouted over the roar of the water, pointing at your feet. But there was no strange gift waiting for us this time. Only a wall of green, with a small opening at the point farthest from the water. Mayo pointed to it.

"This is the way we went," he said. We crawled through what amounted to a tunnel in the vegetation, then left the trees below as we climbed a ridge. It turned into a rill of exposed rock, arcing above the surrounding tree canopy like the back of a dragon. Near the top we passed through a thin cloud layer. Distant ridges came into view.

A whole new level of stillness and awareness seemed to come over Oma then. I'd assumed he was simply finding his way, aiming for a particular place, but there was more to it than that. He was closing in on something. Bending low, he felt for the rocks, and every time he came to a significant outcropping he stopped, crouched, and sniffed.

Isbet could see I was puzzled. *Caves,* she said in Tain'iwa. *Air currents move through them. But the caves near the volcano smell different. Those caves are where the I'iwa live.*

Kit rolled her eyes at me. "This not looking so much the volcano country to me," she said, after I'd translated. I was about to agree with her when you put your hand on my arm.

"There," you said. You were pointing to a spot on the horizon between two peaks. It was maybe five miles away, and another thousand feet above us. "Smoke."

"Is cloud, Daniel," Kit said. "Is just cloud."

But Isbet shook her head. "Tolim eh," she said. *He's right.*

"Not far now, then," Jimmy said. He was talking to Lorna, trying to encourage her, ignoring the absurdity of this alleged volcano, five hundred miles west of where New Guinea's active volcanoes were supposed to be. I could hear her wheezing. We continued, but a few steps later, just before a steep drop-off, you stopped and looked up, a hand held out.

"Rain."

Kit wiped her face with a bandana and looked up at the uninterrupted blue sky. "No, Daniel, I don't think so. Maybe later." But I'd got used to assuming that whatever you said was either true or about to be true. We paused for thirty seconds, feeling the sweat trickle over us, feeling the heat of the air on the insides of our mouths, listening to the electric crackle of the insects. To one side, a small brown stream ran twenty feet below us.

Oma held his face and arms up in a dramatic gesture and muttered, waving a hand. "Trum kel omin," Isbet said to me. *He wants us to hurry.* Oma began to pick his way down ahead of us. He was crouching, using his fingers and toes to feel his way across the fractured surface, like someone reading braille. Dog scampered back and forth between us, as if trying to help or make us move faster. Jimmy and Lorna had taken up a position right ahead of me. She must have put her foot on a loose stone: she slid sideways with a little *ai* of surprise.

"No!" Jimmy cried, and lunged at her. He caught her sleeve, but all that did was pull him off balance too. He spun, fell backward, and hit a finger of rock that ripped the pack from his shoulders. Both of them tumbled toward the stream.

Dog got to them first. Jimmy was lying faceup on the stream bank, motionless. Lorna, thigh deep in mud the color of baby poop, was swearing a blue streak while struggling to extricate herself and get to him. "Och, ye clumsy eejit, Lorna," she was saying to herself. "Why can ye nae luik where yer puttin' yer feck'n feet? Jimmy, are ye a'right? Talk to me, man."

Jimmy was a'right, sort of. His shirt was ripped open, and he had rock rash all over his back; otherwise he was just badly winded. When he recovered, we discovered that Lorna was the bigger problem. She seemed fine, apart from ruined dignity and a grazed arm. But she cried out when we tried to lift her from the muck.

"Knee," she said. "Right feck'n knee."

I bathed away some of the mud and used a knife to cut open the leg of her trousers. There was no visible wound, but she couldn't stand on it.

"Well, this'll sure slow us down," she said.

"It won't slow us down," Mayo said. He'd picked his way down much more slowly and only just arrived on the scene. "We can't afford for it to slow us down. You're not going to make it, so you'll have to go back."

"We'll see about that," she said. Translation: *Start givin' me orders, ye great Aussie git, an' I'll break yer nose.*

It felt odd to agree with Mayo, but he was right. "We don't have much more light," I said. "We'll have to camp here. And your knee isn't the only problem. Jimmy's back is an infection waiting to happen."

Lorna scowled at me. I unpacked the first-aid kit and threw you a tarp to put up. I was cleaning Jimmy's back when you said "Rain" again. Seconds later it began to drizzle. Seconds after that, the drizzle turned into a violent, wind-blown torrent.

It was like having a swimming pool thrown at us. In minutes, my skin went from unpleasantly hot to unpleasantly cold. You followed the lead of Isbet and her father, simply squatting with your backs to a fallen log as if determined to remain motionless however long it lasted. Jimmy and I got a tarp strung up and moved everyone under it. Because nobody could bother to deal with the cooker, Kit and I produced a dinner consisting of chunks of cold Spam knifed onto crackers.

Just as we finished eating, the rain stopped, the wind died, and the mosquitoes showed up in black swarms, impatient for blood. Just as it became fully dark, they went away again—and the rain started again. Dog snuffled around the site—looking for potential dangers or potential leftovers, it was hard to be sure—then came over to lick Spam juice off my fingers. Then it curled up at my feet and immediately started to snore. A long night.

Cold all over. Damp all over. Numb legs and a shoulder aching from where Kit was resting her head on it. Gray light leaking like a pollutant into the blackness. And, out of the corner of my eye, behind the trees, something moving—or was I just imagining it? I had the sense, probably false, that I'd never slept. But I must have dozed off again after that, because I was woken up by the clank of a spoon against a pot, and a sound I'd never heard before: Oma and Isbet, close by, having an argument. At least Jimmy had the cooker working.

"Cold?" he said.

"Freezing."

He handed me a mug of cocoa. I sipped it gratefully and considered pouring it over my head. Kit woke up and took it from me; I saw Jimmy smile.

"How is injuries?" she said.

"Fine."

"Let me look," I said.

"Morag, they're fine. Don't fuss."

"Jimmy," I imitated, "they're probably not fine. And I'm not going to put up with you playing hero just so that you can die of blood poisoning. Show me."

Scabs were forming, but his skin was already bright pink and hot to the touch. "Infected," I said. "You'll have to go back too."

Lorna had woken up. "Jimmy, she's right. Ye got ye'self a right nasty there."

"What about you?" I asked her.

"Just comfy as can be, lyin' here. But I canna walk much an' that's sure. We'll all have to go back down."

Mayo was watching from a log, the gun across his knees. "Morag and I will continue," he said. "We're close enough for me to find the way now. The rest of you can return with Oma and Isbet."

"Forget it," I said. "I came here for Daniel, not for you."

"And I came here for both of them," Kit said.

"Aye," Lorna said, "an' while we're all joinin' the party, let me jus' say I'm no way lettin' you bugger off up there in search of God-knows-what without me, Morag Chen."

"You don't have a choice," I said. "You can't go, and we have to. For Daniel's sake."

"T'iwa," you said. "For everyone."

"I can do it, Mumma. I'm not a child anymore."

"Morag is safe," you said to her, with total conviction.

"What about Isbet and Kit?" I asked you. But you shook your head. You seemed to be saying, *I don't know; my knowledge doesn't go there.*

Isbet stepped between us. *It's decided,* she said in Tain'iwa. *My father will lead your parents back. And I will stay.*

Can he do it? I asked. *Without you to guide him?*

There was an expression in Tain'iwa for doing something the wrong way, or the most difficult way: *walking on your ears.* Isbet used it now: *Now that we've come here,* she said, *he could retrace our path back to the village if he had to walk on his ears.*

"I stay with you," Kit said.

After we'd eaten some rice—with hot sauce squirted on top and the customary sprinkle of bug parts—Jimmy handed me his broken pack. "The usual wilderness stuff. First aid, flashlight, road flares."

"Road flares?"

"I persuaded an angry rhino to get lost with one of those. And there's an avalanche beacon too."

"Oh, *that'll* be useful. So much loose snowpack around here."

"It might be useful. Make sure you're in the open, press the big red button for ten seconds, and it uploads your position to a satellite. You don't have to be in an avalanche to need locating."

"We won't need locating," I said. "We'll be fine. Good luck." You stepped forward and took the pack from me, slipping it on.

As they left, and we were about to lose sight of them in the trees, Lorna turned and looked at me. There wasn't a hint of a smile. "When I spoke to ye on the phone, Morag Chen, I felt entitled to assume that our reunion would last a wee bit longer than thuss. And that it wouldn't end wi' ye disappearin' into a stretch o' unmarked jungle in search o' somethin' that makes the locals mess their undies. Forty-eight hours, gurrl. Not back by then, I'm tellin' ye, we're sendin' in the cavalry."

I didn't want to make her worry more than she was already worrying, so I didn't point out that there would be no cavalry. If anything happened to us in those mountains, and we didn't return, they'd be stuck trying to persuade the other Tainu to come looking. I knew the Tainu. Even with Isbet missing, they wouldn't help us. Oma's dream had changed only his own mind; the rest of them were unsentimental about death and had clear views about their duties to the I'iwa. They'd just look at the ground, mutter about *isula*, which meant "fate," and walk away.

When Jimmy, Lorna, and Oma had gone, Mayo smiled like a mechanic who's just fixed a broken engine. "We'll get along much quicker now," he said. The weather was good again, the terrain easier. And we walked side by side for a while—a fact I managed to use, despite all my anger and instinctive dislike, to get him to answer my most urgent question.

I fell into a whisper; he'd already made it clear that he had a mad idea of us working together, so I thought some conspiratorial info-swapping would appeal to his vanity. Got him to talk about himself. Asked what he thought of this or that issue in cognitive science, gave him an edited version of my conversations with Balakrishnan. I mentioned Iona's name a couple of times too, just to soften him up, then brought up her "thesis" again. As I spoke, I focused my mind on the image of you drawing in the soil that curved line connecting "$\sqrt{1}$" and "$\sqrt{2}$". As if I could will him into saying something.

"I was proud of what Balakrishnan and I were attempting," he said. "At least initially, back when I still thought uploading a mind was more or less a problem of having a big-enough thumb drive. I thought Julius Quinn was just a new-edition holy roller. A second Moses, as Iona said, bringing the Big Message down from the mountain. Easy to make fun of, and I was mildly amused to see that he was, in his confused, religious-mystical way, right about so much! 'Our biology isn't our nature,' he said. Bingo that! 'At the highest level,' he said, 'our biology is a barrier to our nature, because matter is evolving into mind.' Bingo again! I congratulated myself on how much further my understanding had evolved that his."

"But Iona changed that."

"I was making no progress with Route Two. I kept telling Balakrishnan that we only needed a bigger computer, and more money, and a few more years, but privately I'd come to the conclusion that the existing ISOC setup was never going to work. There was something fundamental missing. To capture consciousness in any meaningful way—to liberate consciousness from its prison in the skull, as Quinn might have said—was going to require a technology far more advanced than anything we had. And Iona was the one who made me see two things: how I might find that technology and why it might be curtains for everyone if I failed. You see, her idea was that the Architects weren't necessarily the crazy invention of a half-crazy charismatic and weren't impossible, but that on the contrary, they might be—from a strictly scientific view—*inevitable*."

"And that made your work for ISOC irrelevant? How?"

"She asked a simple question about Route Two. 'OK, David,' she said, 'suppose we buy the whole idea. Suppose some kind of digital immortality really is possible. Maybe it requires better computers than we have, or better mathematics, or something else we've not even thought of yet, but it's almost within reach. Next decade, next century, however long it's going to take, it's out there.' And of course I said, 'It is out there, Iona, I know it is.' 'Fine,' she said. 'So what I don't understand is this. Why assume that we—twenty-first century *Homo sapiens*, an ape living on the third rock out from an average star in an average galaxy in the least fashionable suburbs of the Virgo Supercluster—are the first life in the universe to reach that point? Wouldn't someone out there, or something out there, have learned how to do it first?' And I said, 'What if they had?' 'David,' she said, 'what would the universe look like to us if that were true? How would the universe be if an alien species had already beaten us to the finishing tape and already freed their consciousness from their biology?'"

He stopped and looked at me, as if to see whether I'd got it. Oh, I'd got it, and I was stunned by the simplicity of it.

"If Route Two is possible," I said, "if technological immortality through mind uploading is possible, the best evidence that it's possible won't lie in our existing technology. It'll lie in the existence of the sort of beings who caused us to spend the last five thousand years believing in Route One. So Route One is the best evidence we have that Route Two has already happened. And the Seraphim are worshipping beings who really are immaterial, really are immortal—and were once *creatures*, just like us."

"Iona's thesis," he said. "She didn't know, of course. She just had the imagination to guess, and she was trying to find out whether she was right."

"There's one more thing I don't understand, though. If the Architects are disembodied intelligences—uploaded minds, whatever—why are they a threat to us? Why are they trying to, uh, re-embody? That's what happened at Thera. It's what's kept happening throughout history, if we're to believe the mythology, and it's what we saw at Ararat. Why do they need us?"

"Good question. That's why we're here. You see, these funny little cave people with their unpleasantly sharp spears, they met the Architects at the very beginning, and I think they may have—"

He was interrupted by a short, sharp howl that sounded almost like a human's cry of surprise. Around the next corner, Dog was standing with its tail up, staring into the trees.

"Dota inge?" Isbet said to him. *You smell something?* She hurried forward and put her hand on his head. Next to where he was standing, there was a patch of broken-down grass and vines. It looked as if a heavy bag has been slid sideways off the trail.

"This is near where we were ambushed," Mayo said.

Without hesitating, you walked off the trail into the trees.

CHAPTER 21

TERROR IS THE COLOR OF TEA

Four of them. They were lying in a neat row. The vegetation was so dense that they were easy to miss, even without the hasty screen of branches that had been thrown over them. It was a scene from a weird dream: four sleeping men, all overweight, one with a sapling growing out of his chest. When my eyes adjusted to the gloom, the "sapling" became the shaft of a spear. I also made out a shimmering movement, and that became a clambering, enthusiastic pile of flies.

"Beginning to bloat," Mayo said.

There was silence, broken only by the hum of the insects and the mournful *wauk wauk* of a riflebird. Then—casually, nonchalantly, as if taking a spade out of wet ground—you grabbed the shaft of the spear and pulled. The stone tip didn't want to come out, and you had to use both hands, twisting. There was a sucking sound, and a cup-sized hole appeared, rimmed neatly with a brown-and-white cappuccino froth of maggots.

"Shits," Kit said, holding her hand to her mouth and backing away. "They do this to us also. Maybe we, like, get fuck out of here."

You nodded, but instead of leading the way back to the path, you walked farther in, the spear still in your hand, and pointed with it. Another spear was sticking out of a tree; a fifth body—nearly a skeleton—was pinned there like an insect in a museum display.

"Kurtz," Mayo said. "Must be. You," he said to Kit. "Go back, and take Daniel and the Tainu girl with you. If you stay here, you're only going to get in the way, or get killed, or both. Morag and I don't need guiding now."

She looked at Isbet. Some communication beyond language passed between them.

"How far is cave entrance?" Kit asked.

"Ten minutes."

"We go with you to entrance."

"No," I said.

"Yes. Then at least we know where it is."

⚠

The I'iwa were good hunters, but they hadn't expected Dog.

Moving in silence through the undergrowth at the speed of a sprinter, Dog had spent most of the hike circling us, checking ten times the area we could see. "Is like electron in orbit around us," Kit had said earlier. "Everywhere at once, whoosh!" Sure enough, when we left the bodies behind, the animal vanished again, but minutes later it came up behind us, just in time to howl a warning. I was at the front, with Mayo and his gun right behind me. We turned around to witness a sight that was as strange, in its way, as the Architects themselves.

Three I'iwa were standing in plain sight at the edge of the path we'd beaten through the undergrowth. There were more, maybe a dozen, in a broad arc farther back. And there was no doubt about it: they were like us, but not like us—human, more or less, but oh, so profoundly *narakain*.

The combination of their sameness, and difference, and absolute stillness reminded me of a diorama Bill had dragged us to the American Museum of Natural History Museum in New York. It was the usual evo-junk about how we're "really" Paleolithic creatures, because the savannah-forest margin of a hundred thousand years ago was the scene of our evolution into modern humans. The kind of thing people read about in a science zine, and then stop cooking their food. Idiots.

Sorry.

Anyway, instead of a cave looking out over tundra, with humans wrapped in fur and the inevitable saber-toothed cat, the curators had done a modern street scene: waxwork office types chatting over plastic sandwiches at a fake café table. And the punch line, the big woo-hoo, was that the man in a suit and an open-necked shirt, leaning back with a menu in his hand, and the woman in a skirt and heels, peering at her phone while fiddling with an earring, were Neanderthals. Look how close we are!—that was the message. See how Bob Neander (Marketing) and Betty Thal (Human Resources) need only nice clothes and a haircut to pass for, OK, uglier-than-average *H. sap*.

What I'm saying is it was almost the same with the I'iwa. Their broad faces, deep chests, and muscular arms made me think of wrestlers. Their skin was white, but not that much paler than yours. And their features were regular, pleasing, mostly ordinary. No big brow ridges or missing chins, no nose half the size of the face. But replacing their gray leathery-looking skirts with modern clothes wouldn't have been enough to disguise them. They were totally hairless, for one thing. Androgynous too: you could tell they must be male and female, but you couldn't be sure which was which. And then there were the eyes: not huge, like cartoon-alien huge, but a strange, fiery yellow orange, and just plain *too big*.

The three figures I could clearly see would have looked identical, but each one had a different mark or tattoo in red dye on its chest. One had two parallel lines at an angle, like a tipped equal sign; another had a pizza slice that could have come right off one of the Disks; the third had a vertical line, a horizontal, another vertical, then a small oval at the top, like a stick figure of someone sitting.

The first two held spears. I'd only just taken in the fact that the third one wasn't holding a spear when Kit pulled one from a tree next to her and unhesitatingly waved it back at them, yelling in Russian, *Stay back, little one. Stay back or I make of you nice fat kebab. Understand?*

Her bravado might have been faked, but it was so convincing that at first I thought they were trembling. Hard to describe, but it was as if their bodies kept blurring slightly. Then they became still, and the figure nearest her bobbed its head and made a fluttering motion with one arm. As if receiving an order, the entire group retreated a couple of steps and then began to spread out on either side.

My reaction to what happened next was delayed, distracted, by the thought that was crossing my mind: *Sunil and Vandana. Ildavan. We've been told the I'iwa don't speak—but did I just witness a conversation?*

Kit, on the other hand, saw immediately what was going on: it wasn't her they were interested in, but you.

No way that is happening, guys, she said, still in Russian, and she stepped back quickly so that she was directly in front of you. It was a brave, smart move: they couldn't get to you without attacking her, and they couldn't attack her without endangering you. But you shook your head and stepped around her.

"Don't," you said, stepping back into the opening. Kit was behaving bravely; you, on the other hand, you seemed to know that if you did the right thing, there was no real danger.

"Primitive buggers in some ways," Mayo said under his breath. "But when we get into the caves, you'll see just how misleading that is." He brought the gun up to shoulder height.

"No!" I shouted—and saw one of the I'iwa go down even before I'd registered the noise.

I was convinced in that moment, despite what you'd said, that he'd signed all our death warrants. They outnumbered us at least three to one: Surely they'd just butcher us now? But they didn't attack. The two who were nearest us scooped up the victim by the shoulders, dragged him (or her?) backward, and, as if by magic or evaporation, the whole group blended back into the undergrowth. Mayo loosed off three more shots, aimed at nothing.

"You stupid bastard," I said.

"You stupid, sentimental fool," he replied under his breath. "They have something we absolutely need if any of *our* species is going to survive. Frightening a few dozen of them, or killing all of them for that matter, is a very minor consideration. And, just as the I'iwa will do anything to protect the secret of what makes the Architects tick, I will do anything to get at that secret." He waved his gun at me. "You're going on. And so am I."

Kit looked at the head of the spear, and then at Mayo's head; I could tell she was thinking how well the two of them would fit together. I turned to Isbet, and spoke rapidly with her in Tain'iwa, knowing Mayo couldn't follow it. I was trying to persuade her to take Kit and get out, but she kept looking at Mayo, looking at Kit, and shaking her head.

"Ib delem i'iwa'em," she said. "Keluk andur. Ji'tep awanat, ix'ix em't edaran." *We stay with you until we reach the caves. That way we'll know where the entrance is. And we'll try to stop him somehow.*

She looked at Kit, who nodded as if she'd understood everything. "We come with you," Kit said to me.

"If you get hurt, Yekaterina Cerenkov, I will never forgive myself for getting you involved in this. Do you understand that?"

"I understand perfect, Majka. But what can I do? This guilty-if-I-not-having-protected-you thing, problem with it is it work both ways, yah? You care about another person more than you care about yourself, sure, sometimes this is total pain in the butt. Maybe one day we have chance to get used to it."

I wanted to say something, but not something stolen from a greeting card, so I shut up and just stared at her, as if staring hard enough might make it possible to capture and hold on to the look in her eyes forever.

She touched her hand to my face. "Come on. I smell very strange smell. I think is fake volcano."

She was right that it didn't smell like Ararat. The air around Ararat had smelled of minerals—sulfur and rock: the center of the earth, burning. This was all wood, soil, and animal fat. We picked our way slowly and carefully, scanning every inch of the green leaf-sea that surrounded us. At the top of a rise there was a faint noise in the distance, like a stadium crowd heard from miles away. More rain?

"River," you said.

Oh, just great.

"He's right," Mayo said. "Down here. It's not much more than a stream, though, and there's one of these big beech trees across it. Makes a decent bridge."

Wrong about that.

The river wasn't much—barely a dozen feet across—but it was swollen to maximum capacity, a roaring, powerful, animal thing barely contained within its smooth rock channel. The water was doing twenty knots, and it was the color of builder's tea in a Glasgow café. And the beech tree "bridge" was gone.

"It was right here, I'm certain."

Kit, Isbet, and I stood with our backs to the water, watching. No I'iwa, or none we could see. Mayo hunted for another place to cross. You crouched by the water, looking puzzled, almost as if you could will a bridge into being. But once again I had the sense that you were looking inward, trying to see something that was just outside your mind's grasp.

"Here," Mayo shouted. He'd found another trunk—a small one, slick with moss and moisture. He slung the gun around his neck, grabbed a branch above him, and managed to get a couple of steps out over the water. Dog sat and watched with great interest. I glanced down at the water and tried not to throw up.

"Cross that?" I said. I was talking aloud, to myself. "You have to be absolutely fu—"

"I help you," Kit said, grabbing my hand. "Don't think. Or think only about sky. Nice blue sky, yes, pretty isn't it? I hold your hand, just listen my voice and do what I say. Yes?"

Isbet wasn't focused on helping me: she was focused on getting rid of Mayo, and had sidled to within a few paces of the log's end. She was clearly planning to give it a kick. But when Mayo was about three feet out he slipped anyway. His own weight pushed the trunk sideways. Somehow his flailing arms caught in a vine and he managed to land on our side again as the trunk slumped into the water. One of his legs went in, and it too was tossed sideways by the force of the water, but he flung both arms around a rock and managed to crawl to safety. As he got up, he was looking straight at Isbet. It was obvious what she'd been intending to do.

"The feeling's mutual," he said, getting to his feet and raising the gun. "I should have got rid of you earlier."

Kit and I were standing too far away to do anything, and you were crouched by the water, watching impassively—either not caring what happened, or already knowing the outcome.

I was waiting for the familiar sound of the gun when there was a yellow blur on the ground. The sound I heard next might equally have been the gun going off high over Isbet's head or Mayo's ankle bones snapping like wet sticks as Dog's jaws closed around them.

The I'iwa chose that moment to appear again.

I was running past you—hoping, without much hope, that I'd get the gun before Mayo could use it again. Isbet lunged at him from the opposite direction. Our turn for luck. Just a mite faster, a pace closer, and one of us would have run right through the invisible dotted line, the low parabola, along which the spear was traveling. Instead it thrummed like a hummingbird as it passed through the gap between our heads.

Mayo had bent over double and had his hands around Dog's throat. If he'd been standing, the head of the spear would have caught him in the chest; instead, it entered the top of his left shoulder, in the soft hollow between his collarbone and his shoulder blade. He rose to his full height, bellowing, "Everything! It's everything!"

The shaft of the spear was sticking vertically out of his shoulder, next to his ear, and a dark stain was flooding his shirt lower down. The picture didn't quite make sense at first. Then I saw the spear's tip, poking out in the middle of the stain. It had sliced clear through his shoulder and come out again under his armpit.

That should have been the end for David Maynard Jones. But, like Gilgamesh, he hadn't planned to die, not ever, and he made it very clear that he didn't plan to die now. With his good arm he grabbed me to him. Kit was swinging a punch at him, but he managed to swing the butt of the gun around. It caught her with an audible crack in the side of her head.

I turned and saw her go down. You seemed to know something was wrong, at last, and launched yourself toward us. I heard Isbet cry out— "Oda'xin ga'iwa jam'eyep!" *Kill him, Dog!*—but he lashed out at her; she went down too, and he managed to land a savage kick in Dog's ribs.

He'd had to reach away from me to do that, which gave me some space. I leaned back, allowed my mind to linger for a moment on the thought of him hitting Kit, and, with all the fury I could muster, smashed my head into his chin.

It almost worked.

I was able to wriggle free, sort of, and I moved toward you. But he grabbed me by the hair and pulled me back with such force that I thought my neck would break, turning me round and forcing my face against his.

The scar tissue was like sandpaper against my cheek. "You just don't get it, do you?" he hissed. "Like Bill Calder, you don't get it. This isn't about improving human life. It's about the choice between certain death and eternal life. Eternal life, Morag. Infinite life. What the Seraphim are doing is precisely what the Architects want: it will feed them and make them stronger and stronger. There's no stopping that now, and it means the rest of humanity's toast, defunct. *Homo sapiens* might as well already be extinct. And what does it matter? Every single memory from every single person now living: it's half a trillion years of conscious experience that the Architects will be vacuuming up. What a pity! But it's a drop in the infinite bucket. If Babblers like us can escape—if just one human consciousness can escape and become truly immortal, like them? You do the math."

"I want to fight them, not become one of them."

"Ordinary human beings are finished. The Architects made us what we are so that they could consume us. The end has already begun, and there's nothing you can do for the others. You can only work with me and claim what's yours."

He let go of me long enough to grab the handle of the spear. "Looks bad, this, doesn't it? Superficial tissue damage, though. Muscle and ligaments—easy to repair. If I can just survive the blood loss, and stay alive long enough, we're not going to need tissue anyway."

It might have been halfway believable with a hospital close by. But not here—and anyway, he was wrong about the superficial damage. As I watched him, Lorna's voice came to me, giving a running diagnosis.

Aye, it's true there's a space there, in the shoulder. Spear goes through that gap, an' comes out in the armpit, it's right ugly, an' ye've buggered a

couple o' major muscles, but ye'd survive that, wi' a bit o' luck. T'other hand,
suppose yer out o' luck? Suppose the spear nicks a lung?

Mayo had said himself that he'd used up several lifetimes of luck on
Ararat. Apparently he was all out. The bright red bubble at one corner
of his mouth became a trickle, then a river, then a flood. In the space
of a moment, the look in that one mad eye went from surprise, to rage,
to nothing. A dead man stared at me.

I assumed he'd simply crumple to the ground, but he had one last
act to perform. He went over backward, like a felled tree, but his fingers
didn't let go of me, and the weight of his body kept me moving, turning, overbalancing.

As I fell, I saw in a blur that the I'iwa were standing all around us.
Dozens of them, spears raised, motionless. Each of them had a different
tattoo. I wondered what the tattoos meant.

Mayo crashed backward onto a hummock of rock at the very edge
of the river. I cried out—"No!"—and their expressions changed as they
rushed forward, astonishingly fast, because they had seen what was
about to happen.

His dead hand released me at last. I continued to fall. And it was
already too late.

The water—did I mention this already?—the water in the river,
hurling itself past at an impossible speed, was the color of tea.

With the glaciers in the New Guinea Highlands long gone, you might
expect a river to be warm. Maybe it was warm. But the sensation I
experienced was like lethal cold, or lethal heat—or being electrocuted
by a fire hose. I was in severe, whole-body pain. I couldn't breathe. I
couldn't move a muscle. I was like a silently screaming statue—a helpless Gilgamesh—punched sideways, instantly sucked under, and there
was no way I was ever coming up again.

My back hit the wall of the channel. I was flipped upside down. I was spun sideways, and my head scraped the other wall. I rolled over sideways several times, like a log down a hill. When the currents did spin my face just barely to the surface, it was only for a split second, but I saw sky. I was near the bank, there were overhanging branches, and I tried to reach one, only to find that my arms at my sides were as responsive as wooden oars. I went down again without breathing, and knew my lungs would burst, and knew I was going to die.

I wish I could tell you that at the very end I was thinking of you, of our life together and our life apart, of all the things I'd shared with you and wanted to share with you. But the pure quintessence of terror isn't like that. I was drowning. It was the way of dying I'd always feared the most. I was reduced to wanting only one thing in the world, which was to drown quicker.

I might have got my wish, but the next churn brought me to the surface just in time to be thrust against the opposite bank again. A fallen branch stabbed me in the side of the head and it was like a hot wire being jabbed into my brain: a pain so local and intense that I screamed and took in air.

My hands flung themselves out as if working now entirely on their own, trying to grasp the branch. Way too late: it was already ten yards behind me. But one of my hands closed around a handful of roots instead. The roots stretched and tore, but some of them held against the fierce backward drag of the current and I got the other hand into them too. Because of those roots I was able to look back, and I saw you one last time.

One snapshot. One fragment of consciousness. In that fragment, like a diamond, such a world of detail!

Mayo was lying motionless, with his chest raised up and his arms out, splayed as if crucified. The spear shaft was still poking out of his neck, and an artery must have burst, because the stain spreading into the sunlight around him, already bigger than his body, was bright vermillion, the signature color of a billion oxygen-saturated cells that his muscles and his brain would never get to feed on. Behind him, seen only as vertical flashes of white, were the I'iwa, doing what they seemed to do best—transitioning from visible to invisible as they retreated from the scene. A patch of yellow also disappeared as I saw it, but then it appeared again—Dog, ranging fast along the bank toward me. With its nose an inch from the ground, it was hunting for me, I knew, but it hadn't seen me yet and of course the water would defeat even its brilliant nose. You were a few steps behind, and with the advantage of height you spotted me.

Behind you there was only the endless forest. Isbet had vanished. Kit had vanished too, and I had time, as I hung there in the octopus-grip of the water, to think that I had loved every last thing about her, and that therefore it was a stupid, deep, obvious, and undeniable flaw in the very structure of the universe itself that this was it, that we'd had almost no time together, that she was probably dead, and I was about to die, and we'd never see each other again.

Just as Dog reached me, the roots in my hand gave way and I was swept on, farther and farther downstream. And a bend in the river revealed a wall of rock. And it was the opposite of what we'd seen at the waterfall, because there was a hole in the rock—a toothy, wet, twenty-foot hole like the mouth of a wailing rock star—and the river, instead of flowing out of it, was plunging directly into the mountain.

When the sun went out, there was a noise like insects feeding or a slice of potato frying in oil. I saw one last half-moon of daylight from the mouth of the tunnel. And then, without warning, the all-enclosing water wasn't there anymore. I was falling. And the very last thing I thought was that I would never, never know. And the very last thing I did was scream your name.

"Daniel!"

Epilogue

In the Machine

They had placed her with her hands folded on her chest, on a thick bed of leaves and moss, at the center of an octagonal room. Eight small lamps—bone bowls with long wicks, filled with pools of clear animal fat—glowed from the corners; their yellow light turned her skin the color of honey.

At the sight of her, another memory came back to him, almost undamaged, and clung to him. He was with Iona. No longer quite a child—fourteen, maybe?—and they'd been hiking in green hills somewhere. There were sheep in a field. A steep lane led down into a village. They'd had to climb a low sandstone wall, and when they rounded some old oaks, they found that they were in the far corner of a churchyard. Plain eighteenth-century gravestones and elaborate Victorian ones stood at crazy angles in the grass, the carved angels still there but the words and dates already going down to their inevitable defeat in the battle with time and moss.

The church itself was obviously in regular use, but it was empty just then except for a trapped sparrow panicking among the rafters. They stood together in the aisle, looking up at the choir and cross, and then Iona sat in one of the pews and knelt briefly on a blue embroidered hassock, her chin propped on her hands. It made him uncomfortable, because he didn't know whether she was praying or only trying out the idea of praying. (Later she would say to him, "I'm listening for something, Daniel. I don't know what—I don't even know what kind of what! I'm just listening for something that's out there that we're not noticing. Mathematics and prayer are pretty much the same activities in that respect, as far as I'm concerned.")

He remembered all this now because, in the chancel at the back, they'd found the marble tomb-effigy of an Elizabethan noblewoman, with a brass plaque:

"Anna Hazard, of This Parish. Obiit 1599."

She wore a long dress, a cap, and an elaborately ruffed lace collar. Centuries of dirt and candle soot had darkened the stone until it was the same shade as Morag's skin.

"She looks peaceful, doesn't she?" Iona had said. "As if she's decided death isn't so bad."

At the point where the river had swept her away, allowing the mountain to swallow her, there was no scent for Dog to follow. It was enraged and bewildered by this, for a moment—the loss was like being blinded. But its mind was also not constructed to waste energy on regret; after hesitating for the space of two breaths, it plunged into the trees at right angles to the water, calling with a soft yip-yip for the boy to follow. It wondered if he would understand. Would he persist in some quest of his own, or would he understand that it, with its deep knowledge of the landscape, knew best what to do? Would he have the sense to just follow?

It yipped again, and its heart swelled as it saw him follow. He was slow, but not as slow as some of the others. Dog sensed that this was not a matter of strength but of focus—of the boy knowing what he wanted, and having now an almost-canine capacity to think of nothing but the task ahead.

Once more Dog's nose fell to within an inch of the ground, scanning. Not for her scent, not yet: that wouldn't be here. Her scent was a picture in its mind, a picture as clear and unmistakable as a sunlit snake. But now Dog sought for what the old man had been seeking: the smell of the underworld.

$$\triangle$$

Daniel followed the animal, trusted the animal, but not blindly. He saw, through the mist that hung between the peaks, a glimpse of something thicker and darker that wasn't mist. The smoke again? Dog moved too quickly for him, of course, and often in those first hours, the thought crossed his mind that it might have abandoned him. But every few minutes it came back.

He thought about the scene at the river, and about Isbet and Kit. He also thought about whether he would ever get into the caves and find Morag. That seemed relatively clear. Then he thought about whether they would ever get out again, and what would happen then—that was not clear. But mostly he was able to push these thoughts away, because he knew that what he was doing had to be done; why he knew, or how he knew, didn't matter. He had seen things—*had been given pieces of other people's seeing*: he thought of it that way—and he had to trust the things he'd been given to see, focus on them, and not lose them. Especially now that he could feel his *self* beginning to cohere again.

As he struggled to keep up with Dog, gray parrots cried out as if encouraging him, and giant iridescent butterflies, so blue that they looked like pages torn from the sky, fluttered down through the tree canopy and swam forward through the warm watery air, leading the way. He was bruised, his head ached, and he was thirsty. Small flies kept biting him on the face and neck, and the bites were sharp, with an electrical suddenness like wasp stings. But all his body's discomforts had the feel of something being reported to him. They were like rumors of bad news in a distant country.

Daniel came to a small precipice, and the trees thinned. Stepping forward, he saw that he was on the rim of a large, bowl-shaped depression perhaps half a mile wide and two hundred feet deep. The sides of the bowl were unbroken green forest, and briefly his eyes tricked him into thinking there was a steaming lake in the middle. But the steam on the water was not steam, and the perfect circular blackness at the center of the depression was not water.

He knew at once that he'd been there before, or that some part of his mind (or some part of some mind?) had been there before—and for the first time, right there on the lip of the depression, he was able to grapple briefly with the implications of that thought.

At Ararat he had seen the bright white thing Traditionals liked to call "heaven." The thing Quinn had called "the infinite." He didn't understand it, but he understood enough to know both that it was real—that those who dismissed it were wrong—and that those who believed in it were completely wrong too about what kind of thing it was. Not a *place*, unless that word was just a metaphor to help the mind grasp something ungraspable. And nothing to do with God, or even strictly speaking an afterlife. It was, simply, *everything*. A landscape of unimaginable size built from every thought ever thought, every feeling ever felt, in the present, the past, and the future.

He had seen the future, he thought. Fires. War. Panic. A wide stretch of ocean, covered as far as the eye could see with floating bodies. A tiny Japanese man with a rumpled sweater and round steel glasses, pruning roses in a sunlit garden, who smiled up at him and said, "No, no, Daniel. When I say 'zombie,' I don't mean that kind of thing at all! I'm afraid it's more disturbing than that." A memory of the future, was that really possible? And shouldn't he have known, in that case, about Morag falling into the river?

Iona had said something about this once. "Kurt Gödel," she'd said, showing him an old black-and-white picture that looked like a homeless man. "Mathematician. Crazy as a loon. He and Einstein were big buddies, in their last years. While they were doddering around Princeton one day, discussing time travel, Gödel said, 'If we can travel to other times, then other times aren't times. They're places. In which case time itself, as we understand it, doesn't exist.'"

Dog growled, and Daniel shook his mother's voice from his head, forcing himself to focus on the bizarre scene in front of him.

Volcano.

Something had prompted him to expect it, here in these mountains, but the image he'd attached to the idea was cobbled together from cartoons of volcanoes and old paintings of Vesuvius roaring to life above doomed Pompeiians, and real memories that he hadn't even known were his memories from Ararat. The reality in front of him was nothing like any of these things, and he'd done enough caving to know that this wasn't a real volcano at all. The strange dark *O* in the floor of the little valley was a doline—a hole in the ground that was the vertical entrance to a cave system. Yet there was the thick, pungent gray-white smoke drifting up from it—and something in him kept saying *volcano.*

It was impossible to see down into it. Even with the sun high in the sky, the combination of shadow and smoke obscured whatever was below. And Dog merely sniffed and then ignored it, hurrying around one side of the rim before melting like butter into the forest again. But Daniel knew this meant something, knew this place was the very center of what everything meant, and he was so magnetically drawn to it that he experienced an odd tremor of fear: Might he, if he came too close, throw himself over the edge into the darkness?

Luckily Dog was calling to him, and he knew he must follow, and soon afterward it found another entrance. It had gone far ahead, at least a mile, and hadn't returned. Daniel was anxious again. Then he found it, sitting by a small dark archway, quiet and alert like a fur-coated doorman.

As he stepped toward the archway, he heard his mother again. *Yes. Yes. You're going to be all right now. Just don't give up.*

The sunlight cut through the trees all around him: gold knives on a green velvet cloth. Another of the huge blue butterflies flexed its wings on a branch nearby. Dog looked at him expectantly, its black eyes catching two bright stars of light.

All these things that I see around me are also in me, Daniel thought, feasting his own eyes on the scene. But he was being drawn toward, and needed, whatever was on the other side of the dark cleft in the rock. And he sensed that he would not see any of what was around him—none of the bright colors, and not even the sunlight itself—for a long time.

Δ

The I'iwa knew he was there. A group of them had tracked him all the way, and they let him enter the cave system, the place that was the center of their universe. They weren't worried—on the contrary, they were overjoyed that they'd fended off the threats and that at last he had come to them. But they watched him and didn't help. Even after he had gone into the darkness and had to rely more than ever on the animal's senses, they waited and watched, trying to make his way easier but unwilling to show themselves further until his mind was ready.

They had learned patience the hard way: by waiting. For fifty-seven thousand, one hundred and thirty-three suns, they had waited in these caves. It was a span they had recorded meticulously—and, though the details were less clear before that, their history went back even longer, to the time when their remotest ancestors had lived in the open, always on the move and always about to die, surviving the seemingly boundless time of the Migration.

Seven hundred centuries.

Three thousand generations.

But those were terms from another species, another civilization, and another set of priorities. After the Origin was how they thought of it. In any vocabulary, it was a long time, and all these unimaginable eons, they had kept their own survival secret, kept this place of their survival secret, and kept their skills and their calculations secret—all so that they would be here when the legends said that the tall pale boy and the short dark girl would come.

For sure, there was urgency now, and no time to waste—they knew that the special urgency of *now* was what had carried him here. But they steeled themselves not to interfere. Perhaps he could sense their presence and wondered why they didn't help him—or wondered why they didn't harm him? The legends were silent on that. But they were clear on one thing. Because he had encountered the Architects and been damaged—and because the damage itself had rendered him special—it was necessary for him to find the place for himself. Only then could they discover whether he had brought them what they needed. Only then could they begin to offer the help for which they had spent all the long centuries preparing.

Daniel did sense their presence, dimly, did connect them with the lamps he found burning and the piles of food that were left out for him, but at first he ignored them. The caves and tunnels were what they were: he accepted them as normal. Even after he entered an area of larger galleries and caverns, shaped and smoothed and with all kinds of niches, walls, and stairways, he didn't think it strange at first. He was like a child still: everything was what it was, and his mind offered him nothing to compare it with. But something was shifting, deep inside him. He was beginning to see his own internal picture at last.

It was like watching dawn break over the dark jumbled landscape that, all this time, had been *his own mind*. Instead of merely noticing that certain experiences clung to the tastes, smells, and sights of the I'iwa's subterranean home, he understood that they all clustered around one center. A subject, a *self*. And that this self was a ragged, restitched, but recognizable version of the person he had once been.

A more powerful version too, with more knowledge and more *will*.

"Daniel," he said quietly in one of these spaces.

And then much louder: "Daniel. That is my name, the name I was given by my parents, seventeen years ago when I was born. My name is Daniel Calder."

Finally, with a great struggle, as if heaving a stone up from a deep place of burial, he almost shouted it: "I am Daniel Calder."

The strangeness of the place became clear to him then. He wasn't in a cave system; he was in a cave system that had been turned into an underground city. The phrase itself triggered another memory of his father, who had taken him to Derinkuyu, the underground city in Turkey—a more astounding structure than anything he'd ever seen above ground. It had been carved out of volcanic rock just like this, thirty or thirty-five centuries ago, by people with stone and wood and maybe bronze in their hands, and it was capable of housing thousands. This, the home of the I'iwa, was the same idea, only bigger, older, and more elaborate.

In one of the pools of lamplight, he put down Jimmy's backpack and examined its contents. Space blanket, multi-tool, compass, three energy bars, the ridiculous avalanche beacon, a small flashlight. He wanted to save the flashlight for emergencies, but he turned it on briefly so that he could examine more closely the food they'd left. There were pale roots, like carrots only thinner and longer, that didn't taste of much. There was a spongy green moss, with an intense peppery taste that brought back another memory: making a sandwich at a familiar kitchen counter and completing it by adding chopped arugula. A favorite flavor—but what did *favorite* mean? He had to chase the word around for a moment, like a small animal that wouldn't stay still until cornered, before he could see that it meant *he* had liked the flavor.

He. I. He. Me. My.

In that kitchen, a woman at the table was holding a big mug of tea and a book. *Iona Maclean. My mother.* The idea was still slippery, but it was there.

He couldn't identify the third type of food the I'iwa left. It had a strong smell, somewhere between salami and strong blue cheese, and at first he refused to eat it. Dog ate it with relish. It was the only thing Dog would eat. Daniel discovered soon enough that it tasted good, like beef jerky mixed with fruit.

He never did find out what the roots were, or the moss. But the mystery of the beef jerky was solved in a long, downward-sloping hallway in which the floor, which until now had been increasingly smooth and neat, was carpeted with tiny bones. Each bone had been cleaned meticulously. Not a scrap of flesh remained. Another memory: the smallest bones were like a Victorian toothpick, made from walrus ivory, that his father had once shown him in a museum in England.

A carved oval fissure divided the tunnel from a cave beyond—a genuine cave, this, not shaped and honed like the spaces around it.

The upper half was blocked by a net that had been woven from fine strands of vine, and long black thorns from another plant had been incorporated cleverly into the weave, so that the needle-sharp tips stuck out at all angles. He detached a papery scrap of material from one of the thorns. It felt as fragile as it looked, like charred paper. It was the material out of which the I'iwa had made their skirts.

He took one of the bone lamps and ducked under the net. There was a sound like whispering. The chamber was low, only ten or fifteen feet for the most part, so the rock roof over his head was easily visible. It didn't look like rock, though. It rippled, as if it was coated in a layer of oil or melting rubber.

For a moment he was reminded of the sky above Ararat. But there were no Architects here. He was looking at the I'iwa's source of protein. For who knew how long, they'd been farming here. Farming and eating millions and millions of bats.

The I'iwa had heard Daniel calling his own name, but they attached no special significance to it, having given up spoken language near the very beginning. It had been their way, one way, of protecting themselves from the Architects. Hiding themselves. Camouflaging their very minds from the predatory beings who had come down from the sky and made them what they were, so long ago.

They waited and watched, and, still for a little longer, they waited. Dog began to move faster, whiffling and snorting and looking back to make Daniel hurry, which was hard to do because hurrying made the lamp in his hand flicker. But he tried to hurry because he could tell that Dog had picked something up—that its sensitive nose had discovered, and identified, a one-part-per-billion trace of some organic molecule that didn't belong to the caves, or the bats, or the I'iwa. A molecule that stood out like a sunlit snake in the darkness.

At last, when they had reached the lowest level, Dog began to pant uncontrollably, and at the same time Daniel became fully conscious of being in the I'iwa's presence.

Or: he became fully conscious of *his own being*, in their presence.

When they judged that he was ready, they stepped forward to greet him.

No spears—their hands were empty. The one nearest him had a tattoo that was simply a thick diagonal slash from shoulder to hip. *Stripe*, Daniel thought, and *Stripe* became that I'iwa's name.

Stripe went down on one knee and in a very natural gesture held out the back of his hand. Dog sniffed warily, licked at the pale hand experimentally, and then tossed its muzzle to the left, making a *muh-uuh* noise. Daniel had a hallucinatory sense that it had spoken to him in English: *Here. In here. Come on.* And Dog wasn't mistaken—they had come to the right place. Just a few paces beyond where they had stopped was the octagonal room where Morag lay on her bed of moss like an Elizabethan effigy.

"Morag," he said, kneeling beside her.

One of the I'iwa held a lamp close to her face. In a small current of air, its light flickered over her like the wings of a yellow moth.

"Morag. Can you hear me? Morag? It's Daniel. I'm Daniel. I came to find you."

Or it's not Daniel, he thought. Because the old Daniel Calder, at a moment like this, would have been racked with anguish, seeing her there and not knowing the future. But this Daniel Calder knew, with complete confidence, one more thing he couldn't possibly know.

"Morag. You're going to be OK. Wake up. It's me. You're going to be OK."

She was absolutely still. Even when he stared at her hands, which were folded over her stomach, it was impossible to see any movement. And yet he knew she was alive. He knew she would come back to him.

He sensed that the I'iwa in the room had been looking at her too, almost willing her to wake up, but that their attention had shifted back to him, as if they expected him to perform some specific act. He looked at them, and then back at Morag, puzzled. But then he got it. He leaned back from her makeshift bed, reached into the scuffed and muddied backpack, and brought out the blue binder he'd taken from Rosko.

"Here," he said out loud, because he didn't know how to speak to them yet. "This is for you."

One of the I'iwa took it, closed its eyes as if it was about to faint, and then looked at the others and hurried away.

It was hard for him to know how long she lay there. The I'iwa were meticulous record-keepers, but they were used to thinking either in moments or in eons. They paid a kind of reverend attention to individual experiences, as if whole lifetimes were contained within them, but they also treated years and decades as if they were nothing. In between, the markers of time that humans were so concerned about—hours, days, weeks, and months—seemed to have no meaning for them.

He tried to keep track of the days at first. But, either because it was impossible anyway, or because of the I'iwa's subtle, powerful influence on his mind, he quickly gave up. He thought of those experiments where people volunteer to live in an "apartment" down a mineshaft, with no radio, no light, and no temperature change. It was like that: he knew that his body's natural clock had stopped working. Perhaps he too was sleeping eighteen hours at a time, and then staying awake for forty.

Certainly he and Dog spent whole days by Morag's side, and he slept with Dog curled next to him, on a second heap of moss in the same room—the I'iwa seemed to have guessed that he would want that. But, once he had seen the care and attention with which they nursed her, there were long periods when he and Dog wandered.

He could almost have believed that the two of them were exploring at will, except that they always had a guide. There were things the I'iwa took him to and showed him; there were, he sensed, other things they were not yet prepared to show him. For miles, the galleries went on, and many were decorated with complex groupings of the tattoo symbols. *Decorated*: no, that was the wrong word. They were written, carefully, in precise and dizzyingly long lines. They looked like miles of binary code, or DNA, except that instead of two digits, or four letters, there were dozens of distinct signs, some of them vaguely familiar and some not, in groups of varying length.

Mathematicians, Mayo had said to Morag. The term had made something click in his mind, like a puzzle piece fitting into its place beside something his mother had said to him: *David and his tribe think everything's contained in science. That ultimately everything's contained in physics. Your father's another one. Oh, Daniel, they're so nearly right! But they're also wrong. The quantum world is a world of numbers, not things, and it's numbers that count.*

The little pun—*it's numbers that count*—reminded him painfully of her, of the richness and depth of her personality and her love for him. It was terrible: a panoramic glimpse, as from a mountaintop, of the huge geography of his loss. But he could see that the capacity to experience this emotional pain was a good thing too: the capacity to feel that grief was all a part of his return to himself. And, perhaps only because he was thinking of her, he took it for granted that he was seeing on those walls the record of an unimaginably intricate calculation. The record of an attempt to fight back: of an attempt to break into the minds of the Architects themselves.

But where were these calculations coming from? He kept being puzzled by a nonsensical idea—*the calculations are coming from the volcano itself.* And he sensed, correctly, that the thought was a kind of echo from whatever it was that the I'iwa were not yet ready to show him.

It took time for him to understand that he was not just being shown around as a kindness to pass the time until Morag either recovered or failed to recover. All the walking, all the showing and trying to explain, was part of the reason he'd been brought here. And it was working—it was healing him. The idea was expressed with beautiful simplicity by one of his guides. She (Daniel thought it was *she,* but couldn't say why) took a round, apple-sized rock and broke it. She picked up the neat pieces into which it had split. Laying them in her palm, she indicated first them, then Daniel. Then delicately, as if emphasizing the difficulty and the precision required, she fitted the pieces back together. When she had done so, she held the loose grouping of fragments close to her, as if hugging them, and then took a long inward breath over them, and handed them to him.

This is you, her gestures said. *We are here to cure you. When we have cured you, you will help us.* It wasn't just the context that made him guess this meaning: he'd correctly read her meaning from the gestures, as if she had whispered a full sentence to him. Without thinking, he raised one hand and passed it near his temple, fluttering his thumb as he did so: *I understand.*

How could he understand? Now he saw how: without even suggesting that they were doing so, his guides had been teaching him their language. The old Daniel couldn't hack French; the new Daniel was picking up the strange silent body language of the I'iwa. He wanted to ask, *Who are you?* He wanted to ask, *What happened to you, in the beginning, and what are you doing here among all these symbols? And how am I capable of this?* But he didn't yet know how to ask those questions.

And so the days passed.

They needed to show him the Place of Origin, Stripe told him. But they needed to wait until both of them were ready.

Day after day, he wandered and learned. Day after day, also, he sat by her side, whispering to her about the caves, about her parents and Kit and Rosko, about anything he knew or could half-remember. One day, without opening her eyes, she began to whisper back.

"How long have we been down here?"

He could hardly speak, because he was so relieved to hear her voice at last, but he controlled himself. "A couple of weeks, maybe. A month?"

"You don't know."

"No, I don't."

"But you're back."

"I'm back," he said to her. "I'm with you again. I'm not the same as I was. There are pieces that went missing, and pieces that were added, and I don't understand all of it yet. But I'm back."

"Am I going to live long enough to get to know you again?"

"Yes."

"But Kit's dead. Isn't she?"

"I don't know that."

She fell silent again. He thought she was sleeping.

"What do they mean by 'the Place of Origin,' Daniel?"

"They mean the volcano."

"What do you mean, 'They mean the volcano'?"

"It's still coming into focus. I don't know. I just know it's true."

When at last she recovered enough to stand, and even walk a little, there was a strange role reversal. He knew the I'iwa's body language, and she did not. Also, she was as frail as a person in extreme old age, and spoke very little, in whispers, to save her energy. He had to be at her side constantly. Dog stayed at her side too, looking up, as if planning to catch her if she fell. The I'iwa watched, and nursed her, and waited. Then they told Daniel it was time.

The entrance to the Place of Origin was concealed in plain sight. In a small chamber off an ordinary corridor, there was a pile of large rocks, and behind them a narrow corridor. Stripe entered and signaled for them to follow. Daniel motioned for Dog to go first, then led Morag by the hand. She had little trouble, but it was so narrow that he had to crouch, using his fingertips for balance.

At the end of the tunnel, hundreds of lights flickered against a black background; they might almost have been stars. He had the sense that he was being invited to step out into the blackness, into empty space, and he put out his hands, anxious not to fall. But Stripe was waiting to guide him, and he found himself on a skin-smooth floor of polished stone, with a wall at his back.

The "stars" were lamps. There was also some other source of light from above, because he could make out the surface of the wall. It ran away in a wide arc in both directions, defining a round or oval space the size of a cathedral. It was as if they were nighttime mice, emerging from a hole in the baseboard to step silently into the towering dark emptiness of a room scaled for human beings.

Some of the lamps were in fixtures or niches; others were held by dimly lit moving figures. But immediately in front of them there was a large black nothing—a complete absence of light or detail that didn't make sense. Looking that way, straight ahead, was like opening your eyes under a blindfold.

One of the I'iwa touched Daniel's arm and looked up, drawing his attention to a narrow gallery that had been carved out of the rock about twenty feet above them. It seemed to run all the way around the space in both directions—fifty, a hundred yards perhaps—before curving into or disappearing behind the area of blackness. Above, the walls continued upward into the gloom, arching over them and transforming into a high domed roof.

They went up a narrow staircase that had been carved out of the rock, Daniel holding Morag's arm. At the gallery level, they walked slowly round to the right, stopping frequently for Morag to lean against the rock face and rest. Daniel stayed on the outside in case she stumbled. The gallery was only two or three feet wide and on a subtle incline. By a quarter of the way around, they were fifty feet above the ground.

Now at last he could begin to make sense of what he was seeing. The light was coming from a hole in the top of the cavern, far above them; it was the same circular hole he had mistaken for a lake in the forest, but now he was looking at it from the underside, and sunlight was pouring in through it at an angle. Smoke was pouring upward, from a fire that was burning on the top of the thing that had blocked their view; it rose through the incoming light, graying and veiling it.

The structure was the size of an office building. The sight of it seemed to bring Morag out of her torpor, and she raised her hand, pointing. "Not a volcano. Looks like one, aye, but they always do."

"They?"

"It's a ziggurat, D. The weirdest, most amazing one I've ever seen, but it's a ziggurat all the same. Which is to say, it's a model of a volcano. A memory of a volcano."

Her brain was blessed—cursed, she'd often said to him—with a million lists. *Walking Wikipedia,* Rosko had said, in barely disguised admiration. Ella had made fun of her for it: *Quite the little fact machine, aren't we?* She could have lectured anyone, for an hour or a day, on Djoser, Chogha Zanbil, the Pyramid of the Magician, and all the rest.

"Ziggurats and pyramids are built to wow, aye? Grand monuments in open spaces. The whole point's visibility: impress the yokels, intimidate the foreigners. A slogan in stone, and the message is always the same: 'Look at how powerful we are!' But this? Ship in a bottle, aye? Buried underground. Kept secret. Doesn't make sense to keep a ziggurat secret."

On closer look, though, it did make sense, and the first clue lay in the geometry. There were many stages, each smaller than the one beneath.

No, not "many," Daniel thought: twelve.

And they were circular.

No, octagonal.

No, not octagonal either. They were dodeca—

No.

It was complicated, intricate, magnificent. The lowest and biggest level was a dodecagon: twelve equal sides, twelve equal angles, and the twelve points reached almost all the way to the walls, so that at those points there was only a narrow gap between the ziggurat and the circular cave. The second level was smaller, with eighteen sides. The third was twelve sided again, the next eighteen again, and so on, and each level was turned by a few degrees relative to the one below, so that the whole thing twisted like a corkscrew and the angles never quite overlapped. And each level was taller than the one below, in some ratio he couldn't determine.

The resulting shape was a tower, but also a spiral; motionless, yet spinning; solid, but light. And every surface was covered in dense markings that duplicated the I'iwa tattoos. Daniel hadn't seen all of Morag's ziggurats. But he'd seen the Taj Mahal, and the Sydney Opera House, and Chartres and Wat Arun and the Masjed-e Shah at Isfahan—and this was more beautiful than any of them.

Two I'iwa emerged from the ziggurat itself, on the lowest level. Then three emerged on the second, five on the third, and seven on the fourth. He couldn't see clearly enough to count the groups farther up, but he didn't need to: Morag Chen, Walking Wikipedia, knew the first hundred primes, all the way from two to 541. Another list!

"Thirty-seven on the top level," she said. "That's the twelfth prime. And the total of all those twelve is 197, which is the forty-fifth prime. They're trying to do what Shul-hura imagined doing, and what Archimedes tried to do with the Antikythera Mechanism. Reverse-engineering the Architects! Giving back to ordinary people the power to fight them!"

"I wish Rosko could see this," Daniel said.

"Aye. A computer made out of stone and people. A computer in which the creators of the software become part of the hardware. A computer that's been running for tens of thousands of years, trying to find out how the Architects work."

Stripe motioned for them to follow him farther along the gallery, which sloped down again. At the back of the chamber, a narrow rock bridge arced above the chamber floor, connecting the gallery directly to the ziggurat, or volcano, or computer at its second level. Not daring to look down, Daniel guided Morag across.

The inside of the ziggurat was decorated in a way that seemed even more amazing than the miles of corridors. Instead of large symbols in neat rows, almost every inch of every surface here was covered in a web of interconnected images, paintings the size of fingernails, all bleeding into one another. There were plants and animals. Birds and insects. Landscapes of every kind, many of them clearly local but others with deserts, beaches, oceans, and, repeatedly, the same erupting volcano. Minutely detailed silhouettes of trees, with stars picked out behind them. Some of the more abstract images were maps, Daniel thought. There were individual Tainu too, and groups of Tainu, in equal detail. But most frequent by far were the I'iwa themselves, in tens of thousands of unique images, engaged in every imaginable activity: eating and drinking, and pointing at things, and smelling a leaf or a flower, and making spear tips, and laughing and fighting and peeing and gathering wood and spearing a tree kangaroo and lighting a fire and having sex, and there were even, in a curious act of self-reference that could have been evidence either of humor or of a fanatical desire for completeness or both, I'iwa caught in the very act of painting these images.

"Cave art," he said. But it wasn't like any cave art he knew. He'd seen the world's most famous examples, and these walls made Lascaux, Altamira, and Chauvet look like the interrupted scribblings of children. There was something immense about the scale, the ambition, and the sheer number of images; there was also something fantastically skilled, and orderly, and yet *manic* about the pictures, as if a thousand artists had been told they must keep painting until they'd illustrated everything they'd ever seen, or known, or done; everything they'd ever experienced; and everything they'd ever imagined.

Morag pointed out the image of one particular face. It was an I'iwa sitting on the ground, clutching its jaw in distress. "Toothache?" Daniel said. And he thought, *This is a kind of library. Only not a library of books or texts but of experiences. What was that word Rosko had used?*

Morag might as well have been reading his mind. "Qualia," she said. "The individual units of conscious experience. It's a library of qualia."

They'd been moving up, level by level, inside the ziggurat. Somewhere near the top, they entered a dome-shaped room that seemed to imitate the great space in which it was contained. It had no images, no decorations; in fact there was nothing in it except a model of the ziggurat, ten feet high, in the center. The model looked exact, except that there was no fire burning on top of it; instead, there was something that looked, Daniel thought, like a stone soccer ball.

Several I'iwa were already in the room. Some of them were holding long, burning tapers. Two of the figures in the shadows stepped forward, hand in hand. The one on the right was clearly very old—wrinkled, stoop-shouldered, with bags under the eyes and blotches of purple staining the skin. The one on the left was shorter, whip-slender, and clearly much younger.

Think of us as representing the past and the future, if you like, the old one signed. Daniel thought it was meant as a joke, partly, but he couldn't be sure. *We're here to tell you our story.*

Lamps ringed the room about ten feet up, and they were spaced much closer together than any of the others Daniel and Morag had seen: there were a couple of dozen, only a foot apart, and they had been positioned to flood the top of the model ziggurat with light. Morag and Daniel could see the dark ball at the top now. It was a globe, and it even had a map carved onto it, though it wasn't a modern globe. Most of it appeared to be empty.

There was a stone bench halfway between the entrance and the model ziggurat; Stripe sat on it and gestured for them to join him. For a long time, with Dog sitting alert on the floor between them, Morag and Daniel watched the two I'iwa, the old one and the young one—Daniel trying to keep up with the meaning and whispering a translation as best he could, while Morag's mind, unable for once to connect to the language, rummaged around in its own odd corners, forming and assessing and rejecting hypotheses.

"They're telling us a Babel story," Daniel said. "I can't follow all of it. Many different languages. Many different *kinds*—I think maybe they mean species. And gods, and some sort of punishment for failing to obey. This is seventy thousand years ago. So Mayo was right. They were enslaved, along with—with—"

"Other species, yes," Morag said. "Makes sense. Them and the Neanderthals. And the Denisovans and the Flores hobbits. Others too, I bet. And us, of course. Some of these groups had been in southeast

Asia for a million years, but the first *Homo sapiens* would have been there by then."

"But do we know anything special about seventy thousand years ago?"

"Seventy thousand is the eruption of Mount Toba. A volcano on Sumatra. It was an event thirty, maybe forty times the size of Thera. Screwed the entire planet's climate for a thousand years, and *Homo sapiens* nearly went extinct."

"What about the globe?" he said, pointing.

"It's a map. Southeast Asia. Indonesia, Malaysia, Borneo on the left, and New Guinea joined up to Australia on the right."

"I'm not seeing it."

"That's because it looked this way seventy thousand years ago, when the oceans were a hundred meters lower."

"For me," Daniel said, changing the subject after a pause, "the time since Ararat has been like dreaming. Like being trapped on the other side of a thick glass wall. I could see but not hear, be seen but not make myself heard. I have some catching up to do."

She put her arm through his, leaned against him, and whispered in his ear. "Don't worry," she said. "I'm going to tell you the whole story. Everything you missed, everything you were robbed of, everything that happened at the edge of your understanding when you were present but absent."

The old I'iwa took a taper in her hand. She looked at Daniel, and the signs she made, even though they were made in perfect silence, caused an echo of Iona's voice in the back of his mind: *Stop them. Before it's too late.* Then she stretched upward with her other arm, which trembled with the effort, and touched the tiny flame at the taper's end against the base of the globe.

A thin blue line ran from the flame in both directions around the globe's base. That reminded him of Iona too, because it looked like one of the burners on their gas stove back home.

The ring of sky-colored fire hovered there, flickering, and grew yellow along the top edge. And then there was a sound like an intake of breath, and the whole surface of the globe burst into flames.

It could have been just a symbol or a warning. But Daniel knew it was more than that. It was an insight into the state of things: it was actual knowledge the I'iwa somehow had. Knowledge that the world out there, to which they were about to return, was already burning.

From the Author:
Some Notes on Fact and Fiction

As with the notes for *The Fire Seekers*, I don't recommend you read straight through these. Just browse the headings and dip into whatever sounds interesting. You'll find a more detailed version at my website, www.richardfarr.net.

Fang Lizhi

I'm guessing most readers of this book won't know of Fang Lizhi, a Chinese scientist and activist of great courage who died in 2012. An astrophysicist by trade, he spoke and wrote eloquently on the connections between openness, equality, democracy, and science. "Science begins with doubt" was the first of his five axioms, which attempt to sum up the kind of intellectual environment—respectful of all evidence, skeptical of all authority—that science needs in order to operate effectively. His message, stated briefly, is this: we don't yet know everything there is to know about the world, so science is needed; but this is also true of the human (social, economic, and political) world; therefore, science itself shows us why it's evil for governments to control what their citizens may think and say.

The Chinese Communist Party rewarded Fang Lizhi for this insight in a way that would have been instantly familiar to the guardians of absolute truth (and absolute power over what is to be counted as the truth) in the medieval Catholic Church: prison, "reeducation," and exile.

Of course, the five axioms are about how science *aspires to* work. Fang Lizhi knew very well that it doesn't always live up to its own ideals. Scientists are almost as prone as authoritarian bureaucrats to thinking they know more than they do; see especially the note below on the very word *unscientific*. The great institutional difference between science on the one hand, and both late-medieval Catholicism and China's peculiar brand of pseudocommunism on the other, is that science—usually, eventually—rewards skepticism.

"Become what you are"
The German version, *"Werde, der du bist,"* was a favorite saying of nineteenth-century philosopher Friedrich Nietzsche, who learned it from the Greek poet Pindar. Nietzsche and Pindar are both talking about discovering your real, inner nature and setting that nature free from the social and psychological constraints into which it was born. Both men were highly skeptical of an afterlife, so they'd have been surprised and troubled by the spin being given to the idea here by the leader of the Seraphim: his view is that our true nature will be revealed to us only *in* an afterlife.

Prologue

Bill Calder, the supernatural, and Zeus having a snit

In response to Bill Calder, you could argue that the Greek idea about Zeus and lightning was a perfectly sensible protoscientific theory, until we came along with a better theory that explains what static electricity does inside clouds. In other words, the Zeus theory, which *we* think of as "supernatural," was the only intelligible "natural" option at the time and shows that the Greeks didn't think of Zeus as "supernatural" in our sense—they thought of the gods as a part of the world and interacting with the world. That's probably right, but it doesn't undermine Bill's argument against supernatural explanation.

Let's suppose there are unexplained bumps in the night, and you tell me it's a poltergeist, which you say is "an immaterial or supernatural spirit that can't be explained scientifically." The right response is surely this: either we can make sense of these bumps by doing more scientific or common-sense investigating, or we can't. If we can ("Aha, it was the plumbing all along"), then the evidence that there's a poltergeist vanishes. But if we can't, to say, "See, told you, it was a poltergeist!" is just to dishonestly admit but not admit that as yet we still *have no idea* (repeat: *no* idea) what the cause really is. Evidence for a "poltergeist" would count as evidence only if we could make sense of that term in a way that links it up with the rest of our understanding of the world. ("Tell me more about these polter-thingys. Are they an electromagnetic phenomenon, or not? Do they have mass, or not? Are they ever visible, or not? How do they *work*? And how do you know any of this?") Without good answers to these kinds of questions, the concept is empty, since you've given me no reason not to be *equally* impressed (or unimpressed) by infinitely many alternative theories, like the Well-Hidden Domestic Dragon theory, the Clumsy Dude from Another Dimension theory, and the creepier Undead Wall Insulation theory—to invent and name just three. So instead of saying, "See, told you, it was a poltergeist," you might as well say, "See, told you, it was, um, Something We Don't Know About Yet." And the only response to that is "Precisely. Let's keep investigating."

Notice that some modern believers think God is, as it were, above and beyond the physical—an immaterial creator-spirit who doesn't interact with the world. Others, on the contrary, think that, like Zeus, He makes decisions and then acts on those decisions (by answering your prayer for an easy chem test, drowning Pharaoh's army, etc.). That raises interesting questions about what you commit yourself to when you say that God (or anything, for that matter) is "supernatural." According to Bill's argument, the former doesn't even make sense, because it sounds superficially like a claim about what God's like but really it's a disguised admission that we *cannot* know *anything* about what He's like. On the other hand, the latter seems to have the consequence—weird to most people today, but a commonplace in the eighteenth century—that God's nature is a possible object (even *the* object) of scientific knowledge.

Einstein in delighted free fall

One of the key insights leading Einstein to the general theory of relativity was the equivalence principle, which says that being in a gravitational field is physically indistinguishable from being accelerated at an equivalent rate. A special case of this is that being in *no* gravitational field is indistinguishable from *not* being accelerated. That's free fall, and it's why astronauts say that the transition from the high-g launch phase to the zero-g of orbit is like falling off a cliff.

Khor Virap

Worth looking up (or visiting) for the spectacular location, it's built on the site where Saint Gregory the Illuminator was imprisoned in a pit for thirteen years for trying to convert the Armenians to Christianity.

PART I: AFTERMATH

"Limbo . . . a traffic jam in the afterlife"

Catholic theologians struggled for centuries with the question of what happened to children who died unbaptized. Heaven or hell? Neither seemed to be the right answer, and Limbo, which literally means "border," was conceived of as a place between the two, a sort of celestial no-man's-land where such souls would at least temporarily reside. Vatican theologians more or less abandoned the idea early this century. However, why they *now* think unbaptized souls *don't* go to Limbo seems to me every bit as puzzling as why they previously thought they did. (See the note on futurists, theology, and unicorns.)

"Freshly dead saints in corny baroque paintings"

The florid baroque style in European painting runs from about 1600 to 1725. Morag might be thinking of Sebastiano Ricci's *Apotheosis of Saint Sebastian*, or any of dozens more in the genre. An unexpected "saint" gets a similar treatment more than a century later—though the expression is more constipated than amazed—in John James Barralet's epically unfortunate *The Apotheosis of Washington*.

"Macedonian badass Cleopatra"

Cleopatra VII and her family became perhaps the most famous Egyptians, but they weren't really Egyptian. Like Alexander the Great, they came from Macedonia, on the northern border of Greece—though by Cleopatra's time they'd ruled Egypt for almost three hundred years.

The dynasty was started by Ptolemy I, who had been a general in Alexander's army. In a sense, he and his descendants were even more spectacularly successful than the great conqueror: by taking control of Egypt, they were able to become gods.

"The beast with two backs"

Shakespeare uses this euphemism for sex in *Othello*, but it was invented at least a century earlier. I'm not sure about a gold bed, but it's no fiction that Jules and Cleo were having a very cozy time together; she gave birth to Caesarion—little Caesar—in the summer of the year following his visit.

Caesar and the library

He probably was responsible for a fire at the Library of Alexandria in 48 BCE, but it wasn't devastating: in reality, the institution survived for centuries after that. Alexandria remained a polytheistic city, with many ethnicities and languages and a rich intellectual life, until the middle of the fourth century. In 313, the emperor Constantine may have converted to Christianity. In any case, over the next two decades, until his baptism and death in 337, he made Christianity more and more the semi-official religion of the Roman Empire, with an atmosphere increasingly hostile to the old pagan religions. There was a brief respite for non-Christians after his death, but in 380 the emperor Theodosius I made Christianity the state religion, began to ban pagan rites throughout the empire, passed laws that made it economically difficult and even dangerous to be a non-Christian, and encouraged the destruction of pagan temples. Alexandria's newly monotheist rulers drove out Jews and other non-Christian groups, and—in a startling echo of current policies by radical Sunni Muslims—took it upon themselves to destroy everything pre-Christian in the city, including books, monuments, and even the Serapeum, Alexandria's most magnificent Greek temple. Hatred of the past—and the firm conviction that you're right about everything, and that only the future of your own faith matters—are not new inventions. (See the note "'A recovering fundamentalist'—and what Adam could have learned from Socrates.")

When the great library was finally destroyed or abandoned is unclear, but its contents were probably lost because of piecemeal destruction followed by long neglect, rather than a single great fire. Whatever the exact cause of the loss, during this period most of ancient culture disappeared. You could fill a big lecture hall with the major ancient figures in geography, medicine, history, mathematics, science, drama, poetry, and philosophy from whose writings we have either fragments or nothing. A few examples: Leucippus and Democritus, who invented atomic theory; the mathematician Pythagoras; the philosophers Cleanthes of Assos, Chrysippus, and Zeno of Elea; the great polymath Posidonius of Rhodes, who features in *The Fire Seekers*; the poet Anacreon; and last but not least, the most famous female intellectual of the entire ancient world, the poet Sappho.

The situation in drama sums it up pretty well. Aeschylus, Sophocles, and Menander are famous on the basis of fifteen surviving plays, plus some fragments. But we know from other evidence that between them they wrote over *three hundred* plays. All the rest have vanished. It's like knowing the Harry Potter books from one damaged photocopy of the bits about Hagrid.

Futurists

Morag's dig about futurists and fortune-tellers is probably well deserved, but I've always thought the term has more in common with *theologian*—and *unicorn expert*.

If I claim to know a lot about unicorns, you might reasonably assume this means that I can tell you what shape their horns are supposed to be, which cultures refer to them in their folklore, what magical powers they're alleged to have, and so on. This is perfectly reasonable—and is consistent with the idea that, in another sense, I can't possibly know anything about unicorns, because they're not a possible object of knowledge: they don't exist.

The very idea that there's a legitimate subject called *theology* could be said to trade on a related conflation (or confusion) of two different things the term could mean. The etymology (*theos* = god + *logos* = thought/study/ reasoning) seems clear enough, but it raises the question: Does doing theology result in knowledge *about God*—for example, "Ah: we find, after careful investigation, that He's male, bearded, and eternal; wears an old bedsheet; and kicked Lucifer out of heaven"? Or does it result only in historical knowledge about *what other people have thought they knew about God*—for example: "Martin Luther set off the Protestant Reformation in 1517 by disagreeing with the Catholic Church about their alleged power to influence what He does to souls in purgatory." The second kind of knowledge is unproblematic, or as unproblematic as any kind of historical knowledge can be. But no amount of it shows that the first kind isn't an illusion. And we do at least have reason to worry that the first kind is an illusion, because it's unclear (relative to the ordinary standards we insist on in any other kind of inquiry) what the evidence for that sort of knowledge could possibly be. (See the note about Limbo.)

Similarly, we can ask whether a futurist is (a) someone who charges large sums of money to intellectually naive corporate executives for spouting *opinions* about the future of human technology and society (including, of course, opinions about other futurists' opinions about that future), or (b) someone who actually knows something the rest of us don't know about that future. As with the other two examples, one might worry that (b) is implausible even in principal. (A good starting point for a discussion of this would be the observation that, as a potential object of knowledge, the future shares an important property with unicorns: it doesn't exist.)

In all three cases, if knowledge of type (b) really is illusory, then knowledge of type (a) seems a lot less worth paying for.

"Not even the extent of your own ignorance"

At his trial for impiety in 399 BCE, Socrates shocked the Athenians by claiming, with apparent arrogance, that he was the wisest man in Athens. It must be true, he insisted: no less an authority than the great Oracle at Delphi had said so to his friend Chaerephon! He was puzzled by the oracle's judgment too, he said, so he went about questioning many people who claimed to have some special expertise or knowledge (such as Euthyphro: see the note "'A recovering fundamentalist'—and what Adam could have learned from Socrates"). At last Socrates grasped that the oracle's meaning was simply this: everyone else believed they understood matters that in fact they didn't understand, whereas he, Socrates, *knew how poor and limited his knowledge really was*. (See also the note above on Fang Lizhi, who might equally have said, "Science begins with philosophy, and philosophy begins with doubt.")

But surely, you might say, in most fields there are reliable experts? Yes, Socrates agrees: if you want a box, go to a carpenter; if you want to get across the sea, trust a ship's captain. But we love to think we know more than we do. And, even when we do know a subject well, expertise is paradoxical. In studies Socrates would have loved, Canadian psychologist Philip Tetlock and others have shown that in some areas so-called experts are often systematically *worse* at judging the truth than nonexperts. How is that possible? One reason is "overconfidence bias": amateurs tend to notice when they're wrong and accept that they're wrong, whereas experts have a vested interest in (and are good at) explaining away their past mistakes—and thus persuading even themselves that they were "not really" mistakes.

In short, there are many circumstances in which both "experts" and those who look to them for "enlightenment" can be poor judges of whether what they say is believable.

The Slipher Space Telescope

As a big fat hint to NASA, I've launched this multibillion-dollar fictional planet-hunter in honor of Vesto Slipher, one of the greatest and most inadequately recognized American astronomers. Along with many other achievements, in 1912 he established for the first time the very high relative velocity of the Andromeda Galaxy (then known as the Andromeda Nebula), and thus, along with Henrietta Swan Leavitt and others, paved the way for Edwin Hubble's momentous discovery that the universe is expanding. Hubble was a great man, but he doesn't deserve to be incorrectly credited with both achievements.

Zeta Langley S-8A, and Goldilocks

For how to name an exoplanet—I know you've been dying to find out—see the website of the International Astronomical Union. The conventions are on the messy side, but *Zeta Langley S-8A* can be taken to mean "Slipher discovery 8A, orbiting Zeta Langley," where *Zeta Langley* means the sixth-brightest star, as seen from Earth, in the Langley star cluster.

Like the planet, the Langley star cluster is fictional. Sci-fi nuts may detect here a whisper of a reference to HAL's instructor, as mentioned in the film version of *2001: A Space Odyssey.* ("My instructor was Mr. Langley, and he taught me to sing a song. If you'd like to hear it, I can sing it for you." Oooh, oooh, I love that scene.)

The "Goldilocks Zone" (*not too hot, not too cold, just right*) is the orbital region around a given star in which life as we know it is possible—roughly, the zone within which liquid surface water is possible. Or that's the short version. If you look up "circumstellar habitable zone," you'll find all sorts of stuff explaining why it's far more complicated than that—and then you'll be able to amaze your friends by going on at length about topics like tidal heating, nomad planets, and carbon chauvinism.

Kelvin's basement

William Thomson, 1st Baron Kelvin, got *degrees Kelvin* named after him not because he thought of the idea of absolute zero but because he was the first to accurately calculate its value. But Morag is wrong on the detail: apparently, if you really want to try cryogenic self-storage, the optimal condition for your experiment in time travel is a significantly warmer nitrogen slush.

"Same myths in different forms, over and over"

In *The Fire Seekers*, Bill Calder is struck by the way similar myths emerge in cultures that have had no contact with one another, and in the notes there I mention some interesting cases of other Babel-like myths, or combinations of an Eden / Tree of Knowledge myth with a Babel myth. While writing *Ghosts in the Machine*, I read Sabine Kuegler's memoir about growing up among the Fayu, a tribe in Indonesian West Papua, during the 1980s. Before the Kueglers showed up, the Fayu had had no contact with Western influences such as Christianity, and yet part of their creation myth was the following story. As Kuegler tells the story:

> *There once was a large village with many people who all spoke the same language. These people lived in peace. But one day, a great fire came from the sky, and suddenly there were many languages. Each language was only spoken by one man and one woman, who could communicate only with one another and not with anyone else. So they were spread out over the earth. Among them were a man and a woman named Bisa and Beisa. They spoke in the Fayu language. For days they traveled, trying to find a new home. One day they arrived at the edge of the jungle, and it began to rain. The rain wouldn't stop. Days and weeks it rained and the water kept rising.*

Bisa and Beisa built themselves a canoe and collected many
animals that were trying to escape from the water . . .

Tok Pisin . . . creole

A pidgin is a shared vocabulary that helps users of different languages
communicate. That's how Tok Pisin ("talk pidgin") began in the nineteenth century. But Tok Pisin evolved from a salad of English, German,
Dutch, and Malay words, with bits of Malay grammar, into a full-blown
language of its own, capable of a full range of expression and with a
grammar distinct from any of the parent languages. That's a creole.

A striking feature of Tok Pisin is that it has a very small underlying
vocabulary, and makes up for this with long descriptive expressions.
So for instance *corridor* is *ples wokabaut insait long haus* (literally: place
to walk inside a building), and *embassy* is *haus luluai bilong longwe ples*
(literally: house of a chief from a distant place).

Josef Kurtz

Some readers will suspect, correctly, that I stole the name from Joseph
Conrad's *Heart of Darkness*. Given the novel's central theme—who are
the "savages," really?—it seemed appropriate.

"Upper Paleolithic"

These terms identify (in, unfortunately, a pretty inconsistent and confusing way) different periods of human and prehuman tool use. *Paleolithic*
means "old stone age"—anything from the very beginnings to about
ten thousand years ago. Within that range, Upper Paleolithic is most
recent—from about forty thousand to ten thousand years ago. Stone
tools showing more recent technology than that are either Mesolithic
(from about twenty thousand to five thousand years ago) or Neolithic
(ten thousand to two thousand years ago). The overlaps are partly due
to inconsistency and partly because the relevant technologies developed
at different rates in different regions.

Messier 33

French astronomer Charles Messier was a comet hunter. In the 1750s he began to make a list of annoying objects that were not comets but could easily be mistaken for them; his catalog of "nebulae" ended up listing more than one hundred of the most beautiful objects in the sky.

"A recovering fundamentalist"—and what Adam could have learned from Socrates

In Milton's *Paradise Lost*, Adam asks the archangel Raphael some probing questions about the way God has constructed the universe. He casts the questions as inquiries into astronomy: *Does the earth move or stand still? Why are there so many stars, if all they do is decorate the earth's sky? Why do six of them* (all the known planets, in Milton's time) *wander back and forth among the fixed stars?* But astronomy is really a placeholder for other things; it's Milton's way of expressing, obliquely, the fact that there are deeper questions begging to be asked, none of which Adam quite dares to voice. *How does this whole creation thing work? Who is the mysterious "God" person, really? Where is heaven anyway?* (As Raphael revealingly admits, God has placed heaven an immense distance from the earth partly to ensure His divine privacy.) And you can easily imagine that Adam is itching to ask one more really big one: *Run this by me again, Raph. Can I call you Raph? Great. So take it slow, and tell me again: Why is it that I must obey this "God"?*

Raphael's response to Adam's questions seems indulgent, at first; or, given what's coming, we might say that his tone is greasily flattering. Naturally you are inquisitive, he says, for your divine origin means you've been touched with the intellectual gifts of God Himself! But Raphael quickly turns waspish, and our "first father" ends up getting a sharp slap on the wrist for asking the wrong questions:

> *Sollicit not thy thoughts with matters hid,*
> *Leave them to God above, Him serve and feare . . .*

. . . Heav'n is for thee too high
To know what passes there; be lowlie wise.

"Be lowlie wise": ouch. It carries both the condescending, almost contemptuous meaning "Stay focused on the low, ordinary things that suit your low, ordinary nature" and also a more threatening one: "If you know what's good for you, stop asking questions about what goes on in the executive suite."

Unfortunately, Milton's Adam is all too willing to play his "lowlie" part: after hearing God's messenger put on a display of spectacularly bad reasoning about *why* Adam should be "lowlie wise," he goes all weak at the knees, says he no longer wants to know a thing, and claims to be miraculously "cleerd of doubt." He's grateful, even: total obedience will mean not having "perplexing thoughts" that might "interrupt the sweet of life." He even says, in a toe-curling display of meekness and surrender, "How fully hast thou satisfied me."

It's an embarrassing moment for the human race, and you might wonder how the exchange would have gone if, instead of Adam, Raphael had confronted someone with a better brain and a stiffer spine.

Socrates, for instance?

Wonder no more! Plato, in his dialogue *Euthyphro*, imagines Socrates having just this sort of discussion—though the pompous character with a thing about sticking to the rules is the eponymous Athenian passerby, not an archangel.

As Socrates points out to Euthyphro during a discussion about justice, many people think they should do X and not Y *just because God approves of X and disapproves of Y*. In other words, to know right and wrong, all we need to know is what God commands. That's the position Raphael recommends to Adam.

There's a large problem with this, which Adam really could have raised. *Wait: Aren't we missing a step? Why should I be confident that my understanding of what God approves is what He in fact approves?* But let's leave that aside for a minute. In what has become known as Euthyphro's Dilemma, Socrates argues that there's a deeper problem lurking here, even after we allow ourselves the staggeringly arrogant (and, alas, routine) assumption that we know what God wants. For, Socrates says, to say something is good *just because God approves of it, and for no other reason*, is to say that divine morality is arbitrary.

"So what?" you might reply: "God is God! He can be as arbitrary as He likes! He made the universe. So He gets to make up the rules!"

But, Socrates says, that can't be what you really think. If it were, it would imply that whenever you say "God is good," or "God's judgments are good," or "God is the ultimate good" (which, it seems, everyone does want to do), those judgments must be *mistaken*. Think about it again: if God's judgments are arbitrary, then He just is what He is, and to insist in addition that the way God is "is good," is to say "We judge/believe/accept that God is good." But that implies what we just denied, which is that we can appeal to a standard for what's good that's independent of what God says about it.

Euthyphro's Dilemma leads Socrates to a startling conclusion: even if people *think they think* "X is good just because God approves it," what they must *actually think* is something radically different, namely, "If God approves of X, He does so because He *judges that X is good*." But to say this is to say that God, just like us, appeals to moral reasoning about what's good. And that means goodness is something that must *exist independently of both our judgment and His*.

With this rethinking of moral justification, Socrates opened the door to a powerfully subversive chain of ideas. Part of my exercise of free will is the freedom to base my actions on my own reasoning, including reasoning about what's right and wrong. But that's meaningless unless I can decide whether someone else's alleged justification for controlling or guiding my actions is persuasive or not. And how can I possibly decide whether I should find God's reasoning persuasive (for example, about staying away from the irresistibly yummy-looking fruit on that Tree of

Knowledge) if Wing-Boy is cracking his knuckles and telling me it's naughty and rude and inappropriate to even ask what God's reasons are?

This is important stuff, because arguably our failure to understand Socrates's argument—and our willingness to be bullied by Raphael's—has shaped our entire civilization. The second-century Christian writer Tertullian was trying to mimic the "good," meekly obedient Adam when he wrote that the Gospels contained all truth and that therefore, for the faithful, "curiosity is no longer necessary." This infamous quotation is from *The Prescription of Heretics*, chapter 7. Some Christian commentators say it's misunderstood, so in fairness a fuller version is worth giving:

> Away with those who put forward a Stoic or Platonic or dialectic Christianity. For us, curiosity is no longer necessary after we have known Christ Jesus; nor of search for the Truth after we have known the Gospel. (*Nobis curiositate opus non est post Christum Iesum nec inquisitione post euangelium.*) When we become believers, we have no desire to believe anything else. The first article of our belief is that there is nothing else we ought to believe.

The first sentence might suggest that you can defend Tertullian by arguing that he's not so much saying "Thinking is no longer necessary" as "There's no point going back to *Greek* authors, specifically, and trying to interpret *them*, because everything that matters in *them* is already incorporated into the Gospels." But I don't think this is a plausible way to defend Tertullian, for two reasons.

First: if that is what he's saying, it's hopelessly wrong. The idea that all Greek ethical thought of any value is incorporated into the Gospels may be traditional, and Christians may have been taught for centuries that they ought to believe it, but nobody ought to believe it, because (a) nothing about being a good Christian depends on believing it, and (b) it's unmitigated hogwash.

Second: for reasons that the rest of the passage suggests, it really can't be all Tertullian is saying. He's very clear here that it's not just the wisdom of particular pagan Greeks that we no longer need, but rather the very type of inquiry (call it science, or philosophy, or critical thinking) that they invented.

Why don't we need critical thinking, according to Tertullian? Because the Gospels contain a complete and perfect source of moral truth. And it follows (?) that skeptical questions about the origin and veracity of that truth undermine the ability of the faithful to believe it. And therefore (?) skeptical questions are dangerous and should be condemned as heretical.

This kind of reasoning (a form of which, alas, Saint Augustine shared: see his *Confessions*, chapter 35) is one of history's great intellectual and moral catastrophes. It infected early Christianity, quite unnecessarily, with the guiding principles common to all fundamentalism. Because of Christianity's subsequent success, that fundamentalism went on to shape the viciously anti-pagan, anti-pluralist, anti-intellectual attitudes that dominated so much of the late-Roman and post-Roman world. Its results are illustrated in the fate that, over the next fifteen centuries or so, befell the Library of Alexandria, the entire literary civilization of the Maya (ten thousand codices were destroyed in the 1560s by a single individual, the Spanish bishop Diego de Landa, who thought they were the work of the devil—four of them survive), and a thousand pyres on which it was not mere words that were set alight.

Which brings us back to today's headlines, and to that first large problem, set aside a few paragraphs ago. Fundamentalists think it's arrogant and dangerous to question the will of God. But they are confused. It's arrogant and dangerous *to believe that you already know* the will of God—and no one ever accuses someone of committing the first error without having already committed the second.

"Better rockets?"

Konstantin Tsiolkovsky, born in 1857, was two or three generations ahead of his time: around 1900, he published a large number of papers covering such arcane matters as the minimum velocity needed to reach Earth orbit, how to design multistage rockets and space stations, the use of solid and liquid fuels, and what would be needed for planetary exploration. Unfortunately—so much for all the propaganda we keep hearing about how fast our technology is advancing!—not much has changed in the field of rocketry since Tsiolkovsky invented it. And it's a humbling problem: relative to the scale of interstellar space, never mind intergalactic space, rockets are many thousands of times too expensive, inefficient, and slow to be much use. Exploring the stars is going to require a technology as different from rockets as rockets are from feet.

The Bretz Erratic

The Bretz Erratic doesn't exist, but it seemed like a nice gesture to invent it. J. Harlen Bretz was the brilliant, visionary, stubborn geologist who endured decades of ridicule from his peers for insisting that the amazing geology and topography of Eastern Washington's "channeled scablands" could be explained only by cataclysmic flooding. In an earlier era, no doubt he would have been praised for finding evidence of Noah's flood; instead the experts said his ideas were preposterous—where could all that water have come from?

The answer wasn't the wrath of God, but two-thousand-feet-deep Lake Missoula. Formed repeatedly by giant ice dams during a period roughly fifteen thousand years ago, it emptied every time the ice dams failed. These "Missoula Floods" happened about twenty times, at intervals of about forty years, sending ice-jammed floodwaters, hundreds of feet deep, racing west and south toward the Columbia River Gorge. Boulders embedded in remnants of the ice dams were carried hundreds of miles from the other side of the Bitterroot Range in present-day Idaho and Montana.

Brunhilde

Partridge has named his VW Kombi after Brynhildr, the Valkyrie or warrior goddess of Icelandic legend. She features in various adventures, most famously the *Völsunga Saga*, in which she angers the god Odin. Asked to decide a contest between two kings, she picks the "wrong" man; Odin punishes her by excluding her from Valhalla and making her live as a mortal.

"*Unscientific* is a bully word . . . evidence-free drivel"

Partridge could be thinking of the behaviorist John B. Watson. His immensely influential writings, from 1913 on, persuaded many psychologists and self-styled child development "experts" to be concerned about the alleged danger of too much parental affection. This must have seemed like an interesting hunch, but after so many decades, the shocking truth is still worth emphasizing. First, Watson and his school—while hypocritically vocal about the need for psychology to be rigorously scientific and therefore evidence-driven—had no evidence whatever for a causal connection between affectionate parenting and any particular psychological harm. Second, and more significantly, they seem to have been incapable of even entertaining the intrinsically more plausible "mirror" hypothesis: that if parents were to take such ideas seriously, and change their parenting style as a result of such advice, *this itself* might cause children terrible psychological harm.

Tragically, Watson produced his own body of evidence, treating his own children appallingly, by any normal humane standard. One committed suicide, one repeatedly tried to, and the other two seem to have been consistently unhappy.

Sigmund Freud's follower and rival, Carl Jung, managed to arrive at a similar and similarly baseless and dangerous "scientific theory of parenting" from a different direction. He encouraged parents to worry that close affection would create what Freud had called an "Oedipal attachment" of child to mother. It has been suggested that Jung's advice was partly responsible for the terrible upbringing of Michael Ventris, the ultimate decipherer of the Linear B script, since both his parents were "psychoanalyzed" by Jung, and it seems as though they became even colder and more distant from their son in response to their Swiss guru's "expert" advice.

There are at least three distinct problems with that advice. First: many people have concluded that there's simply "no there there"; on this view, "Oedipal attachment" is like the "black bile" referred to in medieval medical texts, in that it simply doesn't exist. Second: even if it does exist, the people who believe in it have been unable to agree on whether it's a natural and inevitable stage of childhood development or a dangerous perversion of that development. Third: even if it exists, *and* is a dangerous perversion of normal development, there is (at the risk of sounding repetitive) no evidence of any specific causal connections that would justify any advice aimed at improving the situation through a change in parenting style.

If you're in the mood for a big dose of irony, at this point it's worth looking up "refrigerator mother theory," a campaign started in the late 1940s by Leo Kanner and championed endlessly by Bruno Bettelheim, in which mothers of autistic children were assured that their children's problems had all been caused by their parenting *not being warm enough*. This turned out to be another case of bad science—lots of "expert" pronouncement, little or no underlying evidence, a complete unwillingness to take alternative hypotheses seriously, decades of largely unquestioned influence, a vast sea of unnecessary suffering.

For just one more example of psychotherapeutic overreach— allegedly expert, allegedly scientific, and with devastating effects on real families—see *The Myth of Repressed Memory* by Elizabeth Loftus or *The Memory Wars* by Frederick Crews. The "memory wars debate" of the 1990s illustrated particularly well a lamentably common theme in the history of psychiatry: abject failure to distinguish between potentially illuminating *conjectures* (ideas that we have essentially no evidence for yet but that it might one day be possible to confirm or refute) and well-established *theories* (general explanations that we have reason to believe are probably true, because they've survived rigorous testing against all plausible rivals in a context of related theories and bodies of evidence).

The problem with failing to make this distinction is profound. Suppose you inject your patients with a drug after representing it to them as an established method of treatment, when in reality it's a dangerous experiment. This is about the grossest possible violation of medical ethics, short of setting out to murder people. In effect, though, this is what Watson, Jung, Bettelheim, and their many followers were doing to their thousands of victims, all under the phony guise of "my ideas have a scientific basis and yours don't."

Supernova

The ultimate stellar show ought to occur within our galaxy once every few decades, but not one has been observed since Tycho's Star in 1572 and Kepler's Star in 1604; both of these just barely predate the invention of the telescope. Still, if Antares blows, you won't need a telescope: for a few days it will outshine the rest of the Milky Way, and will be visible as a bright dot even during daylight.

PART II: ZONE OF MIRACLES

"Bullshit . . . a philosopher who wrote a whole book about it"

It's true. Harry Frankfurt's *On Bullshit* is a fascinating analysis of what makes liars different from bullshitters. In brief: liars care about steering people away from the truth; bullshitters don't care one way or the other about truth, but only about using cheap rhetoric to sell either themselves or their stuff. So bullshit isn't the opposite of the truth, but a kind of *gilded* truth that's not honest.

Nearly the entire vocabulary of marketing and advertising consists of bullshit in this sense—think of expressions like *all-new, all-natural, farm-fresh, hand-crafted, revolutionary, exclusive, executive, select, luxury, gourmet,* and *artisanal.* Only the most gullible consumer literally believes what these words imply, but we're all happy to engage in a sort of conspiracy of pretending to believe what they imply, because we feel better about spending the money if we're being bullshitted. You could even say that being bullshitted is the service we're paying for. Do you really want them to tell you that your "revolutionary" new phone is—as, I'm sorry to say, it certainly is—pretty much the same as the last model? Or that your "rustic Italian loaf" was baked—as it probably was—from Canadian ingredients in batches of a hundred thousand by Korean robots in New Jersey? Of course not. You'd rather pay for the bullshit. That's why there's so much of it.

Teosinte

Modern corn (maize) shows up as a complete surprise in the archaeological record about nine thousand years ago, as if thrown out of the car window by passing aliens. Where did this bizarre-looking plant come from? In the 1930s, working at Cornell University, George Beadle worked out that it was a domesticated version of teosinte, a grass from the Balsas River in southern Mexico—and it shows up as a surprise because the work of domestication took almost no time at all. Look up a picture of teosinte, and be suitably amazed that its genome is almost identical to that of the fat, juicy bright-yellow botanical freak you just covered in salt and butter.

As the chimp never said to the human, "Isn't it amazing what a big difference small genetic changes can make?"

Breath, nostrils, and the creation of Adam

"And the Lord God formed man of the dust of the ground, and breathed into his nostrils the breath of life; and man became a living soul" (Genesis 2:7).

God's monster and Mary Shelley

Such a story—if I'd made it up, you wouldn't believe it. Hang on to your hat.

In the summer of 1816, the rock star–famous poet Lord Byron was living with his servants and personal physician at Villa Diodati, a grand rented house on Lake Geneva in Switzerland. Six months earlier, his wife, Annabella, had given birth to a daughter and then scandalized England by separating from her husband amid accusations of physical and mental abuse, homosexuality, and incest. (It was probably all true. The last bit was almost certainly true: Byron seems to have been having an affair with his half sister Augusta Leigh, and may have been the father of one of her children.) The publicity was too much even for the flamboyant Lord B, who fled the country in April and never saw mother or baby (or England) again.

Mary Shelley was still Mary Godwin, and still just eighteen years old, when she too fled abroad with her lover, the poet Percy Shelley, who had abandoned his wife, Harriet, and their two children. (He already had two children with Mary. Meanwhile Harriet, back in England, was pregnant with their third, and his—probably, but see below—fifth.)

Mary and Percy went to stay in a house near Byron's. Just to keep things nice and complicated, they were traveling with Mary's stepsister, Claire Claremont, who had been another of Byron's lovers in England—and who, as it turned out, was already pregnant with another of *his* children. She insisted on going to Switzerland with Godwin and Shelley because she wanted to resume her relationship with Byron; he (initially—maybe for about half an hour) insisted he didn't want anything more to do with her.

Lady Caroline Lamb, yet *another* Byron lover from a few years before, had famously described the poet as "mad, bad, and dangerous to know"; this (and his absolute cynicism) comes out especially in the relationship with Claremont. Of being with her again in Geneva he later wrote, "I never loved her nor pretended to love her, but a man is a man, and if a girl of eighteen comes prancing to you at all hours of the night there is but one way. The suite of all this is that she was with *child*, and returned to England to assist in peopling that desolate island."

Claire's daughter Allegra was indeed born in England, but bizarrely enough she was taken by the Shelleys back to Byron, who was by now in Italy. He quickly and rather predictably lost interest in her, and placed her in a convent school, where she died of typhus in 1822. Claire, not unreasonably, more or less accused Byron of murdering her daughter. In a recently discovered memoir, written when she was an old woman, she describes both Byron and Shelley (with whom—take a deep breath— she may *also* have had a child) as "monsters."

But back to 1816. The weather that summer was freakishly cold and gloomy, for reasons the party could not have known—see below. They retreated inside to the fireplace, where they read German ghost stories and Byron suggested that they amuse themselves by writing some of their own. Mary's story became one of the most influential books of the century and perhaps of all time: *Frankenstein; or, The Modern Prometheus.*

Shelley got her subtitle (and the idea of animating dead tissue with electricity) from the philosopher Immanuel Kant's apt description of American genius Benjamin Franklin, in the wake of his experiments with lightning. Both Kant and Shelley were referring to the myth about the Greek Titan who, taking pity on cold and shivering mankind, incurs the wrath of Zeus by bringing celestial fire down to Earth. But she was equally aware of the parallels between her story and the Christian "divine breath" story, as told in Genesis. Victor Frankenstein's "crea-ture" in the story actually finds and reads a copy of Milton's *Paradise*

Lost (lamenting that his fate is even worse than Satan's), and for an epigraph Shelley chose these heartbreaking, plaintive, faintly accusing lines, addressed by Milton's Adam to his creator:

> *Did I request thee, Maker, from my clay*
> *To mould me Man? Did I solicit thee*
> *From darkness to promote me?*

This is the question every child asks, or thinks of asking, when a parent resorts to that phony line "You owe us everything!" In modern English: "I didn't ask to be born. So whose interests were you really serving? Mine, or your own? And if your own, why do I owe you anything?"

For more on Milton's Adam, and the questions he raises (and then meekly drops) about what we should believe, see the note on Socrates and religious fundamentalism. But let's stick with that gloomy summer weather—and how's this for a weird and wonderful connection? The atmospheric conditions that prompted the ghost-story party, and thus *Frankenstein* itself, were caused by the April 1815 eruption of Mount Tambora in the Dutch East Indies (now Indonesia). It was by far the largest eruption in modern history, leaving a crater four miles wide and causing years of global climate disruption, crop failure, and famine. 1816 became known to New Englanders as "the year without a summer": that June, there were blizzards in upstate New York.

As Kit's remarks suggest, the science-fiction riffs on the Frankenstein idea are innumerable. Two of the best are Arthur C. Clarke and Stanley Kubrick's *2001: A Space Odyssey* and Ridley Scott's *Blade Runner* (based on Philip K. Dick's *Do Androids Dream of Electric Sheep?*). Nearly all the writers who have followed in Shelley's footsteps hint at a question she might have expressed this way: "Does the creature move and speak only, or does it have a soul?" In modern terms: "Does it just behave like us? Imitate us? Or is it truly *conscious*?" (For why that distinction is a very big deal, see also the note on Turing. More on this in *The Babel Trilogy, Book Three: Infinity's Illusion*).

By the way, *Frankenstein*'s young inventor was the daughter of radical philosophers William Godwin and Mary Wollstonecraft. After her marriage, she always styled herself Mary Wollstonecraft Shelley, in honor of her remarkable mother, whose own epoch-making book was *A Vindication of the Rights of Woman* (1792).

While we're on the subject of women a century or more ahead of their time, note that the daughter Byron had left behind with his wife in England grew up to be the brilliant mathematician and the world's first "computer programmer," Ada King, Countess of Lovelace (or more popularly, Ada Lovelace). Ada supposedly read her father's work and wasn't impressed, vowing that she would become a better mathematician than he had been a poet. Her achievements were great indeed, but they might easily have disappeared from view if they hadn't become an inspiration to another early programmer, who appreciated their depth and originality—Alan Turing.

Finally, no account of *Frankenstein*'s origins in that amazing summer would be complete without mentioning the fact that the same group, in the same writing session, also invented the modern vampire—and (oh, it's almost too good to be true!) this first vampire was an angry caricature of Lord Byron himself. Byron's "friend" and personal physician at Lake Geneva, John Polidori, had come to hate his employer's success. His own contribution to their ghost story exercise was *The Vampyre*. The main character, Lord Ruthven, is a pale, mysterious London aristocrat with an irresistibly seductive voice; he's bad news, especially for women, and is clearly meant to be Byron.

In a further twist, which horrified and enraged Polidori, a publisher got hold of the manuscript of *The Vampyre* and published it as a new work *by* Byron.

Mary and Percy were married back in England in December. Harriet, his first wife, had killed herself weeks earlier.

"The gray outline of the Institute . . ."

Readers familiar with the University of Washington campus will infer that I had to tear down both Cunningham Hall and Parrington Hall before I could build ISOC. Sorry.

Geist, atman

Geist is German for "spirit"—it's cognate with our *ghost*, from Old English *gast*, "spirit or breath." The Sanskrit for *maha* ("great") and *atman* ("soul, spirit, or consciousness") is where Mohandas "Mahatma" Gandhi got his nickname.

Darwin's *Origin* and changing the question

1859 was the year Darwin published *On the Origin of Species*. Here's how Julian Jaynes glosses that epoch-making event in his own book about origins, *The Origin of Consciousness in the Breakdown of the Bicameral Mind*:

> *Now originally, this search into the nature of consciousness was known as the mind-body problem, heavy with its ponderous philosophical solutions. But since the theory of evolution, it has bared itself into a more scientific question. It has become the problem of the origin of mind, or, more specifically, the origin of consciousness in evolution. Where can this subjective experience which we introspect upon, this constant companion of hosts of associations, hopes, fears, affections, knowledges, colors, smells, thrills, tickles, pleasures, distresses, and desires— where and how in evolution could all this wonderful tapestry of inner experience have evolved? How can we derive this inwardness out of mere matter? And if so, when?*

As the third book of this trilogy will indicate, I think this is partly right and partly wrong. On the one hand, Darwin and evolution make it much harder to see consciousness as all-or-nothing, and we no longer do: we take it for granted that many other organisms are conscious *in some sense*, even if not quite ours. (Dogs and chimps experience hunger and pain, probably also loneliness and anxiety, possibly also joy and grief; they probably don't worry that their children are wasting time, or that God disapproves of them, or that others may say mean things about them after they're dead.) On the other hand, it's misleading to imply that the origin of consciousness is now a purely scientific question. Whether that will turn out to be true depends on what the answer turns out to be, and some philosophers still argue that there's a problem with the very idea that consciousness could be explained by any new scientific finding. When I eat a potato chip, taste receptors on my tongue detect sodium ions and send signals to the brain via specialized neurons, et cetera, et cetera. But the philosopher Gottfried Leibniz had the measure of this three hundred years ago: you can elaborate the physical story as much as you like, get as fine-grained as you like with your description of the mechanism, and still not have an answer to the most basic question of all: Where's the *saltiness*?

Turing among the machines

Alan Turing was born in England in 1912. In the late 1930s, while spending two years in the United States at Princeton, he started to produce original work on logic, the nature of computation, and the concept of an algorithm. He famously spent the Second World War helping to crack German military communications by applying mathematical logic (and some innovative mechanical tinkering) to cryptography in Hut 8, the nerve center of the Government Code and Cypher School at Bletchley Park. Perhaps his most influential work was the paper "Computing Machinery and Intelligence," published in 1950, which essentially created the field of artificial intelligence. It famously begins, "I propose to consider the question, 'Can machines think?'"

In 1952, Turing was arrested for homosexual acts, a criminal offense in the UK at the time. Having been stripped of his security clearance, he was forced to choose between prison and an estrogen treatment "cure"—chemical castration, essentially. He chose to take the drugs, because it would have been impossible to continue his work in prison.

Two years later, he died somewhat mysteriously of cyanide poisoning. Many think this was suicide, brought on by depression over the hormone treatment, but this seems unlikely. He had already completed the treatment some time before his death, was no longer taking estrogen, and was actively engaged in computational work (and experiments involving chemicals that included cyanide).

Since Turing has become something of a cultural icon, it's perhaps unfashionable to say that he has been oversold as the "lonely genius of Bletchley." But many brilliant people worked there—and, contrary to the "cold autistic savant" myth so heavily underlined by the 2014 film *The Imitation Game*, he seems to have been an eccentric but willing (and warmly humorous) collaborator in a giant team effort.

It's even more unfashionable to say that his published ideas on computing and intelligence are anything less than brilliant, but there it is: "Computing Machinery and Intelligence" is a clunky piece of work and surprisingly vague (one is tempted to say confused) on what the "imitation game" or "Turing test" is, how it should be conducted, or what it might be taken to show. (You can get something of the flavor by comparing that famous first sentence, "I propose to consider the question, 'Can machines think?'" with a less famous one that follows soon after: "The original question, 'Can machines think?' I believe to be too meaningless to deserve discussion.")

Fiction tends to make the confusion worse: writers and filmmakers have often been more thrilled by the sound of Turing's idea than by stopping to work out what it really is. So characters in movies and novels tend to throw around the term "Turing test" as if it's a special way of proving that something is conscious—or (a different muddle) as if it's a special way of deciding whether we ought to treat something as if it's conscious.

To see what the Turing test is really about, and what its limitations are, it's useful first to clarify which of two scenarios we're talking about. Are we (as Turing imagined) communicating by text with something that might be a human or might be a machine imitating a human in another room? Or (as per so much science fiction) are we sitting on the couch with a "person" who might be a human or might be a robot/replicant/cyborg/android that's imitating a human? Turing himself raises the "android" version of the story only to dismiss it as a distraction ("We do not wish to penalise the machine for its inability to shine in beauty competitions"). However, given the intervening decades of science fiction, I'll assume it's the "android" scenario we're talking about. In the end it doesn't really matter: as Turing recognized, the point is that these two versions both describe a conversation and a veil (either the wall or the flesh that might be silicon) that stands between me and *knowing what's really going on.*

With that in mind, let me introduce a more important distinction. In one version or understanding of the Turing test, which at first sight seems closer to Turing's intention, the test is designed around the question "Is this entity that I'm interacting with just a machine, built to fool me into thinking it's a human being? Or is it really a human being?" Call this version of the test T1. A different version, which we'll call T2 in honor of a famous cyborg, is designed around a much broader question: "Is the entity just a machine, built to fool me into thinking it has a mind? Or does it really have a mind?"

I think Turing's paper shows clearly that he failed to make this distinction. And the distinction matters, because there may be entities that would fail T1 (showing their nonhumanity all too obviously) but still turn out to have a *mind.* What if your new friend, who seemed ordinary and likeable, suddenly glows purple all over, says "Five out of six of me had a really crummy morning," and then removes the top of her own skull to massage her six-lobed brain? At that point, she fails T1—not because she's a machine, but because she's Zxborp Vood, the ambassador from Sirius Gamma.

What this shows is that "imitation game" is a misleading label for what really interests us. So in what follows I'm going to assume we're talking about T2: not whether the humanoid entity is convincingly human, but whether he/she/it is convincingly *some kind of genuinely conscious intelligence.*

Now, here's the kicker. To say that an entity *fails* T2 is to say that we know it's a mere machine—a simulation of a conscious being rather than the real thing. But then, by a simple point of logic that often gets missed, *passing* T2 means only that *we still don't know, one way or the other.*

That last bit is vital, and people routinely get it wrong, so read it again. OK, don't, but allow me to repeat it in a different way. Failing T2 establishes the absence of consciousness. ("Trickery detected: it's merely a device designed to fool us, and we're not fooled!") But it doesn't follow that *passing* T2 *establishes* consciousness, or even gives us evidence for its probable presence ("trickery ruled out"). Passing T2 only establishes that the question remains open. In the formal language of logic: "A entails B, and A" entails B. But "A entails B, and not-A" entails exactly squat about B.

With that in mind, suppose it's the year 2101, and the latest DomestiBots are so convincingly "human" that your grandchildren really have started to think of their new 9000-series DomestiDave as kind and caring. Or happy. Or depressed. Or tormented by a persistent pain in his left shoulder blade.

(As an aside, I should say that I'm skeptical of the common assumption that even this will happen. Our computers can already be programmed do things that everyone in Turing's day would have counted as impossible for a mere machine—which is to say, *our* computers might well have passed *their* T1. Yet we, having built and spent time with such clever machines, and indeed carried them around in our pockets, aren't even slightly tempted to think of them as conscious. Whence comes the assumption—present in Turing's paper, and now virtually universal in fiction, AI, and popular culture generally—that our grandchildren will be more gullible than we are?)

But OK, just suppose our grandchildren really do find themselves ascribing emotions or intentions to their machines. Remember, remember, remember: that will be a psychological report about them, not about their machines.

The 2015 film *Ex Machina* makes explicit the point I've hinted at here: in the end, Turing's "veil" (wall, disguise) is irrelevant in either form. Ava is a robot who's perfectly capable of passing T2. But her smug inventor, Nathan, already knows that. He wants to find out instead whether his rather feeble-minded employee Caleb will fall for her flirty shtick even when he's allowed to see from the start that she's not a beautiful woman but "just" a machine. "The challenge," Nathan says, "is to show you that she's a robot—and then see if you still feel she has consciousness."

In a way the filmmakers perhaps didn't intend, this awkward line of dialogue exposes the problem at the heart of Turing's idea and any version of the test. For it's an interesting *technological* question whether a "Nathan" will ever be capable of building an "Ava." And, if he does, it'll be an important *psychological* question whether the world's "Calebs" will feel that she truly has (and feel compelled to treat her as if she truly has) emotions and intentions. But the far deeper and more troubling question is an ethical one, and (ironically, given the film's relentless nerdboy sexism) it's a question about Ava, not Caleb. Never mind what the rather clueless Caleb is emotionally inclined to "feel" about her! Leaving that aside, what does it make sense for us, all things considered, to believe she *is*? On that distinction just about everything hangs—and that's why Turing's attitude in his paper, which could be summed up in the phrase "as good as real should be treated as real," is a fascinating idea about computational intelligence but a wholly and disastrously wrong idea when the issue comes to be, say, whether that pain in the left shoulder blade actually *hurts.*

More on this in *The Babel Trilogy, Book Three: Infinity's Illusion.* As my story will ultimately suggest, I believe that in time, we will come to think of Turing's ideas about artificial "thinking machines" and mechanical intelligence as a long blind alley in our understanding of the mind.

Epigenetics, Hominin, et cetera

Genetics is the study of what changes when the genome changes. Epigenetics is the study of inherited changes in the way genes work (or are "expressed") that *don't* depend on changes in the genome. See my note on Jean-Baptiste Lamarck in *The Fire Seekers*; for the full fascinating story, check out Matt Ridley's *Nature via Nurture* or Nessa Carey's *The Epigenetics Revolution.*

If you're confused by *hominid* and *hominin*, welcome to the club. The simple version is this: the great apes (including us) are hominids, and anything in the genus *Homo* (living or extinct, and including us) is a hominin.

The FOXP2 "language gene"

The FOX ("fork-headed box") family of proteins gives its name to the genes that code for it, and FOXP2 is a real protein manufactured by what has been described, misleadingly, as "the language gene."

People are fond of the idea that there's a gene for blue eyes, for anemia, for Tay-Sachs disease, et cetera, as if we're made from a neat stack of children's blocks. In some cases it's like that. But a condition like having bad impulse control, or good eyesight, involves many different genes. And what really makes it complicated is that (see note on epigenetics) we all carry genes that may or may not get switched on. Even environmental factors, like nutrition and radiation, can switch a gene on or off. And that's what FOXP2 does: shaped like a box with a pair of antlers, it's a transcription factor, affecting whether other genes work or not.

The much-studied "KE" family in England is real. About half of them have difficulty understanding sentences where word order is crucial, and show the same tendency to leave off certain initial sounds—for example, saying "able" for "table." A paper published in 2001 identified a mutation in FOXP2 as the culprit.

Babblers share a different mutation on the FOXP2 gene
As far as I know, there's no evidence for a genetic mutation to explain giftedness in languages, and most stories about such giftedness are exaggerated. On the one hand, there are cultures where most people can get by in several languages, and being able to get by in four or five is quite common; on the other hand, there are few people anywhere who maintain full mastery of more than about five languages at any one time.

There's a fascinating tour through the world of hyperpolyglots (actual ones, not Babblers) in Michael Erard's *Babel No More*.

Scanner . . . "this is low resolution, compared with what we can do"
For a sense of how far away this still is, you might take a look at the short video *Neuroscience: Crammed with Connections*, at https://youtu.be/8YM7-Od9Wr8. My own suspicion is that we're way, way, way farther from "complete brain emulation" than even this suggests. (See the note on the Bekenstein bound.)

Language: "a crazy thing that shouldn't exist"
Anyone who knows the literature about "Wallace's Problem," as it's sometimes called, will detect here the influence of linguist Derek Bickerton. See in particular *Adam's Tongue*, in which he argues that, despite misleading similarities, phenomena such as animal warning cries, songs, and gestures have essentially nothing to do with the abstract features underlying human language.

Paradoxically, humans are good at underrating the intellectual, social, and emotional sophistication of other animals—especially when doing so makes it easier to eat them or mistreat them—while being real suckers for the romantic idea that we might one day learn to "talk" to them. Chances are we never will talk to them, because they're just too cognitively distant from us.

One aspect of that distance is particularly telling. Much has been made of the fact that elephants and some other species pass the "mirror recognition test." But nearly all animals, even the most intelligent, fail another superficially easy test. Think how routine it is for humans, even young children, to follow another's pointing hand, and thus demonstrate their ability to make the inference "Ah, she's paying attention to something that she wants me to pay attention to." Human infants start to "get" this when they are as little as nine to fourteen months old. Michael Tomasello, of the Max Planck Institute for Evolutionary Anthropology in Leipzig, has pointed out how striking it is that our closest genetic cousins, the chimpanzees, absolutely never get it. They have many cognitive abilities we once thought they lacked, yet even adult chimps definitively lack this mark of "shared intentionality." That may explain a further critical difference: aside from the exception that some chimps occasionally cooperate to hunt monkeys, nonhuman primates generally lack the human ability to form groups dedicated to cooperating in pursuit of a common goal.

In *The Origin of Consciousness in the Breakdown of the Bicameral Mind*, Julian Jaynes makes a broader point that may be rooted in this cognitive difference. "The emotional lives of men and of other animals are indeed marvelously similar. But . . . the intellectual life of man, his culture and history and religion and science, is different from anything else we know of in the universe. That is fact. It is as if all life evolved to a certain point, and then in ourselves turned at a right angle and simply exploded in a different direction."

The big question is why. For at least a partial answer, check out the TED talk "Why Humans Run the World" (and the book *Sapiens*) by Yuval Noah Harari. For something more technical, specifically on

Wallace's Problem ("How could language ever have evolved?"), see Derek Bickerton's *More Than Nature Needs*.

Oh, but wait: here's a key point on the other side of the cognitive debate. There is at least one species with highly sophisticated "shared intentionality" that routinely does "get" the pointing gesture, perhaps because of its inherently social nature or perhaps because it has spent thousands of years (possibly tens of thousands of years) coevolving with us: *Canis lupus familiaris*, otherwise known as the dog.

For one fascinating possible consequence of that coevolution, see the note "Neanderthals . . . went extinct not much later."

"The Neanderthals had bigger brains than we do"
It's true, just. The later Neanderthals—and their *Homo sapiens* contemporaries, around fifty thousand years ago—were equipped with about 1,500 cc of neuronal oatmeal, on average, whereas we get by on about 1,350 to 1,400 cc. Again, this is on average: the "normal" ranges for the two species are surprisingly large, and overlap—and arguably the differences vanish completely when you take into account body size and other factors.

"We have complete genomes for . . ."
Not yet. We have essentially complete genomes for some Paleolithic *Homo sapiens*, at least one late Neanderthal (a female who died in Croatia approximately forty thousand years ago), and one Denisovan— even though all we have of the entire Denisovan species is a finger bone and a few teeth. (All people of European descent have some Neanderthal DNA; some people of Melanesian, Polynesian, and Australian Aboriginal decent have some Denisovan DNA.) Intriguingly, the Denisovan genome suggests they interbred with *H. sapiens*, *H. neanderthalensis*, and yet another, unidentified human species.

We have nothing yet for the Red Deer Cave people and don't even know for sure that they're a separate species. Some experts have suggested that they were the result of interbreeding between Denisovans and *H. sapiens,* but a recently rediscovered thigh bone, dated to fourteen thousand years old, suggests that the Red Deer Cave people are, like *H. floresiensis* perhaps, a long-surviving remnant of a more primitive population, probably *H. erectus.*

The bit about FOXQ3 is pure invention—a claim that some knowledgeable readers may find hard to believe. I had Natazscha "discover" it in a draft of this chapter that I wrote while reading some of the research on FOXP2 in early 2015. But there really is a gene called FOXO3 (associated with human longevity, no less, and of great interest to the real-world people I make some fun of here as the "Extenders"). I found out about the real FOXO3, quite by chance, more than a year after I'd invented FOXQ3.

The Great Leap Forward

The carving of a woman known as the Venus of Hohle Fels (Venus of the Hollow Rock, discovered in 2008) comes from this period. At forty thousand years old, it's the most ancient representation of a human being currently known.

The Bekenstein bound

Is nature ultimately grainy or smooth? Is it made of indivisible units, or is it smooth and infinitely divisible? This may be the most profound question in science, and it's been debated since at least 500 BCE, when the philosopher Leucippus, and his student Democritus of Abdera, invented the idea that everything was constructed from elementary particles that were *atomos*—indivisible.

The modern "atom," first conceived of by John Dalton around 1803, was supposed to be *atomos*, and then it turned out not to be. But quantum mechanics is a return to Democritus in that it too claims there's a very, very tiny "smallest possible thing"—an indivisible ultimate unit of space itself, the Planck length.

If that size really is an *absolute minimum*, then there's a huge but finite number of ways to arrange the contents of space. Think of a cube-shaped "toy universe" consisting of eight dice, seven of which are red and one of which is yellow; there are only eight possible ways for this universe to be. If quantum mechanics is right about graininess, then any volume of space—including both the whole universe, the visible universe, and the much smaller bit of the universe that has the special honor of being the inside of your head—is subject to the same principle.

Physicist Jacob Bekenstein's interest was in entropy and black holes. But his quantum-based idea—that any region of space contains a finite amount of information—seems to have implications for the debate over consciousness and the physical basis of the mind. If I can create an exact copy of my brain down to the last Planck unit, then everything about that copy will be identical too: *that* brain (that I?) will also dislike loud noise, love the taste of figs, remember falling out of a tree on a summer afternoon in England decades ago, and wish it were smart enough to understand quantum mechanics; it will be me, in fact—or, at least, it will be wholly convinced that it's me.

Notice the very big *if*, way back there at the beginning of that last overpacked sentence. And, if you don't have anything more pressing to do right now, look up "Boltzmann brain."

PART III: AN ALTERNATIVE TO GOD

Linear B

The scripts known as Linear A and Linear B were discovered on Crete at the beginning of the twentieth century, shortly before the Phaistos Disk was found. They're closely related syllabaries—which is to say, they're physically similar, and, as in much of Egyptian hieroglyphic script, each symbol represents one syllable. But think of English and

Finnish: despite the visual similarity, which makes it clear the *scripts* are related, Linear A and B encode two entirely unrelated languages.

Linear A is believed to be the written form of a pre-Greek indigenous Cretan language, but any other knowledge of it is lost. It was used only for a relatively short time, between about 1750 BCE and 1450 BCE, and apparently only for routine bureaucratic purposes, which suggests that we see in it the first emergence of a writing system—a way of keeping lists, for instance—in an otherwise preliterate culture.

Linear B was used for several centuries, beginning just before the end of the Linear A period. Finally cracked in 1952, it should really be called "Mycenaean Linear B," because what it encodes is not a Cretan language but the earliest written form of Greek.

The Mycenaean Greeks (from the Peloponnese, the big peninsula in southern Greece) brought their language across the Mediterranean to Crete when they invaded the island around 1550 BCE, in the wake of the Thera eruption. Presumably they also had no writing at that time and adapted the recently invented local system, Linear A, as a vehicle for their own language.

Centuries later, after the fall of Mycenaean influence during the Bronze Age Collapse, Greeks adopted from the Phoenicians the completely different alphabetical writing system (alpha, beta . . .) we're familiar with.

The whole story of how the truth about Linear B was recovered, mainly by Alice Kober and Michael Ventris, is told brilliantly by Margalit Fox in *The Riddle of the Labyrinth*.

"Kraist . . . someone he's never even met"

I cribbed the Tainu's response to Kurtz from a real tribe in the Brazilian Amazon, the Pirahã (pronounced PIR-aha). I admit that, being inclined to atheism, I find it an initially plausible and tempting response—but on second thoughts it's far from persuasive.

Linguist and former missionary Dan Everett has lived among the Pirahã for decades. He says that he lost his Christian faith partly because he found their skepticism about his own beliefs compelling. ("Wait—you've been going on and on about Jesus, and you want us to believe all this stuff about him, and yet now you admit that you never even *met* the guy?")

For Everett's own account, search "Daniel Everett losing religion" on YouTube, or read the last sections of his fascinating and moving book about his fieldwork, *Don't Sleep, There Are Snakes*. But, before you walk away with the idea that the Pirahã have a knockdown argument for the silliness of religious belief, consider an obvious response. Wouldn't their reasons for being skeptical about Everett's Jesus *also* force them to be skeptical about my claiming to know that Henry VIII had six wives, or that Abraham Lincoln was once president of the United States? And yet, in any sane view of what knowledge is, I do know these things. As Everett himself attests, the Pirahã have no records of their own past, and thus little sense of history. So maybe they were right not to believe what Everett said about Jesus or maybe they weren't, but the mere fact that Everett hadn't walked with him by the Sea of Galilee seems to be a poor basis for that skepticism.

Smoked ancestors

This is (or was) true of the Angu (or Anga) people, who live in the Morobe Highlands of far western Papua New Guinea. The practice has been frowned upon by missionaries, who have attempted to ban it. For some vitriolic commentary on the damage that banning traditional burial rites does to indigenous people, see Norman Lewis, *The Missionaries*. By the way, Lewis's revulsion at the influence missionaries were having on indigenous people led to the creation of the organization Survival International.

Ghostly ancestors and first contact

The last truly uncontacted New Guineans were Highlanders who encountered early Australian prospectors in the 1930s. They had been cut off from the outside world for millennia, and had invented farming at roughly the same time as it arose in Mesopotamia.

There are remarkable photos and film clips online of what happened when these dark-skinned Melanesians first encountered bizarre white-skinned beings with knee socks and rifles—particularly from Dan Leahy's first expeditions. The appearance of the Caucasians was terrifying, partly because pale skin fit right into their existing stories: many of them believed that the dead retained their bodies but that their skin turned white. One historic (and disturbing) clip shows Leahy shooting a tethered pig to convince the villagers of his power; see http://aso.gov.au/titles/documentaries/first-contact. In her book about New Guinea, *Four Corners*, travel writer Kira Salak describes seeing this clip:

> "It is like the fall of Eden in that moment, recorded for posterity on grainy black and white. When I first saw it, I was riveted. It is actually possible to sit down and watch on a television screen an abbreviated version of foreign encroachment and destruction, a chilling glimpse of what has happened to nearly every native group "discovered" in the world. It is almost as if I were watching the arrival of Judgment Day. Thirty years later in the western half of New Guinea, the Indonesians would already have their foothold and begin the massive deforestation and genocide of the tribes. Thirty years from beginning to the arrival of the end."

For more on Indonesia and "the arrival of the end," see the note "Giant mines (and a short polemic on the relationship between wealth, government, colonialism, racism, and terrorism)."

"Paint their bodies with clay . . . a tribe near Goroka does that"
Morag's referring to the "Asaro mudmen." It's the masks that are really wild—look them up!

"Homer was a blind storyteller . . ."
There are many legends about Homer, but we know virtually nothing about him for sure. He may or may not have been blind, and may or may not have been illiterate; he probably lived on the coast of Asia Minor (modern Turkey) around 750 BCE, or up to a couple of centuries earlier. But it's also possible that he's just a legend, and that the great epics under his name were the work of many people.

"Five miles high on peyote"
Peyote, a cactus native to Mexico, contains powerful psychoactive alkaloids, including mescaline. The spiritual significance of their effects is nicely captured in the descriptive noun *entheogen*, which was invented for these substances in the 1970s to replace the earlier *hallucinogen* and *psychedelic*. *Entheogenic* literally means "producing a sense of the divine."

Nuxalk, and what Raven did
The Pacific Northwest is one of the world's five top hot spots for language extinction, with over two hundred critically endangered languages, including Nuxalk, Kutenai, Klallam, Yakama, Snohomish, Spokane, Quileute, Siletz Dee-ni, and Straits Salish. (The other four major hot spots are Central and South America; Northern Australia, especially the Cape York Peninsula; the American Southwest; and East Siberia.) Nuxalk is spoken only in one village at the mouth of the Bella Coola River in British Columbia. Its strange phonemes, and its distaste for vowels, make it especially difficult for anyone who starts out with a European language. You can hear it spoken here: https://www.youtube.com/watch?v=Jkk-8Ti057U.

Here I have altered slightly the version of the Raven story I found at firstvoices.com—a great site for learning about Native American language and culture.

Physicists . . . three big theories . . . junk

The attempt to reconcile general relativity and quantum mechanics into a coherent theory of quantum gravity has already sucked up many whole careers with no end in sight; string theory, which many thought would elegantly solve the impasse, can't offer any testable predictions at all, according to its critics, and seems to come in up to 10^{500} equally plausible versions, which is a few too many.

"A thousand years of human habitation"

Scientists disagree about when Polynesians from the southwest first arrived in the Hawaiian Islands; around 1000 CE is probable.

Gilgamesh and the lion

To see the original, search "Louvre Gilgamesh."

"A trapdoor function . . . even our best computers will gag on it"

Modern cryptography (and therefore the entire Internet, the world banking system, and a whole lot else) depends on trapdoor functions, mathematical operations that are intrinsically harder to compute in one direction than another. Even simple addition is a sort of trapdoor function: you can solve "$123 + 789 = x$" quicker than "$123 + x = 912$." But some functions are (or they become, when the numbers are large) *much much much* harder one way than the other.

The key example is prime factors. "What's 13×17?" is easy: 221. But "Here's a number, 221; what are its two prime factors?" is significantly harder. What if, instead of two-digit primes, I start with a pair of *two-hundred-digit* primes? Your computer can still multiply them together in a flash. But the reverse process, finding the primes with nothing but the result to go on, isn't merely more difficult: it's practically impossible, even with all the computing power in the world.

This fact makes it possible to use systems in which you publish a "public key" that anyone can use to encode a message to you; only you own, and never need to transmit, the "private key" capable of decoding those messages.

The idea of public keys based on trapdoor functions was the biggest advance in cryptography since hiding things under rocks, and goes back to publications by Whitfield Diffie and Martin Hellman in 1976.

Archimedes

See my note on him in *The Fire Seekers*. The newest research makes a good case that the Antikythera Mechanism was manufactured in about 205 BCE, which makes it slightly too recent for Archimedes—he had his terminal encounter with a Roman soldier during the sacking of Syracuse in 211 BCE—but it could have been based on his design.

Socrates and knowing how ignorant you are

The point was also made by the great Chinese sage Lao-tzu, or Laozi. Speaking of ignorance, I've always thought it fascinating that Socrates and Lao had so many things in common, and were near contemporaries, but had no idea that each other's entire civilizations existed.

The Voynich Manuscript

The Voynich is easily the oddest and most beautiful of all the great "mystery" texts, in my opinion—take a look at the many pages reproduced online. It is, contrary to my fictional history, still in the Beinecke Library at Yale. "Solutions" to the mystery are legion; good luck.

"Let there be light": What's involved in creating a universe?

If you don't know it, listen to the first part of Joseph Haydn's oratorio *Die Schöpfung* (*The Creation*), with the volume turned way, way up. The

C-major chord on the word *light* is a real spine tingler. In the English version, the crucial words are "And God said, 'Let there be light,' and there was light"—which suggests to me a chain of three events: He decided that light would be a good idea, He reached for the switch, and the light came on as a result of His action. The German text seems to do a better job of hinting at a less ordinary, more appropriate idea. *"Und Gott sprach: 'Es werde Licht!' Und es ward Licht"*: literally, "And God said it would be light—and *that was the light.*" On this view, more broadly, God doesn't cause the universe to exist, because His idea of the universe *is* the universe. So we exist in the mind of God. (I'm grateful to Henry Newell for introducing me to both the oratorio and this insight about the text many years ago.)

See the note on Hegel—and, if you're interested in a grand intellectual detour, look up "the simulation argument," a more recent and perhaps rather creepier take on the idea that we, and the universe, might be nothing more that someone else's idea.

Religion, immortality, and equating consciousness with the soul that survives death

Balakrishnan is giving a very simplified view here, and one that sounds much more like Christianity (or perhaps Islam) than religion in general. The Greeks seem to have a very ambivalent view of whether or in what sense the dead survive; so does Judaism; Buddhism and Hinduism perhaps even more so, since they think of survival after death in term of reincarnation—and they think of reincarnation as something to be escaped.

Einstein . . . "the theory has to be right"

Though Einstein's two great theories were published in 1905 and 1915, it was in 1919 that he became world famous. That was when Arthur Eddington used a total solar eclipse to show that the sun's gravity "bends" starlight just as general relativity predicts. Einstein joked that

it would have been a pity if the experiment had gone the other way—
not because that would have disproved his theory, but because it was
"correct anyway." That's not arrogance; it expresses the perfectly sound
idea that even a new theory needs more than one contrary "fact" to
defeat it, especially if it's profoundly convincing in other ways. Science
works through a balance of evidence about what to believe overall, and
theories guide what it makes sense to believe just as much as facts do.

Descartes's ghost

The great French mathematician and philosopher René Descartes outlined his version of mind-body dualism in *The Passions of the Soul*, 1649.
According to his view (or, arguably, an unfair simplification of it), the
body is analogous to a mechanical device—a robot, we might say—controlled or piloted by an immaterial and immortal substance that resides
within it. Descartes believed the world was made up of two fundamentally different kinds of stuff, matter and thought. (Or three, really:
matter, thought, and God.) Matter is *res extensa*—"extended stuff," or,
literally, stuff that takes up space. Thinking stuff, *res cogitans*, has no
extension in space. But we human beings are uniquely dual: physical
objects that think.

The big problem for dualism—closely related to Bill Calder's skepticism about the very idea of "the supernatural"—seems to be this: How
can we make sense of the idea that the mind/soul and matter interact?
There has never been a good answer to that question, and in *The Concept
of Mind* (published exactly three centuries after *The Passions of the Soul*,
in 1949), English philosopher Gilbert Ryle dismissed "Cartesian dualism" as the "ghost in the machine" theory.

Ryle's work ushered in an era in which few philosophers took dualism seriously; instead, various forms of physicalism or naturalism or
materialism, which might collectively be called "all machine, no ghost"
theories, reigned supreme. They still do, despite the fact that purely
materialist theories are also beset by deep problems. In particular: If

matter is all there is, as Bill Calder and Mayo both think, how can we make sense of the idea that mind or soul or consciousness (the reality of which we experience directly every moment of our waking lives) even exists? The question has driven some philosophers, such as Daniel Dennett, to propose in all seriousness the apparently self-contradictory "eliminative materialist" doctrine that consciousness itself is an illusion. By way of illustrating how deep the trouble is, another philosopher, Galen Strawson, has memorably described this as "the silliest view that anyone has held in the whole history of humanity."

See also the note on Turing, and on "Our biology is a barrier to our nature, because matter is evolving into mind."

Of course, there may be another option. Patience, grasshopper.

Haole . . . buried him at sea

The word *haole* implies pale-skinned, and it's now used in the sense of a white person from the mainland, but that's not what it originally meant. Probably (no one seems sure) it meant "without breath," and this had to do with Europeans not following Hawaiian customs involving breathing. One theory is that Hawaiians traditionally greeted one another by touching noses and in effect intermingling their breaths, and Europeans failed to do that.

Middle Eastern street . . . hijabs . . . abayas

A burqa is the fullest garment: it covers the whole body, with a mesh screen for the eyes. Chadors and abayas are full-body hooded cloaks, worn over other clothes. A niqab is a veil for the face only, usually with a slit for the eyes. A hijab is basically a scarf that covers the hair but not the face, and is often worn with what is otherwise Western-style clothing. Morag is guilty of cliché, as she suspects: Jordan is one of the most liberal Islamic countries, and many women there, especially in the cities, wear either the hijab or no head covering at all.

PART IV: GHOSTS

Giant mines (and a short polemic on the relationship between wealth, government, colonialism, racism, and terrorism)

The island of New Guinea is rich in minerals; the open-pit mines at Ok Tedi and Porgera in Papua New Guinea, and the Freeport mine at Grasberg on the Indonesian side of the border, are among the largest man-made holes on Earth. (Use Google Earth to look up Puncak Jaya, the tallest peak in New Guinea. The Grasberg mine is the set of concentric rings clearly visible just to the west of it.) It's a classic example of what economists call the "resource curse," in which poor, vulnerable people have their lives made immeasurably worse, rather than better, by the discovery of mineral wealth on their own land. Almost none of the vast profits from these mines have gone to indigenous groups, mine tailings have poisoned once-pristine major rivers like the Strickland and Fly, and violence has blossomed in the jungles like a big new crop.

Unfortunately for the people of Papua New Guinea and West Papua, the biggest problem isn't even foreign mining (and logging) corporations, but corrupt governments that find those corporations to be an irresistible sources of cash. As Nobel Prize–winning economist Angus Deaton has pointed out, one of the biggest factors separating the most fortunate people in the world from the least fortunate is the matter of living under relatively stable, transparent, competent, corruption-free governments—and those of Indonesia and Papua New Guinea rank a miserable 107th and 145th out of 175 on Transparency International's global corruption index.

Around the world, governments at this level are a lot like the bully in the school corridor: reliably stupid, but also reliably strong, selfish, pitiless, and violent. For all its failings, at least the government of Papua New Guinea is indigenous. The government of West Papua (formerly Irian Jaya), on the contrary, is one of the most brutal, most ruthless, most overtly racist exercises in colonial domination in history, comparable to the worst excesses of the European powers in Africa in the nineteenth century.

The former Dutch territory was forcibly annexed by Indonesia during a drive for independence from 1961 to 1969. As zoologist Tim Flannery drily remarked (writing in 1998, shortly after the area had been renamed "Irian Jaya" by the Indonesian government):

> "Surely it is a perverse twist of fate that has put a nation of mostly Muslim, mostly Javanese, people in control of a place like Irian Jaya. You could not imagine, even if you tried, two more antipathetic cultures. Muslims abhor pigs, while to a Highland Irianese they are the most highly esteemed of possessions. Javanese have a highly developed sense of modesty . . . for most Irianese, near-nudity is the universally respectable state . . . Javanese fear the forest and are happiest in towns . . . Irianese treat the forest as their home."

This is a short quote from a long list of opposites, and bad things could have been predicted to flow from them. But alas, *bad* is far too weak a word, as it is not really even the Indonesian government that rules West Papua, but the Indonesian military—which, after enjoying decades of generous support, supplies, training, and diplomatic shielding by the United States, Australia, and even the United Nations, *has one of the worst human-rights records of any entity on earth*. In the fifty years since the brutally violent annexation, many tens of thousands of West Papuans (over five hundred thousand, according to the group International Parliamentarians for West Papua) have been murdered by Indonesian forces, with thousands more imprisoned, raped, tortured, and "disappeared," in a campaign of terror that arguably amounts to genocide.

About that word *terror*. We're encouraged to think that terrorism is a very big deal, but what is it? The US State Department recognizes more than sixty terrorist organizations around the world. It would appear that what unites the listed organizations is their willingness to pursue political goals by using violence to intimidate and kill innocent people—and they are doing so at an unprecedented rate, mainly in Afghanistan, Iraq, Nigeria, Pakistan, and Syria. Currently the world's worst example is Nigeria's Boko Haram, an especially bloodthirsty Islamic extremist group affiliated with ISIS/ISIL. It's on the list and in the news for murdering 6,664 people in 2014, more even than the rest of ISIS/ISIL worldwide. (Figures are from the Institute for Economics and Peace, 2015 Global Terrorism Index.) But since 1963 the Indonesian military has murdered up to *seventy times* that many people in Irian Jaya/West Papua alone, out of a population of just 4.5 million. It continues to imprison, torture, and murder West Papuans today, making something of a specialty of pro-democracy activists, otherwise known as "rebels" (look up, for example, the cases of Yawan Wayeni and Danny Kogoya), and farmers and children (see, but be warned of very disturbing images at, freewestpapua.blogspot.com). Yet Indonesia's army doesn't even make it onto the State Department's terrorist list.

Possibly this is evidence that the United States government is a fan not only of our "ally," Indonesia, but also of Lewis Carroll. For, as Humpty Dumpty famously tells Alice, "When I use a word . . . it means just what I choose it to mean—neither more nor less."

You can find out more about what's going on in West Papua in this article from the *Diplomat*, http://thediplomat.com/2014/01/the-human-tragedy-of-west-papua, and at the websites of Human Rights Watch, International Parliamentarians for West Papua, Cultural Survival, Survival International, and Amnesty International.

839 languages

New Internationalist magazine lists 253 tribal languages for the Indonesian province of West Papua and states that the island as a whole accounts for 15 percent of all known languages—so that's a total of about eight hundred to one thousand. Zoologist Tim Flannery gives a similar number. Let's say eight hundred. By way of comparison, Ethnologue lists 166 for all of Europe and Scandinavia combined.

Singing dog

The New Guinea singing dog (*Canis lupus hallstromi*) is actually a shy, rare, and genuinely wild relative of the Australian dingo; hunting dogs in the Highlands are descended (at any rate partly) from them.

Giant rat

He doesn't just mean it's a big one. The Bosavi woolly rat, a species discovered in 2009, is one of many "giant rat" species of the genus *Muridae* in New Guinea, and it may be the largest of all: it's almost three feet long and weighs about three and a half pounds. Rats like this are a common food source for many tribes in New Guinea. The Bosavi woolly rat, by the way, was found living in the crater of an extinct volcano.

Lost tribes . . . "the Hagahai, the Fayu, the Liawep"

These are just three real New Guinea tribes that as recently as the 1980s or 1990s had had little or no contact with Westerners, and relatively little contact even with other local tribes. There's good information on the Hagahai at culturalsurvival.org; for the Fayu, see Sabine Kuegler's memoir *Child of the Jungle* and Jared Diamond's *Guns, Germs, and Steel*; for the Liawep, see Edward Marriott's *The Lost Tribe*. Several other tribes with very little outside contact are described in Tim Flannery's memoir *Throwim Way Leg*—including both the Miyanmin and the Atbalmin, whose territory is approximately where I've set the Chens' encounter with the Tainu. Survival International claims there are forty such groups in West Papua alone.

Many tribes or groups referred to as "uncontacted" in places like New Guinea and the Peruvian and Brazilian Amazon are better characterized as having responded to contact with neighboring populations and the "outside world" by making it clear that they wish to minimize or avoid any more of it.

Humans arriving in Australia/Melanesia "fifty thousand years ago"
Jimmy could be wrong. The best current evidence strongly suggests fifty thousand years at least, and sixty thousand or more is quite possible. (The sea level was so much lower back then that Australia, Tasmania, and New Guinea were one landmass, known to geographers as Sahul, and the coastal areas where you'd expect to find the earliest evidence of settlement now lie under the Timor and Arafura Seas.)

"Neanderthals . . . went extinct not much later"
At one point the Neanderthals ranged from east of the Caspian Sea to southern England and southern Spain, and recent evidence puts them at least occasionally as far east as the Altai Mountains in Siberia. By about fifty thousand years ago, their range was shrinking, and, while there's been some apparent evidence of a remnant population hanging on in southern Europe until twenty-four thousand years ago, recent research is pushing the date of final extinction back in the direction of forty thousand years.

After showing up from Africa, *Homo sapiens* may have lived alongside Neanderthals for tens of thousands of years, but some argue that there was little or no interaction until about forty-two thousand years ago. If that's right, and the Neanderthals really did die out forty to thirty-eight thousand years ago, the overlap is suspiciously narrow. Did we bring disease to them? Slaughter them? Slaughter them and eat them? A new theory, outlined in Pat Shipman's book *The Invaders*, suggests rather that we outcompeted them for food resources by showing up ready-armed with a lethal new hunting technology: semi-domesticated dog-wolves. Some clever statistical research on skulls from ancient and modern *Canidae* (wolves and dogs) suggests that our ancestors first domesticated wolves into dogs not seven to ten thousand years ago— or fifteen thousand years ago, which until recently was an "extreme" date—but as long as thirty to forty thousand years ago. And dogs make hunting big game much, much easier. (See also the note "Language: 'a crazy thing that shouldn't exist.'")

Homo floresiensis and the legend of the *ebu gogo*

Remains of the dwarf hominin species *Homo floresiensis*, immediately nicknamed "the hobbit," were discovered in 2003 in a cave on the Indonesian island of Flores, about 1,300 miles west of New Guinea. *H. floresiensis* reached the Flores area hundreds of thousands of years before modern humans did and thrived, partly on a diet of now-extinct pygmy elephants, long after the Neanderthals went extinct in Eurasia. (An even more recent discovery, in 2016—stone tools well over one hundred thousand years old on the island of Sulawesi—indicates that yet other groups of early hominins also beat *Homo sapiens* to the area.)

Modern people on Flores tell of the *ebu gogo*, small hairy people who live in caves in the forest and come out to steal pigs and even children. (The names means something like "greedy granny" in the local language.) It's a similar story to the Orang Pendek ("short person") legend on Sumatra. The most recent alleged sightings of *ebu gogo* are from the nineteenth century; still, if *H. floresiensis* was the cause of those reports, then the species hung on at least ten thousand years longer than current fossils indicate. And maybe they did—jungles are notoriously bad environments for fossil preservation. Anyway, that's what gave me the idea for the I'iwa.

"Our biology is a barrier to our nature, because matter is evolving into mind"

That we might evolve from pure matter to pure mind—that that is the whole universe's trajectory, in fact—is the philosopher Hegel in a nutshell. It's a fascinating idea; too bad it's buried in *The Phenomenology of Spirit*, one of the most unreadable books ever written. But you can say this much for Hegel: at least he took the reality of ideas seriously and accepted that the relationship between things and thoughts was a genuine and deep mystery. In the past century, most cognitive scientists and psychologists, and many philosophers, have managed to persuade themselves that it isn't a deep mystery. Which is tragic, really: being mistaken, they've condemned themselves to playing in the shallows. (See also the note on "Let there be light" and the simulation argument.)

Paleolithic evolution and "idiots" not cooking their food

A trifle harsh, but it's easy to see where Morag's impatience is coming from. A lot of pop science gives the impression that we evolved into modern human beings one Wednesday afternoon on the African savannah a hundred thousand years ago—as if some magical change made us anatomically and biologically what we are, now, right then. But evolution is continuous, and while some people claim we've evolved little since the mid-Paleolithic, the most recent evidence suggests the opposite: epochal revolutions like the domestication of cattle, the invention of agriculture, mass migration, and industrialization have probably *accelerated* the pace of human genetic change. So there's little reason to think that what was normal or natural for our ancestors one hundred thousand years ago is an especially good guide to what's best for us now. As for cooking dinner: our bodies became adapted to this vastly more efficient way of getting calories at least three hundred and fifty thousand years ago, and possibly two million years ago. In either case, that's long before *Homo sapiens* even evolved.

"I make of you nice fat kebab"
That might sound odd, coming from a Russian, but kebabs, or shashlik, have been a popular fast food in Russia ever since they were introduced from Central Asia over a century ago.

Time for Gödel
Gödel was one of the most important mathematicians of the twentieth century and one of the most important logicians since Aristotle. Like Iona, he was a mathematical Platonist: he believed mathematical objects existed in an independent reality outside the mind, and had to be discovered; they were not mere inventions. His own work contributed strong new reasons for believing so.

Modern physics seems to agree with him on the unreality of time. Einstein called it "a stubbornly persistent illusion." And when John Wheeler and Bryce DeWitt tried to combine general relativity with quantum mechanics by giving a quantum-mechanical description of the universe as a whole, they found that "time" dropped out of the picture. Look up "Wheeler-DeWitt equation" for more on this.

Iona's "crazy as a loon" comment is a reference to the fact that Gödel was paranoid about being poisoned and would only eat food that had been prepared for him by his wife. When she became too ill to do this, he stopped eating and essentially starved himself to death. He died in 1978.

The underground city at Derinkuyu
In case you think the I'iwa's home too fanciful, look this up. Derinkuyu once held thousands of people and their cattle, and it's just one of several dozen underground settlements in Cappadocia, carved out by the Hittites and/or Phrygians. I visited the area many years ago; I was already writing about the I'iwa before I realized it was *those* interiors populating my mind's eye. The earliest written reference to the

Cappadocian rock settlements is already familiar to readers of *The Fire Seekers*: Xenophon visited them during his campaigns with Cyrus the Great and mentions them in *Anabasis*.

Lascaux, Altamira, and Chauvet

These are the three best-known sites for early cave art. At Altamira, in Spain, the paintings discovered in 1879 were originally dated at twelve to fifteen thousand years old, which seemed astonishing enough—but Lascaux in France was discovered in 1940, with apparently older images, and some of those at Chauvet in France (discovered 1994) were clearly older still. Subsequent research has shown that most of these sites were occupied in waves over tens of thousands of years; at Chauvet, and also another Spanish cave, El Castillo, the oldest images are now believed to be as much as 37,000 to 40,000 years old. That puts them near the time when *H. sapiens* arrived in Europe and the Neanderthals vanished.

The most amazing aspect of the cave paintings isn't their age but their staggering skill, beauty, and power. When Altamira was discovered, the images were dismissed as fakes on the grounds that "primitive" people could not possibly have produced such things. Funny, but understandable—some of the animals, in particular, take your breath away. For a private tour of Chauvet, see Werner Herzog's documentary *Cave of Forgotten Dreams*.

Some Dates

Let me repeat my warning from *The Fire Seekers*: what follows is mostly accurate, but even then, many of the dates are rough approximations. Some are highly speculative—and I've thrown in an outright invention or two just to keep you awake.

600,000 BCE: *Homo heidelbergensis*, the first human species with a roughly modern brain size, has evolved in Africa; some *H. heidelbergensis* leave Africa and enter Eurasia about this time.

400,000–300,000 BCE: Neanderthals, Denisovans, and other human species are evolving from and alongside *H. heidelbergensis* in Eurasia.

200,000 BCE: *Homo sapiens* is evolving from the African branch of *H. heidelbergensis*.

120,000–75,000 BCE: Small numbers of *H. sapiens* leave Africa for the Middle East, possibly in multiple waves, and spread north and east into Europe and Asia. Here they encounter their "cousins," the Neanderthals, Denisovans, and others, for the first time. (60,000–40,000 BCE was given as a plausible "out of Africa" date for *H. sapiens* until recently, but now looks too conservative; anything before 75,000 BCE remains controversial, but is supported by some recent genetic and tool evidence.)

72,000 BCE: Mount Toba, a giant stratovolcano on what is now the island of Sumatra, erupts in probably the largest explosion on Earth in the past twenty-five million years. The eruption ejects 2,500–3,000 cubic kilometers of material—perhaps thirty to forty times as much as Strongyle/Thera (c. 1628 BCE) and Tambora (1815), 150 times as much as Krakatoa (1883), and at least three thousand times as much as Mount Saint Helens (1980). (Lake Toba, which now fills the caldera, is over a thousand square kilometers in area and five hundred meters deep.) The effect on the global climate is catastrophic, and populations of many larger terrestrial species, including both *Homo sapiens* and the Neanderthals, plunge to within a whisker of extinction.

60,000–30,000 BCE: The "Great Leap Forward" is characterized by an apparently sudden acceleration in the sophistication of human culture, including carving, cave art, ritual burial, and flutes made from vulture and mammoth bones. Humans also cross from Southeast Asia to populate Australasia during this time; due to lower sea levels, Australia and New Guinea are one landmass, Sahul.

40,000 BCE: Extinction of the Neanderthals, probably because they are outcompeted for resources by *H. sapiens*; the date of the extinction of the Denisovans is unknown.

24,000 BCE: Controversial later date for a remnant population of Neanderthals in southern Europe.

13,000 BCE: Toomba lava flow at what is now the Great Basalt Wall, Queensland, Australia.

17,000–12,000 BCE: Last known survival of *H. floresiensis* ("the hobbits") on the island of Flores in Indonesia. The date is disputed, and some evidence suggests that a local volcanic eruption around 10,000 BCE was the final cause of their destruction.

8,000 BCE: Rising seas separate Sahul into Australia, New Guinea, and other islands.

7,000 BCE: A new civilization emerges in the eastern Mediterranean on the island known as Strongyle (later Thera). Strict social hierarchies emerge for the first time, along with city-building, written language, and the very idea of organized religion. For at least a thousand years, the civilization develops in isolation; then a powerful priestly caste begins exporting its language, and its revolutionary new religious and cultural ideas, across the eastern Mediterranean and Mesopotamia.

5000–4000 BCE: First wave of city-building in the ancient world.

4000–3200 BCE: True writing emerges almost simultaneously in Sumer, the Indus Valley, early Minoan Crete, and Egypt.

2800–2500 BCE: Explosive growth in the number of languages in the region, including Akkadian, Assyrian, Babylonian, Minoan, and others. During the middle of this period, Gilgamesh is king of Uruk, in Mesopotamia.

1628 BCE: A massive volcanic eruption, perhaps four or five times the scale of Krakatoa, destroys the island of Strongyle/Thera.

1300 BCE or earlier: The original Great Ziggurat at Babylon is built.

1250–1150 BCE: The Bronze Age Collapse begins with a series of devastating library fires and culminates in the mysterious, violent destruction of whole cities and civilizations throughout the Mediterranean; many "myths" about violent, angry gods returning to commit acts of retribution, for instance the Nineveh "Deluge Tablets" in *The Epic of Gilgamesh*, date from this time.

600 BCE: The Great Ziggurat at Babylon, repeatedly destroyed and reconstructed, is rebuilt for the last time.

560–550 BCE: Authorship of the book of Genesis by Jewish scholars during their exile in Babylon; the Roman statesman Solon visits Egypt, where he hears the story of Atlantis—an echo of the destruction of Strongyle/Thera.

399 BCE: The Athenian soldier, historian, and philosopher Xenophon takes part in the epic retreat from Mesopotamia of the army of the Ten Thousand, and describes his experiences in the original *Anabasis*; back in Athens, the philosopher Socrates, a relentless critic of Athenian society, is executed for "corrupting the youth" and "atheism" (teaching false views about the gods).

△

1829 CE: The first Neanderthal bones are discovered; the specimens that gave the species its name, from the Neander Valley in Germany, are discovered in 1856; the species name, *Homo neanderthalensis*, is given in 1864.

1900 CE: The last reports from Flores, Indonesia, of the *ebu gogo*, a hairy, one-and-a-half-meter-tall possible hominin reportedly seen in the jungle by the Nage people of Flores.

1979 CE: Hominin remains discovered at Red Deer Cave in Guangxi Zhuangzu, southern China; they may or may not be a distinct human species surviving until as recently as 11,500 years ago.

2003 CE: Discovery of *Homo floresiensis* on the island of Flores, in Indonesia; *H. floresiensis is* apparently another new human species that survived until 50,000 years ago or less (from direct skeletal evidence), may have continued to exist until between thirteen thousand and eleven thousand years ago (from indirect evidence such as tool fragments), and may even have existed much more recently, if the legendary *ebu gogo* was a remnant population.

2008 CE: First hominin bone discovered in Denisova Cave, Russia, later identified as another new human species, *Homo sp.* Altai (the Denisovan).

2013 CE: The unearthing of bones by recreational cavers in the Dinaledi Chamber of the Rising Star cave system in South Africa led to paleoanthropologist Lee Berger identifying a new hominin species, *Homo naledi.*

THANKS

I'm grateful to copyeditors Rebecca Brinbury and Chris Henderson-Bauer for saving me from a multitude of errors, to proofreader Janice Lee for saving me from yet more, and to Eva Stabenow for correcting my German. My undying gratitude also to the usual crew—including, now, Jason Kirk at Amazon; I probably owe the most to a remarkable group of women who I think should consider forming a rock band called the Voiceless Velar Stops (go on, look it up, you're not that busy): Clarissa, Courtney, Kate, and Kerry.

About the Author

Richard Farr is the author of *The Fire Seekers* (The Babel Trilogy, Book One) and several other books. He lives in Seattle. You can find him at www.richardfarr.net.